A LIADEN UNIVERSE® CONSTELLATION
✧ Volume 2 ✧

BAEN BOOKS
by Sharon Lee & Steve Miller
✧✧✧
The Liaden Universe®
Fledgling
Saltation
Mouse & Dragon
Ghost Ship
Dragon Ship
Necessity's Child
Trade Secret

The Dragon Variation (omnibus)
The Agent Gambit (omnibus)
Korval's Game (omnibus)
The Crystal Variation (omnibus)
A Liaden Universe® Constellation: Volume1
A Liaden Universe® Constellation: Volume 2

The Fey Duology
Duainfey
Longeye

by Sharon Lee
Carousel Tides
Carousel Sun
Carousel Seas (forthcoming)

A LIADEN UNIVERSE®
CONSTELLATION
✧ Volume 2 ✧

SHARON LEE &
STEVE MILLER

A LIADEN UNIVERSE ® CONSTELLATION: VOLUME 2

This is a work of fiction. All the characters and events portrayed in this book are fictional, and any resemblance to real people or incidents is purely coincidental.

"Veil of the Dancer" originally appeared in *Absolute Magnitude* #19, Summer/Fall 2002. "Quiet Knives" originally appeared in *Quiet Knives* , SRM Publisher, Ltd., November 2003. "This House" originally appeared in *Stars: Original Stories Based on the Songs of Janis Ian*, edited by Janis Ian and Mike Resnick, DAW, August 2003. "This House" lyrics used with permission of the author. "Lord of the Dance" originally appeared in *With Stars Underfoot*, SRM Publisher, Ltd., November 2004. "Necessary Evils" originally appeared in *Necessary Evils*, SRM Publisher, Ltd., November 2005. "The Beggar King" originally appeared in *Necessary Evils*, SRM Publisher, Ltd., November 2005. "Fighting Chance" originally appeared in *Women of War*, edited by Tanya Huff and Alexander Potter, DAW, July 2005. "Prodigal Son" originally appeared in *Allies*, SRM Publisher, Ltd., November 2006. "Daughter of Dragons" originally appeared in *Dragon Tide*, SRM Publisher, Ltd., December 2007. "Dragon Tide" originally appeared in *Dragon Tide*, SRM Publisher, Ltd., December 2007. "Shadow Partner" originally appeared in *Eidolon*, SRM Publisher, Ltd., November 2008. "Persistence" originally appeared in *Eidolon*, SRM Publisher, Ltd., November 2008. "Misfits" originally appeared in *Jim Baen's Universe*, December 2007. "Hidden Resources" originally appeared in *Halfling Moon*, SRM Publisher, Ltd., December 2009. "Moon on the Hills" originally appeared in *Halfling Moon*, SRM Publisher, Ltd., December 2009. "Skyblaze" originally appeared in *Skyblaze*, SRM Publisher, Ltd., February 2011.

A Baen Books Original

Baen Publishing Enterprises
P.O. Box 1403
Riverdale, NY 10471
www.baen.com

ISBN: 978-1-4516-3944-5

Cover art by Stephen Hickman

First Baen printing, January 2014

Distributed by Simon & Schuster
1230 Avenue of the Americas
New York, NY 10020

Printed in the United States of America

10 9 8 7 6 5 4 3 2 1

✧ Table of Contents ✧

A LIADEN UNIVERSE® CONSTELLATION

✧ Volume 2 ✧

✧ Foreword ✧

WRITERS MAKE MONEY, naturally enough, by selling what they write.

Mostly, if the writers in question are wild and crazy freelance fiction writers, like ourselves, we write the story that's begging to be written . . . and then we submit it to various venues, hoping that one will send us a check and print the story.

Sadly, most of the stories writers produce in this way are never purchased and published. This is not, necessarily, because the stories are bad stories, but because there are too many stories, and not enough venues to offer them homes.

Now, we . . .

But wait. "We" are Sharon Lee and Steve Miller, and together we've written (as of Right Now, which is the end of April 2012) twenty novels, most of them set in a fictional place called the Liaden Universe®, a space-opera geography of our own devising.

We've also written dozens of short stories in that same universe. You're holding the *second* volume of those stories in your hand right now. The total number of stories collected in both volumes is . . . thirty-three.

Most of those stories—in fact, all but ten—first appeared in chapbooks published by SRM Publisher, Ltd., a micropublisher that we owned. From 1995 to 2011, we annually published at least one chapbook containing a novella, or two (rarely three) short stories.

Twenty-three of the stories first saw print in one of SRM's *Adventures in the Liaden Universe*® chapbook.

That means that all of our Liaden shorts made it into print. All of them.

For this, we thank our fans. Without their encouragement and support, we might not have created the first chapbook. We certainly wouldn't have created *seventeen* chapbooks.

It's worth saying here that this isn't a solution that everyone can—or ought—to embrace. Saying more then would require an article—or a discussion panel.

We do want to take a moment to talk about those ten stories—those ten *lucky* stories—that were placed with paying markets.

Actually, we want to take a moment to talk about the *markets*.

Between Summer of 1999 and Fall of 2002, *Absolute Magnitude* magazine published four Liaden Universe® stories: "Balance of Trade," "A Choice of Weapons," "Changeling," and "Veil of the Dancer."

Absolute Magnitude was a market for space opera in the grand ol' SF style. One of the stories we placed there—"Balance of Trade"—grew up to be a novel. Another—"Changeling"—showed up on the preliminary Nebula ballot.

Absolute Magnitude is no longer a market.

That means, it's out of business.

"A Matter of Dreams" appeared as a text story in the graphic serial publication, *A Distant Soil* #27. While Colleen Doran is still writing, drawing, and publishing this long-running and awesome comic, it's no longer a market for text stories.

In spring 2002, *3SF*, a British magazine, purchased "Sweet Waters" for its premier issue. *3SF* aimed to present quality stories from all over the science fiction and fantasy spectrum, at a variety of word lengths.

3SF is no longer a market.

Three of the remaining four stories were by invitation. An "invitation story" is a story that an editor has specifically asked to be written to fit the theme of an upcoming anthology or magazine issue.

So, that's "Naratha's Shadow," in Lee Martindale's *Such a Pretty*

Face; "This House," in Janis Ian's *Stars* anthology; "Fighting Chance" in Tanya Huff and Alex Potter's *Women of War*.

Theme anthologies are pretty often one-offs, and so it was with these. We had fun, we got paid; the anthologies, every one of them, are, excellent, but—not a repeat market.

The last of the ten, "Misfits," was also an invitation story, though we were allowed to pick our subject and write as long as the story needed. "Misfits" appeared in *Jim Baen's Universe* . . .

. . . which is no longer a market.

You might be asking yourselves at this point just why we're going on about this market thing at such length. Are we trying to tell you that publishing is a hard business, from almost any side you'd like stand on?

Well . . . no.

Everybody knows that while there are many benefits attached to writing as a career, riches beyond the wildest dreams of avarice is rarely one of them.

And as for publishing, who hasn't heard the old joke: "Hey! Know how to make a million bucks in publishing?

". . . Start with two million!"

So, yes, publishing is hard; writing is hard, and yet . . . people—quite clever people who don't really lack for common sense—continue to write, and continue to publish what others write.

And you might ask yourself, with such a rate of failure and so many odds stacked against the entire crazy enterprise, why anyone would even make the attempt to become a writer or invest time, money and sweat to set up as a publisher.

And the answer to that?

Is love.

Writers love to write. They love to tell stories. They love to *tell you* stories.

Yeah, *you*.

And publishers, most of them, most notably the small and indie publishers who haven't been swallowed up by megacorps, they love to put stories into the hands of people who are going to enjoy them. They believe in stories; in the power of word and imagination.

So that's that. That's why you have a compilation of sixteen short stories in your hand, twelve of them originally self-published—a tangible and visible collaboration of human love, and belief.

For you.

Enjoy.

—**Sharon Lee and Steve Miller**
Waterville, Maine
April 2012

✧ Veil of the Dancer ✧

IN THE CITY OF IRAVATI on the world of Skardu, there lived a scholar who had three daughters, and they were the light and comfort of his elder years.

Greatly did the scholar rejoice in his two elder daughters—golden-haired Humaria; Shereen with her tresses of flame—both of these born of the wives his father had picked out for him when he was still a young man. Surely, they were beautiful and possessed of every womanly grace, the elder daughters of Scholar Reyman Bhar. Surely, he valued them, as a pious father should.

The third—ah, the third daughter. Small and dark and wise as a mouse was the daughter of his third, and last, wife. The girl was clever, and it had amused him to teach her to read, and to do sums, and to speak the various tongues of the unpious. Surely, these were not the natural studies of a daughter, even the daughter of so renowned a scholar as Reyman Bhar.

It began as duty; for a father must demonstrate to his daughters that, however much they are beloved, they are deficient in that acuity of thought by which the gods mark out males as the natural leaders of household, and world. But little Inas, bold mouse, did not fail to learn her letters, as her sisters had. Problems mathematic she relished as much as flame-haired Shereen did candied *sventi* leaves. Walks along the river way brought forth the proper names of birds and their kin; in the long-neglected glade of Istat, with its ancient sundial and moon-marks she proved herself astute in the motions of the planets.

Higher languages rose as readily to her lips as the dialect of women; she read not only for knowledge, but for joy, treasuring especially the myths of her mother's now-empty homeland.

Seeing the joy of learning in her, the teaching became experiment more than duty, as the scholar sought to discover the limits of his little one's mind.

On the eve of her fourteenth birthday, he had not yet found them.

• • • ◇ • • •

WELL THOUGH THE SCHOLAR loved his daughters, yet it is a father's duty to see them profitably married. The man he had decided upon for his golden Humaria was one Safarez, eldest son of Merchant Gabir Majidi. It was a balanced match, as both the scholar and the merchant agreed. The Majidi son was a pious man of sober, studious nature, who bore his thirty years with dignity. Over the course of several interviews with the father and the son, Scholar Bhar had become certain that Safarez would value nineteen-year-old Humaria, gay and heedless as a *flitterbee*; more, that he would protect her and discipline her and be not behind in those duties which are a husband's joy and especial burden.

So, the price was set, and met; the priests consulted regarding the proper day and hour; the marriage garden rented; and, finally, Humaria informed of the upcoming blessed alteration in her circumstances.

Naturally enough, she wept, for she was a good girl and valued her father as she ought. Naturally enough, Shereen ran to cuddle her and murmur sweet, soothing nonsense into her pretty ears. The scholar left them to it, and sought his study, where he found his youngest, dark Inas, bent over a book in the lamplight.

She turned when he entered, and knelt, as befit both a daughter and a student, and bowed 'til her forehead touched the carpet. Scholar Bhar paused, admiring the graceful arc of her slim body within the silken pool of her robes. His mouse was growing, he thought. Soon, he would be about choosing a husband for her.

But not yet. Now, it was Humaria, and, at the change of season he would situate Shereen, who would surely pine for her sister's companionship. He had a likely match in mind, there, and the husband's property not so far distant from the Majidi. Then, next year, perhaps—or, more comfortably, the year after that—he would look about for a suitable husband for his precious, precocious mouse.

"Arise, Daughter," he said now, and marked how she did so, swaying to her feet in a single, boneless move, the robes rustling, then falling silent, sheathing her poised and silent slenderness.

"So," he said, and met her dark eyes through the veil. "A momentous change approaches your life, my child. Your sister, Humaria, is to wed."

Inas bowed, dainty hands folded demurely before her.

"What?" he chided gently. "Do you not share your sister's joy?"

There was a small pause, not unusual; his mouse weighed her words like a miser weighed his gold.

"Certainly, if my sister is joyous, then it would be unworthy of me to weep," she said in her soft, soothing voice. "If it is permitted that I know—who has come forward as her husband?"

Reyman Bhar nodded, well-pleased to find proper womanly feeling, as well as a scholar's thirst for knowledge.

"You are allowed to know that Safarez, eldest son of Majidi the Merchant, has claimed the right to husband Humaria."

Inas the subtle, stood silent, then bowed once more, as if an afterthought, which was not, the scholar thought, like her. He moved to his desk, giving her time to consider, for, surely, even his clever mouse was female, if not yet full woman, and might perhaps know a moment's envy for a sister's good fortune.

"They are very grand, the Majidi," she said softly. "Humaria will be pleased."

"Eventually, she will be so," he allowed, seating himself and pulling a notetaker forward. "Today, she weeps for the home she will lose. Tomorrow, she will sing for the home she is to gain."

"Yes," said Inas, and the scholar smiled into his beard.

"Your sisters will require your assistance with the wedding preparations," he said, opening the notetaker and beginning a list. "I will be going to Lahore-Gadani tomorrow, to purchase what is needful. Tell me what I shall bring you."

Mouse silence.

"I? I am not to be wed, Father."

"True. However, it has not escaped one's attention that tomorrow is the anniversary of your natal day. It amuses me to bring you a gift from the city, in celebration. What shall you have?"

"Why, only yourself, returned to us timely and in good health," Inas said, which was proper, and womanly, and dutiful.

The scholar smiled more widely into his beard, and said nothing else.

· · · ✦ · · ·

HUMARIA WEPT WELL INTO THE NIGHT, rocking inside the circle of Shereen's arms. At last, her sobs quieted somewhat, and Shereen looked to Inas, who sat on a pillow across the room, as she had all evening, playing Humaria's favorite songs, softly, upon the lap-harp.

Obedient to the message in her sister's eyes, Inas put the harp aside, arose and moved silently to the cooking alcove. Deftly, she put the kettle on the heat-ring, rinsed the pot with warm water and measured peace tea into an infuser.

The kettle boiled. While the tea steeped, she placed Humaria's own blue cup on a tray, with a few sweet biscuits and some leaves of candied *sventi*. At the last, she added a pink candle, sacred to Amineh, the little god of women, and breathed a prayer for heart's ease. Then, she lifted the tray and carried it to her sister's couch.

Humaria lay against Shereen's breast, veils and hair disordered. Inas knelt by the end table, placed the tray, and poured tea.

"Here, sweet love," Shereen cooed, easing Humaria away from her shoulder. "Our dear sister Inas offers tea in your own pretty cup. Drink, and be at peace."

Shivering, Humaria accepted the cup. She bent her face and breathed of the sweet, narcotic steam, then sipped, eyes closed.

Shereen sat up, and put her head scarf to rights, though she left the *ubaie*—the facial veils—unhooked and dangling along her right jaw.

"Our young Inas is fortunate, is she not, Sister?" Humaria

murmured, her soft voice blurry with the combined effects of weeping and the tea.

"How so?" asked Shereen, watching her closely, in case she should suddenly droop into sleep.

"Why," said Humaria, sipping tea. "Because she will remain here in our home with our father, and need never marry. Indeed, I would wonder if a husband could be found for a woman who reads as well as a man."

Shereen blinked, and bent her head, fussing with the fall of the *hijab* across her breast. Inas watched her, abruptly chilly, though the night was warm and no breeze came though the windows that stood open onto the garden.

"Certainly," Shereen said, after too long a pause. "Certainly, our father might wish to keep his youngest with him as long as may be, since he shows no disposition to take another wife, and she knows the ways of his books and his studies."

"And certainly," Humaria said, her eyes open now, and staring at Inas, where she knelt, feeling much like a mouse, and not so bold, so bold at all.

"Certainly, on that blessed day when the gods call our father to sit with them as a saint in Heaven, my husband will inherit all his worldly stuffs, including this, our clever sister Inas, to dispose of as he will."

At her father's direction, Inas had read many things, including the Holy Books and domestic law. She knew, with a scholar's detachment, that women were the lesser vessel and men the god-chosen administrators of the universe the gods had created, toyed with and tired of.

She knew that, in point of law, women were disbarred from holding property. Indeed, in point of law, women were themselves property, much the same as an ox or other working cattle, subject to a man's masterful oversight. A man might dispose of subject women, as he might dispose of an extra brood cow, or of an old and toothless dog.

She knew these things.

And, yet, until this moment, she had not considered the impact of these facts upon her own life and self.

What, indeed, she thought, would Safarez the merchant's son, do with one Inas, youngest daughter of his wife's father? Inas, who read as well as a man—a sinful blot so dire that she could not but be grateful that the Holy Books also stated that the souls of women were small, withered things, of no interest to the gods.

Humaria finished the last of her tea, and sat cradling the blue cup in her plump, pretty hands, her eyes misty.

"There now, sweet, rest," Shereen murmured, capturing the cup and passing it to Inas. She put her arm around Humaria's shoulders, urging her to lie down on the couch.

Inas arose and carried the tray back to the cooking alcove. She washed and dried the teapot and cup, and put the crackers back in their tin. The *sventi* she left out.

She was wise in this, for not many minutes later, Shereen slipped into the alcove, veils dangling and flame-colored hair rippling free. She sighed, and reached for the leaves, eating two, one after the other, before giving Inas a swift glance out of the sides of her eyes, as if Shereen were the youngest, and caught by her elder in some unwomanly bit of mischief.

"Our sister was distraught," she said softly. "She never meant to wound you."

"She did not wound me," Inas murmured. "She opened my eyes to the truth."

Shereen stared, *sventi* leaf halfway to her lips.

"You do not find the truth a fearsome thing, then, Sister?" she asked, and it was Inas who looked away this time.

"The truth is merely a statement of what is," she said, repeating the most basic of her father's lessons, and wishing that her voice did not tremble so. "Once the truth is known, it can be accepted. Truth defines the order of the universe. By accepting truth, we accept the will of the gods."

Shereen ate her leaf in silence. "It must be a wonderful thing to be a scholar," she said then, "and have no reason to fear." She smiled, wearily.

"Give you sweet slumber, Sister. The morrow will be upon us too soon."

She went away, robes rustling, leaving Inas alone with the truth.

• • •✦• • •

THE TRUTH, BEING BRIGHT, held Inas from sleep, until at last she sat up within her *chatrue*, lit her fragrant lamp, and had the books of her own studies down from the shelf.

In the doubled brightness, she read until the astronomer on his distant column announced the sighting of the Trio of morning with his baleful song.

She read as a scholar would, from books to which her father, the elder scholar, had directed her, desiring her to put aside those he might wish to study.

The book she read in the lamplight was surely one which her father would find of interest. A volume of Kenazari mythology, it listed the gods and saints by their various praise names and detailed their honors.

Nawar caught her eye, "the one who guards." A warrior's name, surely. Yet, her mother had been named Nawar. A second aspect of the same god, Natesa—"blade dancer"—in the Kenazari heresy that held each person was a spirit reincarnated until perfected, alternatively taking the form of male and female. The duty of the god in either aspect was to confound the gods of order and introduce random action into the universe, which was heresy, as well, for the priests taught that the purpose of the gods, enacted through mortal men, was to order and regulate the universe.

Inas leaned back against her pillows and considered what she knew of her father's third wife. Nawar had been one of the married women chosen as guardians of the three dozen maiden wives sent south from Kenazari as the peace tithe. Each maiden was to be wed to a wise man or scholar, and it had been the hope of the scholars who had negotiated it that these marriages would heal the rifts which had opened between those who had together tamed the wildlands.

Alas, it had been a peace worked out and implemented locally, as the Holy Books taught, and it had left the mountain generals unsatisfied.

Despite the agreement and the high hopes of wise men, the generals and their soldiers swept through Kenazari shortly after the rich caravan of dowries and oath-bound girls passed beyond the walls of the redoubt. Fueled by greed, bearing off-world weapons, they murdered and laid waste—and then dispersed, melting back into the mountains, leaving nothing of ancient, wealthy Kenazari, save stone and carrion.

The priests of the south found the married escorts to be widows and awarded them to worthy husbands. Reyman Bhar had lately performed a great service for the priests of Iravati, and stood in need of a wife. Nawar was thus bestowed upon him, and it had pleased the gods to allow them to find joy, each in the other, for she was a daughter of an old house of scholars, and could read, and write, and reason as well as any man. Her city was dead, but she made shift to preserve what could be found of its works, assisted gladly by her new husband.

So it was that numerous scrolls, books, and tomes written in the soon-to-be-forgotten language found their way into the house of Scholar Bhar, where eventually they came under the study of a girl child, in the tradition of her mother's house . . .

The astronomer on his tall, cold column called the Trio. Inas looked to her store of oil, seeing it sadly depleted, and turned the lamp back 'til the light fled and the smoky wick gave its ghost to the distant dawn.

She slept then, her head full of the myths of ancient Kenazari, marriage far removed from her dreams.

. . . ⬦ . . .

THEIR FATHER SENT WORD that he would be some days in the city of Lahore-Gadani, one day to west across the windswept ridges of the Marakwenti range that separated Iravati from the river Gadan. He had happened upon his most excellent friend and colleague, Scholar Baquar Hafeez, who begged him to shed the light of his intellect upon a problem of rare complexity.

This news was conveyed to them by Nasir, their father's servant, speaking through the screen in the guest door.

Humaria at once commenced to weep, her face buried in her hands as she rocked back and forth, moaning, "He has forgotten my wedding! I will go to my husband ragged and ashamed!"

Shereen rushed to embrace her, while Inas sighed, irritable with lack of sleep.

"I do not think our father has forgotten your wedding, Sister," she said, softly, but Humaria only cried harder.

As it happened, their father had not forgotten his daughters, nor his mission in the city. The first parcels arrived shortly after Uncu's prayer was called, and were passed through the gate, one by one.

Bolts of saffron silk, from which Humaria's bridal robes would be sewn; yards of pearls; rings of gold and topaz; bracelets of gold; *ubaie* fragile as spider silk and as white as salt; hairpins, headcloths, and combs; sandals; needles; thread. More bolts, in brown and black, from which Humaria's new dayrobes would be made, and a hooded black cloak, lined in fleece.

Additional parcels arrived as the day wore on: a bolt each of good black silk for Shereen and Inas; headcloths, *ubaie*; silver bracelets and silver rings set with onyx.

Humaria and Shereen fell upon each new arrival with cries of gladness. Shereen ran for her patterns; Humaria gave the saffron silk one last caress and scampered off for scissors and chalk.

Inas put her silk and rings and bracelets aside, and began to clear the worktable.

Across the room, the guest screen slid back and a small package wrapped in brown paper and tied with red string was placed on the ledge.

Inas went forward, wondering what else was here to adorn Humaria's wedding day, even as she recognized her father's hand and the lines that formed her own name.

Smiling, she caught the package up and hurried, lightfooted, to her room. Once there, she broke the red string and unwrapped the brown paper, exposing not a book, as she had expected, from the weight and the size, but a box.

She put it aside, and searched the wrapping for any note from her father. There was none, and she turned her attention back to his gift.

It was an old box of leather-wrapped wood. Doubtless, it had been handsome in its day, but it seemed lately to have fallen on hard times. The leather was scuffed in places, cracked in others, the ornamental gilt work all but worn away. She turned it over in her hands, and rubbed her thumb along a tear in the leather where the wood showed through—gray, which would be ironwood, she thought, from her study of native product.

She turned the box again, set it on her knee, released the three ivory hooks and lifted the lid.

Inside were seven small volumes, each bound in leather much better preserved than that which sheathed the box.

Carefully, she removed the first volume on the right; carefully, she opened it—and all but laughed aloud, for here was treasure, indeed, and all honor to her father, for believing her worthy of so scholarly a gift. She had read of such things, but this was the first she had seen. A *curiat*—a diary kept of a journey, or a course of study, or a penance.

These . . . Quickly, she had the remaining six out and opened, sliding the *ubaie* away from her eyes, the better to see the handwritten words. Yes, these detailed a scholar's journey—one volume dealt with geography, another with plants, another with minerals, still another with animals. Volume five detailed temples and universities, while volume six seemed a list of expenditures. The seventh volume indexed the preceding six. All were written in a fine, clear hand, using the common, or trade, alphabet, rather than that of the scholars, which was odd, but not entirely outside of the scope of possibility. Perhaps the scholar in question had liked the resonances which had been evoked by writing in the common script. Scholars often indulged in thought experiments, and this seven-volume *curiat* had a complexity, a layering, that suggested it had been conceived and executed by a scholar of the highest learning.

Carefully, she put volumes two through seven back in the box and opened the first, being careful not to crack the spine.

"Inas?" Shereen's voice startled her out of her reading. Quickly, she thrust the book into the box and silently shut the lid.

"Yes, Sister?" she called.

"Wherever have you been?" her elder scolded from the other side of the curtain. "We need your needle out here, lazy girl. Will you send your sister to her husband in old dayrobes?"

"Of course not," Inas said. Silently, she stood, picked up the box, and slipped it beneath the mattress. Later, she would move it to the secure hidey hole, but, for now, the mattress would suffice.

"Well?" Shereen asked, acidic. "Are you going to sleep all day?"

"No, Sister," Inas said meekly and pushed the curtain aside.

· · ·✧· · ·

THE DAYS OF THEIR father's absence saw a frenzy of needlework. At night, after her sisters had fallen, exhausted, into their beds, Inas read the *curiat*, and learned amazing things.

First, she learned that the geographical volume mislocated several key markers, such as the Ilam Mountains, and the Sea of Lukistan. Distrustful of her own knowledge in the face of a work of scholarship, she stole off to her father's study in the deep of night, and pulled down the atlas. She compared the latitudes and longitudes given in the *curiat* volume against those established by the geographical college, verifying that the *curiat* was off in some areas by a league, and in others by a day's hard travel.

Next, she discovered that the habits of certain animals were misrepresented—these, too, she double-checked in the compendium of creatures issued by the zoological college.

Within the volume of universities and temples were bits of myth, comparing those found in Lahore-Gadani to others, from Selikot. Several fragments dealt with the exploits of the disorderly Natesa; one such named the aspect Shiva, another Nawar; all set against yet a third mythic creature, the Coyote of the Nile.

Then, she discovered that the whole of volume five had been machine printed, in perfect reproduction of the fine hand of the scholar. So the *curiat* was not as ancient as it appeared, which gave her cause to marvel upon the scholar who had created it.

Minerals—well, but by the time she had found the discrepancies in the weights of certain ores, she had made the discovery which explained every error.

She had, as was her habit, waited until her sisters retired, then lit her lamp, pulled up the board under the carpet, and brought the box onto her *chatrue*. She released the three ivory hooks, opened the lid— the box overbalanced and spilled to the floor, books scattering every which way.

Inas slipped out of bed and tenderly gathered the little volumes up, biting her lip when she found several pages in the third book crumpled. Carefully, she smoothed the damaged sheets, and replaced the book with its brothers inside the box.

It was then that she noticed pieces of the box itself had come loose, leaving two neat, deep, holes in the wood, at opposite corners of the lid. Frowning, she scanned the carpet, spying one long spindle, tightly wrapped in cloth. The second had rolled beneath the *chatrue,* and by the time she reached and squirmed and had it out with the very tips of her fingers, the cloth covering had begun to unravel.

Daintily, she fingered it, wondering if perhaps the cloth held some herb for protection against demons, or perhaps salts, to insure the books kept dry, or—

There was writing on the inside of the cloth. Tiny and meticulous, it was immediately recognizable as the same hand which had penned the *curiat.*

Exquisitely careful, breath caught, she unrolled the little scroll across the carpet, scanning the columns of text; heart hammering into overdrive as she realized that she had discovered her nameless scholar's key.

Teeth indenting her bottom lip, she unrolled the second scroll next to the first, and saw that she had the complete cipher.

Breathless, she groped behind her for the box, and extracted a book at random.

Slowly at first—then more quickly as her agile mind grew acquainted with the key—she began to read.

Illuminated by the cipher, it was found that the volume geographical did not concern itself with mountain ranges and rivers at all, but was instead a detailed report of a clandestine entry into the city of Selikot, and a blasphemous subterfuge.

I regret to inform you, oh, brother in arms, that our information regarding this hopeful world was much misleading. Women are not restricted; they are quarantined, cut off from society and commerce. They may only travel in the company of a male of their kin unit, and even then, heavily shielded in many layers of full body robes, their faces, eyes and hair hidden by veils. So it is that the first adjustment in our well-laid plans has been implemented. You will find that your partner, Thelma Delance, has ceded her route and her studies to a certain Scholar Umar Khan. And a damnable time I had finding a false beard in this blasted city, too. However, as you know to your sorrow, I'm a resourceful wench, and all is now made seemly. Scholar Khan is suitably odd, and elicits smiles and blessings wherever he walks. The project continues only slightly impeded by the beard, which itches. I will hold a copy of this letter in my field notes, in the interests of completeness.

Farewell for now, brother Jamie. You owe me a drink and dinner when we are reunited.

· · · ⋄ · · ·

INAS WAS SLOW WITH her needle next morning, her head full of wonders and blasphemies.

That there were other worlds, other peoples, variously named "Terran" and "Liaden"—that was known. Indeed, Selikot was the site of a "spaceport" and bazaar, where such outworlders traded what goods they brought for those offered by the likes of Merchant Majidi. The outworlders were not permitted beyond the bazaar, for they were unpious; and the likes of Merchant Majidi must needs undergo purifications after their business in the bazaar was concluded.

Yet now it seemed that one—nay, *a pair*—of outworlders had moved beyond the bazaar to rove and study the wider world—and one of them a woman. A woman who had disguised herself as a man.

This was blasphemy, and yet the temples had not fallen; the crust of the world had not split open and swallowed cities; nor had fires rained from the heavens.

Perhaps Thelma Delance had repented her sin? Perhaps Amineh, the little god of women, had interceded with his brothers and bought mercy?

Perhaps the gods were not as all-seeing and as all-powerful as she had been taught?

Within the layers of her at-home robes, Inas shivered, but her scholar-trained mind continued its questions, and the answers which arose to retire those new and disturbing questions altered the measure of the world.

"Truth defines the order of the universe," she whispered, bending to her needlework. "When we accept the truth, we accept the will of the gods."

Yet, how if accepting the truth proved the absence of the gods? Why had her father given her such a gift? Had he read the *curiat* before sending it to her? Did he know of the hidden—

Across the room, from the other side of the guest screen, Nasir's voice intruded.

"The Esteemed and Blessed Scholar Reyman Bhar is returned home and bids his daughter Inas attend him in the study."

· · ·✧· · ·

HER FATHER WAS AT HIS DESK, several volumes open before him, his fingers nimble on the keypad of the notetaker. Inas waited, silent, her hands folded into her sleeves. The light of the study lamps was diffused into a golden glow by the *ubaie*, so that her father seemed surrounded by the light of Heaven. He was a handsome man, dark, with a masterful beak of a nose and the high forehead of a scholar. His beard was as black and as glossy as that of a man half his age. He wore the House turban, by which she knew he had been home some hours before sending for her, and the loosened braid of his hair showed thick and gray.

He made a few more notes, turned a page of the topmost book, set the notetaker aside, and looked up.

Inas melted to her knees and bowed, forehead to the carpet.

"Arise, Daughter," he said, kindly as always.

She did so and stood quiet once more, hands folded before her.

"Tell me, did my packet arrive timely?"

"Father," she said softly, "it did. I am grateful to you for so precious a gift."

He smiled, well-pleased with her. "It is a curiosity, is it not? Did you mark the pattern of the errors? Almost, it seems a farce—a plaything. What think you?"

"Perhaps," Inas said, her breath painfully short, "it is a test?"

He considered it, black brows knit, then nodded, judiciously. "It could be so. Yes, I believe you have the right of it, Daughter. A test devised by a scholar of the higher orders, perhaps to teach discipline." He paused, thinking more deeply. Inas, waiting, felt ill, wondering if he knew of the hidden scholar's key and the blasphemies contained in the revealed text.

"Yes," he said again. "A test. How well the scholar must have loved the student for which it was devised!"

"Yes, Father," Inas whispered, and gathered together her courage, lips parting to ask it, for she must know . . .

"As you progress in scholarship, you will learn that the most precious gifts are those which are more than they appear," her father said, "and that hidden knowledge has power." He bowed, seated as he was, scholar to scholar, which was a small blasphemy of its own, face as austere as a saint's.

And so, Inas thought, she was instructed. She bowed. "Yes, Father."

"Hah." He leaned back in his chair, suddenly at ease, and waved her to the stool at his feet.

"Sit, child, and tell me how the arrangements for your sister's wedding progress."

* * * ✧ * * *

THE *CURIAT* BUOYED HER, frightened her, intrigued her. She spent her nights with it, and every other moment she could steal. She stored it now in the long-forgot sand-wood drawer—the hidden pass-through where it stood long out of use—where she could, if she wished, reach it as easily from the garden or her room.

Thelma Delance—she heard the woman's voice in the few hours of sleep she allowed herself—a loud, good-natured, and unwomanly voice, honest as women could never be, and courageous.

Inas read, and learned. Thelma Delance had been a scholar of wide learning. There were recipes for medicines among her notes; recipes for poisons, for explosives, and other disasters, which Inas understood only mistily; and lessons of *self-defense*, which held echoes of her mother's name. There was other knowledge, too—plans for establishing a *base*.

And there was the appalling fact that the notes simply ended, and did not pick up again:

They're on me. I've got one more trick up my sleeve. You know me, Jamie Moore, always one more trick up Thelma's wide sleeve, eh? We'll see soon enough if it's worked. If it has, you owe me—that's my cue. They're shooting . . .

There was nothing more after that, only the box, and the wound it bore, which might, Inas thought, have been made by a pellet.

She wondered who had wished to kill Thelma Delance—and almost laughed. Surely, that list was long. The priests—of a certainty. The scholars—indeed. The port police, the merchant guild, the freelance vigilantes . . .

And Inas realized all at once that she was crying, the silent, secret tears that women were allowed, to mourn a sister, a mother, a friend.

· · · ✧ · · ·

THE DAY BEFORE HUMARIA was to wed, Inas once again attended her father in the study, where she was given the task of reshelving the volumes he had utilized in his last commissioned research. By chance their proper places were in the back corner of the room, where the convergence of walls and shelves made an alcove not easily seen from the greater room.

She had been at her task some time, her father deep in some new bit of study at his desk, when she heard the door open and Nasir announce, "The Esteemed and Honorable Scholar Baquar Hafeez begs the favor of an audience with the Glorious and Blessed Scholar Reyman Bhar."

"Old friend, enter and be welcome!" Her father's voice was cordial and kindly—and, to his daughter's ear, slightly startled. His chair skritched a little against the carpet as he pushed away from the desk, doubtless rising to embrace his friend.

"To what blessed event do I owe this visit?"

"Why, to none other than Janwai Himself!" Scholar Hafeez returned, his voice deeper and louder than her father's. "Or at the least, to his priests, who have commissioned me for research at the hill temple. There are certain etched stones in the meditation rooms, as I take it?"

"Ah, are there not!" Reyman Bhar exclaimed. "You are in for a course of study, my friend. Be advised, buy a pair of nightsight lenses before you ascend. The meditation rooms are ancient, indeed, and lit by oil."

"Do you say so?" Scholar Hafeez exclaimed, over certain creaks and groanings from the visitor's chair as it accepted his weight.

Inas, forgotten, huddled, soundless and scarcely moving in the alcove, listening as the talk moved from the meditation rooms to the wider history of the hill temple, to the progress of the report on which her father and Scholar Hafeez had collaborated, not so long since.

At some point, Nasir came in, bearing refreshments. The talk wandered on. In the alcove, Inas sank silently to her knees, drinking in the esoterica of scholarship as a thirsty man guzzles tea.

Finally, there came a break in the talk. Scholar Hafeez cleared his throat.

"I wonder, old friend—that *curiat* you bought in Hamid's store?"

"Yes?" her father murmured. "A peculiar piece, was it not? One would almost believe it had come from the old days, when Hamid's grandfather was said to buy from slavers and caravan thieves."

"Just so. An antique from the days of exploration, precious for its oddity. I have no secrets from you, my friend, so I will confess that it comes often into my mind. I wonder if you would consider parting with it. I will, of course, meet what price you name."

"Ah." Her father paused. Inas pictured him leaning back in his chair, fingers steepled before his chin, brows pulled together as he considered the matter. In the alcove, she hardly dared breathe, even to send a futile woman's prayer to the little god for mercy.

"As much as it saddens me to refuse a friend," Reyman Bhar said softly, "I must inform you that the *curiat* had been purchased as a gift for a promising young scholar of my acquaintance."

"A strange item to bestow upon a youth," murmured Baquar Hafeez, adding hastily, "but you will, of course, know your own student! It is only that—"

"I most sincerely regret," Scholar Bhar interrupted gently. "The gift has already been given."

There was a pause.

"Ah," said Scholar Hafeez. "Well, then, there is nothing more to be said."

"Just so," her father replied, and there was the sound of his chair being pushed back. "Come, my friend, you have not yet seen my garden. This is the hour of its glory. Walk with me and be refreshed."

Inas counted to fifty after the door closed, then she rose, reshelved the two remaining volumes, and ghosted out of the study, down the hall to the women's wing.

· · ·✦· · ·

HUMARIA'S WEDDING WAS BLESSED and beautiful, the banquet very grand to behold, and even the women's portions fresh and unbroken, which spoke well for her new husband's generosity.

At the last moment, it was arranged between Reyman Bhar and Gabir Majidi that Shereen would stay with her sister for the first month of her new marriage, as the merchant's wife was ill and there were no daughters in his house to bear Humaria company.

So it was that Scholar Bhar came home with only his youngest daughter to companion him. Nasir pulled the sedan before the house and the scholar emerged, his daughter after him. He ascended the ramp to the door, fingering his keycard from his pocket—and froze, staring at a door which was neither latched nor locked.

Carefully, he put forth his hand, pushing the door with the tips of his fingers. It swung open onto a hallway as neat and as orderly as always. Cautiously, the scholar moved on, his daughter forgotten at his back.

There was some small disorder in the public room—a vase overturned and shattered, some display books tossed aside. The rugs and the news computer—items that would bring a goodly price at the thieves market—were in place, untouched. The scholar walked on, down the hall to—

His study.

Books had been ripped from their shelves and flung to the floor, where they lay, spine-broke and torn, ankle-deep and desolate. His notepad lay in the center of the desk, shattered, as if it had been struck with a hammer. The loose pages of priceless manuscripts lay over all.

Behind him, Scholar Bhar heard a sound; a high keening, as if from the throat of a hunting hawk, or a lost soul.

He turned and beheld Inas, wilting against the door, her hand at her throat, falling silent in the instant he looked at her.

"Peace—" he began and stopped, for there was another sound, from the back of the house—but no. It would only be Nasir, coming in from putting the sedan away.

Yes, footsteps; he heard them clearly. And voices. The sudden, ghastly sound of a gun going off.

The scholar grabbed his daughter's shoulder, spinning her around. "Quickly—to the front door!"

She ran, astonishingly fleet, despite the hindrance of her robes. Alas that she was not fleet enough.

Baquar Hafeez was waiting for them inside the front hallway, and there was a gun in his hand.

• • ◇ • •

"AGAIN," Scholar Hafeez said, and the large man he called Danyal lifted her father's right hand, bent the second finger back.

Reyman Bhar screamed. Inas, on her knees beside the chair in which Scholar Hafeez took his ease, stared, stone-faced, through her veil, memorizing the faces of these men, and the questions they asked.

It was the *curiat* they wanted. And it was the *curiat* which Reyman Bhar was peculiarly determined that they not have. And why was that? Inas wondered. Surely not because he had made it a gift to a daughter. He had only to order her to fetch it from its hiding place and hand it to Baquar Hafeez. What could a daughter do, but obey?

And yet—*hidden knowledge has power.*

"The *curiat*, old friend," Scholar Hafeez said again—patient, so patient. "Spare yourself any more pain. Only tell me who has the *curiat*, and I will leave you and your household in peace."

"Why?" her father asked—a scholar's question, despite his pain.

"There are those who believe it to be the work of infidels," Scholar Hafeez said smoothly, and yet again: "The *curiat*, Reyman. Where is it?"

"It is not for you to know," her father gasped, his voice hoarse from screaming, his left arm useless, dislocated by Danyal in the first round of questions.

Scholar Hafeez sighed, deeply, regretfully.

"I was afraid that you might prove obstinate. Perhaps something else might persuade you."

It happened so quickly, she had no time to understand—pain exploded in her face and she was flung sideways to the floor, brilliant color distorting her vision. Her wrist was seized and she was lifted. More pain. She tried to get her feet under her, but she was pulled inexorably upward, sandals dangling. Her vision spangled, stabilized—Danyal's face was bare inches from hers. He was smiling.

Somewhere, her father was shouting.

"Your pardon, old friend?" Scholar Hafeez was all solicitude. "I did not quite hear the location of the *curiat*?"

"Release my daughter!"

"Certainly. After you disclose the location of the *curiat*. Such a small thing, really, when weighed against a daughter's virtue."

"Inas—" her father began, and what followed was not in the common tongue, but in that of her mother, and they were uttered as a prayer.

"Opportunity comes, Daughter, be stout and true. Honor your mother, in all her names."

Scholar Hafeez made a small sound of disappointment, and moved a hand. "The *ubaie*, Danyal."

Inas saw his hand move. He crumbled the fragile fabrics in his fist and tore them away, unseating her headcloth. Her hair spilled across her shoulders, rippling black.

Danyal licked his lips, his eyes now openly upon her chest.

There was a scream of rage, and from the corner of her eye she saw her father, on his knees, a bloody blade in his least-damaged hand, reaching again toward Hafeez.

Danyal still held her, his attention on his master; Inas brought both of her knees up, aiming to crush his man-parts, as Thelma Delance had described.

The villain gasped, eyes rolling up. His grip loosened, she fell to the floor, rolling, in order to confound the aim of the gun, and there was a confusion of noises, and her father shouting "Run!"—and run she did, her hair streaming and her face uncovered, never looking back, despite the sounds of gunfire behind her.

· · · ✧ · · ·

THE HOUSE WAS IN the merchant district of the city of Harap, a walk of many days from the prefecture Coratu, whose principal cities, Iravati and Lahore-Gadani, had lately suffered a sudden rash of explosions and fires and unexplained deaths. There were those who said it was a judgment from the gods; that Lahore-Gadani had become too assertive and Iravati too complacent in its tranquility. The priests had ordered a cleansing, and a month-long fast for the entire prefecture. Perhaps it would be enough.

In Harap, though.

In Harap, at that certain house, a boy crossed the street from out of the night-time shadows and made a ragged salaam to the doorman.

"Peace," he said, in a soft, girlish voice. "I am here to speak with Jamie Moore."

The doorman gave him one bored look. "Why?"

The boy hefted the sack he held in his left hand. "I have something for him."

"Huh." The doorman considered it, then swung sideways, rapping three times on the door. It opened and he said to the one who came forward, "Search him. I'll alert the boss."

* * * ✧ * * *

THE SEARCH HAD DISCOVERED WEAPONS, of course, and they had been confiscated. The bag, they scanned, discovering thereby the mass and material of its contents. Indeed, the search was notable in that which it did not discover—but perhaps, to off-worlders, such things mattered not.

The door to the searching chamber opened and the doorman looked in.

"You're fortunate," he said. "The boss is willing to play."

So, then, there was the escort, up to the top of the house, to another door, and the room beyond, where a man sat behind a desk, his books piled, open, one upon the other, a notetaker in his hand.

Tears rose. She swallowed them, and bowed the bow of peace.

"I'm Jamie Moore," the man behind the desk said. "Who are you?"

"I am Inas Bhar, youngest daughter of Scholar Reyman Bhar, who died the death to preserve what I bring you tonight."

The man looked at her, blue eyes—outworlder eyes—bland and uninterested.

"I don't have a lot of time or patience," he said. "Forget the theatrics and show me what you've got."

She swallowed, her throat suddenly dry. This—this was the part of all her careful plans that might yet go awry. She opened the bag, reached inside and pulled out the *curiat*.

"For you," she said, holding it up for him to see, "from Thelma Delance."

There was a long silence, while he looked between her and the box. Finally, he held out his hands.

"Let me see."

Reluctantly, she placed the *curiat* in his hands, watching as he flicked the ivory hooks, raised the lid, fished out a volume, and opened it at random.

He read a page, the next, rifled to the back of the book and read two pages more. He put the book back in the box and met her eyes.

"It's genuine," he said and gave her the honor of a seated bow. "The Juntavas owes you. What'll it be? Gold? A husband with position? I realize the options are limited on this world, but we'll do what we can to pay fair."

"I do not wish to marry. I want . . ." She stopped, took a breath, and met the bland, blue eyes. "My father was a scholar. He taught me to be a scholar—to read, to reason, to *think*. I want to continue—in my father's memory."

He shrugged. "Nice work, if you can get it."

Inas drew herself up. "I speak five dialects and three languages," she said. "I am adept with the higher maths and with astronomy. I read the mercantile, scholarly and holy scripts. I know how to mix the explosive *skihi* and—" The man behind the desk held up a hand.

"Hold up. You know how to mix *skihi*? Who taught you that?"

She pointed at the *curiat*. "Page thirty-seven, volume three."

He whistled. "You found the cipher, did you? Clever girl." He glanced thoughtfully down at the box.

"You wouldn't have used any of that formula, would you? Say, back home or in Lahore-Gadani?"

Inas bowed, scholar to scholar. "They killed my father. He had no sons to avenge him."

"Right."

More silence—enough that Inas began to worry about the reasoning going on behind those blue out-worlder eyes. It would, after all, be a simple thing to shoot her—and far more merciful than the punishment the priests would inflict upon her, were she discovered dressed in a boy's tunic and trousers, her face uncovered, her hair cut and braided with green string.

"Your timing's good," Jamie Moore said abruptly. "We've got a sector chief checking in tomorrow. What I can do, I can show you to the chief, and the two of you can talk. This is sector chief business, understand me?"

Inas bowed. "I understand, Jamie Moore. Thank you."

"Better hold that until you meet the chief," he said, and the door opened behind her, though she had not seen him give a signal.

"We'll stand you a bath, a meal and a bed," he said, and jerked his head at the doorman. "Get her downstairs. Guard on the door."

He looked at her once more. "What happens next is up to you."

. . . ⟡ . . .

SHE SAT ON THE EDGE of the *chatrue*—well, no she didn't. Properly a *chatrue*, a female's bed, would be hidden by a curtain at a height so that even a tall man could not see over. This was hardly a bed meant for a woman . . .

She sat on the edge of the bed then, with the daybreak meal in dishes spread around her, amazed and appreciative at the amount of food she was given to break her fast.

But, after all—she had come to the house in the clothes of a boy, admitted to taking a son's duty of retribution to herself; and agreed to meet with the *sector chief*. These were all deeds worthy of male necessities; hence they fed her as a male would be fed, with two kinds of meat, with porridge of proper sweetness and with extra honey on the side, with fresh juice of the gormel-berry—and brought her clean boy's clothes in the local style, that she might appear before the sector chief in proper order.

She had slept well, waking only once, at the sound of quiet feet in the stairway. Left behind when she woke then was a half-formed dream: In it she had lost her veils to Danyal, but rather than leer, he had screamed and run, terrified of what he had seen revealed in her face.

Too late now to run, she thought as she slipped back into sleep, both Danyal and her father's false friend had fallen to her vengeance. And the *curiat* was in the hands of the infidel.

Inas ate all the breakfast, leaving but some honey. There had been too many days since her father's death when food had been scarce; too many nights when her stomach was empty, for her to stint now on sustenance.

"Hello, Child!" A voice called from outside the door. There followed a brisk knock, with the sound of laughter running behind it. "Your appointment begins now!"

· · ·✧· · ·

THE NAME OF JAMIE Moore's boss was Sarah Chang. She was small and round, with crisp black hair bristling all over her head, and slanting black eyes. Her clothing was simple—a long-sleeved shirt, open at the throat, a vest, trousers and boots. A wide belt held a pouch and a holster. Her face was naked, which Inas had expected. What she had not expected was the jolt of shock she felt.

Sarah Chang laughed.

"You're the one pretending to be a boy," she commented, and Inas bowed, wryly.

"I am an exception," she said. "I do not expect to meet myself."

"*Here*, you're an exception," the woman corrected, and pointed at one of the room's two chairs, taking the other for herself. "Sit. Tell me what happened. Don't leave anything out. But don't dawdle."

So, she had told it. The gift of the *curiat*; the visit of Scholar Hafeez to her father; Humaria's wedding; the violation of her father's study, and his brutal questioning; her escape into the night, and return to a house of the unjustly murdered—father, books and servant. Her revenge.

"You mixed a batch of skihi, blew up a couple buildings, disguised yourself as a boy and walked away from it," Sarah Chang said, by way of summing up. She shook her head. "Pretty cool. How'd you think of all that?"

Inas moved her hands. "I learned from Thelma Delance. The

recipe for *skihi* was in her *curiat*. She disguised herself as a man in order to pursue her scholarship."

"So she did." The woman closed her eyes. "Any idea what I should do with you?"

Inas licked her lips. "I wish to be a scholar."

"Not the line of work women usually get into, hereabouts." Sarah Chang's eyes were open now, and watching carefully.

"Thelma Delance—"

"Thelma was an outworlder," the boss interrupted. "Like I am. Like Jamie is."

This woman possessed a man's hard purpose, Inas thought; she would do nothing for pity. She raised her chin.

"Surely, then, there is some place where I, too, would be an outworlder, and free to pursue my life as I wish?"

Sarah Chang laughed.

"How old are you?" She asked then.

"Fourteen winters."

The boss tipped her head. "Thirteen Standards, near enough. Regular old maid. And you've got a nice touch with an explosive.

"*Skihi*, for your information, is an extremely volatile mixture. Many explosive experts have the missing fingers to prove it." She bounced out of her chair and shook her head.

"All right, Inas, let's go."

She stayed in her chair, looking up into the slanting black eyes. "Go where?"

"Out-world," the boss said, and moved an impatient hand, pointing upward, toward the sky—and beyond.

✧ Quiet Knives ✧

THE TURTLES HAD CANCELED, the tidy kill-fee deposited to ship's funds just before the message had hit her in box.

Just as well, thought Midj Rolanni, wearily. She sagged back into the pilot's chair and reached for the cup nestled in the armrest holder. She'd hadn't really wanted to reconfigure the flight deck for two turtles, anyway.

The 'toot wasn't exactly prime grade and being cold didn't improve it. She drank it anyway, her eyes on the screen, but seeing through it, into the past, and not much liking what she saw.

She finished the cold 'toot in a swallow, shuddered and threw the cup at the recycler. It hit the unit's rim, shimmied for a heartbeat, undecided, and fell in, for a wonder. Midj sighed and leaned to the board, saving the turtles' cancellation with a finger-tap, and accessing the stored message queue.

There wasn't much there besides the turtles' message—the transmittal, listing the cargo she'd paid Teyope to carry for her and the credit letter from the bank, guaranteeing the funds, half on cargo transmittal, half on delivery.

And the letter from Kore. Pretty thin letter, really, just a couple of lines. Not what you'd call reason for off-shipping a perfectly profitable cargo onto a trader just a little gray—". . . just a little gray," she repeated the thought under her breath—and Teyope *did* owe her, which even he acknowledged, damn his black heart; so the cargo was in a fine way to arriving as ordered, where ordered, and not a line of the guarantees found in violation.

She hoped.

Her hand moved on its own, fingers tapping the access, though she could have told the whole of Kore's note out from heart. Still, her eyes tracked the sentences, few as they were, as if she'd never read them before.

Or as if she hoped they'd say something different this time.

Her bad luck, the words formed the same sentences they had since the first, the sentences making up one spare paragraph, the message of which was—trouble.

Midj. You said, if I ever changed my mind, you'd come. Cessilee Port, Shaltren, on Saint Belamie's Day. I'll meet you. Kore.

"And for this," she said out loud, hearing her voice vibrate against the metal skin of her ship. "For this, you shed cargo and take your ship—your home and your livelihood—onto Juntavas headquarters?"

It wasn't the first time she'd asked the question since the letter's receipt. Sometimes, she'd whispered it, sometimes shouted. *Skeedaddle*, now. Her ship didn't tell her nothing, but that she needed to go. She'd promised, hadn't she?

And so she had—promised. Half her lifetime ago, and the hardest thing she'd done before or since was to close the hatch on him, knowing where he was going. She'd replayed their last conversation until her head ached and her eyes blurred, wondering what she could have said instead, that would have made him understand . . .

But he *had* understood. He'd chosen, eyes open, knowing her, knowing how she felt. He'd said as much, and say what you would about Korelan Zar, he was no liar, nor ever had been.

"You go, then," the memory of her voice, shaking, filled her ears. "If this job is so important you gotta take up the Juntavas, too—then go. I ain't gonna stop you. And I ain't gonna know you, either. Walk down that ramp, Korelan, and you're as good as dead to me, you hear?"

She remembered his face: troubled, but not anything like rethinking the plan. He'd thought it through—he'd told her so, and she believed him. Kore'd always been the thinker of the two of them.

"Midj," he said, and she remembered that his voice hadn't been precisely steady, either. "I've got to. I told you—"

"You told me," she'd interrupted, harsher maybe in memory than in truth. She remembered she'd been crying by then, with her hand against the open hatch, and the ramp run down to blastcrete, a car waiting, its windows opaqued and patient, just a few yards beyond.

"You told me," she'd said again, and she remembered that it had been hard to breathe. "And I told you. I ain't comin' with you. I ain't putting *Skeedaddle* into Juntavas service. You want to sell yourself, I guess you got the right. But this ship belongs to me."

His face had closed then, and he nodded, just once, slung his kit over his shoulder and headed down the ramp. Chest on fire, she'd watched him go, heard her own voice, barely above a whisper.

"Kore . . ."

He turned and looked up to where she stood, fists braced against her ship.

"You change your mind," she said, "you send. I'll come for you."

He smiled then, so slight she might've missed it, if she hadn't known him so well.

"Thanks, Midj. I'll remember that."

In the present, Midj Rolanni, captain-owner of the independent tradeship *Skeedaddle*, one of a dozen free traders elected as liaison to TerraTrade—respectable and respected—Midj Rolanni drew a hard breath.

Twenty Standards. And Kore had remembered.

* * * ◇ * * *

SHE SET DOWN AS PREARRANGED in Vashon's Yard and walked over to the office, jump-bag on her shoulder.

Vashon himself was on the counter, fiddling with the computer, fingers poking at the keys. He looked up and nodded, then put his attention back on the problem at hand. Midj leaned her elbows on the counter and frowned up at the ship board.

Rebella was in port—no good news, there—and *BonniSu*, which was better. In fact, she'd actively enjoy seeing Su Bonner, maybe buy her a beer and catch up on the news. Been a couple Standards since they'd been in port together, and Su had bought last time . . .

"Sorry, Cap," Vashon said, breaking into this pleasant line of thought. "Emergency order, all good now. What'll it be?"

All spacers were "Cap" to Vashon, who despite it was one of the best all-around spaceship mechanics in the quadrant—and maybe the next.

"Ship's *Skeedaddle*, out of Dundalk," she said, turning from the board. "Got an appointment for a general systems check. Replace what's worn, lube the coils, and bring her up to spec—that's a Sanderson rebuild in there, now, so the spec's 're—"

"Right, right . . ." He was poking at the keys again, bringing up the records. "Got it all right here, Cap. How're them podclamps we fitted working out for you?"

"Better'n the originals," she said honestly, which was no stretch, the originals having seen a decade of hard use before *Skeedaddle* ever came to her, never mind what she'd put on 'em.

"Good," he said absently, frowning down at his screen. "Now, that Sanderson—we have it on-file to tune at ninety-percent spec, that being efficient enough for trade work, like we talked about. You're still wantin'—"

"Bring her up to true spec," Midj interrupted, which she'd decided already and, dammit, she wasn't going to second-guess herself at this hour. If she was a fool, then she was, and it wouldn't be the first time she'd made the wrong call.

Not even close.

Vashon was nodding, making quick notes on his keypad. "Bring her to true spec, aye, Cap, will do." He looked up.

"You'll be wanting the upgraded vents, then, Cap? If you're going to be running at spec, I advise it."

She nodded. "Take a look at the mid-ship stabilizer, too, would you? Moving her just now, I thought I noticed a slide."

" 'Cause you come in without cans," he said, making another note. "But, sure, we'll check it—ought to ride stable, cans or no cans." He looked up again.

"Anything else?"

"That's all I know about. If you find anything major that needs fixing, I'll be at the Haven."

"Haven it is," he said, entering that into the file, too. "Cash, card, or ship's credit?"

"Ship's credit."

"Right, then." He gave her a crabbed smile. "She ought to be good to go by the end of the week, barring we find anything unexpected. You can check progress on our stats channel, updated every two hours, local. Ship's name is your passcode."

"Thanks," she said, and shifted the bag into a more comfortable position on her shoulder. "I'll see you at the end of the week, barring the unexpected."

They each nodded to each other and she let herself out the door that gave onto the open Port.

· · ·✧· · ·

"GOING *WHERE*?" Su Bonner paused with her beer halfway to her mouth.

"Shaltren," Midj repeated, trying to sound matter-of-fact, and not at all reassured by the other woman's decisive headshake.

"Shaltren's not the place you want to be at this particular point in time, Captain Rolanni, me heart." Su put her beer down on the table with an audible thud. "Trust me on this one, like you never have before."

"I trust you plenty," Midj said, spinning her own beer 'round the various scars on the plastic tabletop, that being a handy way to not meet her friend's eyes. "You know I do."

"Then you've given over the idea of going to Shaltren." Su picked up her beer and had a hefty swallow. "Good."

Midj sighed, still navigating the bottle through the tabletop galaxy. "So, what's wrong with Shaltren? Besides the usual."

"The usual being that it's Juntavas Headquarters? That'd be bad enough, by your lights and by mine. Lately, though, there's more. Chairman Trogar, they say, is not well-loved."

Frowning, Midj glanced up. "Must break his heart."

"Not exactly, no." Su had another swallow of beer and shook two fingers at the bartender. "What I heard is, he means to keep it that way. Anybody who talks across him or who doesn't rise fast enough when he yells 'lift!'—they're dead right off. He's got himself an aggressive expansion plan in motion and he doesn't mind spending lives—that's anybody's but his own—to get what he wants."

Midj shrugged. "The Juntavas always grabbed what they could."

The new beers came, the 'keeper collected Su's empty, looked a question at Midj and was waved away.

"Not always." Su was taking her last comment as a debating point. "I'm not saying every decent spacer should sign up onto the Juntavas workforce, but I will say they've been getting carefuller in later years. They're still trading in all the stuff nobody ought, but they haven't been as gun-happy as they were back in the day . . ." She raised a hand, showing palm.

"Cold comfort to you and yours, I grant. The fact remains, there was a trend toward less of that and more . . . circumspection—and now what rises to the top of the deck but Grom Trogar, who wants a return to the bad old days—and looks like getting them."

"Well." Midj finished her beer, set the bottle aside, and cracked the seal on the second.

"*So,*" Su said into the lengthening silence. "You changed your mind about going to Shaltren, right? At least until somebody resets Mr. Trogar's clock?"

Midj sighed and met her friend's eyes. "Don't see my business waiting that long, frankly."

"What business is worth losing your ship, getting killed, or both?"

Trust Su to ask the good questions. Midj kept her eyes steady.

"You remember Korelan Zar," she not-asked, and Su frowned.

"Tall, thin fella; amber eyes and coffee-color skin," she said slowly. "I remember thinking that skin was so pretty-looking." She fingered her beer. "Your partner, right? He was the one that told you one day he take you to Panore for a vacation, right?"

Midj nodded, said nothing.

Su's sip was nearly a chug, then she continued into the silence.

"Right. Always wondered what happened to him. Never got around to asking. Must be—what? Fifteen, eighteen Standards?"

"Twenty." Her voice sounded tight in her own ears. "What happened to him was he figured he had to sign on with another crew—he had reasons, they seemed good to him, and that's all twenty

Standards in the past. Thing is, I told him, if he ever needed to ship out—call, and I'd come get him."

Su was quiet. Midj had a swig of beer, and another.

"And where he is, is Shaltren," Su said eventually, after she enjoyed a couple of swigs, herself. "Midj—you don't owe him."

"I owe him—I promised." She closed her eyes, opened them. "He asked me to come."

"Shit." More quiet, then—"How soon?"

St. Belamie's Day had begun as a joke; at need, it had become a code—he'd remembered that, too, and trusted her to do the same. It was a moving target, calculated by finding the square root of the diameter of *Skeedaddle*, multiplying by the Standard day on which the message was sent and dividing by twelve. Accordingly, she had about twenty Standard Days on Kago before she lifted for Shaltren.

She'd wanted to time it closer, but there was the ship to be brought up to spec, and she daren't gamble that Vashon would find nothing wrong. Likely he wouldn't, but it wasn't the way to bet, not with Kore waiting for her, with who knew what on his dance card.

"Couple weeks, local," she said to Su, and the other woman nodded.

"Let's do this again before I ship out," she said, and finished off her beer in one long swallow. She thumped the bottle to the table. "For now, gotta lift. Business."

"I hear that," Midj said, dredging up a grin. "I'm at the Haven for the next while, then back on-ship. Gimme a holler when you know you got time for dinner. I'll stand the cost."

"Like hell you will," Su said amiably. She got her feet under her and was gone, leaving Midj alone with the rest of her beer and the tab.

• • • ✧ • • •

HE WALKED DOWN THE RAMP easy, not hurrying, a pilot on his way to his ship, that was all. He turned the corner and froze, there on the edge of the hallway, still out of range of the camera's wide eye— and the woman leaning against the wall, gun holstered, waiting.

Waiting for him, he had no doubt. He knew her—Sambra Reallen—who hadn't been anybody particular, and now ran in Grom

Trogar's pack; high up in the pack, though not so high that calling attention to herself might be fatal. If she was here, calmly waiting for him go through the one door he had to go through—then he was too late.

He nodded once, turned, and went back up the hall, walking no faster than he had going down, and with as little noise.

Too late, he thought, as he reached street-level. *Damn*.

* * * ⋄ * * *

THERE WERE TWO WAYS to play it from here, given that he'd sworn not to be a damn fool. The strike for the ship, that might've been foolish, though he'd had reason to hope that the fiction of the Judge's continued residence would cover him. The judge's absence would still serve as cover, since he *was* the Judge's courier. But the fact that one of Chairman Trogar's own had been waiting for him—that was bad. He wondered how bad, as he ran his keycard through the coder.

If they'd been waiting for him at the ship, then they likely knew some things. They probably knew that the judge and most of the household were gone, scattered, along with all the rest of the judges and staff who had managed to go missing before Grom Trogar thought to look for them. It was unlikely that they knew everything—and they'd figure that, too. Which meant he had a bad time ahead of him.

Nothing to help it now—if he ran anywhere on Shaltren, they'd catch him, and the inconvenience would only make his examination worse. If he waited for them, and went peaceably—it was going to be bad. Chairman Trogar would see to that.

If they'd been at the ship, they'd be *here* soon, if they weren't already.

The door to the house slid open.

He stepped inside, playing the part of a man with nothing to fear. His persona had long been established—a bit stolid, a bit slow, a steady pilot, been with the judge since his itinerant days.

He flicked on the lights—public room empty. So far, so good. They'd take their time coming in—Judges and their crews, after all, had a reputation for being a bit chancy to mess with.

There was some urgency on him now. He'd planned for back-up; it was second nature anymore to plan for back-up. At the time it had seemed prudent and, anyway, he'd meant to be gone before it came to that.

Meant to, he thought now, walking quickly through the darkened rooms, heading for the comm room and the pinbeam. *Meant to isn't 'will.'*

He'd put a life in danger. Might have put a life in danger. If the first message had gotten through. If she hadn't just read it and laughed.

I'll come for you, she whispered in his memory, the tears running down her face, her eyes steady on his. He moved faster now, surefooted in the dark. She'd come. She'd promised. Unless something radical had happened in her life, altering her entirely from the woman he had known—Midj Rolanni kept her promises.

He'd had no right to pull her in on this. *Especially* this. Even as a contingency back-up that was never going to be called into play. No right at all.

He slapped the wall as he strode into the comm center. The lights came up, showing the room empty—but he was hearing things now. Noises on his back path. The sound, maybe, of a door being forced.

Fingers quick and steady, he called up the 'beam, fed in the ID of the receiver. The noises were closer now—heavy feet, somebody swearing. Somewhere in one of the outer rooms, glass shattered shrilly.

He typed, heard feet in the room beyond, hit *send*, cleared the log, and spun, hands up and palms showing empty.

"If you're looking for the High Judge," he said to the man holding the gun in the doorway, "he's not home."

· · · ◇ · · ·

VASHON NOT FINDING anything about to blow down in *Skeedaddle*'s innards, and the vent upgrade going more smoothly than the man himself had expected, Midj was back on-board in good order inside of eight local days.

She stowed her kit and initiated a systems check, easing into the pilot's chair with a sigh of relief. The ship was quiet; the only noises were those she knew so well that they didn't register with her anymore, except as a general sense of everything operating as it should. Of all being right in her world, enclosed and constrained as it was.

When she ran with a 'hand—never with a partner, not after Kore—the noises necessarily generated by another person sharing the space would distract and disorient her at first, but pretty soon became just another voice in the overall song of the ship.

And whenever circumstances had her on-port for any length of time, she came back to the ship with relief her overriding emotion, only too eager to lower the hatch and shut out the din of voices, machinery and weather.

Hers. Safe. Comfortable. Familiar. Down to the ancient *Vacation on Incomparable Panore* holocard Kore'd given her as a promise after one particularly hard trade run.

She'd thought before now that maybe it was time to start charting the course of her retirement. Not that she was old, though some days she felt every Standard she'd lived had been two. But she did have a certain responsibility to her ship, which could be expected to outlive a mere human's span—hell, it had already outlived two captains, and there wasn't any reason it wouldn't outlast her.

She ought to take up a second—a couple of the cousins were hopeful, so she'd heard. The time to train her replacement was while she was still in her prime, so control could be eased over gradual, with her giving more of her attention to TerraTrade, while the captain-to-be took over ship duty, until one day the change was done, as painless as could be for everyone. That's how Berl took *Skeedaddle* over from Mam, who had gone back to the planet she'd been born to for her retired years, and near as Midj had ever seen on her infrequent visits, missed neither space nor ship.

Berl, now. Midj shook her head, her eyes watching the progress of the systems check across the board. In a universe without violence— in a universe without the Juntavas—Berl would've been standing captain yet, and his baby sister maybe trading off some other ship. Maybe she'd been running back-up on *Skeedaddle*, though that wasn't the likeliest scenario, her and her brother having gotten along about as well as opinionated and high-tempered sibs ever did.

Still and all, he hadn't deserved what had come to him; and she hadn't wanted the ship that bad, having found a post that suited her on the Zar family ship. Suited her for a number of reasons, truth told, only one of them being the younger son, who came on as her partner once she'd understood Berl was really dead, and *Skeedaddle* was hers.

Full circle.

The board beeped; systems checked out clean, which was nothing more than she'd expected. She had a cold pad spoke for at the public yard; some meetings set up across the next couple days—couple of independents on-port she still needed to get to regarding their views on TerraTrade's proposed "small-trade" policies. She'd write that report before she lifted, send it on to Lezly, in case . . .

In case.

Well.

She reached to the board, opened eyes and ears, began to tap in the code for the office at the public yard—and stopped, fingers frozen over the keypad.

In the top left corner of the board, a yellow light glowed. Pinbeam message waiting, that was.

Most likely it was TerraTrade business, though she couldn't immediately call to mind anything urgent enough to require a 'beam. Still, it happened. That's why emergencies were called emergencies.

She tapped the button, the message screen lit, sender ID scrolled—not a code she recognized, off-hand—and then the message.

Situation's changed. Don't come. K

* * * ✧ * * *

THE ROOM WAS SOFTLY LIT, his chair comfortable. For the moment, there were no restraints, other than those imposed by the presence of the woman across the table from him.

"Where is the High Judge, Mr. Zar?"

She was courteous, even gentle, despite having asked this selfsame question at least six times in the last few hours.

"Evaluation tour, is what he told me," he answered, letting some frustration show.

"An evaluation tour," his interlocutor repeated, a note of polite disbelief entering her cool voice. "What sort of evaluation?"

"Of the other judges," he said, and sighed hard, showing her his empty hands turned palm-up on his knee. "He was going to visit them on the job, see how they were doing, talk to them. It's a regular thing he does, every couple Standards." That last at least was true.

"I see." She nodded. He didn't know her name—she hadn't told him one, and she wasn't somebody he knew. She had a high smooth forehead, a short brush of pale hair and eyes hidden by dark glasses. One of Grom Trogar's own—his sister, for all Kore knew or cared.

What mattered was that she could make his life very unhappy, not to say short, unless he could convince her he was short on brains *and* info.

"It seems very odd to me," she said now, conversationally, "that the High Judge would embark on such a tour without his pilot."

They'd been over this ground, too.

"I'm a courier pilot," he said, keeping a visible lid on most of his frustration, "not a big-ship pilot. I fly courier work, small traders, that kind of thing. I stay here, in case I'm needed."

She hesitated; he could almost taste her weighing the question of the rest of the household's whereabouts against his own actions. Questions regarding his actions won out.

"You went to the courier shed this afternoon, is that correct?"

"Yes," he said, a little snappish.

"Why?" Getting a little snappish, herself.

"I had a 'beam from the judge, with instructions."

"Instructions to lift?"

"Yes."

"And yet you didn't lift, Mr. Zar. I wonder why not."

He shrugged, taking it careful here. "There was a guard on the door. It smelled wrong, so I went back to the house and sent a 'beam to the judge."

"I see. Which guard?"

He had no reason to protect the woman who'd been waiting for him. On the other hand, he had no reason to tell this woman the truth.

"Nobody I'd seen before."

She shook her head, but let that line go, too. Time enough to ask the question again, later.

"Once more, Mr. Zar—where is the High Judge?"

"I told you—on evaluation tour."

"Where is Natesa the Assassin?"

She was trying to throw him off. He gave an irritable shrug. "How the hell do I know? You think a courier assigns Judges?"

"Hm. What was the destination of the lift you did not make?"

He shook his head. "High Judge's business, ma'am. I'm not to disclose that without his say. If you want to 'beam him and get his OK . . ."

She laughed, very softly, and leaned back in her chair, sliding her dark glasses off and holding them lightly between the first and middle fingers of her right hand. Her eyes were large and pale gray, pupils shrinking to pinpoints in the dim light.

"You are *good*, Mr. Zar—my compliments. Unfortunately, I think you are not quite the dull fellow you play so well. We both know what happens next, I think? Unless there is something you wish to tell me?"

He waited, a beat, two . . . .

She shook her head—regretfully, he thought, and extended a long hand to touch a button on her side of the table. The door behind her slid open, admitting two men, one carrying a case, the other a gun.

The woman rose, languidly, and motioned them forward. Kore felt his stomach tighten.

"Mr. Zar has decided that a dose of the drug is required to aid his memory, gentlemen. I'll be back in ten minutes."

* * * ✧ * * *

DON'T COME . . .

Midj stared at the message, then laughed—the first real laugh she had in—gods, a Standard.

"Don't come," she snorted, leaning back in the chair in the aftermath of her laugh. "Tell me another one, Kore."

Shaking her head, she got up, went down the short hall to the galley and drew herself a cup of 'toot, black and sweet.

Sipping, she walked back to the pilot's chamber and stood behind the chair, looking down at the message on the screen.

"Now, of all the things he might've expected me to remember, wouldn't that have been one of 'em?" She asked her ship. There was no answer except for the smooth hum of the air filtering system. But, then, what other answer was needed? *Skeedaddle* knew Kore as well as she did.

As well as she *had*.

Twenty-six years ago, Midj Rolanni had been taken up as trader by Amin Zar, and working beside the least of Amin's sons, one Korelan, who also had a head for trade. Their eighth or ninth stop, they were set to meet with one of the Zar cousins, who was a merchant on the port. Taking orbit, they collected their messages, including one from the cousin: "Don't come."

Amin Zar took a look at that message, nodded, broke open the weapons locker and issued arms. They went down on schedule, whereupon Amin and the elder sibs disembarked, leaving Kore, Midj, and young Berta in care of the ship.

Several hours later, they were back, Amin carrying the cousin, and a few of the sibs bloodied—and Midj still had bad dreams about the lift outta there.

After it all calmed down, she'd asked Kore why they'd gone in, when they'd clearly been warned away.

And he'd laughed and told her that "Don't come" was Zar family code for "help."

She sipped some more 'toot, took the half-empty cup over to the chute and dumped it in.

The time, she thought, going back and sitting in her chair, had come to face down some truths.

Truth Number One: she was a damn fool.

Truth Number Two: so was the Korelan Zar she had known, twenty Standards ago. Who but a damn fool left the woman, the ship and the life that he loved for a long shot at changing the galaxy?

And who but a damn fool let him go alone?

What came into play now were those same twenty Standards and what they might have done to the man at his core.

She noted that he never had said he'd changed his mind, in that first, brief call for her to come get him. The Kore she knew had never been a liar, preferring misdirection to outright falsehoods. It looked like he'd kept that tendency, and its familiarity had been the one thing that had convinced her the letter was genuine; St. Belamie giving her a second.

And this—this was the third validation, and the most compelling reason to continue on the course she had charted, in case she was having any last minute doubts.

"You gonna die for twenty Standards ago?" She asked herself, and heard her voice echo off the metal walls of her ship.

You gonna turn your back on a friend when he needs your help? Her ship whispered in the silence that followed.

No, she thought. No; she'd done that once, and it had stuck in her craw ever since.

One good thing—she could go on her own time, now, since the way she saw it, "don't come" trumped St. Belamie.

Smiling, she reached to the board and opened a line.

"Tower, this is *Skeedaddle*, over at Vashon's Yard. How soon can I lift outta here?"

* * * ✧ * * *

THERE WERE RESTRAINTS this time, uncomfortably tight, and a violent headache.

So, he thought, laboriously, *you wanted to make the guy with the gun use it, and he did. Quitcherbitchin.*

"He's back," a man's voice said breathlessly from somewhere to the left.

He'd managed to land some blows of his own, which didn't comfort him much, since he was still alive.

A man moved into view, his right cheek smeared with blood and a rising shiner on his left eye.

Good, he thought, and then saw the injector. *Not good*.

He tried to jerk away, but the cords only tightened, constricting his breathing—some kind of tanglewire, then. He might be able to—

"No, you don't, flyboy," the man with the injector snarled, and grabbed his chin in an iron grip, holding him immobile while the cold nozzle against his neck.

There was a hiss, a sharp sting, and the injection was made. The man with the black eye released him and stepped back, grinning.

He closed his eyes. *Fool*, he thought.

The drug worked fast. The irritation of the wire was the first thing to fade from his perception, then the raging headache. He lost track of his feet, his fingers, his legs, his heartbeat, and, finally, his thoughts. He hung, limbless, without breath or heartbeat, a nameless clot of fog, without thought or volition.

"What is your name?" A voice pierced the fog.

"Korelan Zar," another voice answered, slowly. Inside the fog, something stirred, knew the voice and the name. He recognized, dimly, peril.

"Good," said the first voice. "Where is the High Judge?"

"I don't know," he heard himself say.

"I see. Why were you going to your ship?"

"Orders."

"What orders?" He was listening in earnest now, interested in the answer; expecting to hear another, "I don't know . . ."

"Orders to get out, if it looked like all was going to hell." *Well*, he thought, inside the thinning fog, *that certainly makes sense*.

"And things in your opinion were going to hell?"

He'd said so, hadn't he? "Yes."

"Ah," said the voice. That not being a question, he found himself speechless. Time passed; he felt the fog growing dense about him again.

"What," the voice said, sharp enough to shred the fog and cut him where he hung, defenseless. "What was the text of the last message you sent to the High Judge?"

"Situation stable," he heard himself answer.

"When was that?"

"Four weeks ago, local."

More silence; this time, he found he was able to concentrate and thin the fog further. He could feel the shadows of the tanglewire binding him to the chair; a breath of headache . . .

"You were at the comm when we located you earlier this evening. Who did you send to?"

A question had been asked; the drug compelled him to answer with the truth, but the truth had facets . . ..

"An old girlfriend."

"Indeed. What's her name?"

The answer formed; he felt the words on his tongue, swelling, filling his mouth, his throat . . .

"Impressive," the voice didn't-ask, releasing him. Exhausted, he fell back into the fog, felt it close softly around him, hiding the restraints, the pain, the sense of his own self.

"What," the voice asked, soft now, almost as if it were part of the fog, "is the code of the last receiver to which you sent a pinbeam?"

Calmly, his voice told the code, while he sank deeper into the fog and at last stopped listening.

• • • ✧ • • •

SHE SET *Skeedaddle* down in the general port, calling some minor attention to herself by requesting a hot pad. Tower was so bland and courteous she might have been back on Kago, which didn't comfort her as much as maybe it should have.

Sighing, she levered out of the pilot's chair and stretched, careful of her back and shoulders, before moving down the hall.

She pulled a pellet pistol from the weapons locker, and a needle gun—nothing more than a trigger, a spring and the needle itself. Completely illegal on most worlds, of course, though she'd come by it legally enough: It had been with Berl's body when it came back, with his ship, to his sister.

She slipped the needle gun into a hideaway pocket, and clipped the pistol to her belt. That done, she straightened her jacket, sealed the locker and went back to the galley for a cup of 'toot and a snack while the hull cooled.

• • • ✧ • • •

THE FACT THAT THEY hadn't killed him was—worrisome. That they kept him here, imprisoned, but not particularly misused, indicated that they thought there was more he could tell them.

He'd had time to consider that; time to weigh whether he ought to file his last flight now and preserve what—and who—he could.

The end of that line of consideration was simply that he wanted to live. His one attempt toward suicide had failed and he couldn't say, even considering present conditions, that he was sorry on that score. If it came down that he died in the line of doing something useful, then that was how it was. But to die uselessly, while there were still cards in play—no.

That decision left open the question of what he could do of use, confined and maybe being used as bait. Not that the judge would fall for bait, but Grom Trogar might not know that. In fact, Chairman Trogar might well see the Judge's concern for his household and his courier as a weakness to be exploited. Big believer in exploiting other people's weaknesses, Mr. Trogar.

Having the time, he thought about his life past, and what he might've done different, if he hadn't been your basic idealistic idiot. Put that way, he could see himself staying with Midj, leading a trader's prosperous life, raising a couple of kids, maybe getting into politics. There were more ways to change the galaxy than the route he had chosen. And who was to say that change was the best thing?

He'd been so sure.

. . . ◈ . . .

SHE HAD A PLAN, if you could call it that. Whoever had fixed the alias for the pin-beam Kore had sent his last message from had been good, and if she'd started with no information, she'd right now be on a planet known as Soltier, somewhere over in the next quadrant. Knowing that Kore was on Shaltren made the exercise of tracking the 'beam somewhat easier, and she thought she had a reasonable lock on his last location.

Nothing guaranteed that he'd still be at that location, of course, but it was really the only card she had, unless she wanted to go calling on the chairman, which she was holding in reserve as her Last Stupid Idea.

For her first trick, she needed a cab.

There was a cab stand at the end of the street, green-and-white glow-letters spelling out *Robo Cab! Cheap! Quick! Reliable!*

Right.

She leaned in, hit the call button, and walked out to the curb to wait.

Traffic wasn't in short supply this planet-noon, and the port looked prosperous enough. If you didn't know you were on galactic crime headquarters, in fact, it looked amazingly normal.

Up the street, a cab cut across three lanes of traffic, angling in toward her position, the green-and-white Robo Cab logo bright in the daylight. It pulled up in front of her, the door opened and she stepped in.

Mistake.

"Good afternoon, Captain Rolanni," said the woman pointing the gun at her. "Let's have lunch."

The door snapped shut and the cab accelerated into traffic.

* * * ⋄ * * *

IT WAS GOING TO take a bit to disable the camera, but he thought he had a workable notion, there. The hard part was going to be getting out the door. After that, he'd have to deal with the details: scoping out where, exactly, he was, and how, exactly, to get out.

He'd read somewhere that it was the duty of prisoners taken in war to attempt to escape, in order, so he guessed, to make the other side commit more resources to keeping their prisoners where they belonged. It had occurred to him at the time that the efficient answer to that might be to shoot all the troublemakers at hand and institute a policy of taking no prisoners. On the other hand, with Mr. Trogar having erred on the side of prisoner-taking, he supposed there was a certain usefulness to confounding the home guard.

Or, as the Judge was a little too fond of saying, "Let's throw a rock in the pond and see who we piss off."

* * * ⋄ * * *

SURPRISINGLY ENOUGH, it *was* lunch, and if there was a guard mounted outside the door of the private parlor and her host was armed, no one had gotten around to taking the gun that openly rode on her belt, or searched her for any hidden surprises she might be carrying.

Lunch was simple—premade sandwiches, hand pastries, coffee, and some local fruit.

To hear her tell it, the host's name was Sambra Reallen, which was as good as any other name. She professed herself a not-friend of the current chairman, on which point Midj reserved judgment, considering the manner of their meeting. Since she also seemed to hold some interesting information, Midj was willing to listen to her for the space it took to eat a sandwich and savor a couple of cups of the real bean.

"You're here for Korelan Zar," Sambra Reallen said. It was disturbing to hear that fact stated so baldly, no "am I right?" about it.

There was no use playing games, so Midj nodded slowly and sipped her coffee. "Man asked me to give him a ride off-world. That against the law?"

The other woman grinned, quick and feral. "At the moment, the law here is the chairman's whim. Given that—yes, I'm afraid it is."

"That's too bad," Midj said, hoping she sounded at least neutral.

"You could say that," Sambra Reallen agreed. She wasn't drinking coffee, and she hadn't even bothered to look at the sandwich in front of her. "Captain Rolanni, do you have any idea who Korelan Zar *is*?"

Well, that was a question, now, wasn't it? Midj shrugged. "Old friend. Called in a favor. I came. That's how we do things, out where the chairman's whims count for spit."

Another quick grin. "I'll take that as a long 'no,'" she said. "Korelan Zar is the High Judge's courier."

Midj sipped coffee, considering. She decided that she didn't really care what the Juntavas had to do with judges or judging, and looked up to meet Sambra Reallen's sober gaze.

"Kore was a hell of a pilot," she said, which was nothing but the truth.

The Juntava snorted. "So he was and so he is. He's also been with the High Judge for twenty Standards—maybe more. The two of them came out of nowhere—the High Judge, he wasn't a judge then; the closest we had to judges were the enforcers—and that wasn't close at all. He sold the Justice Department idea to the then-chairman—the chairman that the present whimsical guy we've got replaced, you understand. The two of them—Zar and the judge—they set up the whole system, recruited judges, trained 'em and set 'em loose. I don't know how many judges there are now—the last number I heard was thirty, but I think that's low—very low. The High Judge isn't a man who shows you all the cards he's got in his hand—and Korelan Zar's just like him."

It was a fair description of Kore, all things weighed. And the project itself jibed with the one he'd tried to sell her on, sitting across from her in *Skeedaddle*'s tiny galley, holding her hands so hard she felt the bones grinding together. Bunch of crazy talk, she'd thought then. Now . . . well, say the years had given her a different understanding of what was necessarily crazy.

"Not that I'm disinterested in your problems," she said now to Sambra Reallen, "but I'm not quite grasping what this has to do with me."

The other woman nodded vigorously. "Thank you, yes. You do need to know what this has to do with you." She leaned forward, face intent, eyes hard.

"The High Judge, his household, all the judges I know about and all those I don't—are gone. Say that they are not blessed with the chairman's favor. I don't doubt—I *know*—that the High Judge had a plan. He must have foreseen—if not the current situation, at least the *possibility* of the current situation. He would have planned for this. His very disappearance forces me to conclude that he *does* have a plan, and has only withdrawn for a time to marshal his forces and his allies."

Midj shrugged. "So?"

"So." Sambra Reallen leaned deliberately back in her chair. "About a month ago, local, the chairman realized the High Judge had not been seen in some while. That, indeed, the entire network of judges, as far as they are known, had slipped through the hands of his seekers. He realized, indeed, that the sole member of the High Judge's household remaining upon Shaltren was—"

"The courier." Midj put down her cup, all her attention now focused on the other woman.

Sambra Reallen nodded. "Precisely. The word went out that Korelan Zar should be brought to the chairman. How Zar heard of the order, I don't know, but I'm not surprised that he did. He made a strike for his ship, as I was sure he would, and I waited for him there, hoping to divert him to a safe place. Something must have spooked him; he returned to the High Judge's house—and was taken into custody shortly thereafter."

"Hm. How 'bout if it was you who spooked him?" Midj asked.

"I'm thinking that altruism isn't exactly your style. What'd you want from Kore in exchange for the safe berth?"

The other woman's face tightened. "Information! The High Judge must be planning something—I must know what it is! The chairman can't be allowed to continue—he's already lost us ground on three significant worlds and will loose Stelubia entirely if he's not stopped. All of that would be reason enough, if there weren't Turtles in the mix, too!"

Midj blinked. "Turtles? Clutch Turtles?"

"There's another kind?"

"Not that I know of. These would be two, and asking after the health of a couple of humans they adopted, am I right?"

Sambra Reallen nodded, sighed.

"Indeed," she said finally, finding her pastry's icing a fascinating diversion from the discussion as she weighed some inner necessity.

"These things are too big to be secret," she continued, "no matter how hard any of us wish to hide them. Here you are, fresh in, and already the word is out."

The pilot relaxed slightly, realizing that the Juntava was apparently too focused on her own set of woes to pursue Midj's familiarity with the doings of the Clutch.

"I've been reading history, Captain Rolanni. The vengeance that these two beings may visit upon the entire organization if their petition is mishandled—and there is no possibility that the chairman will *not* mishandle it—doesn't bear thinking about. I—action needs to be taken. But I must know what the High Judge is planning."

"And you think Kore knows."

"Yes."

"But Kore's been taken by the chairman," Midj pointed out, trying to keep the thought—and its implications—from reaching real nerve endings. "If he's as ruthless as you say, he's already cracked Kore's head open and emptied out everything inside." *Including my name, my ship's name, and the fact that I was coming for him.* That *did* touch nerve, and she picked up her cup, swigging down the last of the cold coffee.

"The chairman tried to do exactly that," Sambra Reallen said. "Mr.

Zar's defenses are formidable—also, as I discover from my study of the session transcript, he wasn't asked the right question."

"You got my name from the transcript, then."

"No." The Juntava shook her head. "I got your pinbeam receiver ID from the transcript. Mr. Zar could not be persuaded to part with your name, though he was obviously experiencing some . . . discomfort for withholding the information."

The receiver ID was enough to sink her—present company being evidence—but she'd made it extra easier for them by coming on-world—and the joke was on her, if she'd taken an honest warn-away for code.

"So, what do you want from me?" Might as well ask it straight out, though she thought she had a good idea what it would be.

"I want you to pull him out of custody. I can provide you with his location, weapons if you need them, and a safe place to bring him to."

Yup, that was it. Midj shook her head.

"And what do I get?"

The Juntava pushed the untouched sandwich away and leaned her elbows on the table.

"What do you want?"

Just like that: name a price and the Juntavas would meet it. No problem. She felt a hot flash of fury and the words, *I want my brother back* rising; she kept them behind her teeth with an effort. Sat for a couple of heartbeats, breathing. Just that.

When she was sure she could trust her voice, she met the other woman's bland eyes.

"What I want is Kore, free and in shape to leave, if that's what he still wants. And I want us both to have safe passage out of here, and a guarantee that neither of us will be pursued by the Juntavas after."

There was a pause.

"I could promise you these things," Sambra Reallen said eventually, "but until I hear what Korelan Zar has to tell me—if he will tell me anything—I can't know if my promise will hold air." She raised a hand, palm out. "I understand that you have no reason to love the Juntavas, Captain. The best I can promise at this point is that, if Chairman

Trogar leaves the game, I will do my best to ensure that your conditions are met."

About what she'd figured and as good as she was going to get with no time to negotiate anyway, not with Kore's life on the line.

"Why hasn't the chairman killed him?" she asked.

The Juntava shrugged. "It could be that the chairman thinks Korelan Zar still retains some potential for amusement."

Right. Midj sighed.

"I'll need a diversion. If Kore's high-level, then there are high-level people interested in him who'll have to be drawn off."

Sambra Reallen nodded. "I'll call a department chair meeting."

Midj blinked. "You can do that?"

The Juntava smiled, letting a glimmer of genuine amusement show. "Oh, yes," she said. "I can do that."

· · · ◇ · · ·

GETTING OUT THE DOOR hadn't been so hard after all, though there was going to be hell to pay if—well, there was going to be hell to pay. It wasn't any use thinking there could be a different outcome to this.

He was sorry he wouldn't be on hand to see the finish of it, since he'd been in on the beginning. It had been a grand, beautiful scheme, so logical, so—simple. Introduce a justice system into Juntavas structure. Feed and nurture and protect it and its practitioners for twenty, thirty, fifty Standards—they hadn't been sure of the timing, but hoped to see results within their lifetimes—easily that. Lately, he thought they'd been optimistic—and not only of the timing.

Still, he had a gun, courtesy of a guard even more stupid than he was, and he knew where he was, and where he was going, more or less right down to his final breath. It was . . . freeing in a way. He felt at peace with himself, and with his purpose. If he could kill Grom Trogar, then he would depart as happy as a man filled full of pellets could be, and the plan—his plan, that he'd given up his life of small happinesses to see through—would have a second chance at continuing.

It was convenient that his holding room was in the chairman's building. Convenient that he had committed the layout of that building, along with several others, to memory years ago. He knew where the secret stair was and he knew the code that opened the hatch. He eased the panel shut behind him and began to climb.

He paused to catch his breath just below the fourteenth landing. Only one more landing, if his memory could be relied upon, and since he'd already decided that it could, why worry about it now? The hatch opened in what used to be a supply closet in the chairman's suite. He steeled himself for the unpleasant truth that he might need to kill blameless people before he got to his target. He wasn't an assassin; even killing Mr. Trogar, himself, as much as it was needed, wasn't going to be a joy. The important thing was not to freeze, not to hesitate. To acquire his target and shoot. He might get only one shot, and it was important to make it count.

Leaning against the wall, he once again went over his stolen gun. It was a good gun, loaded, well-oiled with an extra clip of pellets riding in the handle. The guard had taken good care of his weapon. Points for the—

Above him and to the left, where the ongoing flight angled off the landing, there was a noise. A very slight noise, not immediately repeated, as if someone had scuffed a boot against the edge of a step.

He went down on one knee on the step, raised the gun in two hands, and waited, breathing slow. *Easy . . .*

Another scuff, and a shadow on the dim wall of the landing. His finger tightened on the trigger. Silence—

And a sudden appalling rush of sound as a dark figure hurtled and hit the landing, flat-footed, gun out and pointing at his head. He had a moment to feel anger, then—

"Kore!"

He blinked and stared up into a pale face and dark brown eyes, short dark hair showing a blaze of gray at the temple.

"Midj?" Slowly, he lowered the gun. "What the hell are you doing here?"

"Back atcha." She lowered her own weapon and stood, a little stiffly, he thought. "But it's gonna hafta to wait. I'm supposed to be getting you out of here, to a safe place."

He frowned. "Safe by whose standards?"

"Woman by the name of Sambra Reallen."

He thought about it, shook his head. "Can't trust her."

"Can't not trust her." she countered. "She picked me up in port. Could've just as easily been the chairman, the way I hear it. She wants him gone and she don't want to jinx the High Judge's play, if he has a play. Which you're supposed to tell her."

He snorted. "She wouldn't believe me." He thought again. "How were you supposed to get me out of here?"

"Same way I came in," she said, jerking her head up the stairs. "We walk up to the roof. There's a monowing waiting to lift us out."

"OK," he said, and came to his feet. He smiled, then, and it felt like his soul was stretched so wide it might burt a seam.

"Midj, thank you."

"No problem."

· · ·✧· · ·

THEY WERE TWO STEPS below the fifteenth landing when the alarm went out. Kore threw himself onto the landing, fingers moving rapidly on the code bar. The panel slid open as Midj came up beside him.

"What's going on?"

"Damned if I know. But the doors will seal in ten seconds—go!" He pushed her through and followed, into the dimness of the supply room.

"Where are we?"

Trust Midj to ask the question. "Chairman Trogar's office."

"Great."

"Could be worse. Let's see . . ."

Carefully, he eased open the closet door. The receptionist's desk was empty, but he could hear voices out in the hall. He slipped forward, barely hearing Midj's curse as she followed him.

He crept to the hall door, peered around—and abruptly gave up stealth.

In the center of the hall, surrounded by gaping humans, stood two large green—persons. On the floor beyond them, he could see a form, a shock of white hair, a widening pool of blood, a—weapon, though what sort of weapon he scarcely knew.

The largest of the two green persons—sang. There was a flash of pinpoint light, a snap of sound and the weapon was molten metal, mixing with liquid red. There followed a stifled scream from the crowd and a shifting of bodies, and then, from the crowd, one stepped forward and bowed.

"I am called Sambra Reallen, Chairman Pro Tem," she said softly. "How may I serve you, Aged Ones?"

* * * ✧ * * *

SKEEDADDLE WAS WELL AWAY, on course for Clarine to chat with Teyope, should he have actually happened to deliver the cargo as commissioned. At least, that's what Sambra Reallen knew. It was the least of what Sambra Reallen knew, and Midj hoped she had joy in her new status. Talk about being in a position to honor promises.

"She'll have to be certified by the department heads." Kore sat down on the edge of the co-pilot's chair and held out a steaming cup. "'toot?"

"Thanks." She took it, spinning her chair to face him. She drew a breath, thinking she might be about to say something, found her mouth dry, and drank some 'toot instead.

"I wanted to say." Kore was holding his cup between both palms, staring down as if the hot liquid were a navigation screen. "I wanted to say—I'm sorry. I had no right to pull you into that, Midj, knowing what you—knowing what it could become. My arrogance. I thought I was ahead of the trouble."

"Well," she said, softly. And then again, "Well."

He looked up, amber eyes wary. The black hair showed some shine of silver, his face marked with the lines of responsibility and worry.

"Your plan. I mean your *old* plan. Is that playing out the way you'd hoped?"

He tipped his head, considering. Had a sip of 'toot.

"Not exactly. There were compromises needed. Somehow, I hadn't thought of there needing to be compromises. Some good people died, and I never meant for that to happen. Justice . . ." The ghost of a laugh. "Justice isn't always easy to cipher. I didn't expect that at all." He sighed.

"That said—we've made progress. In some direction. We've introduced another player into the game, and another set of rules. Is that a good thing, a bad thing, or of null value?" He shrugged. "Don't know."

Right.

Midj sipped her 'toot; used her chin to point at the board.

"Course is set for Clarine. It's easy to change, if you're expected somewhere. Or I can set you down where you say. . . or, you can stay on."

There, it was out in the open.

Kore was looking at her like he thought hard.

"Stay on?"

"If you want to." The cup of 'toot trembled a bit in her hand, belying her attempt at a casual tone.

She cleared her throat and met his eyes square. "Thinking over it all—I had the idea we'd been a damn-good team, Kore. Had the idea we might be again, if you're wantin' it."

She felt a moment of panic then—a moment brought on in part by twenty years of the nagging voice in her head telling her, *He joined up with his eyes open, Midj—they'll never let him go*—

"That is," she said with a challenge, "if you want it and if they'll *let* you . . ."

A pause, getting long while he—and she—sipped at their cups. Then . . .

"There isn't anything I want more," Kore said slowly. "But I—Midj, maybe we need to do this in stages. First, I gotta get back to the Judge. I've got to let him know where I am, how it is with me. And—I'd like you to meet him. Talk with him."

Meet the Juntava who had stolen away Kore and twenty years of their life? She felt the anger rise—shook it off as he kept talking.

"Then, well, I got a couple Standard years' of vacation time coming. We could go somewhere . . . like maybe Panore."

He favored her suddenly with a grin that made her sway as she laughed.

"A couple years' vacation? On Panore, is it? What did you do? Loot the strongbox?"

His grin faded, and Midj felt a chill. *Suppose he had looted the joint?*

"Nah," he admitted wryly, "I didn't. It's just that I never really took much time off. I mean the Judge project, it kept me pretty busy. And . . ."

"But Panore? I'd have thought you would have forgotten that . . ."

He shook his head then, and snorted a quiet laugh, and kind of talked into his cup for a minute like he was afraid, or too shy, to look at her.

"Nah. I always *did* mean to get out to Panore, you know. And I always kept hoping there'd be some way I could maybe get you to go with me. So when I got a chance, I put some of my money into a condo-building out there . . . one unit's mine."

He looked up, caught the look of amazement that had left her mouth half-open. She felt the words spill out unbidden.

"What? Panore's for fatcats! Do you have any idea of what it costs to live on a place like that? I, I . . ."

He signed a quick *yes* in pilot's hand-talk as he finished his 'toot.

"So yeah, I do know. But now that you brought it up, why don't we find us a cargo or two that'll take us out that way, make sure we can still work together. Then, we can make sure we can still play together."

He put the cup down and unexpectedly reached his hand out for hers. "Tell me it's a deal, and I'll sign the book as co-pilot right now."

"Deal," she said, and squeezed his hand before pulling the logbook out on its trip tray.

✦ This House ✦

I built this house out of cedar wood
and I laid the beams by hand
One for every false heart I had known
One for the true heart I planned
—from *This House* by Janis Ian

IT WAS SPRING AGAIN.

Mil Ton Intassi caught the first hint of it as he strolled through his early-morning garden—a bare flutter of warmth along the chill edge of mountain air, no more than that. Nonetheless, he sighed as he walked, and tucked his hands into the sleeves of his jacket.

At the end of the garden, he paused, looking out across the toothy horizon, dyed orange by the rising sun. Mist boiled up from the valley below him, making the trees into wraiths, obscuring the road and the airport entirely.

Spring, he thought again.

He had come here in the spring, retreating to the house he had built, to the constancy of the mountains.

Turning his back on the roiling fog, he strolled down the pale stone path, passing between banked rows of flowers.

At the center of the garden, the path forked; the left fork became a pleasant meander through the lower gardens, into the perimeter wood. It was cunning, with many delightful vistas, grassy knolls, and shady groves perfect for tête-à-têtes.

The right-hand path led straight to the house, and it was to the house that Mil Ton returned, slipping in through the terrace window, sliding it closed behind him.

He left his jacket on its peg and crossed to the stove, where he poured tea into a lopsided pottery mug before he moved on, his footsteps firm on the scrubbed wooden floor.

At the doorway to the great room, he paused, looking to his right at the fireplace, the full wall of native stone, which they had gathered and placed themselves. The grate wanted sweeping and new logs needed to be laid. He would see to it later.

Opposite the doorway was a wall of windows through which he could see the orange light unfurling like ribbons through the busy mist, and, nearer, a pleasant lawn, guarded on the far side by a band of cedar trees, their rough bark showing pink against the glossy green needles. Cedar was plentiful on this side of the mountain. So plentiful that he had used native cedar wood for beam, post, and floor.

Mil Ton turned his head, looking down the room to the letterbox. The panel light glowed cheerfully green, which meant there were messages in the bin. It was rare, now, that he received any messages beyond the commonplace—notices of quartershare payments, the occasional query from the clan's man of business. His sister—his delm—had at last given over scolding him, and would not command him; her letters were laconic, noncommittal, and increasingly rare. The others—he moved his shoulders and walked forward to stand at the window, sipping tea and staring down into the thinning orange mist.

The green light tickled the edge of his vision. What could it be? he wondered—and sighed sharply, irritated with himself. The letterbox existed because his sister—or perhaps it had been his delm—asked that he not make himself entirely unavailable to the clan. Had she not, he would have had neither letterbox, nor telephone, nor newsnet access. Two of those he had managed, and missed neither. Nor would he mourn the letterbox, did it suddenly malfunction and die.

Oh, blast it all—*what* could it be?

He put the cup on the sill and went down the room, jerking open the drawer and snatching out two flimsies.

The first was, after all, an inquiry from his man of business on the subject of reinvesting an unexpected payout of dividend. He set it aside.

The second message was from Master Tereza of Solcintra Healer Hall, and it was rather lengthy, outlining an exceptionally interesting and difficult case currently in the care of the Hall, and wondering if he might bring himself down to the city for a few days to lend his expertise.

Mil Ton made a sound halfway between a growl and a laugh; his fingers tightened, crumpling the sheet into an unreadable mess.

Go to Solcintra Hall, take up his role as a healer once more. Tereza, of all of them, should know that he had no intention of ever—he had told her, quite plainly—and his had never been a true healing talent, in any case. It was a farce. A bitter joke made at his expense.

He closed his eyes, deliberately initiating a basic relaxation exercise. Slowly, he brought his anger—his panic—under control. Slowly, cool sense returned.

Tereza had been his friend. Caustic, she could certainly be, but to taunt a wounded man for his pain? No. That was not Tereza.

The flimsy was a ruin of mangled fiber and smeared ink. No matter. He crossed the room and dropped it into the fire grate, and stood staring down into the cold ashes.

Return to Solcintra? Not likely.

He moved his shoulders, turned back to the window and picked up the lopsided cup; sipped tepid tea.

He should answer his man of business. He should, for the friendship that had been between them, answer Tereza. He should.

And he would—later. After he had finished his tea and sat for his dry, dutiful hours, trying to recapture that talent which *had* been his, and which seemed to have deserted him now. One of many desertions, and not the least hurtful.

* * * ⟡ * *

SPRING CREPT ONWARD, kissing the flowers in the door garden into dewy wakefulness. Oppressed by cedar walls, Mil Ton escaped down the left-hand path, pacing restlessly past knolls and groves, until at last he came to a certain tree, and beneath the tree, a bench, where he sat down, and sighed, and raised his face to receive the benediction of the breeze.

In the warm sunlight, eventually he dozed. Certainly, the day bid well for dozing, sweet dreams and all manner of pleasant things. That he dozed, that was pleasant. That he did not dream, that was just as well. That he was awakened by a voice murmuring his name, that was—unexpected.

He straightened from his comfortable slouch against the tree, eyes snapping wide.

Before him, settled casually cross-legged on the new grass, heedless of stains on his town-tailored clothes, was a man somewhat younger than himself, dark of hair, gray of eye. Mil Ton stared, voice gone to dust in his throat.

"The house remembered me," the man in the grass said apologetically. "I hope you don't mind."

Mil Ton turned his face away. "When did it matter, what I minded?"

"Always," the other replied, softly. "Mil Ton. I told you how it was."

He took a deep breath, imposing calm with an exercise he had learned in Healer Hall, and faced about.

"Fen Ris," he said, low, but not soft. Then, "Yes. You told me how it was."

The gray eyes shadowed. "And in telling you, killed you twice." He raised a ringless and elegant hand, palm turned up. "Would that it were otherwise." The hand reversed, palm toward the grass. "Would that it were not."

Would that he had died of the pain of betrayal, Mil Ton thought, rather than live to endure this. He straightened further on the bench, frowning down at the other.

"Why do you break my peace?"

Fen Ris tipped his head slightly to one side in the old, familiar gesture. "Break?" he murmured, consideringly. "Yes, I suppose I deserve that. Indeed, I know that I deserve it. Did I not first appeal to Master Tereza and the healers in the Hall at Solcintra, hoping that they might cure what our house healer could not?" He paused, head bent, then looked up sharply, gray gaze like a blow.

"Master Tereza said she had sent for you," he stated, absolutely neutral. "She said, you would not come."

Mil Ton felt a chill, his fingers twitched, as if crumpling a flimsy into ruin.

"She did not say it was you."

"Ah. Would you have come, if she had said it was me?"

Yes, Mil Ton thought, looking aside so the other would not read it in his eyes.

"No," he said.

There was a small silence, followed by a sigh.

"Just as well, then," Fen Ris murmured. "For it was not I." He paused, and Mil Ton looked back to him, drawn despite his will.

"Who, then?" he asked, shortly.

The gray eyes were infinitely sorrowful, eternally determined.

"My lifemate."

Fury, pure as flame, seared him. "You dare?"

Fen Ris lifted his chin, defiant. "You, who taught me what it is to truly love—you ask if I *dare*?"

To truly love. Yes, he had taught that lesson—learned that lesson. And then he had learned the next lesson—that even love can betray.

He closed his eyes, groping for the rags of his dignity . . .

"Her name is Endele," Fen Ris said softly. "By profession, she is a gardener." A pause, a light laugh. "A rare blossom in our house of risk-takers and daredevils."

Eyes closed, Mil Ton said nothing.

"Well." Fen Ris said after a moment. "You live so secluded here that you may not have heard of the accident at the skimmer fields last relumma. Three drivers were killed upon the instant. One walked away unscathed. Two were sealed into crisis units. Of those, one died."

Mil Ton had once followed the skimmer races—how not?—he had seen how easily a miscalculated corner approach could become tragedy.

"You were ever luck's darling," he whispered, his inner ear filled with the shrieks of torn metal and dying drivers; his inner eye watching carefully as Fen Ris climbed from his battered machine and—

"Aye," Fen Ris said. "That I was allowed to emerge whole and hale from the catastrophe unit—that was luck, indeed."

Abruptly it was cold, his mind's eye providing a different scene, as the emergency crew worked feverishly to cut through the twisted remains of a racing skimmer and extricate the shattered driver, the still face sheathed in blood—two alive, of six. Gods, he had almost lost Fen Ris—

No.

He had already lost Fen Ris.

"I might say," Fen Ris murmured, "that I was the most blessed of men, save for this one thing—that when I emerged from the unit, Endele—my lady, my heart . . ." His voice faded.

"She does not remember you."

Silence. Mil Ton opened his eyes and met the bleak gray stare.

"So," said Fen Ris, "you did read the file."

"I read the summary Tereza sent, to entice me back to the Hall," he corrected. "The case intrigued her—no physical impediment to the patient's memory, nor even a complete loss of memory. Only one person has been excised entirely from her past."

"Excised," Fen Ris repeated. "We have not so long a shared past, after all. A year—only that."

Mil Ton moved his shoulders. "Court her anew, then," he said, bitterly.

"When I did not court her before?" the other retorted. He sighed. "I have tried. She withdraws. She does not know me; she does not trust me." He paused, then said, so low Mil Ton could scarcely hear—

"She does not want me."

It should have given him pleasure, Mil Ton thought distantly, to see the one who had dealt him such anguish, in agony. And, yet, it was not pleasure he felt, beholding Fen Ris thus, but rather a sort of bleak inevitability.

"Why me?" he asked, which was not what he had meant to say.

Fen Ris lifted his face, allowing Mil Ton to plumb the depths of his eyes, sample the veracity of his face.

"Because you will know how to value my greatest treasure," he murmured. "Who would know better?"

Mil Ton closed his eyes, listening to his own heartbeat, to the breeze playing in the leaves over his head, and, eventually, to his own voice, low and uninflected.

"Bring her here, if she will come. If she will not, there's an end to it, for I will not go into the city."

"Mil Ton—"

"Hear me. If she refuses Healing, she is free to go when and where she will. If she accepts Healing, the same terms apply." He opened his eyes, and looked hard into the other's face.

"Bring your treasure here and you may lose it of its own will and desire."

This was warning, proper duty of a healer, after all, and perhaps it was foretelling as well.

Seated, Fen Ris bowed, acknowledging that he'd heard, then came effortlessly to his feet. "The terms are acceptable. I will bring her tomorrow, if she will come."

Mil Ton stood. "Our business is concluded," he said flatly. "Pray, leave me."

Fen Ris stood, frozen—a heartbeat, no more than that; surely, not long enough to be certain—and thawed abruptly, sweeping a low bow, accepting a debt too deep to repay.

"I have not—" Mil Ton began, but the other turned as if he had not spoken, and went lightly across the grass, up the path, and away.

* * * ⟡ * * *

MIL TON HAD STAYED UP LATE into the night, pacing and calling himself every sort of fool, retiring at last to toss and turn until he fell into uneasy sleep at dawn. Some hours later, a blade of sunlight sliced through the guardian cedars, through the casement and into his face.

The intrusion of light was enough to wake him. A glance at the clock brought a curse to his lips. Fen Ris would be arriving soon, if, indeed, he arrived at all.

Quickly, Mil Ton showered, dressed, and went on slippered feet down the hall toward the kitchen. As he passed the great room, he glanced within—and froze in his steps.

A woman sat on the edge of the hearth, a blue duffel bag at her feet, her hands neatly folded on her lap. She sat without any of the cushions or pillows she might have used to ease her rest, and her purpose seemed not to be repose, but alert waiting.

Her attention at this moment was directed outward, toward the window, beyond which the busy birds flickered among the cedar branches.

He took one step into the room.

The woman on the hearth turned her head, showing him a round, high-browed face, and a pair of wary brown eyes.

Mil Ton bowed in welcome of the guest. "Good day to you. I am Mil Ton Intassi, builder of this house."

"And healer," she said, her voice deeper than he had expected.

"And healer," he allowed, though with less confidence than he once might have. He glanced around the room. "You came alone?"

She glanced down at the blue duffel. "He drove me here, and opened the door to the house. There was no need for him to wait. He knew I did not want him. You did not want him either, he said."

Not *entirely* true, Mil Ton thought, face heating as he recalled the hours spent pacing. He inclined his head.

"May I know your name?"

"Bah! I have no manners," she cried and sprang to her feet. She bowed—a completely unadorned bow of introduction—and straightened.

"I am Endele per'Timbral Clan—" her voice faded, a cloud of confusion passed briefly across her smooth face.

"I am Endele per'Timbral," she repeated, round chin thrust out defiantly.

Mil Ton inclined his head. "Be welcome in my house, Endele per'Timbral," he said, seriously. "I am in need of a cup of tea. May I offer you the same?"

"Thank you," she said promptly. "A cup of tea would be welcome."

She followed him down the hall to the kitchen and waited with quiet patience while he rummaged in the closet for a cup worthy of a guest. In the back, he located a confection of pearly porcelain. He poured tea and handed it off, recalling as she received it that the cup, the sole survivor of a long-broken set, had belonged to Fen Ris.

Healers were taught to flow with their instincts. Mil Ton turned away to pour for himself, choosing the lopsided cup, as always, and damned both Healer training and himself, for agreeing to . . .

"He said that you can heal me." Endele spoke from behind him, her speech as unadorned as her bow had been. "He means, you will make me remember him."

Mil Ton turned to look at her. She held the pearly cup daintily on the tips of her fingers, sipping tea as neatly as a cat. Certainly, she was not a beauty—her smooth forehead was too high, her face too round, her hair merely brown, caught back with a plain silver hair ring. Her person was compact and sturdy, and she had the gift of stillness.

"Do you, yourself, desire this healing?" he asked, the words coming effortlessly to his lips, as if the year away were the merest blink of an eye. "I will not attempt a healing against your will."

She frowned slightly. "Did you tell him that?"

"Of course," said Mil Ton. "I also told him that, if you wish to leave here for your own destination, now or later, I will not impede you. He accepted the terms."

"Did he?" The frown did not disappear. "Why?"

Mil Ton sipped tea, deliberately savoring the citrus bite while he considered. It was taught that a healer owed truth to those he would heal. How much truth was left to the healer's discretion.

"I believe," he said slowly, to Endele per'Timbral's wary brown eyes, "it is because he values you above all other things and wishes for you only that which will increase your joy."

Tears filled her eyes, glittering. She turned aside, embarrassed to weep before a stranger, as anyone would be, and walked over to the terrace door, her footsteps soft on the wooden floor.

Mil Ton sipped tea and watched her. She stood quite still, her shoulders stiff with tension, tea cup forgotten in one hand, staring out into the garden as if it were the most fascinating thoroughfare in Solcintra City.

Sipping tea, Mil Ton let his mind drift. He was not skilled at hearing another's emotions. But the Masters of the Hall in Solcintra had taught him somewhat of their craft, and sometimes, if he disengaged his mind, allowing himself to fall, as it were into a waking doze—well, sometimes, then, he could see . . .

Images.

Now he saw images and more than images. He saw intentions made visible.

Walls of stone, a window set flush and firm, tightly latched against the storm raging without. Hanging to the right of the window was a wreath woven of some blue-leaved plant, which gave off a sweet, springlike scent. Mil Ton breathed in. Breathed out.

He felt, without seeing, that the stone barrier was all around the woman, as if she walked in some great walled city, able to stay safe from some lurking, perhaps inimical presence . . .

A rustle of something and the stones and their meaning faded.

"Please," a breathless voice said nearby. He opened his eyes to his own wood-floored kitchen, and looked down into the round face of Endele per'Timbral.

"Please," she said again. "May I walk in your garden?"

"Certainly," he said, suddenly remembering her profession. "I am afraid you will find it inadequate in the extreme, however."

"I was charmed to see your house sitting so comfortably in the woods. I am certain I will be charmed by your garden," she said, and turned to place her cup on the counter.

He unlocked the door and she slipped through, walking down the path without a look behind her. Mil Ton watched her out of sight, then left the door on the latch and poured himself a second cup of tea.

· · · ◇ · · ·

BY TRADE, HE WAS A STORYTELLER. A storyteller whose stories sometimes went . . . odd. Odd enough to pique the interest of the masters, who had insisted that he was healer, and taught him what they could of the craft.

He was, at best, a mediocre healer, for he never had gained the necessary control over his rather peculiar talent to make it more than an uncertain tool. Sometimes, without warning, he would tell what Tereza was pleased to call a True Story, and that story would have—an effect. Neither story nor effect was predictable, and so he was most likely to be called upon as a last resort, after every other healing art had failed.

As now.

Mil Ton thought about the woman—the woman Fen Ris had taken as lifemate. He remembered the impassioned speech on the subject of this same woman, on the night Fen Ris had come to tell him how it was.

He sighed then, filled for a moment with all the grief of that night, and recalled Fen Ris demanding, *demanding* that Mil Ton take no Balance against this woman, for she had not stolen Fen Ris but discovered him. Among tears and joy, Fen Ris insisted that they both had been snatched, unanticipated and unplanned, out of their ordinary lives.

And now, of course, there was no ordinary life for any of them.

He wondered—he very much wondered—if Endele per'Timbral would choose healing.

Her blue bag still lay by the hearth, but it had been many hours since she had gone out into the garden. More than enough time for a sturdy woman in good health to have hiked down to the airport, engaged a pilot and a plane and been on her way to—anywhere at all.

Mil Ton sighed and looked back to his screen. When he found that he could no longer practice his profession, he had taught himself a new skill. Written stories never turned odd, and before his betrayal, he had achieved a modest success in his work.

The work was more difficult now; the stories that came so grudgingly off the tips of his fingers were bleak and gray and hopeless. He had hoped for something better from this one, before Fen Ris had intruded into his life again. Now, he was distracted, his emotions in turmoil. He wondered again if Endele per'Timbral had departed for a destination of her own choosing. Fen Ris would suffer, if she had done so. He told himself he didn't care.

Unquiet, he put the keyboard aside and pulled a book from the table next to his chair. If he could not write, perhaps he could lose himself inside the story of another.

· · ·◇· · ·

SHE RETURNED TO THE HOUSE with sunset, her hair wind-combed, her shirt and leggings rumpled, dirt under her fingernails.

"Your garden *is* charming," she told him. "I took the liberty of weeding a few beds so that the younger flowers will have room to grow."

"Ah." said Mil Ton, turning from the freezer with a readimeal in one hand. "My thanks."

"No thanks needed," she assured him, eyeing the box. "I would welcome a similar meal, if the house is able," she said, voice almost shy.

"Certainly, the house is able," he said, snappish from a day of grudging, grayish work.

She inclined her head seriously. "I am in the House's debt." She held up her hands. "Is there a place where I may wash off your garden's good dirt?"

He told her where to find the 'fresher and she left him.

· · ·◇· · ·

DINNER WAS ENLIVENED by a discussion of the garden. She was knowledgeable—more so than Mil Ton, who had planted piecemeal, with those things that appealed to him. He kept up his side only indifferently, his vision from time to time overlain with stone, and a storm raging, raging, raging, outside windows tight and sealed.

When the meal was done, she helped him clear the table, and, when the last dish was stacked in the cleaner, stood awkwardly, her strong, capable hands twisted into a knot before her.

Mil Ton considered her through a shimmer of stone walls.

"Have you decided," he said, careful to keep his voice neutral—for this was *her* choice, and hers alone, so the master healers taught—"whether you are in need of healing?"

She looked aside, and it seemed that, for a moment, the phantom stones took on weight and substance. Then, the vision faded and it was only clean air between him and a woman undecided.

"They say—they say he is my lifemate," she said, low and stammering. "They say the lifeprice was negotiated with my clan, that he paid it out of his winnings on the field. They say we were inseparable, greater together than apart. His kin—they say all this. And I say—if these things are so, why do I not remember him?"

Mil Ton drew a deep, careful breath. "Why should they tell you these things, if they were not so?"

She moved her shoulders, face averted. "Clearly, it *is* so," she whispered. "They—he—the facts are as they state them. I saw the announcement in the back issue of the *Gazette*. I spoke to my sister. I remember the rooms which are mine in his clan house. I remember the gardens, and the shopkeeper at the end of the street. I remember his sister, his brothers—all his kin! Saving him. Only him. My . . . lifemate."

Her pain was evident. One needn't be an empath to feel it. Mil Ton drew a calming breath . . .

"I am not a monster," she continued. "He—of course, he is bewildered. He seems—kind, and, and concerned for my happiness. He looks at me . . . I do *not* know him!" she burst out passionately. "I owe him nothing!" She caught herself, teeth indenting lower lip. Mil Ton saw the slow slide of a tear down one round cheek.

She was sincere; he remembered Tereza's report all too well:

This is not merely some childish game of willfulness, but a true forgetting. And, yet, how has she forgotten? Her intellect is intact; she has suffered no trauma, taken no drugs, appealed to no healer to rid her of the burden of her memories . . .

"And do you," Mil Ton asked once more, "wish to embrace healing?"

She turned her head and looked at him, her cheeks wet and her eyes tragic.

"What will happen, if I am healed?"

Ah, the question. The very question. And he owed her only truth.

"It is the wish of your lifemate that you would then recall him and the life you have embarked upon together. If you do not also wish for that outcome, deny me."

Her lips tightened, and again she turned away, walked a few steps down the room and turned back to face him.

"You built this house, he said. You alone." She looked around her, at the bare wooden floor, the cedar beam, the cabinets and counter in-between. "It must have taken a very long time."

So, there would be no healing. Mil Ton sighed. Fen Ris. It was possible to feel pity for Fen Ris. He bought a moment to compose himself by repeating her inventory of the kitchen, then brought his eyes to her face and inclined his head.

"Indeed, it took much longer than needful, to build this house. I worked on it infrequently, with long stretches between."

"But, why build it at all?"

"Well." He hesitated, then moved his hand, indicating that she should walk with him.

"I began when I was still an apprentice. My mother had died and left the mountain to myself alone, as her father had once left it to her. There had been a house here, in the past; I discovered the foundation when I began to clear the land." He paused and gave her a sideline look.

"I had planned to have a garden here, you see—and what I did first was to clear the land and cut the pathways . . ."

"But you had uncovered the foundation," she said, preceding him into the great room. She sat on the edge of the hearth, where she had been before. Fen Ris had himself perched precisely there on any number of evenings or mornings. And here was this woman—

Mil Ton walked over to his chair and sat on the arm.

"I had uncovered the foundation," he repeated, "before I went away—back to the city and my craft. I was away—for many years, traveling in stories. I made a success of myself. My tales were sought after; halls were filled with those who hungered for my words.

"When I returned, I was ill with self-loathing. My stories had become . . . weapons—horribly potent, uncontrollable. I drove a man mad in Chonselta City. In Teramis, a woman ran from the hall, screaming . . ."

On the hearth, Endele per'Timbral sat still as a stone, only her eyes alive.

"That I came here—I scarcely knew why. Except that I had discovered a foundation and it came to me that I could build a house, and keep the world safely away."

Oh, gods, he thought, feeling the shape of the words in his mouth, listening to his voice, spinning the tale he meant, and yet did not mean, to tell . . .

"I built the house of cedar, and laid the beams by hand; the windows I set tight against the walls. At the core, a fireplace—" He used his chin to point over her shoulder. "Before I finished that, the healers came to me. News of my stories and the effects of my stories had reached the Masters of the Guild and they begged that I come to be trained, before I harmed anyone else." He looked down at his hand, fisted against his knee, and heard his voice continue the tale.

"So, I went and I trained, and then I worked as a healer in the hall. I learned to write stories down and they did not cause madness, and so took up another craft for myself. I was content and solitary until I met a young man at the skimmer track." He paused; she sat like a woman hewn of ice.

"He was bold, and he was beautiful; intelligent and full of joy. We were friends, first, then lovers. I brought him here and he transformed my house with his presence; with his help, the fireplace went from pit to hearth."

He closed his eyes, heard the words fall from his lips. "One evening, he came to me—we had been days apart, but that was no unknown thing—he followed the races, of course. He came to me and he was weeping, he held me and he told me of the woman he had met, how their hearts beat together, how they must be united, or die."

Behind his closed eyes, he saw image over image—Fen Ris before him, beseeching and explaining, and this woman's wall of stone, matching texture for texture the very hearth she sat on.

"Perhaps a true healer might have understood. I did not. I cast him out, told him to go to his woman and leave me—leave me in peace. I fled—here, to the place which was built for safety . . ."

"How did you abide it?" Her voice was shrill, he opened his eyes to find her on her feet, her body bowed with tension, her eyes frantic. "How did you abide loving him? Knowing what he does? Knowing that they might one day bring his body to you? Couldn't you see that you needed to lock yourself away?"

His vision wavered, he saw stones falling, felt wind tear his hair, lash rain into his face. In the midst of chaos, he reached out, and put his arms around her, and held her while she sobbed against his shoulder.

Eventually, the wind died, the woman in his arms quieted.

"I loved him for himself," he said softly, into her hair. "And he loved the races. He would not choose to stop racing, though he might have done, had I asked him. But he would have been unhappy, desperately so—and I loved him too well to ask it." He sighed.

"In the end, it came to *my* choice: Did I bide and share in our love, for as long as we both remained? Or turn my face aside, from the fear that, someday, he might be gone?"

In his arms, Endele per'Timbral shuddered—and relaxed.

"As simple as that?" she whispered.

"As simple, and as complex." Words failed him for a moment—in his head now were images of Fen Ris laughing, and of the ocean waves crashing on stone beneath the pair of them, of arms reaching eagerly—

He sighed again. "I have perhaps done you no favor, child, in unmaking the choice you had made, if safety is what you need above all."

"Perhaps," she said, and straightened out of his embrace, showing him a wet face, and eyes as calm as dawn. "Perhaps not." She inclined her head. "All honor, Healer. With your permission, I will retire, and tend my garden of choices while I dream."

He showed her to the tiny guest room, with its thin bed and single window, giving out to the moonlit garden, then returned to the great room.

For a few heartbeats, he stood, staring down into the cold hearth. It came to him, as from a distance, that it wanted sweeping, and he knelt down on the stones and reached for the brush.

· · ·◇· · ·

"MIL TON." A woman's voice, near at hand. He stirred, irritable, muscles aching, as if he had slept on cold stone.

"Mil Ton," she said again, and he opened his eyes to Endele per'Timbral's pale and composed face. She extended a hand, and helped him to rise, and they walked in companionable silence to the kitchen for tea.

"Have you decided," he asked her, as they stood by the open door, inhaling the promise of the garden, "what you shall do?"

"Yes," she said softly. "Have you?"

"Yes," he answered—and it was so, though he had not until that moment understood that a decision had been necessary. He smiled, feeling his heart absurdly light in his breast.

"I will return to Solcintra. Tereza writes that there is work for me, at the Hall."

"I am glad," she said. "Perhaps you will come to us, when you are settled. He would like it, I think—and I would."

He looked over to her and met her smile.

"Thank you," he said softly. "I would like it, too."

✧ Lord of the Dance ✧

IT WAS SNOWING, of course.

The gentleman looked out the window as the groundcar moved quietly through the dark streets. His streets.

And really, he said to himself irritably, *you ought to be able to hit upon some affordable way of lighting them.*

"What are you thinking, Pat Rin?" His lady's voice was soft as the snow, her hand light on his knee. And he was a boor, to ignore her most welcome presence in worries over street lamps.

He leaned back in the seat, placed his hand over hers, and looked into her dark eyes.

"I was thinking how pretty the snow is," he murmured.

She laughed and he smiled as the car turned the corner—and abruptly there was light, spilling rich and yellow from all the doors and windows of Audrey's Whorehouse, warming the dark sidewalks and spinning the snowflakes into gold.

• • • ✧ • •

"BOSS. MS. NATESA." Villy bowed with grace, if without nuance, and pulled the door wide. "You honor our house."

Great gods. Pat Rin carefully did not look at his lady as he inclined his head.

"We are of course pleased to accept Ms. Audrey's invitation," he murmured. "It has been an age since I have danced."

The boy smiled brilliantly. "We hoped you'd be pleased, sir." He pointed to the left, blessedly returning to a more Terran mode.

"You can leave your coats in the room, there, then join everybody in the big parlor."

"Thank you," Pat Rin said, and moved off as the bell chimed again, Natesa on his arm.

"Who," he murmured, for her ear alone, "do you suppose has been tutoring Villy in the Liaden mode?"

"Why shouldn't he be teaching himself?" she countered, slanting a quick, subtle look into his face. "He admires you greatly, Master."

"Most assuredly he does," Pat Rin replied, with irony, and paused before the small room which served as a public closet for the clients of Ms. Audrey's house. Natesa removed her hand from his arm and turned, allowing him to slip the long fleece coat from her shoulders. The remains of snowflakes glittered on the dark green fabric like a spangle of tiny jewels. He shook it out and stepped into the closet.

The hooks and hangers were crowded with a variety of garments: oiled sweaters, thick woolen shirts, scarred spaceleather jackets, and two or three evening cloaks in the Liaden style.

Pat Rin removed his own cloak and hung it carefully over Natesa's coat. Shaking out his lace, he stepped back into the hallway, where his lady waited in her sun-yellow gown.

He paused, his heart suddenly constricted in his chest. Natesa's black eyebrows rose, just slightly, and he moved a hand in response to the question she did not voice.

"You overwhelm me with your beauty," he said.

She laughed softly and stepped forward to take his arm again.

"And you overwhelm me with yours," she answered in her lightly accented High Liaden. "Come, let us see if together we may not overwhelm the world."

· · · ⋄ · · ·

THE DOORS BETWEEN the public parlor and the visitors' lounge had been opened and tied back; the furniture moved out of the public parlor and the serviceable beige rug rolled up, revealing a surprisingly wide expanse of plastic tile in a deep, mostly unscarred brown. A refreshment table was placed along the back wall, directly beneath—

Pat Rin blinked.

When not pressed into duty as a dance hall, the public parlor of

Ms. Audrey's bordello displayed certain . . . works of art . . . as might perhaps serve to beguile the mind away from the cares of the day and toward the mutual enjoyment of pleasure.

This evening, the walls had been—transformed.

The artwork was gone, or mayhap only hidden behind objects, which, had anyone dared challenge Pat Rin to describe twelve items belonging to Korval that he least expected to find on public display, he would certainly have placed within the top six.

Nursery rugs, they were—the design based upon a star map. Three rugs together formed the whole of the map, the original of which he had himself seen, preserved in Korval's log books.

One rug had lain on the floor of the nursery at Jelaza Kazone. The second, in the schoolroom at Trealla Fantrol. The third—the third had covered the floor in the small private parlor the boy, Pat Rin, had shared with his fosterfather, Luken bel'Tarda. And yet on the wall directly across from him—the rug, the very rug, from Trealla Fantrol. And on the wall to his right, the rug from Jelaza Kazone.

Carefully, Pat Rin turned his head, and—yes, there on the wall behind them was the rug from his childhood, looking just as it always had, close-looped and unworn, its colors as bright as—

"Pat Rin?" Natesa murmured. "Is something amiss?"

He shook himself, and turned his head to smile at her.

"Merely—unexpected, let us say." He waved a languorous hand. "What a crush, to be sure!"

This was not strictly the case. Still, the big parlor was comfortably crowded, the conversation level somewhat louder than one might perhaps have expected at a similar gathering in Solcintra. Bosses of several of the nearer territories were present, including Penn Kalhoon, as well as the Portmaster, and a good mix of local merchants.

Across the room, white hair gleaming in the abundant light, his cousin Shan stood in deep conversation with Narly Jempkins, chairman of the nascent Surebleak Mercantile Union.

"We arrive among the last, as suits our station," Natesa said softly, which bait he ignored in favor of inclining his head to their hostess, who was approaching in a rustle of synthsilk, her pale hair intricately dressed, and an easy smile on her face.

"Boss. Natesa. I'm real glad you could come."

"Audrey." Natesa smiled and extended a hand, which the older woman clasped between both of hers.

"Winter has been too long," Natesa said. "How clever of you to think of a dance!"

Audrey laughed. "Wish I could say it was all my idea! Miri was the one who put the seed in my head, if you want the truth. Said she had too much energy and no place to spend it, which I'll say between the three of us ain't the usual complaint of new-birthed mothers."

"Miri is an example to us all," Pat Rin murmured, which pleasantry Audrey greeted with another laugh.

"Ain't she just—and your brother's another one! When I invite a man to a dance and I don't expect him to bring his keyboard and set up with the band. That's just what he's done, though—take a look!" She pointed down the room, where was collected a fiddle, a guitar, a drum set, a portable omnichora—and several musicians wearing what passed for stage finery on Surebleak, clustered about a slender man in a ruffled white shirt and formal slacks that would have been unexceptional at any evening gather in Solcintra.

It had been . . . disconcerting . . . to find that Audrey, with the rest of Pat Rin's acquaintance on Surebleak, assumed that Val Con, his cousin and his delm, was in fact his younger brother, brought in to care for the transplanted family business while the boss undertook the important task of putting the streets in order.

As the misapprehension only amused Miri, and Val Con's sole comment on the matter was a slightly elevated eyebrow, Pat Rin gave over attempting to explain their actual relationship and resigned himself to having at his advanced age acquired a sibling.

"For a time, he and Miri sang for their suppers," he said now to Audrey. "Perhaps he misses the work."

"Could be," she answered, as the sound of footsteps and voices grew louder in the hall behind them. She sent a look over his shoulder, extended a hand and patted his sleeve lightly.

"The two of you go on in and circulate. Dancing ought to be starting up soon."

Thus dismissed, Pat Rin followed Natesa deeper into the parlor.

• • •✦• • •

MS. AUDREY'S BIG PARLOR, already crowded, grew more so. Deep in a discussion with Etienne Borden and Andy Mack, which involved free-standing solar batteries, and the benefits of light level meters over mechanical timers, Pat Rin still registered an abrupt lowering of the ambient noise and looked around, thinking that the promised music was at last about to begin. But no.

It was his mother entering the room, on the arm of no one less than Scout Commander ter'Meulen, dressed for the occasion in High House best, his face oh-so-politely bland, and his mustache positively noncommittal.

Pat Rin, who had all his life known Scout ter'Meulen, could only wonder at the reasons behind such a display—not to mention the why and wherefore of Lady Kareen accepting his arm for anything at all. They were neither one a friend of the other, though it had always seemed to Pat Rin that the greater amusement was on Clonak's side and the greater dislike on his mother's. Surely—

Audrey bustled forward to welcome these newest arrivals, her high, sweet voice easily rising above the other conversations in the room.

"I *knew* you'd turn the trick, Mr. Clonak!" she said gaily, patting him kindly on the shoulder. This was apparently a dismissal, as Clonak adroitly disengaged himself from the lady's arm, took two steps into the parlor and was lost in the general crush.

Audrey turned to face Kareen squarely, and Pat Rin's stomach tightened, as he contemplated disaster. Even had he not counted Audrey a friend, he thought, it was surely no more than his duty to stand between her and Lady Kareen yos'Phelium, in the same way that it was his duty as Boss to stand between the residents of his streets and mayhem.

He murmured something quick and doubtless unintelligible to the colonel and the assistant portmaster, and slipped through the press of bodies, moving as quickly as he was able.

"Lady Kareen," Audrey said clearly. "Be welcome in my house."

It was the proper sentiment, properly expressed, thought Pat Rin, working his way forward. Though what—and from whom—his mother might exact as Balance for being made welcome at a whorehouse—

"Well met, Cousin!" Val Con murmured, astonishingly slipping his arm through Pat Rin's. "Where to in such a rush?"

"If you would not see a murder done—or worse—" Pat Rin hissed into the frigid silence that followed Audrey's greeting—"let me tend to this!"

"Nay, I think you wrong both our host and your lady mother," Val Con said tranquilly, his grip on Pat Rin's arm tightening. "Besides, the hand is dealt."

"You know what my mother is capable—"

"Peace," his cousin interrupted. "My aunt is about to play her first card."

"Who speaks?" Lady Kareen's Terran was heavily accented, but perfectly intelligible; her tone as frigid as the wind in high winter.

It was of course quite mad to even consider that he might extricate himself from the brotherly embrace of one who was both a pilot and a scout. Nonetheless, Pat Rin took a careful breath to camouflage his shift of weight—and felt warm fingers around his unencumbered hand. He looked down, equally dismayed and unsurprised to see Miri grinning up at him, gray eyes glinting.

"Take it easy, Boss," she whispered. "Audrey's good for this."

He began to answer, then closed his mouth tightly. The fact that this had been planned—that Audrey had been coached on form and manner . . .

"That's right," their host was saying equitably to his mother. "You won't know that. I'm Audrey Breckstone, boss of this House. I'm happy to see you."

Not for nothing did Lady Kareen stand foremost among the scholars of the Liaden Code of Proper Conduct. She not only knew her Code, but she practiced it, meticulously. Rather too meticulously, as some might think. But there was perhaps, Pat Rin thought now, an advantage—to Audrey, to the House, and to Kareen herself—in an extremely nice reading of Code in regard to this particular circumstance.

It was not for a mere son to say what weights and measures were called into consideration as his mother stood there, head tipped politely to one side, face smooth and emotionless, but surely the unworthy scholar who had studied Code at her feet might make certain shrewd and informed guesses.

Whether Audrey possessed the native genius to have added that guileless, "I'm happy to see you," to her introduction, or whether she had been coached in what she was to say mattered not at all. That she had uttered the phrase in apparent sincerity placed her *melant'i* somewhat in regard to the *melant'i* of Kareen yos'Phelium. Here was, in fact, a delm—at most—or a head of Line—at least—so secure in her own worth and the worth of her House that she not only welcomed, but was *happy to receive*, the burden of a visit from high stickler who might ruin her and hers with a word.

Or, to phrase the matter in the parlance of Surebleak, Audrey had in essence said to Kareen: *I see that you're armed, and I'm your equal.*

"I am pleased to accept the greeting of the House," Lady Kareen stated, and bowed—expert to expert—which allowed a certain limited equality between herself and her host, and placed a finer measuring into the future, after more data had been gathered and weighed.

To her credit—or that of her tutor—Audrey did not attempt to answer the bow. Instead, she smiled, and offered her arm.

"There's going to be music and dancing for the youngers in just a bit, now," she said. "But I'm betting that a woman of good sense would like to have a glass of wine in her hand."

There was a slight hesitation as Kareen performed the mental gymnastics necessary to untangle this, then she stepped forward and placed her hand lightly on Audrey's sleeve.

"Thank you," she said austerely. "A glass of wine would be most welcome."

The two ladies moved off toward the refreshment table as the rest of the guests shook themselves and returned to interrupted conversations.

Pat Rin remembered to breathe.

"See?" Miri gave his hand a companionable squeeze before releasing him, and sending another grin up into his face. "Piece o' cake."

"As an author of the joke, you might well say so," he replied, with feeling. "But consider how it might seem to those who had no—"

"Indeed, it was ill-done of us," Val Con murmured, slipping his arm away. "We had not taken into account that your duty would place you between the two ladies."

Pat Rin turned to stare, and Val Con inclined his head, for all the worlds like a proper Liaden, and murmured the phrase in High Liaden—"Forgive us, Cousin. We do not intend to distress you, but to attain clarity."

Sighing, Pat Rin also inclined his head. "It is forgotten," rising reflexively to his lips.

"Next time, we'll send you a clue ahead of time," Miri said.

He eyed her. "Must there be a next time?"

"Bound to be," she answered, not without a certain amount of sympathy. Her eyes moved, tracking something beyond his shoulder.

"Band's settin' up," she said to Val Con.

"Ah," he returned, and lifted an eyebrow. "Cousin, I am wanted at my 'chora."

"By all means, go," Pat Rin told him. "Perhaps Ms. Audrey will induce my mother to stand up with Andy Mack."

The band played surprisingly well, and in a rather wider range than Pat Rin had expected, fiddle and guitar at the fore, Val Con's omnichora weaving a light, almost insubstantial, background.

At Ms. Audrey's insistence, he and Natesa had stood up for the first dance—a lively circle dance not dissimilar to the *nescolantz*, which had been a staple at young people's balls when he had been considerably younger. He spied Ms. Audrey, with Lady Kareen and Luken bel'Tarda at her side, observing the pattern of the dance from the edge of the rug. Further on, Clonak ter'Meulen was in animated conversation with Uncle Daav and Cheever McFarland.

At the end of the first dance, he relinquished Natesa to Priscilla with a bow, and started for the refreshment table. He'd scarcely gone three steps before his hand was caught.

"Come," said his cousin, Nova. "I claim you for the next dance!"

"Ah, do you?" He laughed, and allowed himself to be led back onto the floor. "Then let us hope the band pities me and produces a less-spirited number!"

Alas, his wish had not reached the ears of the band leader, for the next dance was something akin to a jig, requiring intricate footwork which he learned from step to step by the simple expedient of observing Nova and reproducing her movement.

He'd done the same thing many times in the past, of course—a person of *melant'i* would naturally take care to acquire the movements of a variety of dances, so that he might do his proper duty as a guest; however, no one but a scholar of the form could hope to know the intricacies of all possible dances. A quick eye and a flair for mimicry were, therefore, skills that a young person who wished to move without offense through Solcintra's party season would do well to acquire.

Having survived the jig unbloodied, Pat Rin bowed to his fair partner, handed her off to his Uncle Daav, and turned, setting his sights on a glass of wine and perhaps more discussion of solar arrays with Andy Mack, who he could see speaking with Clonak to the left of the refreshment table.

This time, he was claimed by a smiling Villy, who led him back out onto the floor with something very like a skip in his step. At least, Pat Rin thought, the gods were at last kind: it was a square dance, with he and Villy facing off as sides one and two, while Shan and Priscilla taking up the third side and the fourth.

The slower pace was more than balanced by a complex, cumulative pattern of exchanges with one's partner, thus: step forward, touch right hands, step back/step forward, touch right hands, then left, step back—and so on, until the tune turned on itself and one began to subtract a gesture at the exchange, and each dancer was at last back in their place, having regained all that had been given.

The music stopped the instant the second partner pair fell back into place. There was a moment of tension, as if the dancers awaited another phrase from the musicians—then laughter, and light applause. Their little square evaporated, Pat Rin moving with determination toward the refreshment table, Shan and Priscilla amiably keeping pace. He was sincerely thirsty now, and thinking in terms of a glass of cool juice.

"Do you find the party agreeable?" he asked Priscilla.

"Perfectly agreeable," she said, with a seriousness that was belied by the glimmer of a smile in her eyes. "Ms. Audrey said that she meant to host the dance of the winter."

"Which we thought would be no great challenge," Shan continued. "There being so few dances held in the winter. Or the summer. Or the spring, come to belabor it."

Pat Rin considered him. "If you find a lack, Cousin, you might host a ball or two yourself."

"Well, I might," Shan allowed. "If it weren't for the fact that the delm has some foolish notion in his head about bringing Surebleak up to a mid-tier spaceport, with a timetable of roughly *right now*. Perhaps he's spoken to you on the subject?"

"He has," Pat Rin said, "and I must say that the delm and I are as one on the matter."

"Well, then, what choice have I—a mere master trader!— commanded as I am by both the Delm of Korval and the Boss of Surebleak? Duty, as always, must bow before pleasure, and so it is that tomorrow I regretfully shake the snow of Surebleak from my boots and betake myself to Terran Trade Commission headquarters, to enlist their aid in the delm's necessity. There will be no dances held at yos'Galan's house—had we a house, which of course, we don't—until my task is done. Unless, Priscilla, you would care to host a ball or six while I'm gone?"

"I thought I'd go with you, instead," his lifemate replied in her calm deep voice. "To keep you and Padi out of trouble."

This was news. Pat Rin looked up. "Your heir accompanies you on this mission?"

Shan grinned, silver eyes glinting. "Now, pity me, truly. Bearding the Terran Guild is as nothing when measured against the prospect of introducing one's daughter to the intricacies—not to say the politics— of trade."

They had reached the refreshment table. Pat Rin poured wine for the two of them, and a glass of cider for himself. He then inclined his head as Shan moved off to answer a hail from Portmaster Liu—and again a moment later as Priscilla was called over to join Thera Kalhoon, Penn's lady wife.

Momentarily alone, Pat Rin sighed, had another sip of cider, and closed his eyes. Now that he had extricated himself from dancing, the band was—of course!—playing smooth and undemanding strolling music, the voice of the omnichora somewhat stronger than it had been previously.

Opening his eyes, Pat Rin looked out over the crowded dance floor. Uncle Daav was dancing with Natesa, Nova with Clonak ter'Meulen, and Villy with Etienne Borden. He sipped more cider and reminded himself that it was a boon to be warm in the depths of Surebleak's winter.

"Hey, there, Boss." Miri's cheerful voice interrupted his reverie. "Feeling OK?"

He considered her gravely, one eyebrow up, which only widened her grin.

"You look like Daav when you do that," she said, reaching around him for the cider bottle.

"There's punch, if you'd rather," Pat Rin murmured, and Miri laughed as she poured cider into a cup.

"Think I don't know better'n Audrey's punch?" she asked.

"The wine, then," Pat Rin countered. "It's quite pleasant."

She sent a sparkling glance up into his face. "Oughta be, considering it came out of our cellar." She sipped. "That's good," she sighed, and gestured vaguely with the cup. "Only way we could get Shan to come was to promise there'd be something drinkable on the table."

"Doubtless," Pat Rin said dryly, and she laughed again.

"Cut a fine figure out on the floor," she commented, her eyes on the languid dancers. "Bet you could dance all night, if there was need."

It was his turn to laugh, softly. "I hope that I do not shame my host or my lady," he murmured. "But I have long since given over dancing until dawn."

"Not quite 'til dawn, I'm guessing," Miri said, as the music swept into a crescendo, the 'chora's voice suddenly and achingly clear. She knocked back the last of her cider and put the cup on the table.

Pat Rin glanced at his cup, finished the last swallow and thought about pouring another before he went in search of Andy Mack, and—

"Over here!" Miri called, and put her hand on his arm.

Pat Rin went still. "What?" he snapped.

"Easy. It ain't nothin' more than this special dance Audrey's had it in her head we all gotta do together. Family thing."

"I have already danced—"

"One more!" Villy cried, arriving in a swirl of exuberance. "You have to, sir! You're the Boss!"

"Ah." He considered the boy's flushed face. "How if I appoint Boss Kalhoon to stand up in my place?"

"Won't work," Miri said. "Penn gets the least bit warm and his glasses fog up on him."

"Besides not being family?" he asked, but she only grinned, and nodded toward the floor, where stood surely all the members of Clan Korval present at the party, saving herself, Val Con, and Lady Kareen, who was at the edge of the rug, between Clonak ter'Meulen and Andy Mack, her face so perfectly bland that Pat Rin shivered.

"Miri . . ." He began, but she was gone, walking toward the group assembled in a loose circle at the center of the floor.

"Come on, sir!" Villy tugged his hand. "They're waiting for you!"

It was on the edge of his tongue to snap that they might wait for him until the snow melted. However, good manners overcame bad grace, and he allowed himself to be led out onto the floor. Hoots and whistles came from some of the spectators on the rug, and Lady Kareen's face grew blander still.

At the edge of the circle, Villy relinquished his hand, bowed his liquid, meaningless bow, and skipped back toward the refreshment table.

Pat Rin gave a sigh—and another as Natesa came forward to put her hand on his arm.

"A round dance, my love," she murmured, as she eased him into the circle. "Audrey has asked us most especially to honor her."

If one's host desired it, there was nothing more to be said. And certainly he was able for one more dance. Still . . . He looked into Natesa's eyes.

"Do I know this dance, I wonder?" he murmured.

She smiled. "I believe you will find that you do," she answered, and guided him to a gap in the circle between Nova and Priscilla. Having seen him situated, she moved away, slipping into place between Luken and Daav, and smiling at him across the circle.

The drummer beat out a rapid tattoo, sticks flashing, and struck the cymbal a ringing blow, the sound quickly muffled by a cunning hand on the rim.

The room stilled admirably as Ms. Audrey walked out onto the floor, head high, back straight, as proud and as easy as any delm might be within the jewel of her own entertainment.

She raised her hands and spun slowly, showing herself to all gathered.

"You might be wondering," she said conversationally to the room at large, "why it is that I decided to throw a party in the middle of the winter. One reason is that Miri Robertson over here was getting the silly-stirs, her being a woman who had to go off-world to find enough going on to keep her busy—" She paused to let the general laughter die back, then tipped her head and smiled.

"There's two other reasons for this gathering, though. And I'm thinking they're both important enough to want some explaining.

"So, the next reason for the party is that we're in the middle of a special kinda winter. The first winter in my memory and in all of yours where there ain't a turf war going on, when the road to the spaceport stands open for its whole length, and where there are not less than five bosses in this room right now."

Much shouting, stamping, and whistling erupted. At the edge of the rug, Andy Mack reached out, grabbed Penn Kalhoon's arm and yanked it high into the air. Here and there around the room, the other bosses were being given similar treatment. The applause ebbed, then swelled again, going on until the drummer rapped out a short, sharp rebuke.

Ms. Audrey waited while the room quieted, then held up her hands. Silence fell, more or less immediately, and she grinned broadly.

"That's right. Now, you'll remember I said *three* reasons and here's the third—" She turned, bringing the room's attention to the circle of Korval, standing ready at the center of the dance floor.

"Boss Conrad and his organization are the reason we can have this party, now, in the middle of winter, without worrying we'll attract the attention of a rival fatcat." She looked around the room, spinning slowly on her heel.

"Remember this. Remember this night, this party. And remember who made it all happen."

The room was utterly quiet for the beat of three, then Andy Mack called out from Lady Kareen's side, "First of many nights just like it!"

"First of many!" The room took up the cry, hurled it against the ceiling, sustained it—

Once again, the drummer intervened. The shouting subsided slowly, and by the time quiet was more or less achieved, Ms. Audrey was making one of the little group about Lady Kareen, her arm tucked companionably through Clonak's, and Cheever McFarland had waded out of the rugbound observers and onto the dance floor.

It was rare, Pat Rin thought, that one saw Cheever McFarland dressed in other than utilitarian clothing—tough sensible trousers and shirt in neutral colors, sturdy boots, and the inevitable jump-pilot's jacket. Tonight, however, tonight, the big Terran positively turned heads as he moved toward their small circle.

The theme was black—a silk shirt so deep that it shone like onyx with no ruffles or ballooning sleeves which might entangle a pilot, while the trousers were not so tight as to bind should a pilot need to move quickly, nor the shiny black boots too snug should a pilot need to run. Over the shirt was not the usual battered spaceleather jacket but a vest in opal-blue brocade, embroidered with silver rosebuds.

Someone from the group on the rug whistled; Pat Rin suspected Andy Mack. Cheever only grinned his easy grin and raised a big, unringed hand.

"Now, what we're going to be doing here is something like what's called a round dance in Boss Conrad's hometown, and what they called a cue dance back when I learned how, at pilot school. Either name makes sense—a round dance on account it moves 'round in a circle and a cue dance on account there's somebody stands outside the circle, who's got what you might call the big picture, and they're the one responsible for shouting out signals about what steps to dance." He put his hand on his chest, and the drummer executed a long, showy roll, which got a laugh from those watching, and a grin from Cheever himself.

"Boss Conrad and his kin, they learned round dancin' because where they come from, it's what polite people learn to dance. Me, I learned in a piloting seminar because we was bored and needed some legal way to work it off. That being the case, the cues are a little different.

"So, what we're gonna do is show you a round dance like Boss Conrad learned it, and then a cue dance like I did."

"Where'd Miri learn how?" somebody—Pat Rin didn't recognize the voice—called from the back.

"From the boss' brother," Miri sang back. "You?"

The drummer hit the block twice and struck the cymbal hard, to general laughter.

"Any more questions?" Cheever called, and continued without taking a breath. "Fine. We're ready whenever the band gets around to it."

Immediately, the omnichora launched six bright notes, like skyrockets, toward the hidden winter sky, the fiddle player spun clear around and enthusiastically put her bow across the strings, the guitarist plucked out a quick pattern of sound and the drummer beat the rim, counting out three, six, twelve.

The music shifted, twisted, slowed . . .

"Bow to your partner," Cheever directed, against the mannerly rising of *Tiordia's Stroll*.

Pat Rin received Nova's bow, bowing to her in turn. At Cheever's instruction, they joined hands, crossed, turned, and slid two steps forward, two steps right, three steps backward, three left, crossed, turned, and changed partners. Pat Rin's left hand slipped out of Nova's as his right hand met Priscilla's. He and his new partner stepped together, then apart, changed sides and danced four steps left and five steps back, six steps forward, four steps right . . .

Relaxed and smiling, Pat Rin performed his part in the dance with ease, warmed and oddly comforted by the familiar movements. He did, in that portion of his mind neither attentive to nor lulled by the dance, own himself astonished to find Cheever McFarland so able a dance master. *Truly*, he thought, as he and Priscilla crossed and turned; *there is no end to the good pilot's talents . . .*

The dance continued its pleasant course until each dancer had partnered with every other dancer in the set. Perfectly on cue, he left Luken's side, his hand finding Nova's precisely on the beat. They turned, crossed, and dropped hands to the caller's commands, and bowed, holding it for twelve beats, and straightening just as the last note from the 'chora trembled into silence.

The room was entirely quiet as they straightened, and in that moment, Pat Rin saw his mother, attended now by no one less than Portmaster Liu. Her face was calm, perhaps even relaxed, as if the dance had soothed her as well. She inclined her head slightly in his direction, then turned to address the portmaster.

A wholly unexceptional procedure, Pat Rin thought, and not at all too much effort to expend for the pleasure of one's host. He was slightly warm, but nothing that another glass of cider couldn't put—

"All right," Cheever McFarland was saying, his big voice shattering the quiet. "That's what a round dance looks in Boss Conrad's old turf. Now we're gonna show you how I learned it. First thing you'll notice different, are the cues. Pilots, they can't leave anything alone if there's a way to maybe tweak it. Next thing you'll notice is there's some extra bits added in, 'cause pilots tend toward boredom and makin' trouble if they don't have six things to do at the same time."

Pat Rin frowned and turned to cock an eyebrow at Nova, who replied with a bland glance that would have done justice to his mother.

"Last thing," Cheever was saying, "is that pilots? They're competitive. So this dance, it's a kind of a contest, too."

Contest? thought Pat Rin, feeling his stomach tighten. He looked across the circle for Natesa, but she was turned away, watching something in the room beyond.

"Just as soon as the band's ready," Cheever said.

The drummer snapped out a twelve-count, then the guitar came in, followed by the fiddle, the omnichora singing softly in support. The tune was somewhat brisker than *Tiordia's Stroll*—and completely unfamiliar.

"Acknowledge your co-pilot," Cheever instructed, and Pat Rin turned to exchange bows with Nova, who smiled at him.

"Comp—" he began, but—

"Check your board," Cheever called, which Pat Rin's feet somehow knew to be a glide and change sides.

"Bring up the screens!"

Warned by the set of Nova's hip, Pat Rin managed to spin as instructed, though raggedly.

"Strap in," Cheever instructed. Nova's hand moved, Pat Rin caught it in his; they turned, separated—

"Lift!"—each danced six steps to their right—"Establish orbit!"— a half-turn, so Pat Rin was looking over Nova's shoulder at the starry rug that had covered the floor in Luken's small private parlor in their quarters above the warehouse—

"Outer ring adjust," Cheever said. Pat Rin kept his place while Nova slid three steps to left. His view of the rug was now unimpeded.

"Lay in coords!" Cheever called.

Lay in—

But Cheever was giving the coordinates. Rapidly. Pat Rin focused on the rug—on the *map*—found the first coord, slid forward two steps, located the second, slipped to the left three steps, the third—the third? There!—and forward again, four steps.

"Roll starboard!" came the instruction, and Pat Rin spun to the right with the rest, noting in a sort of mental gasp that the music was moving quicker now, that the 'chora's voice was louder, and the fiddle's entirely gone.

"Lay in coords!"

This time, it wasn't a complete shock; Pat Rin had time to face the map—the less familiar rug that had graced the school-room floor at Trealla Fantrol—and focus before Cheever intoned the first coord, then another, and another—a set of six full coordinates this time, and Pat Rin slipped, spun, circled, and lunged as directed, finishing the sequence damp and limp, but oddly triumphant. He hadn't missed a step!

Luken, however, had not had the same good fortune. Pat Rin spied him walking away from the circle, Andy Mack leaving the crowd at the edge of the rug to meet him—then Cheever called them to roll once more and he was facing the map from Jelaza Kazone.

The music was much too quick now, Pat Rin thought, tucking up his lace, and shaking his hair out of his eyes. More a jig than a round dance, which the 'chora gave shape in a continuing twisty flow of brilliantine notes.

Val Con must be ready to drop, he thought—and there was another thought, linked to that—but it was lost in the need to accept the coordinates, and he plotted his course with his feet and his hips, barely registering when Miri dropped out at the eighth coord—and Priscilla, at the twelfth.

The next round came and as he glimpsed the nearest celestial rug, he all but felt the controls beneath his hands; in truth he missed the cabin of *Fortune's Reward*, as he missed the thrust against his back, and the comfort of sitting First Board. The rug was before him, and another as he danced, and the calculations went thus and so and turn and step, and by rights now there should be jump-glare and stars on the screens ahead, and stars behind, with stars underfoot, and a planet to find.

But the dance—

"Orient!" Cheever called, and the four remaining dancers came together in the center, joined hands, ran—*too fast!* Pat Rin thought, with a sudden spike of panic—'round, three times, six—

"Establish orbit!"

As one, they dropped hands, each spinning away from every, two-four-six revolutions, and came to rest, facing—the entranced spectators.

At the fore of them all stood his mother, considering him with a sort of distant interest, as one might inspect an insect.

"Check your board!" Cheever directed, and Pat Rin executed the required glide and change, aware of the weight of his limbs. It was hot, and his head ached, and, really, he had every reason to be tire—

The omnichora shouted, notes streaming like lift beacons, and there was Miri next to his mother, and Priscilla approaching—

"Lay in coords!"

There was no map this time. Pat Rin closed his eyes.

Cheever chanted the coordinates—a short set of three. Forward, back, turn left—

"Sign your co-pilot!"

Pat Rin extended a hand—and his eyes snapped open in astonishment as it was caught in a warm grip.

"Well done!" Uncle Daav whispered, under cover of the music, and—

"Clear your board!"

The two of them crossed, separated, and came back together.

"Lock it down!"

Natesa's fingers wove comfortably with his. Shan, on her other side, extended his hand and caught Daav's free hand.

"Dim the lights," Cheever said softly, and the four of them walked sedately widdershins, three times, the 'chora slowing, slowing, almost down to a proper round . . .

"Open hatch."

Obediently, they dropped hands.

"Go to town," Cheever all but whispered, and the four of them turned to face the rug and those watching, as the 'chora finished with a flurry and a flare—and the shouts and whistles began.

· · · ◇ · · ·

PAT RIN SHOOK HIS LACE OUT and reached for his glass. With Natesa's connivance, he'd slipped through the crowd to the back room that had been set aside for the band's use. Finding a bottle of autumn wine before him, he poured and sipped, and sipped once again before making the attempt to make himself seemly.

The dance—the dance had been an odd thing, to be sure; in memory not nearly so harrowing as in actuality. Had it gone on much longer, he had no doubt but that he would have joined Luken, Miri, and Priscilla at his mother's side.

He paused, frowning, recalling the moment when he had met his mother's eyes . . .

"Ah, here he is, keeping the wine to himself!" Clonak ter'Meulen's voice overfilled the little room. Pat Rin sighed, and turned to face not only the portly scout, but Luken and Daav, and Shan, Priscilla, Natesa, Andy Mack, Nova, Cheever, Miri—and Val Con, green eyes sparkling, the renegade lock of hair sticking damply to his forehead.

"Well met, Cousin," he murmured, and Pat Rin held out his glass.

"I thought the 'chora was overextended," he said. "Drink."

"My thanks." Val Con took the glass and sipped; sighed. Pat Rin considered him, doing a different sort of calculation.

"More clarity?" he asked, but it was Miri who answered.

"No complaints, Boss. Sent you a clue, fair and square," she said.

He eyed her. "Hardly in advance."

"But in advance, nonetheless," Val Con said, with a note of finality in his quiet voice. "Come, let us not bicker. There is business to be done—and quickly, so that Clonak is not long kept from the wine."

"That's a touching regard for my well-being," Clonak said, and suddenly pulled himself up straight, looking not so pudgy, nor foolish at all.

"Pat Rin yos'Phelium Clan Korval," he intoned, the syllables of the High Tongue falling cool and sharp from his lips, "has stated in the hearing of pilots and of master pilots not once but several times that he holds a first-class limited license under false pretenses. The pilot's solo rating flight was conducted in a Korval safeship, programmed to fly, should there be no pilot available. Pat Rin yos'Phelium has stated his belief that it was the ship which overcame the challenges of the pilot's solo, not the pilot." Clonak gave Pat Rin a level look.

"These are serious concerns and the pilot erred not in laying them before master pilots. Therefore, and after consultation, it was agreed that a retesting should be done. The testing is now completed, and I call upon the master pilots present to render their opinions: is Pat Rin yos'Phelium Clan Korval a pilot or does he hold a license wrongly? Speak, Masters!"

Daav stepped forward, black eyes serious.

"Though he is perhaps not as conversant with the basic coord book as might be desirable, it is my estimation as a master pilot that

Pat Rin yos'Phelium is worthy of the license he carries." He fell back a step, cocking an eyebrow at Andy Mack, lounging against the wall. The lanky pilot shook his head, white hair moving softly across his shoulders, and took a sip of his beer.

"Been sayin' it, ain't I? Boy's a pilot. Tell by lookin' at him."

Shan stepped forward. "It is my estimation as a master pilot," he said seriously, "that Pat Rin yos'Phelium is worthy of the license he carries." He fell back a step, and Priscilla came forward, then Nova, Cheever and at last Natesa, who made her declaration with the cool, emotionless intonation of a Judge, then smiled at him and stepped forward to take his hand.

"You did well, Pat Rin," she murmured.

"In fact," said Clonak, "he did. I say this as one who doubted the damn dance would work out at all, but young Shadow carried the day. So," he looked sharply at Pat Rin. "In my estimation as a master pilot, having observed the whole of the testing, Pat Rin yos'Phelium is worthy of the license he carries and I'll thank you to stop doubting yourself, you young whippersnapper! Between you and your lady mother, you're a devil's brew, make no mistake!"

Pat Rin blinked. "My mother?"

"It happens," Priscilla said surprisingly, "that Lady Kareen is, after all, of the *dramliz*. She appears to have only one talent, which is rare, but not unknown."

Pat Rin looked at her, foreknowing . . . "And that talent is?"

Priscilla smiled at him. "She may impose her will—to a very limited extent—upon the unwary." Her smiled deepened. "And now that you are warned, you are armed."

His mother a *dramliza*? It was only slightly mad, Pat Rin thought, considering the facts of Shan and Anthora in the present generation. But that one talent . . .

"I think you are saying that it was my mother's influence that kept me from qualifying as pilot?"

"At first, boy-dear," Luken said, gently. "By the time you had failed two or three times, you were quite able to fail all on your own." He smiled, sadly. "It was my sorrow, my boy, that I could never allow you to see anything other than your own unworthiness."

Pat Rin blinked against tears; Natesa's finger's tightened around his. "You did so much else, Father . . ."

A small pause, and then was Val Con abruptly before him, raising his hand so that Korval's Ring gleamed.

Pat Rin lifted an eyebrow. "Korval?"

"You will," Korval stated, "arrange time to study with Clonak ter'Meulen. You will learn the core coordinates, and such protocols as Scout ter'Meulen finds worthy. You will come to your delm inside of one local year and submit to such verification as may be demanded."

"Ah. And my streets? My duties as Boss?"

Val Con smiled, and put his hand on his lifemate's shoulder.

"You'll think of something," he said.

Pat Rin drew a breath—to say what he hardly knew, or perhaps he meant only to laugh. The opportunity for either, however, was snatched from him by Cheever McFarland.

"Right then," the big man said. "Time to finish it up."

* * * ⟡ * * *

THE FIDDLER PROVIDED a sprightly, skipping little melody as they filed into the parlor and took up position on a clear space on the rug, Val Con leaving them at the last to tend his 'chora once more.

Pat Rin stood in the first row of pilots, Natesa on his right, Luken on his left, Daav directly behind. The room was quiet, all eyes on them. Especially, Pat Rin saw, were Lady Kareen's eyes on them, from her position between Audrey and Penn Kalhoon. His mother's face betrayed the faintest hint of boredom, as would perhaps be worthy of an adult who had been teased into attending a gathering of halflings.

The fiddler finished her tune as Cheever McFarland and Miri Robertson stepped up before the rest of them, mercifully blocking Pat Rin's view of his mother's face. From behind, the 'chora began to whisper a faint line of a tantalizingly familiar song. Pat Rin strained his ears, trying to identify the music—then forgot about it as Cheever began to speak.

"I'm going to impose on your patience once more, here, if Ms. Audrey'll let me," he said.

In the first row, Audrey laughed, and called out, "It don't strain my eyes any looking at you, Mr. McFarland! Speak on!"

"Thank you, ma'am." The big man bent a little at the waist—*a bow*, Pat Rin thought, *Cheever McFarland style*—then raised his voice so that it carried to the far corners of the room—and likely the rooms abovestairs, as well.

"Now, I know you all heard me say that pilots is competitive, and you might've thought that just meant that them who missed their steps had to drop outta the dance. But there was a little more to it than that. We was also looking to judge who among the pilots dancing had danced best, according to their level, their flight time, and their training. Miri here—you all know Miri's partnered with the Boss' brother, right? And when there's a question comes before either of them, they got this arrangement where both are understood to answer? Makes the family business run smoother. Anyhow, Miri here's gonna announce the winner."

Whistles, hoots, and stamping filled the room. The drum tried to bring order, without success, until—

"PIPE DOWN!" Miri ordered, loud enough to make Pat Rin's ears ring—and silence fell like a knife.

"That's better," she said, in a more conversational tone. "I won't take long. Just want to say that it's the judgment of the master pilots we assembled here to watch that the winner of tonight's competition is—Boss Conrad!"

More noise erupted, shaking the rugs hung against the walls, and he walked forward to stand between Miri and Cheever. Smiling hugely, Villy danced forward with a bouquet of dried leaves tied with bright ribbons and presented it with a bow.

Pat Rin inclined his head, received the offering, and stood while the cheering went on, his eye inexorably drawn to the place where his mother stood, silent and bland-faced.

She met his eyes, her own as hard as stones—and turned her face away.

Pat Rin took a breath, sighed it out, and looked up with a smile as his lady came to his side.

"Shall we go home, love?" she asked, slipping her arm through his.

He looked into her face, and then around the room, heard the drummer begin his count—and looked back to her.

"I believe," he said, smiling, "that I would like to dance with my lifemate. There are still some hours until dawn."

✧ The Beggar King ✧

THE FRONT OFFICE of Triplanetary Freight Forwarding was empty, which he'd expected, considering. He hadn't called ahead, and they'd only known he was on his way, not when he'd arrive. Which turned out to be just as well, because he hadn't done all that good a job coordinating his arrival with local downtime; the cabbie who'd brought him from the shipyard had spent no energy at all hiding his surprise that any Terran would wander here by himself at this sunless time.

The files . . . the front-office files were in order, up-to-date, and accessible to his code, which—given one thing and another—he hadn't expected. The boss' office, what he supposed he'd be calling *his* office for as long as might be, was locked, which didn't mean anything except that staff was conscientious.

He used the key he'd been given and stood to one side, shoulder against the wall, hands in the pockets of his leather jacket, while the door slid open and the lights came up in the room beyond.

Since there weren't any immediate hostilities initiated, he eased 'round the wall, hands still in his pockets, and stood just beyond the threshold, taking a long careful look at everything there was to see.

The office was pretty much like he remembered it from his last visit, excusing the lack of clutter obscuring the expensive red wood of the desk, and the sharp, infuriating presence of Lela Toonapple behind it.

"Well, now," he said conversationally, tarrying yet by the door.

"Already you've outlasted Replacement Number Three. That ought to ease you."

In fact, it didn't ease him in the least, nor was he a man who usually talked to himself, despite that being a common trait of courier pilots. Replacement Number One had apparently bought his ticket out by congratulating himself aloud upon entering this very office. The sound waves had triggered a razorfall rigged into the ceiling and, hey, presto! Replacement Number One was freshly bleeding meat. He fancied he could see a stain of dried blood, dull against the gleaming crimson wood. Fancy only, he assured himself; staff here were efficient, having been trained by Herself, who would never have tolerated bad housekeeping.

According to the reports, Replacement Number Two had gotten herself done within ten planet days by a local bent on revenge, what they called *Balance* hereabouts. Occupational hazard, that was. Or not. He considered himself warned.

And, he acknowledged, finishing his visual scan and stepping into the office, the fact remained that each of the three replacements before him had gone down their own road to meet death very soon after planetfall, the only obvious link between them that they'd struck Sector Boss Ailsworth as a threat to his position; enough of a threat that they'd been shuffled out of the high-visibility zone and dropped in a place where, apparently, there was no advancement. Hard to know who to blame, there, if anyone—they'd all accepted the job, after all.

Same, he admitted wryly to himself, shrugging his shoulder pack off and putting it on the desk, as Number Four.

"Nice going, Clarence," he muttered, and pulled his left hand and the bug-finder out of its pocket. He scrutinized the read-out, with its cheery blue lights proclaiming *safe-safe-safe*, and set it down next to his pack. Sighing, he slipped the gun out of his right pocket, snapped on the safety and put it decently away into its holster.

The temp was set a little low for his liking, so he kept the jacket on as he pulled the chair into a comfortable spot before sitting and adjusted the armrests so he wouldn't bang his elbows too hard (because he knew he was one that used his armrests)—ergonomics be damned—and bent over to bring the comp on-line.

First file up was addressed to him. A roster it was, listing names and contact numbers for staff, couriers, day-labor and such. It also gave the address and contact codes for the round-the-clock office, whose work he'd seriously not wished to impinge upon as his first act on-planet. The second file was something else. He frowned, scanned through, then went back to the top, one hand already reaching for the desk-comm.

He punched up the first number on the contact page; a woman answered, sounding surprised. Hers was, after all, a purposefully quiet office on a purposefully quiet planet.

"Tora Belle here."

"This is O'Berin," Clarence told her, firm and quiet. "Contact staff and let 'em know there's a meeting at headquarters when the port goes dayside. I want everybody here, sharp and ready to work."

"Yes, *sir*," Tora Belle said. "Day-labor, too?"

"Everybody," Clarence confirmed, letting her hear a touch of impatience.

"Yes, *sir*," she answered. "Anything else?"

"Bring yourself here an hour before the others. I fancy I'll be having some questions for you."

She drew a breath, slow and not quite steady.

"Questions," he said to that minor sound of dread. "You can expect from me what you had from Herself, for the same cause and reasons. Fair?"

Out the breath came, stronger. "*Yes*, sir," she whispered.

"Tomorrow, then. O'Berin out." He cut the connection and turned back to the screen and its tangled skein of news. It was going to be a long night.

Sighing, he peeled out of his jacket and adjusted the gain on the screen. He checked to make sure the telltales would talk to him in case anyone unexpected—which was just about anyone at all—tested the defenses, and reached automatically for the cup still likely sitting on his desk at Landofar.

He should've asked Belle to bring along coffee tomorrow, he thought ruefully, if there was coffee to be had. Well, and it would be interesting to see, as Herself would have had it, what Belle might think of on her own.

• • •◇• • •

"MORE TEA, MOTHER?" Daav asked, reaching for the pot.

"Of your considerable goodness." Chi yos'Phelium held out her cup with a smile.

He served her, and then himself, replacing the pot on the warmer. They shared a late breakfast on the patio overlooking the so-called wilderness. To Daav's eye, and no doubt to his mother's, the well-grown and cared-for strip of trees looked rather overly domesticated. No matter, the view was pleasant, and if it were somewhat tame, at least they could be assured that no wild animals, nor wild men, for that matter, would come roaring down upon them to smash up the porcelain and make all untidy.

"Really, Daav," his mother murmured as she took her cup in hand, "you have become extremely useful. I wonder that I allow you to return to the scouts."

He sipped his own tea, outwardly unperturbed. "Surely, ma'am, you must know that my usefulness is directly attributable to the knowledge that I am not long for Liad. Were you to deny me the scouts, I make no doubt that I should soon revert to the surly fellow we both know me to be."

"It is true," Chi said, as if the thought had just occurred to her, "that you are far from sweet-tempered, my son. Doubtless you are correct, and I would tire of your company in a few days under such changed circumstance." She put her cup, gently, on the table. "Well, then, back to the scouts you shall go, when your leave is done." She shot him a quick, mischievous glance from beneath thick golden lashes. "Now, own yourself relieved, sir!"

"Reprieved!" he exclaimed in obligingly melodramatic tones. "So near it was that my heart fair stuttered in my breast, and very nearly was I unmanned! Yet, Doom stayed her fair hand, and turned her face aside. Surely, I am the most fortunate of men!"

His mother laughed, and brought her hands together in a Terran clap of appreciation. "Well-played, sir! Truly, Daav, you should have sought the stage, rather than the scouts."

"A traveling troupe, ma'am?" he asked her, and she sent him another glance, this one sharp and serious.

"You will need to come to terms at some point," she commented. "I will say no more, other than to note that the point grows nearer, not more distant."

That this was undoubtedly true did nothing to ease Daav's feelings regarding the matter of his recent ascent to nadelm, the heir in fact to the delm. His mother advised him that he would, in time, grow accustomed to his rank and, when duty required it of him, to a life lived primarily on Liad.

Daav took leave, privately, to doubt it.

"I wonder, my son," his mother said, selecting a fruit from the bowl between them, "if you might dispatch a small errand for me at the Low Port."

Daav blinked, and sent her a look, half-expecting to meet more mischief in her face, though her voice had been serious enough.

The glance he met was likewise serious.

"At the Low Port, ma'am?" he repeated, neutrally.

His mother considered him blandly. "Quite a small thing, really, Daav. If you would be so good."

"Of course you know I can deny you nothing," he replied. "I shall be . . . perhaps *delighted* is not precisely the word which expresses my state of mind, but don't have a care for that! What may I be honored to bring you from the Low Port, Mother?"

"The answer to a riddle," she said composedly, and Daav felt his interest prick, despite himself. Riddles at the Low Port were often . . . compelling. And, sad to own, the Low Port itself was rather more to his liking than almost any other location on Liad, saving his clanhouse or at his brother's side.

"And the riddle?" he inquired, feigning boredom, which he was fairly certain deceived his parent not at all.

"Where do the pilots who visit Ilgay's Hell and Janif's Game Palace go after they depart the pleasures of the house?"

Daav considered her. "Surely, to their rightful berths, or to their clanhouses, the guildhall, or to the arms of a lover. Come, ma'am, this is not worthy of you! Hardly a riddle at all!"

"But if they do not arrive at their clanhouses, if their captains fill their berths from the will-call list, their lovers weep for their absence, and the guild assesses a fine against their licenses, and still they do not reappear? Does the riddle seem less tame then?"

Daav frowned. "Less tame and all but terrifying," he said slowly, considering the plural. "How many?"

"Eight, over the last two relumma," she replied. "The full particulars are on the computer in the study, if you find yourself interested."

"Interested," he allowed. "But is this not a matter, perhaps, for your acquaintance at Mid-Port?"

"It would seem to be so. Alas, several relumma past, my acquaintance was kind enough to inform me that she was removing herself from her position—having achieved what she was pleased to term 'sufficient time in grade to make it stick'—and the last two replacements have not lasted even long enough for one to request a meeting upon neutral ground."

Daav frowned again. "If the Balance is not firm at that juncture . . ." he murmured.

"Precisely!" his mother said, with a wide smile. "The thing wants examination from a number of angles, my child." She rose, waving a languid hand in the general direction of the study.

"Please, make yourself familiar with the particulars. I repose all faith in your ability to unravel this for me." Another brilliant smile and she was gone, dropping a light touch on his shoulder as she passed.

Daav sighed, and finished his tea, wishing he had as much confidence in his abilities as his parent pretended to. Still, he owned, it was an appealing problem—and not only for its locale. And pilots . . . pilots were the proper care of Korval, after all.

· · · ✧ · · ·

THE START OF IT WAS EASY ENOUGH, needing only a choice, and it was at Ilgay's Hell that he chose to begin his investigations.

Ilgay's was fortunately located hard by a port employment kiosk, at the center of a narrow street bracketed by food stalls and tea stands. There were folk enough about, and of various sort, so that the presence of an additional, and slightly ragged, pilot was nothing to turn heads.

First, he betook himself to the hiring kiosk, patiently waiting his turn in line for a chance at one of the three available terminals. He scrolled down the scanty offerings, frowning, then sighed, as would a man who had been disappointed not so much as vindicated, and left without even requesting a printout.

On the street again, he became one with the loose amble of those from the hiring hall, stopping at one stand to buy a rice ball and at another to purchase a paper cup of watery tea. Others, slightly plumper in pocket than the ragged pilot, bought synthasoy burgers, and sweet buns. All eventually moved down to the center of the street to take up leans and crouches where they might study the door to Ilgay's Hell.

The number of patrons entering this establishment increased as the portgate times cycled by; some were handlers or crew off-duty coming for the nearest respite, and some were those whose workday had included only the need to not lie alone in a cheap room, watching the local free vid-feed.

Some few vehicles passed by, this being a roadable place, no matter that the way was thin and the populace not all that attentive to the needs of those well-off enough to go other than on foot.

Among the ragtag group of watchers among whom Daav had placed himself there was a hierarchy. Some huddled together, passing small words and small containers between themselves, backs to the planet. Those were crewfolk left behind perhaps, or day-labor never off-world, but they shared the chance that today might be better than yesterday.

Some, more desperate, attempted the occasional gambit and even the occasional offer to sell this or that item or service to those about to enter the Hell. Here, at least, dignity and *melant'i* were still in force. Here, if there was actual begging, it was done quietly and out of view of others.

The few pilots among the watchers, were, thankfully, none that Daav recognized. That worked both ways, for his face was long away from port, which he suspected now had weighed in his mother's decision to send him to accomplish this bit of work, rather than come herself. In any wise, it was not the face, then, but the jacket that kept the more unruly of the watchers from stretching *melant'i* enough to ask for a favor or a handout. These *were* port folk, after all, and they knew that a pilot staring into the distance was not to be disturbed, for he might be thinking, calculating, might in fact be *doing* something and not simply be as lost as he or she looked. You spoke to a pilot, here, if he spoke to you, or if you were his equal.

Eventually, as he had hoped, Daav was noticed by several people going into the club—seen to be a pilot, waiting—and by several more, some of whom eyed him speculatively before going in. He amused himself by determining which of the burly doorfolk were basic security and which was the day-shift bouncer.

He had determined to make his own entrance when the day-shift bouncer ceded his post to the night-shift. In fact, that event was imminent, and he was gathering his lanky form to move across the street and through the door when he paused, head tipped in order to more clearly hear the approaching ruckus. About him, the other watchers stirred, straightened, shook themselves slightly. The very air changed—from *waiting* to *anticipation*.

From around several corners then, came, noisily, an advance crew—obviously working together, obviously security of some kind, well-armed and well-fed. They settled themselves about the crowd, and the sense of anticipation grew, edged with something that Daav hesitated to name as *hope*, but still as if the event bearing down upon them was the beginning of what they'd been waiting for this past clock-count, be it day or year.

The ruckus came on, and 'round the corner by the tea shop came a large, even an opulent, vehicle, ostentatiously fan-lifted above the narrow street, its mirror finish reflecting sky, worn faces, and old boots in egalitarian elegance.

Daav drifted toward the back of the crowd, ears and eyes alert. Words moved around him, heard in snatches: "New boss . . .", "free food, sometimes!", and "Possibly Juntavas, but work is work—" and not all the words were Liaden.

The car stopped and two of the traveling security force moved forward to open the door. A man alighted, moving with pilot grace, his body language eloquently alert. The clothes he uneasily wore were those of a prosperous merchant of no discernible clan. His copper-colored hair was slightly shorter than current fashion, and brushed severely back from a pale, round face. His eyes were very blue.

That electric blue glance swept the crowd and he bowed an encompassing bow, saying a few words to those closest. His hands moved subtly, coins and perhaps vouchers appearing between his fingers, vanishing as quickly, and the word moved through the crowd: "Day-work tomorrow . . . "

Perhaps it was the jacket, though certainly his was not the only leather on the street. Perhaps it was merely his height, notable even in this mixed company. Whichever, those very blue eyes paused in their efficient scan of the crowd, lingering a moment, and a moment more, on Daav's face. Daav held his breath, hoping he hadn't been recognized—and the man turned away.

Security moved to enter the club, the man following, two more security at his back. The car swept away, spitting city-grit at the legs and faces of the unwary. Daav joined those who followed at a respectful distance; the night bouncer nodded at his jacket and let him enter the precincts of joy.

· · ·◇· · ·

WITHIN, there was some slight disarray, as the copper-haired man was ushered to a table hastily swept and settled for him near the center of the floor. Gravely, he sat, flanked by his security, as one of the staff ran for the bar and others came forward in ones and twos and made their bows, for all the worlds as if the delm of gaming hells had come to sit among them, and take their census.

Daav slipped to the right before those sharp eyes might find him again, and made his way to the back of the room, and the various wheels of fortune.

· · ·◇· · ·

"BUY SOME LUCK, PILOT?"

The person who asked it was very nearly as tall as he was, with lush, if improbable, violet hair, and in such a state of expansive undress as must surely have put her health at risk, chilly as the house was kept.

Daav considered his small pile of chips wryly, and glanced back to her. He'd spent a good deal of energy over the last few hours carefully building the pile, and then making it dwindle.

"I'll be needing more than luck to turn this night around," he said gruffly, keeping to his character. "And nothing to spare for random results."

She smiled, to his eye honestly amused, and slid bonelessly between him and the next player.

"A bargain, then," she murmured, wrapping her hands around his arm. "If your luck changes for the better across the next three spins, you'll own I know my business and pay me double my usual fee."

He grunted, considered his small holdings once more, and snapped his fingers. "Done," he said. "See you do your work well, to mutual profit." He divided what remained of his holdings into thirds with overcareful fingers, and dropped the first third onto the ship symbol. The lady wrapped 'round him and reached down a long, naked arm to heft his empty glass.

"Wine for my pilot!" she called across to the smaller bar, and in a twinkling a fresh glass was by his hand.

"Do you pay for that out of your fee?" he asked, and she laughed, rubbing her cheek against his shoulder, violet hair ticking his chin.

"Winners drink free," she murmured.

"The stakes keep rising," he commented, and she laughed again, low in her throat.

"That's life."

"All bets frozen!" the croupier called and spun the wheel with a will.

Lights flashed merrily, the ebon ball dancing among them. His provisional luck extended her slender hand and picked up the wine glass, sipping languidly before raising it to his lips.

"To winning big," she murmured. Daav sipped, unsurprised to find the vintage much superior to that of his first glass, and she drank again before replacing the glass in its holder.

The wheel stopped; there was a moment of stillness—and then an eruption of chimes as the wheel and the square claimed by his small pile of chips began to flash a matching, exuberant green.

"We have," the croupier called, "a winner!"

His luck let loose with an ear-splitting whoop, and reached up to cuddle his cheek in her palm. Her fingers were, surprisingly, calloused; the same pattern of callouses his own hands bore.

The croupier paid out of the bank two golds and a stack of silvers. Daav had tripled his wager on that run, and he had no doubt the next two would be winners, as well. After which, if matters progressed along the usual pattern of such things, his luck would undertake to get him drunk or elsewise besotted, and then stand by as her confederates relieved him of the house's money.

It was usual in such cases, he knew, that the victim would then be left to wake up on his own and chart a no doubt unsteady course for home. There was no benefit to the house in murder, after all.

Unless, of course, one's luck was a freelancer. In which case, she might be . . . interested in his mother's riddle.

"Will you not wager again, Pilot?" his luck murmured from her affectionate nestle, one hand dropping from his arm to his thigh. "Our agreement was for profit over three spins." Her voice dropped. "Unless you have no need of the money . . ."

The lady, Daav conceded, knew her business, and certainly he had gone to some pains to appear a pilot in . . . unfortunate financial circumstances. His boots were perhaps a bit more than respectably worn, portions of his dark trousers showed as much shine as his boots.

Daav swept his palm on the worn fabric at his knee, just slightly lower than the spot on his leg his luck was gripping.

He glanced at her; nodded at the croupier.

"Let it ride," he growled, and his luck whooped. "My pilot knows how to play the game!" she shouted to the room at large.

"Have done," he said, sharp and surly under the racket of the wheel spinning. "Unless you want to be relieved of your earnings by those whose profit is taken from the pockets of others? I assure you, I have a better use for my portion than losing it to a wolf pack."

She laughed low in her throat. "Are you afraid of wolf packs, Pilot?"

"If I was afraid of losing my winnings to a wolf pack," he answered, "I wouldn't have come here."

He glanced about, hand negligently indicating the riff-raff about them, and carefully *not* including the semi-official head table where still sat the high-roller, done receiving his subjects now, bereft of his security, but having acquired a companion of his own to help him drink his wine.

"Mmm," his luck murmured, twining so nearly 'round him it seemed she would soon be inside his jacket with him. What else she might have said, if anything, was lost in a explosion of light and sound as the wheel and the square holding his second wager declared him again a winner.

"Excellent!" his luck shouted, and raised the wine glass to his lips. Drink he did, though not as deeply as she urged him, and she finished the last herself, before holding the glass high again.

"More wine for my pilot!" she called, and scarcely had the words rang out than the glass arrived, larger than the last, Daav saw at a glance, and filled to the top.

"Peace," his luck breathed into his ear, as she raised the glass for a sip. "I know you would be quiet, but I must advertise my skill for those others who might wish to employ me. I swear I will make only as much noise as will advance my own cause. Done?"

"Done," he answered, and obligingly sipped from the glass she held up to him. Again, he drank rather less than she would have had him, and was pleased to see her drink again, and deeply, before returning the glass to the table.

Himself—he considered his winnings, and of a sudden leaned forward, awkwardly, for being bound by his luck, and pushed the two-thirds of his original amount that he had held in reserve onto the ship square.

"Let it all ride," he said, slurring his words slightly.

His luck sighed so deeply her entire body quivered. The rest of the players pushed their wagers forward in silence. The croupier called the freeze and spun the wheel. Hard.

It seemed the entire house held its breath while the wheel danced 'round, and at last came to rest, winner flashing.

"A third win!" screamed his luck, forsaking his arm to propel herself into the air with a push on his shoulder, her fists beating the air. "Luck is where you find it!" she crowed.

Daav turned slightly and she came to rest with her breasts pressed against his chest, and her arms around his shoulders. She came up on her toes, pressing into him and whispered in his ear.

"Come over to my table, Sweeting, and buy me a drink."

"My winnings . . . " he protested, and she laughed, turning her head to look at the croupier. "Bring the pilot's winnings to Zara Chance's table," she commanded.

"It shall be done at once!" The croupier swore, and turned to give orders to certain of the house's other employees, who were standing nearby. Zara Chance wove her fingers with Daav's and led him away from the wheel, passing through a wide and curious throng, some of whom made to touch her. She slapped those questing hands away, laughing her rich, lazy laugh.

"Free luck is worth what you paid for it! Let us pass! Make way for Zara Chance and her winner!"

* * *◇* * *

IF THE SURLY, black-haired pilot wasn't alert at his board, his lady luck was going to undress him right in the booth, Clarence thought. Not that he didn't seem an adroit lad, and not a quarter so drunk as he was letting it be seen. But if the lady was one with the rumor he and his crew'd been chasing all over Low and Mid-Port this last while . . .

"You have a fancy for exotic hair, Boss O'Berin?" his own companion asked.

"Could be," he answered, giving her a straight look. He'd asked for somebody who knew the news, whereupon the floor boss had gone to the back and ushered her out, introducing her as, "Mistress Ilda, quarter-owner."

"Tell me about her," he said to Ilda now, angling his chin at the pair grappling in the booth.

"Her name is Zara Chance," Mistress Ilda said promptly. "She is not one of our regulars, and if it was in my power, I would ban her entirely."

"Shorts the house, does she?" Clarence asked.

"Not in the least," Ilda returned primly. "Very prompt in paying her percentage, is Zara Chance, and lays down extra for the good wine, too."

"But you don't like her," Clarence persisted when she paused, his eyes on the couple in the booth. The pilot had managed to untangle himself from the lady, and was engaged in counting his winnings, which was not, Clarence thought, quite so adroit. He considered the man more closely, but he didn't have the look of either a port-cop or a bounty-hunter.

"I don't like her," Ilda agreed. "Zara Chance's winners have a way of disappearing, once she has had her way with them. Losing customers is, as I'm sure you'd agree, Boss O'Berin, bad for business." She sighed, and shrugged, reaching for her glass. "But she does not overfish the waters, you see, and my partners are inclined to turn a blind eye, out of respect for her percentage." She sipped. "Zara Chance knows her business; and her winners always win big."

"Hm." Clarence picked up his own glass and had a sip, to be sociable. "Tell me about him."

"I've never seen him before," Ilda answered, sounding just a thought regretful. "And I doubt I'll see him again."

At the booth, the pilot had done fiddling with his coins. He pushed a sizable pile over to Zara Chance and slipped the remainder away into various pockets. Where the lady put her share, Clarence couldn't have said, but she leaned over, her hand on the pilot's arm, and her lips against his ear.

The pilot moved his shoulders; Zara Chance threw back her head and laughed, then slid out of the booth, pulling him with her.

Out of the corner of his eye, Clarence saw Belle and Huang notice the pair of them, and ease into position.

"Thank you," he said to Ilda. "You've been very helpful. I'm doing a full review, just to acquaint myself with the local franchises—staff'll be contacting you about a time for a business meeting. Right now, though—"

Ilda nodded, leaning back in her chair. "My partners and I will be pleased to see you, Boss," she said formally. "And, speaking only for myself, if you can arrange it so that Zara Chance never comes to this Hell again, I'd be much obliged."

"I'll see what I can do," Clarence told her, and stood up.

The pilot and Zara Chance were out the door, Belle and Huang on their trail.

"'Til next time," he said and moved toward the door, not hurrying, both hands in plain sight. At the door, he exchanged nods with the bouncer and stepped out into the street.

He paused in the thin spill of light from Ilgay's sign and brought his arm up, a man checking the time, that was all. The tell-tales gave him Belle and Huang's position, some meters to the right, and on an intersecting course with the points occupied by Urel and Gounce.

"Gotcha," he breathed, and ambled down the dark street, hands in pockets, the fingers of the right curled 'round the butt of his gun, not that he expected he'd need it. Staff knew what to do, now that the quarry was in sight. And it had been Belle, after all, who'd put together the pattern of the freelance luck and overlaid it with the pattern of pilots gone missing.

By rights, Clarence acknowledged, he should have let staff handle the whole job. He'd weighed it, wondering if he'd be sending the message that there was a certain lack of trust in staff's abilities. In the end, though, he'd opted to take a personal interest, showing staff he wasn't afraid to put his gun where his orders were. Showing 'em that he was the boss and that he took his port serious, just as serious as Herself had done. Pilots going missing on *her* watch? Not bloody likely.

From up ahead came the sudden sound of a scuffle. He heard Belle's voice, raised, and a shot.

Swearing, he leapt into a run, gun out, damn it all, and swung 'round the corner, dodging into the cover of a broken doorway.

* * * ✧ * * *

"WE'RE FOLLOWED," Zara Chance said, low, and sent Daav a glance so hard he felt it strike the side of his face in the darkness. "Your backup, Pilot?"

If he had thought that tonight would have been anything other than a simple reconnoiter run, it might well have been his backup,

Daav thought. Though his people might not have been quite so noisy.

Still, it was nice to be able to tell the lady the truth.

"None of mine. Most likely they're sent from the house to recover its loss."

A small pause while she gave that consideration. "It may be so," she allowed, eventually, "though Ilgay isn't known for bringing its business to the street."

"They might change policy," he offered. "For a stiff loss."

"Hm," she answered, and suddenly grabbed his arm, swinging him 'round to face back the way they'd come, and the silence between them was filled with a vibroblade's grim promise.

Blast. Well, and it likely *was* recovery crew from the house, or a wolf pack with its nose on cash. Either way, fighting at the lady's side could only increase her regard for him, which must be to his advantage. Daav slipped a slim dagger from his boot, the sound of hasty footsteps growing louder.

A man came briskly 'round the corner, stuttered to a halt, and then danced back as Zara Chance lunged, vibroblade humming like a live thing. She pursued, and he swung to one side, missing the kick, slapping at his vest, and around the corner came his mate, shouting, gun out. A shot went over Daav's head and he swept forward, meaning to knock the gun away, when yet another person arrived, copper hair gleaming in the meager light, gun out and leveled.

"Put the knife down and stand away from the pilot, hands where I can see them," he said in calm, no-nonsense Trade. "Make me ask twice and it won't be so civil."

"Since we are being civil . . ." She thumbed her weapon off, crouched to place it on the ground, and flung herself sidewise, hitting Daav hard enough to send him staggering toward the man with the gun. Startled, he tucked and hit the ground rolling, heard a shot whine somewhere overhead and heard the red-haired man snap, "I'll mind him—don't lose her!"

There came the sound of boots against gritty tarmac, and Daav continued his roll, snapped to his feet, turned to pursue—and froze, the sound of a safety being disengaged ludicrously loud.

"I have," he said over his shoulder, "business with the lady."

"Mine comes first," the red-haired man answered. "Drop the knife, why not?"

Daav sighed and turned to face him. "Because I happen to be fond of it and don't want to risk nicking the edge, if you must know."

A grin flickered, ghostly, across the pale face. "Put it away, then. Tell me where."

"Left boot," Daav said obligingly, and bent to slip the blade home. He could no longer hear sounds of the chase, and silently cursed himself for losing his contact like an idiot.

"That lady's bad trouble," the man with the gun said, when he straightened. "You get on home or to the guildhall or wherever you're wanted and let us take care of her."

Daav felt his temper flicker, not to mention a lively spurt of curiosity about his solicitous captor.

"Perhaps you think *I'm* not bad trouble," he said, allowing his voice to take an edge. "That would be a mistake."

The other man cocked his head to one side, hair glinting like metal in the dim light. He shifted the gun, but notably did not snap the safety on. "What's your name, Trouble?"

"Daav," he said shortly, feeling the curiosity rise above his irritation. "And your own?"

"Clarence. Your ladyfriend is a link to a bunch of pilots going missing on this port. That's my concern. I can't afford to lose pilots— it's expensive and it's bad for business, and it's going to stop."

"I agree with you upon every point. Stopping it is precisely the reason I am here, exactly the reason I agreed to go with Zara Chance to meet her 'recruiter', and—"

"Where's your backup?" Clarence interrupted. Daav blinked, and said nothing.

"You came down here *by yourself, without backup*?" The safety went on with an emphatic snap and the gun disappeared into a pocket as if Clarence no longer considered him a threat. Daav was inclined to feel insulted.

"I'll tell you what," Clarence said sharply, "that's *stupid*, hear me? I don't ever want to hear about you taking that kind of risk on my port again. I hear it and you're still alive, you'll wish you weren't. You reading me, Trouble?"

It seemed the red-haired man was genuinely angry. And the claim of it being *his* port nothing short of suicidal, when speaking with one of—

Oh, Daav thought, recalling his state of deliberate shabbiness.

"Let me be clear," he said, speaking with gentle care. "My name is Daav yos'Phelium Clan Korval. I am rather inclined to believe that this is *my* port, far more than it is yours."

He felt, rather than saw, the other man stiffen, heard the soft exhalation of breath that sounded peculiarly like "fuck," before Clarence raised his hand, said, "Look . . . " and hesitated.

Daav, fair ablaze with curiosity, waited, posture conveying nothing other than polite interest.

Clarence sighed, and lowered his hand. "It was still stupid," he said, firmly.

"Since you put it like that," Daav said, feeling an unexpected jolt of relief, "I agree. It was stupid. In my defense, I hardly expected contact tonight. My information on the missing pilots indicates that they were patrons of two different establishments—"

"Five," Clarence interrupted. "We've got her charted. Seems to have only been the one woman, but she was careful not to—overfish the waters, like my friend back at Ilgay's has it." He paused. "We should probably merge info."

"Though perhaps," Daav murmured, "not on the open street."

"Point." Clarence sighed. "I'm the new Juntavas Boss, by the way. Clarence O'Berin."

"I had thought you must be, as soon as I saw you dance in as Beggar King, though you seem young for the office," Daav said dryly, and around an unaccountable feeling of regret. He liked this Clarence, with his blunt good sense and competent planning. Which was, he acknowledged, just like his perversity. "You must be quite accomplished."

Clarence snorted. "No. Just the last in a set of people who let the sector boss get scared of 'em." He sighed. "So, you see, I know something about stupid."

"Ah," said Daav. "What—" Clarence held up a hand, and he swallowed the rest of his question as the other fished a comm out of his pocket and brought it to his lips.

"Go."

He listened, briefly, murmured, "Out," and stowed the unit with a nod.

"My team's got Zara Chance locked down. Interested in hearing what she has to say for herself?"

"Very," Daav answered, and fell in beside his new . . . associate.

• • •◇• • •

DAAV YOS'PHELIUM'S long legs easily kept the pace Clarence set to Belle's coordinates. The lanky pilot made about as much noise as a shadow, which got Clarence to reviewing what he knew of the individuals who made up Clan Korval, while keeping a wary eye on the street.

Chi yos'Phelium, delm, was in Herself's deep notes, attached to a long list of warnings and qualifiers for the education of those who might come after. Near as he could figure, the delm was Herself's age, give or take five Standards. At a guess, Daav was right around Clarence's age, too young, and likely of too low a rank to be any of Herself's concern. Boss would, naturally, talk to boss. On Liad even more than anywhere else.

Clarence looked at his companion, what could be seen of him in the general dimness.

"I'd have thought Chi'd come herself, since the issue was pilots," he said, more or less a shot at random.

Daav made a soft sound that might have been a laugh.

"My mother," he said, "would have been . . . conspicuous, let us say. Besides, she wishes to train me for my lifework, when she is through with being delm, and I am ever as much a pilot as she, in these days." There was a small pause before he continued. "I would have thought Boss Toonapple would have left *her* port in better repair. Perhaps her . . . withdrawal . . . was hasty?"

"Herself, Boss Toonapple as you have her, retired, all peaceful and legal, and left the business in good order. Last message I had from her said she was going someplace where she didn't have to look at a Liaden for a dozen years." He sent a quick glance at the other's profile. "Sorry."

"No need," his companion replied. "Indeed, I am much in sympathy with the boss. I infer, then, that there was some lapse of time before you were appointed to take her place?"

"There were a couple others sent first, by that sector boss I was telling you about. They didn't manage to survive too long. Staff tried to hold the line, but things started slipping with nobody at first board, if you take me. Most of what I've been doing since I got here is showing the flag to the locals and tightening up systems that slipped due to lack of repair. Like this one." The tracker shook against his wrist, and he reached out to put a hand on Daav's sleeve, stopping him.

"This is my gig, all right? You're here to witness and report back to your boss—delm."

"Agreed," Daav answered, and it might have been the truth. Clarence hoped so; he didn't warm to people much, but he found himself liking Daav yos'Phelium.

* * * ◇ * * *

THERE WERE PASSED THROUGH to the room where Zara Chance was held, secluded from the others that Clarence's people had surprised and secured. She looked up as they came in, and smiled when she saw Daav.

"So, Pilot," she said, her voice husky and languid. "Want to buy some luck?"

"I believe you may wish to husband what you have," he answered. "But I thank you for your concern."

Her laugh was cut off as Clarence stepped forward, her expression shifting toward disgust.

"Terran," she spat.

"That's right," Clarence said, calmly. "Nice to meet you, too. I've got some questions for you, and I'm going to give you a chance to answer them on your own. If you don't want to play nice, then Mr. Urel here will be happy to introduce you to our particular brand of happy juice. I'm told it's sometimes unpleasant, but not fatal."

Zara Chance stared at him, but did not respond.

"Listen close. I've got a list of ten pilots gone missing out of five gambling houses; four were seen with you on the nights they vanished." Clarence jerked his head toward Daav. "This pilot here has similar data linking you to the disappearance of pilots. You're made, is what I'm saying. Now, what I want from you is the name and location of your boss, your access codes, and the details of what happened to those pilots, as far as you know them."

"Is that all?" she asked politely, and Daav saw her shudder, minutely. "Alas, I am not able to—"

"Poison!" He snapped and jumped forward, reaching for the kit that wasn't on his belt. He grabbed her shoulder. "What is it?"

She laughed again, breath suddenly short, and stared up at him in defiance.

"Why, it is fatal, Pilot. What . . . else . . . would you have of poison?" Her face was sheeted in sweat, and she was gasping in earnest now. "Soon, you will know your reliance on the Code for the culture . . . idiocy . . . it—"

She gurgled, eyes rolling up in her head. Daav caught her, and eased her body to the floor.

"Dammit!" Clarence swore behind him, and Daav reached out to close her eyes.

"Indeed."

* * * ✦ * * *

"I . . . SEE," his mother said slowly. "So, my son, you tell me that your errand is unfulfilled?"

"It is the judgment of Mr. O'Berin and myself that we have but cut off one head of a hydra," he admitted.

"Thus warning the others to be more circumspect," his mother said tartly, and Daav inclined his head.

"Alas, that is also our conclusion." He sighed and reached for his cup. "Mr. O'Berin professes himself to be alert for new disappearances, though he believes—and I agree with him—that there will be a period of waiting, in the hopes that he will become busy with other of his business, and that Korval will turn its eye elsewhere."

"I see." She tapped the disk he had given her lightly against her knee. "And the contact information for the so-excellent Mr. O'Berin is made available to me. I assume that mine has likewise been made available to him."

"It seemed reasonable," Daav said, "especially as I am soon to return to the scouts."

"Just so. Well, we do not always succeed at the first outing." Chi yos'Phelium sighed and slipped the disk into her pocket before picking up her cup and sipping her tea. "Your impression of Mr. O'Berin seems largely positive."

"I found him organized, level-headed, and committed to his duty," Daav agreed. "I could wish to find his like on my next team."

"Hah. Recall to what he owes his allegiance, my son, and tread warily. I will own to a certain—respect—for Mistress Toonapple, and I flatter myself that she returned my regard. Had our situations been otherwise, it is perhaps not too far afield to say that we might have been friends. Alas, the old agreement between Korval and the Juntavas must forever stand between such relationships."

"Of course," Daav said, and rose to make his bow. He dropped a kiss on her cheek as he passed her chair.

"Goodnight, Mother."

"Goodnight, Child."

. . . ⬦ . . .

CLARENCE CAME 'ROUND his desk with his hand out and a smile on his face.

"Come in, sit down. Got a couple things to clean up here, then we can go to lunch, if you've got time."

Daav returned the smile, and met the hand willingly, relishing the other's firm grip.

"Not this time, I think," Daav said seriously, "as some matters are pressing."

Clarence's smile dimmed thoughtfully.

"This because you can't be seen with a Terran? Can't be seen with the—what did you call me? The Beggar King?"

Daav laughed softly.

"Forgive me, please; it was not meant as an insult. I'm told that I am too harsh on Liadens and too lenient on the entirety of the universe otherwise. And as it happens to call you the Beggar King was a lapse of accuracy, for on some worlds thieves and smugglers are guilded and acknowledged rather than hidden. Indeed, a city lacking a Beggar King is a poor one and likely more violent and dangerous as a result. If only the Council of Clans would give over its playacting . . . but there, you see—I am a scout, after all, and far too aware that the Clan grandmother was a smuggler."

Daav mused on that a moment, continued.

"I, of course, do have that heritage, and the necessity to care for pilots; the others on Liad are . . . passengers, if you will. Almost wards. And until I am Delm and able to make the clan's own direction closer to mine own, if I may, until then the city and the port will run as they do, with only the most minor meddling on my part. I do not despise smugglers and thieves as long as they are not bent on stealing my Clan's goods and smuggling them away . . .

"And thus it is not politics nor society standing in the way of lunch. I am, alas, on my way to my posting and only stopped by to give you this." He produced a disk from his vest pocket and held it out.

Clarence gave it due consideration before accepting it and stood weighing it in his hand. "More contacts?" he asked, and Daav inclined his head.

"Indeed. The portmaster, the scout commander, the Master of the Pilots Guild. With Korval general House passwords. If you have need—use them."

Clarence tipped his head, and sent a blue glance as sharp as the edge of a knife into Daav's face.

"What's the Balance?"

Daav laughed, delightedly.

"Asked like a Liaden! The Balance is only this: keep your ears and eyes open—which you and I both know you will do. If you hear or see anything that might have bearing on the . . . continued harmonious flow of business—more pilots disappearing, eh? An incipient riot, rumor of an Yxtrang invasion—let those contacts know, would you?"

"Yxtrang invasion," Clarence repeated. "You get those often?"

Daav moved his shoulders. "It's a rich world. The defense net ought to be sufficient, but—*ought to* isn't always *is*."

Another period of silence while Clarence communed with whatever loyalties and pressures of duty weighed upon him, then he nodded once, crisply, and moved over to the desk, slipping the disk into a drawer, and locking it with a thumbprint.

"I can do that," he said, straightening. "So, where are you off to that you can't stop for lunch with a friend?"

Daav hesitated, lifted his hand, let it fall.

"Clarence, your duty and my own lie at odds. We cannot be friends."

"If you say so. Where I'm from, though, what I do on my own time is my business."

"Ah. I will meditate upon that during my next tour of duty. To answer your question, though, I am returning to the scouts, and will be gone for . . . a few years, if the gods smile. Perhaps, in fact, you will have moved to a more convivial posting by the time I return."

Clarence snorted. "I think you'll find me right here," he said, and held out his hand again. "If you're on a deadline, don't let me keep you. Until again."

It was a farewell such as he might have had from one to whom he had ties. And, Daav thought suddenly, meeting that wiry hand again with a will, he and Clarence were tied, dark to light, each the mirror image of the other.

"Until again, Clarence," he said, and smiled.

✧ Necessary Evils ✧

The House of vel'Albren
Jectova

"THERE IS SOMEONE NEW among the vines," the eldest rasped, though the speaking cup was between Pinori's palms, and half-raised to her lips. Being no fool, the youngest paused before she drank, and sent a frown to their middle sister, Katauba.

She moved her fingers slightly, signing that Pinori should wait. It was rare enough, this while, that the Old One spoke at all, even with the cup in-hand. That she spoke now, and out of turn, indicated a level of alarm that must engage her sisters' closest attention. Still, there was protocol and—

Unbidden, Pinori leaned forward and offered the cup. The Old One received it, her gnarled fingers caressing the worn ceramic, and raised it to her lips, drinking deeply.

"Someone new, Auntie?" Pinori asked, which was according to their custom, now the cup was in the proper hands. "'Mong our own vines?"

"If she were anywhere else, what care would I have for her or her doings?" the Old One snapped. "Deep in my own fief I saw her, snipping and thinning, as if she had the right and the duty of it!"

"Trimming!" Katauba stared, for that was a clear breach of the ancient agreement between themselves and the House. "How—"

"But who was it, Auntie?" Pinori interrupted ruthlessly. "One of the Family?"

"Do I know the face and name of every bland human with ties to the House?" the Old One asked peevishly, then sighed, turning the cup in brown fingers and staring down into its depths.

"Truly, Child," she said, more temperately, "she appeared a stranger, with pale hair and quiet hands. It seemed to me that she had the heart of a gardener, for the vines balked and drew blood as I watched, but she made no complaint, nor handled them with aught but care. The row she worked was one I had myself marked to trim, so she has done no harm. Thus far. However, those vines are *mine*, to protect and to nourish, and I did not ask her aid. Nor do I wish for it."

"Well, then," Pinori said soothingly, "'tis likely only some small oversight which has sent this gardener into the wrong quarter. We should speak to the House and remind them of our accord."

Katauba stirred. "It is perhaps not well to recall our presence to the House," she murmured.

The Old One inclined her head, and raised the cup in salute. "In these days and times, I agree. The vines are ours, the wine which the grapes produce are ours. We are charged with protection and nourishment. Therefore, the punishment of this intruder clearly falls to us."

"But, if we punish her, the House will surely take note of us!" Pinori objected.

"And it is possible," Katauba added, slipping the cup out of the Old One's hands, "even, as our sister says—likely—that there is honest error here, either on the side of the House or on that of the gardener, herself." She paused to sip, savoring the spicy red wine.

"Perhaps," she suggested, "our duty might extend to instruction."

"Instruction?" The Old One considered her out of port-red eyes. "And how shall we instruct her?"

"Why, we will ask our sweet sister, Pinori, to seek the stranger gardener out upon the morrow, whereupon she will make her known to those vines which fall within the House's honor—and warn her away from those which are in our care." Katauba extended the cup to the youngest of them all, with a smile and a lifted brow.

Sighing, Pinori took the cup, though she did not drink. "Why must it be me?" she asked, irritably.

"Because, of we three, it is you who look most like the houselings," the Old One cackled.

"True," Katauba said briskly, seeing mutiny in the youngest's face. "And, so you are less likely to cause alarm, if indeed this strange gardener is not of the House, but some mere employee who has misunderstood her orders."

"The plan our sister proposes is prudent," the Old One stated, leaning back into her bower, with a rustle and a wave of a hand. "Let it be done as she has said."

Pinori frowned, as if she might stamp her foot and allow her temper rein. After a moment, though, she only sighed again, drank, and inclined her head.

"Let it be done as my sisters suggest," she said, though more snappish than conciliatory. "Tomorrow, I shall seek out the stranger and speak with her."

• • • ◇ • • •

THE DAMNED VINES had a will of their own.

Seltin vos'Taber swallowed a curse as she considered her lacerated fingers. Anyone would think that the plants didn't want to be trimmed.

Sighing, Seltin took a firmer grip on her shears. Trim, was the order and take the samples back to the lab, whereupon she was required to analyze vine, leaf, and fruit, keeping a log of her findings until—

Until, she thought, one hand rising involuntarily to her throat, unsteady fingertips caressing the ceramic threads woven into her skin . . . *until my master gives me other work*.

She bit her lip, fingers curling into a fist. As a general rule of life, it was not well to look too far into the future. Certainly, it was beyond folly for a bond-slave to do so.

Indeed, it were best for such persons to cultivate a short memory indeed, and an indifference to all except her master's pleasure— especially those who found themselves bonded to a master whose pleasure derived chiefly from another's pain.

Well.

Once again, she bent to the vines, taking a firm grip just below the node and bringing the shears to bear. She could swear that the plant writhed in her fingers, seeking escape. Not impossible, according to the stories whispered here and there. For though House vel'Albren had made its considerable fortune in wine and custom blends, it was whispered that, in the not-so-recent past, they, like others of the formerly Closed Houses, had also specialized in the production of . . . custom organisms. Given that her master's character seemed representative of the character of his House, it was not— unfortunately—impossible to imagine that the vines *did* object to being trimmed, and that such action gave them pain.

Which consideration, fact or fancy, had nothing, she thought sternly, to do with herself. Her sole concern was to avoid such personal pain as she might, and endure what she could not avoid. If trimming the vines gave them pain, well, then, it—it was the master's will. She was nothing more than a tool of the master's will, as devoid of choice as the shears in her hand.

The vine was severed with a snick, the sample dropped into the basket at her feet. Two more snips and she was done with the day's sampling. She slid the shears into their holster, lifted the basket, turned, and—

"Eeep!" Her voice quavered upward in surprise, and she jumped, feeling the vengeful talons of the vine she had just trimmed gouge her back through her thin shirt.

The woman before her tipped her head, pale eyes puzzled in a grave, pale face. She extended a small, neat hand as if to offer assistance, and moved a step forward. Seltin stood her ground, feeling more than a little foolish.

"Oh!" the woman said, her voice so soft it scarcely made itself heard over the din of breeze through leaf. "I did not want to frighten you."

Seltin had her breath back now, and some measure of her wits. She threw herself to her knees and bent her head, keeping withal a firm grip on the basket.

"Mistress," she said, humbly, for everyone here—and elsewhere, for that matter—was her better. "Please forgive me."

"Ah!" The other clapped her hands, in irritation or in summons

Seltin knew not. She kept her head low, and her back bent, and tried not to think.

She felt pressure, then—light, not hurtful—on her head. It took a moment to realize that the other must have placed her hands so, as if in benediction.

"You show proper respect," the woman said in her soft voice, and the pressure was gone as she took her hands away. "That is well. Truly, you are forgiven, Child. But you must not come again to these vines which are under our care. We shall do what is needful here. And you shall turn your ministrations to those vines which are under the care of the humans of the House. Is it agreed?"

What?

Kneeling, Seltin blinked. Kneeling still, she dared to raise her head and look up into the other's face.

Pale she was, but not unnaturally so; her eyes of so light a green they appeared nearly colorless. Her hair was an extremely light brown, fine as cobwebs, silken strands rising and dancing in the small breeze. She wore, not the heavy purple robes which were the standard dress of the House, nor yet the crimson shirt and tights of a slave, but a drift of iridescent fabric from shoulders to mid-thigh. Her arms and legs and feet were bare, and she wore no rings or other ornaments. She was young, and comely, and in all ways desirable.

"Forgive me," Seltin said again, hearing her voice crack. "I am commanded to trim here and in other places specifically shown to me by my master." She moved an unsteady arm, meaning to indicate the vines among which she knelt, and beyond, to the east and the south.

"Not so," the other woman said, gently. "That is in violation of our accord. Go you and say to your master that the Kapoori yet tend what is theirs."

There was something . . . very compelling about those colorless eyes, that pale, emotionless face, and it was only with a major application of will that Seltin was able to look aside, her fingers rising of their own accord, to touch the marks of her slavery.

"Forgive me," she whispered, for a third time. "My master's instructions were extremely clear. If I say to him that the Kapoori warn him away from what is theirs, he will only . . . beat . . . me and have me back here tomorrow."

Silence, long enough for Seltin to reflect upon her status as a bond-slave—and wilt where she knelt in the dirt.

Cool fingers fingers slipped beneath her chin turning her face gently, but with unexpected strength, until she looked up once more into those still, peculiar eyes. The fingers moved, brushing the threads woven into her throat. Seltin shivered, and bit her tongue, lest she cry out.

"Your master is harsh, if he will beat you for carrying a message," the other commented. "What are you called, Child?"

"Seltin," she whispered. "Seltin vos'Taber."

A frown marred the smoothness of the other woman's face. "That is no name from within the House," she said. "What is your craft?"

"I am—I was a chemist, with a specialty in exotic foodstuffs and—and inebriants."

The frown deepened. "One would believe that the House has an overabundance of chemists, and no need to add more." She moved her shapely shoulders, as if to cast off curiosity. "What is your master called, then?"

"Zanith vel'Albren," Seltin answered, hating even to speak the syllables.

"And that *is* name from within the House, in truth, though he who bears it is unknown to me."

She stepped back, her hands falling to her side.

"This bears consideration," she said solemnly, and moved a hand toward the house. "Go thou, and trouble our vines no more this day."

That, at least, she was able to do. Seltin bowed until her forehead touched the ground and she breathed in the smell of humus and leaf.

"I will, Lady," she stammered and dared to look up. "Lady, what is your—" she began, but the words died in her mouth.

She was alone with her samples and the breeze in the living vines. There was not so much as the impression of a dainty bare foot in the spongy soil to bear witness to the fact of her visitor.

· · · ⋄ · · ·

"SHE IS HIGHT SELTIN VOS'TABER," Pinori said from her seat on the old stone fence, keeping a respectful distance from Katauba and her work. "She is not of the House, though she serves one of the House. I found her both humble and mannerly."

"This is happy news," Katauba said, the vines she worked upon undulating in pleasure. "So, she will no longer interfere in our domain?"

Pinori bit her lip, looked down at her hands, and said nothing.

Katauba turned her head, amber eyes piercing. "Do you say that she defies your command? I would scarce hold that mannerly or humble."

"Nay, nay!" Pinori looked up hastily. "She is not mistress of her own life! She does as she is commanded by her master—and will, I warrant, whether or no she would, until the doom is drawn from her skin."

Her sister frowned, and straightened. The vines reached after her, twining about her hands, her wrists. "You say to me that this person is a mere kobold?"

"A natural human, as I judge her," Pinori stood, her own hands raised before her, fingers spread wide. "Here, I tell my tale badly. It would seem that Seltin vos'Taber, natural human though she be, is bound in service to one of the House, and his will she dares not cross, for cause of the threads woven into her throat." She paused, meeting her sister's stare with a lift of the chin. "I would have had her deliver to her master a message, that the Kapoori yet tend their tithe."

Katauba raised her brows. "That were bold, when we had agreed between us not to recall us to the House."

Pinori shrugged. "Bold or not, she would not carry my word. Her master would beat her, she said, and make no alterations in his course."

"Hah." Katauba pressed her lips together, and pulled her hands gently from the grip of the vines. "What is the name of this master?"

"Zanith vel'Albren, so she had it," Pinori said, and went forward a step as her sister thrust out a vine-sheathed hand.

"Do you know him?"

Silence, while Katauba stared, her pupils the merest black slits bisecting her wide golden eyes.

"Sister?" Pinori dared another step forward, though the vines coiled and reached, plucking at her.

"Of him," Katauba murmured, in a strained voice unlike her usual rich tones. "I know of him."

"And . . ." Pinori ventured when yet more silence had grown between them, "is it . . . an ill knowing, Sister?"

"Ill?" Katauba's eyes suddenly sharpened, blazing bright. "It may be ill, certainly, from such a Houseling. Well it was, Sister, that your respectful, humble human refused your order."

Pinori considered that. "Surely," she said at last, brushing her hands down her garment, and shooing the vines away. "It is of no matter if she would take my word or refuse it. This Houseling—this Zanith—deliberately sets her 'mong our honor and forbids her to trim elsewhere. I would judge that to mean that the House has recalled us well, and, therefore, we may deliver our message personally."

"Ah," said Katauba, turning back to her vines. "Perhaps . . . perhaps that would be best. We shall speak of it at twilight, over the cup."

That was clear dismissal, and in truth, she was wanted among her own vines, yet Pinori hesitated. "I might go myself," she offered. "Now, and see the thing done. I—I fear what might transpire, should the Old One find Seltin in the vineyard."

"The Old One agreed that you would speak to the human today," Katauba said, her attention already focused on her work. "She will not act before the day has gone and the cup has passed between us."

This was true enough, Pinori owned; the Old One was almost too odd for her to comprehend, root and kin though they were, but she kept most scrupulously to the very least syllable of her word. Seltin would be safe, should she venture back into the vineyard before the day was done.

Pinori bowed. "Until day's end, Sister," she said, and moved off through the wistful vines, to that portion of the vineyard which was particularly under her care.

* * * ⋄ * * *

SELTIN SAVED HER DATA and stretched, careful of her back. Her life before her arrest and conviction had been reasonably active, but the time she had spent in the tank, between sentencing and Zanith vel'Albren's purchase of her bond, had robbed her muscles of tone. Happily, her master saw fit to put her to hard labor immediately upon her revival, she thought wryly, so that soon she would be as musclebound as any kobold.

She stretched again, high on her toes this time, finding an obscure comfort in the movement of the long muscles, aches or no.

All about her was darkness, her little island of industry the only light in the cavernous lab. By rights—by reason—she should be gone herself within the next few moments. All that remained was to seal the file, log off and go—upstairs, where her master awaited her.

Even as she reached for the chording wand, she saw again the woman who had spoken to her in the vineyard that afternoon. The Kapoori, and before she had time to think, her fingers had moved along the wand, and the House library interface was opening in a subscreen.

The subscreen—that was clever, she thought, detached, as if her fingers belonged to someone other than herself. If he checked the log—and he would—the master would only see that her workspace was active, and that she had accessed the library, which was consistent both with the lateness of the hour and the as-yet-unsealed file.

Her fingers moved again on the wand, and across the subscreen there scrolled a list of open articles related to the House's past in Designed Sentients. She had, of course, reviewed this material prior to beginning the task assigned to her. It had—amused—her master, that she had been so thorough, and he had made her a sarcastic little bow.

"I had forgot," he'd said, his voice smooth and cultured, "when you were human, you had been an artist of excellence." He'd straightened and smiled at her, that smile that made her stomach clench and her breath grow short in anticipation of agony.

"Pity," he'd said, and left her to scan the data.

His pleasure that night had been cruel, by even his standards.

In the dark lab, protected by her small pool of light, Seltin sorted swiftly through the data. Of the Kapoori, there was no mention, though she found reference to a certain class of being which were dubbed "Mothers of the Vine." How many of those custom designs had been made, what their duties and skills were—the library did not yield those secrets to a quick and furtive search.

What did come forth, however, was the nugget she had half-remembered from her former search.

House Albren had moved out of custom biologics and more firmly into wines and specialty blends not simply because wine brought the House more profit. Indeed, if she read the doc aright, it would seem that several of the House's designs proved to be flawed, and fatally so. For the customers of the House.

As the two most catastrophic failures of design were demonstrated in those biologics the House had designed for its direct competitors in wine, it was at first speculated that the flaws had been deliberate. Indeed, those who had lost kin to Albren designs argued that point most vociferously before a guild judge.

In the end, however, nothing was proven. The accusing Houses each paid a fine to the court; House Albren paid a fine to the court and the case was dismissed. So was justice served in the Spiral Arm. By and by, House Albren quietly withdrew from the business of designing sentients, its standing among the Great Houses of the Vine having risen . . . considerably.

Which, Seltin thought, was interesting, but illuminated the Kapoori not at all. She glanced at the time in the corner of her screen and felt her throat tighten. Gods, the time! He would—

She picked up the wand, closed the subscreen, and sealed her notes, in a flurry of finger strokes.

"Quickly, quickly," she whispered to herself. "You must go . . . "

"Must you at once?" a sibilant voice asked from the darkness at her back. Gasping, Seltin dropped the wand, and spun, back pressed against her worktable, hands out before her.

"Who's there?" she called, voice quavering and high. "Show yourself!"

"No need to shout," the voice chided her. The darkness yielded a movement, and the movement became a woman—or a sort of woman. Her hair was long and vibrantly green, her skin brown. She was small and rounded, a brief skirt her only garment. Tattoos in the pattern of grape vines twined up and down her forearms and across her heavy breasts. Her eyes were amber, and they glowed in the dimness, like cat eyes.

Seltin remembered to breathe.

"Who are you?" she whispered, then, a not-question: "Another of the Kapoori."

"My sister speaks too freely," the woman murmured. "It is a failing of youth. Do you have the same failing?"

"I speak when I'm spoken to," Seltin said, and tasted bitterness along her tongue. "If you've come to ask me to bear a message to Zanith vel'Albren, I—"

"Indeed, indeed." The other raised her hands, smoothing the dim air with broad, calloused fingers. "Regain your peace, I beg you. I have come to be sure that you will *not* bear any message at all to Zanith vel'Albren, nor even whisper that you have seen us."

Seltin looked down, awash with humiliation.

"Unfortunately, I cannot promise that, either."

"Repine not. I can make that promise for you." The other woman drifted forward, silent on brown, naked feet.

Seltin considered her curiously. She should, she thought distantly, be afraid. Instead, she felt only curiosity, and a sort of anticipatory relief. If this tattooed woman should end her life, would it not also end the suffering, the degradation, and—

Out of the darkness came the hiss of a door opening, and a man's mild voice: "Seltin?"

She spun, knees wobbling, hands rising uselessly before her, breath rattling in a throat already tight.

"Seltin?" the voice came again, faintly chiding. "What keeps you here so late?"

"Your work, Master," she gasped, hating the high breathiness of fear she heard in her own voice. "Only your work. I—I was just now finished, and—"

"Just now finished?" he asked, and she heard him moving toward her through the dark. Even in her terror, she spared a thought, flung a look over her shoulder—but there was only darkness, all around. The tattooed Kapoori had, wisely, made an escape.

"The usage stats show you logged off whole minutes ago, and still

I find you dallying here. Is it possible that you thought to shirk your evening duties, Seltin?"

No, she thought hopelessly. She had long since given up any pretext of resistance. And yet—knowing her danger, she had tarried, as if—

"You do not answer," her master said, softly, sadly—and the agony struck.

• • • ✧ • • •

SHE ROUSED TO THE SOUND of someone gasping painfully for breath, and scrabbled after unconsciousness, foreknowing the nightmare of waking.

Alas, the stupor continued to lighten, and she knew the gasping for her own, her abused throat working painfully; her muscles shivering with residual agony.

Gradually, she came to know that she was lying on her side on a cold, hard surface, which could be anywhere. Once, he had left her naked outside when he had done with his pleasure, and it was only her bad luck that she had woken before she froze.

This time . . .

Warm, rough fingers brushed sticky hair away from her cold forehead, then touched her cheek gently.

"Wake, Little Mother," the voice of the second Kapoori whispered. "He is gone, and here is one with the means to aid you."

Cautiously, she pried her eyes open, and stared into the strong, brown face.

"Will you kill me?" she whispered, the words fractured and desperate. She raised a trembling hand and gripped the Kapoori's strong wrist. "Please."

Hot amber eyes burned into hers. "If there is no other choice, I swear that I will grant you death. However, you must rely on my judgment when I say that today despair is not the victor. Today, I will give you ease and comfort, and some small tithe of strength. Trust me."

She bent forward and placed her lips against Seltin's in a firm kiss. Seltin lay, shivering, too tired to fight, too worn to care, even when the Kapoori's tongue slid into her mouth, and the kiss grew deeper, waking a—glow, an effervescence, a feeling of health and of joy . . .

Languidly, the Kapoori ended the kiss, sitting back with a smile on her wide mouth.

"To your good health, Little Mother," she murmured, and moved her hand, brushing the palm down across Seltin's eyes. "Sleep now."

· · · ✧ · · ·

"THEY SHOULD ALL BE GIVEN to the vines," the Old One said coldly, "so that we may continue our work in peace."

"Nay!" Pinori cried, out of turn, and in apparent alarm. "Auntie, surely we should do no such thing!"

"Pah!" the Old One answered, a sentiment with which Katauba found herself in some accord. However—

"Our sister speaks truly," she said, forcing herself to calmness, forcing herself to consider calmly that which she had seen and heard in the course of the young mother's torture. "We must not act in haste." She extended a hand and slipped the cup from the Old One's hand. She took the ritual sip and closed her eyes, savoring the complex flavors, before opening her eyes once more.

"Nor," she said, "must we forget our purpose—the purpose for which the House saw us created."

"The vines!" the Old One cried, in a tone of curious triumph.

Katauba inclined her head. "Indeed. The House created us to tend the vines, and to coax from them the finest grapes that could be had, which the House then presses into wine, and sells abroad—"

"To the benefit of the House!" Pinori interrupted, passionately. "Thus, we are of value to the House, and to speak of, of—"

"Correct," Katauba said crisply. "Those of the House are necessary to us, as we are to the House. There should be respect and accord between us, as we all work toward and for the same goals."

"There ye have it aslant," the Old One said, interrupting in her turn. Katauba frowned at her.

"I don't understand."

"We care for the vines, and the fruit that comes to them," the Old One said. "Right enough ye are. The House, though, the House cares nothing for the vines, nor yet the grapes, excepting as those things are a means to amassing more for the House."

Katauba blinked. This was a long and unusually complex speech for the Old One, and as such bore thinking upon.

"More?" Pinori asked, who was apparently thinking rapidly, or not at all. "*More what*, Auntie?"

"Power," the Old One answered, and nodded wisely.

Katauba thought of the man standing in the pool of light, fingers stroking the gems set into his bracelet, smiling and aroused as the woman writhed and strangled at his feet. She shuddered, and took an unprecedented second sip from the cup.

"Sisters," she said, and marked the unsteadiness of her own voice. "Perhaps the time has come for us to reassess our position. Thinking upon our sister's words, it comes to me that we are at a disadvantage, for without the protection, the contacts and the supplies provided by the House, we are vulnerable in ways that the House is not, did we merely—" Her throat closed, but she forced the words out anyway, "did we merely stop tending the vines."

There was silence, as the other two thought. Katauba put the cup down on the rock at her side, and in due time Pinori leaned over and picked it up.

"If we are in danger," she said slowly, "perhaps we should leave."

"Leave the vines!" cried the Old One. "That's not possible, younger!"

"It *is* possible," Pinori answered hotly. "I have done so!"

"Now, that is true," Katauba said, remembering. "You went with the senior seller on a trip to promote the House's wines, some many seasons ago." She turned and caught the Old One's eye. "You recall it, Sister."

"I do." She shrugged one sticklike shoulder. "It was why they designed her to look as they do." She stood, shifting from one strong foot to another. "So, one of us might leave. If she wished to," she said. "Solves nothing."

. . . and Katauba had to admit that she was right.

* * * ⟡ * * *

"HOW GOES THE WORK?"

The one who asked it was Garad vel'Albren, the master vintner, and, as usual, he addressed Zanith, giving slightly less attention to

Seltin, who was doing the actual work, as he might to a chair, or a crucible. Indeed, she thought, meticulously noting the latest sugar levels in the fruits she had harvested that morning, it seemed that the master vintner considered her not only blind and deaf, but dead.

"The work proceeds," Zanith murmured in answer behind her. "I do not believe that anything in the analysis has proven beyond our capability to duplicate—and so we establish that They are endowed with no special magic, such as the ignorant and the Housebound would have us believe. Would you like a copy of the log, yourself?"

Garad, predictably, hesitated, and Seltin bent closely over her table, making sure that her motions were slow and fumbling, as they should be after such a night as she had endured.

That she was *not* weakened, ill, clumsy and stupid was—interesting. Indeed, she felt not only well, but *very well*, a state so alien to her late situation that she had known a moment of alarm upon rising—and before she had recalled that the Kapoori had been with her when she had regained consciousness.

And if the Kapoori were able to reverse the damage of extended neural overload with a simple kiss, then perhaps they did partake somewhat of the "magic" her master so scorned.

"If Their techniques and abilities are only what may be reproduced in the laboratory," Garad was saying, in uncanny echo of her thought, "why were They created in the first place?"

"It was the vogue at one time to design creatures adept at one or two necessary and repetitive tasks, and thus free time for other, more complex pursuits," Zanith answered with the airy insolence that characterized him. "I believe that the House encompassed less members in those days, thus creating spare hands made a certain amount of sense.

"The sums of the past, however, are not those of the present. Now we have learned that such designed creatures may take distempers, and turn upon those who gave them life, and duty. Clearly, it is our own duty to rid the House of such a menace to itself, despite those who would have us cling to the old ways."

"Indeed, indeed," Garad said hastily. "It was not my intention to malign the work, or to withdraw my support . . ."

Idly, Seltin wondered what it was that Zanith held over the head of his cousin and co-conspirator, who was clearly of a timid nature, and none-too-adroit at any thinking that did not involve vines and vintages.

Garad took a breath. "I would very much like to have a copy of the log, Cousin," he said, with uncharacteristic firmness. "I have a number of test vines, and it is none too soon, perhaps, to try your findings in the field."

Now, that, Seltin thought, startled, was actually sensible. Zanith believed in numbers, tests, and analyses, and tended to ignore the fact that the practical application of those results might be . . . difficult to effect. Extensive field testing of their findings—into several years— was only prudent before the system in place was declared obsolete.

Not that anyone had asked her. Nor were likely to do so.

"Very well then," Zanith said to his cousin. "I will transmit the log as soon as today's results are recorded. Test well—and you will find that what I have said is nothing more than truth. The universe is built on fact, Cousin, not on magic."

* * * ⟡ * * *

THE SUNLIGHT LAY HEAVY on the vineyard. Despite herself, Seltin found her head drooping and her eyes slipping shut in the fragrant, friendly heat. The urge to lie down beneath the sample vine, curl up on the warm ground and go to sleep was—almost— overpowering.

Surety of what Zanith would do to her if she should succumb to the temptation to nap kept her upright, though she worked as a woman in a dream. She had not been abused since the night of the Kapoori's kiss—the longest such time since Zanith vel'Albren had bought her bond. She did not question why he withheld himself from his pleasures; she tried instead to enjoy the gift of even so limited an amount of freedom—and not look beyond the hour in which she found herself.

The two Kapoori had also been absent from her life since that night, though she dared to cuddle the promise the second had made her. Foolish it was, but it comforted her against the shadows of the future of which she dared not think.

Snip, went the shears, and she added another specimen to her pile.

That was enough, she judged, from this particular section. She slipped the shears away, bent to the basket—

Perhaps the vines rustled. Perhaps, having been kissed, she had acquired an affinity for their presence. Either, both or neither—it really made no difference.

Seltin straightened, turned to the left, and met the light eyes of the Kapoori who had first spoken to her, here in this very section of vineyard.

"Goodday," she said, surprised that her voice was calm, even cordial.

"Goodday to you, Seltin vos'Taber," the other replied, her smile as soft as her voice. "I trust I find you well?"

"You do," Seltin said, and touched her tongue to lips suddenly dry before adding. "I am in the debt of—another of the Kapoori—I regret that I do not know her name. She succored me some nights ago. Please, if it does not offend, I ask that you carry my gratitude to her."

"She is my next eldest sister and her name is Katauba. I shall gladly carry your words to her."

Seltin inclined her head, then looked up. "There is something—" she blurted, and stopped, horrified.

The other tipped her head. "Yes? And that is?"

Seltin took a hard breath. "I—what are you called, Lady?"

"I am Pinori. But that was not what you had been going to say, I think."

"It—was not . . . " She was shivering, her hand rose and she fingered the threads woven into her skin. She dared not, Zanith would kill her, by slow degrees, laughing all the while—

Honor, she thought.

She had been honorable, once. Before a frivolous accusation and a wrongful conviction had destroyed her faith in order and decency. Before she had been sold to a man who delighted in her degradation and pain. She was beyond honor now—or so she had told herself. Slaves cannot afford such things.

And, yet—

"It may be of interest," she said slowly, and her voice was by no means steady now. By no means whatsoever.

"It may interest yourself and . . . Katauba . . . to know that Zanith vel'Albren and Master Vintner Garad hope to learn the ways and means of your . . . care of the vines." She was trembling, her stomach roiling. She could not, she thought, in panic, do this!

She drew a hard breath. *Yes*, she told herself, *I can*.

"That is the work they have set me to—the purpose of my sampling here." Her voice failed entirely, and she simply stood there, panting in terror.

Pinori inclined her head. "We had deduced as much."

"Yes," Seltin whispered, shakily. "Yes, of course. But have you also deduced that they intend to . . . to—" To *what*, she thought wildly: *Dismantle? Deactivate? Cancel?*

". . . kill you when they feel confident that the vines can be tended by themselves alone?"

Pinori's light eyes changed, like dark wine swirling into a glass. Her fine features pulled tight, and of a sudden she did not seem so young, nor so comely—nor in any way human.

Seltin swallowed, and abruptly knelt in the dirt, her legs abruptly too weak to bear her weight. She forced herself to speak another sentence.

"Perhaps—forewarned—you may leave before this—before this terrible calamity comes to pass," she whispered.

"Perhaps we might," Pinori said, and her light voice was as cold as snow. She looked down and it seemed to Seltin that she made an effort to smooth the anger from her face. She extended a hand, and lay it lightly on Seltin's hair.

"You do the Kapoori a great service, Seltin vos'Taber. You will not be forgotten."

She lifted her hand, turned and was gone, one moment there, and the next not, as if the vines themselves had swallowed her.

• • •✧• • •

THE LAB AGAIN, and hers the only light in a sea of darkness. The log was open, awaiting her final notations; notations she was not yet ready to make. Her findings of this day were—not impossible, clearly, but surely unanticipated. Unprecedented.

Yesterday, the sample vines had been healthy, heavy with fruit, their tannins and sugars quivering on the edge of maturity.

Today, the vines were drooping, the fruits wrinkled. Her analysis had shown the sugars dried, the tannins soured, the vines themselves ill as if from blight, though if it were blight, it was one unknown to her or to the encyclopedia of the vine.

This, she thought, *is what the Kapoori can do, that we cannot.* Lay waste to a vineyard in the course of one night, leaving no clue to either cause or cure? It was impossible. *It was*, Seltin thought, running her fingers through her already disordered hair—*it was as if the thing had been done by magic—a pass of hands, a mutter of secret words, and hey, presto! The crop has failed.*

She was a scientist. Every trained nerve rebelled against such a thought, and yet, if *not* magic, than what?

A breeze moved through the lab, ruffling her hair and bearing scents of growing things. She breathed in appreciatively, then spun, heart in her mouth, for she knew that the windows were sealed, the doors barred—

The lights came up, slowly, nibbling at the edges of the dark like dawn, until the room was dim and cozy, like a garden on a comfortably overcast morning.

Across the lab, now, came her master, though not as she had ever seen him.

Zanith vel'Albren was a decisive man; he strode, he spoke firmly, he etched himself into the very molecules of the air. Not for him the hesitant step, the faltering whisper, the shrinking posture.

The man who came down the room—he shuffled, and seemed not entirely in control of his movements. He had one arm thrown about the shoulders of—of a monster, plainly put: tall, she was; her hair a brown and green tangle of leaf and twig; her fingers were long and gnarled like roots. Her face was sharp, and all covered in pale green down. She wore a short, sleeveless white shift, which revealed more than it hid of a corded brown body.

All at once, Zanith came to a halt. He grabbed the vine woman's shoulder and pulled her 'round against to him.

"More . . . " he moaned, and she laughed, rich and intoxicating. She raised her stick-fingered hand and slid it into his hair, disordering it.

"Greedy manling," she crooned. "You shall have more—and more than ever you would want."

Zanith moaned again, in pain or in urgency it was impossible to tell. The Kapoori pulled his head down, ungently, and kissed him, hard, deep, and deeper still—then let him go all at once, and caught his arm, pulling him with her.

"Come, the vines require such healing such as you alone may give them. Would you keep them waiting?"

"Never," Zanith slurred, docilely following his captor. "Never keep them waiting."

The Kapoori pulled him onward, straight to Seltin's table, and paused a moment, looking at her out of port-red eyes, set deep beneath wild brows.

"You may wish to follow, Little Mother. The vines have a gift for you as well."

Seltin stared at her, and then at Zanith.

"What have you—what have you done to him?" she whispered.

The Kapoori laughed and Seltin felt her senses swim.

"Only kissed him, Little Mother. You saw." She shifted, and placed one brown hand on the worktable. "Come or not, as you alone will it. In either wise, bear the thanks of the Kapoori with you."

She inclined her wild head and passed on, guiding Zanith as if he were a child. Seltin stared after them until they passed down the row of tables and out through the door which should have been—which had been!—locked against the night.

She bit her lip and glanced down at her table, giving a gasp as she saw what the Kapoori had left for her.

A wide ceramic bracelet set with a number of gem-colored nodes. The controller, tuned to the threads woven into her skin, which Zanith vel'Albren had so delighted to use . . .

She snatched it up and thrust it into her pocket. Then, heart hammering, she went after the Kapoori.

* * * ◇ * * *

AT FIRST, laughter guided her. She moved carefully, stalking it in the dimness, noting that the vines shifted and danced among the shadows, though there was neither wind nor breeze.

Perhaps, Seltin thought, they had merely been disturbed by the passage of the Kapoori and her captive. If that were so, then they were not so far ahead of her, she should catch them in a moment or two—

That was when she heard the first scream, hoarse and horrible.

Heedless of the danger, Seltin ran.

The vines seemed to writhe out of her way, no stick or stone tripped her. There came a second scream, so near she would have screamed herself, had she any breath to spare.

She was in an area of the vineyard where she had never been; the vines here were wild and unrestrained, heavy with fruit, the avenue thin and twisty.

A third scream came, the avenue widened, and Seltin fell to her knees, horrified. Ecstatic.

Zanith vel'Albren lay naked in the dirt, arms and legs spread wide, held by vines as thick as Seltin's forearm. The Kapoori who had led him to this place stood at his feet, her arms crossed beneath her breasts, her wild face merciless. At his head stood the one called Katauba, the vines Seltin had thought mere tattoo twisting and waving in the still air. Of the third Kapoori . . .

"I am here," the light voice murmured in her very ear. "Have a care, Seltin vos'Taber; the vines are not always discerning."

"What—" Seltin whispered. "What will happen to him?"

"Watch," the other said, and moved a few steps forward, toward the undiscerning vines, the grim Kapoori and the man, screaming and begging in the dirt.

"Please, please!" he shouted in a hoarse and trembling voice. "Tell me what you want! Anything the House can give will be yours. Anything—"

"We wish only to nourish the vines, Child of Flesh," the wildest of the Kapoori told him, in her rich, intoxicating voice. "It is what we do."

"No!" Zanith shouted. "No, you cannot—"

"You believe the old tales, then?" Katauba asked him. "I had heard otherwise."

"Please, I—I will give you a stay. I swear it! None will harm you or, or take you from your work while I—"

Pinori gestured, a ripple of the fingers only, yet it drew Seltin's eye, and she gasped, heart stuttering, as she saw the vines creeping across the ground. A tendril slid across his chest, leaving a thin line of blood in its wake. Another slipped over his hip, and wrapped itself around his straining manhood.

Zanith screamed again, wordless, and fought his bounds.

"Best accept it," the Wild One advised. "It will go easier for you."

"Though it must be said," Katauba added, "that the vines treasure an exuberant spirit."

More tendrils, more blood, and now his face was covered, the screams muffled, and the creeping vines sliding delicate feelers into his ears.

Seltin gagged, and Pinori glanced back to her, her face showing nothing but friendly concern.

"Come," she said, and put her hand on Seltin's arm, drawing her away from the impossible.

· · · ◇ · · ·

ON BALCHIAPORT, in the Street of Epicures, a new sign hangs, crisp under the faintly blue light of midday: *Kapoori Fine Wines and Custom Foodstuffs.*

Inside, two walls hold racked bottles, while a third supports a stasis-case displaying a few of those advertised custom foodstuffs.

The proprietors are young women. Pinori specializes in the wines; her partner, Seltin, will produce any food you can imagine, and some beyond anyone's imagining. It is said that Seltin was once a slave; if you look closely at her throat, you will, indeed, see a rumpled scar, as if bond-threads had been removed.

No one believes that, of course. But it makes for an interesting story.

✧ Fighting Chance ✧

"TRY IT NOW," Miri called, and folded her arms over her eyes.

There were a couple seconds of nothing more than the crunchy sound of shoes against gritty floor, which would be Penn moving over to get at the switch.

"Trying it now," he yelled, which was more warning than his dad was used to giving. There was an ominous sizzle, and a mechanical moan as the fans started in to work—picking up speed until they were humming fit to beat and yet there hadn't been a flare-out.

Miri lowered her arms carefully and squinted up into the workings. The damn splice was gonna hold this time.

For awhile, anyhow.

"Pressure's heading for normal," Penn shouted over the building racket. "Come on outta there, Miri."

"Just gotta close up," she shouted back, and wrestled the hatch up, holding it with a knee while she used both hands to seat the locking pin.

That done, she rolled out. A grubby hand intersected her line of vision. Frowning, she looked up into Penn's wary, spectacled face—and relaxed. Penn was OK, she reminded herself, and took the offered assist.

Once on her feet, she dropped his hand and Penn took a step back, glasses flashing as he looked at the lift-bike.

"Guess that's it 'til the next time," he said.

Miri shrugged. The 'bike belonged to Jerim Snarth, who'd got it off a guy who worked at the spaceport, who'd got it from—don't ask don't tell. Miri's guess was that the 'bike's original owner had gotten fed up with it breaking down every third use and left it on a scrap pile.

On the other hand, Jerim was good for the repair money, most of the time, which meant Penn's dad paid Miri on time, so she supposed she oughta hope for more breakdowns.

"Must've wrapped every wire in that thing two or three times by now," she said to Penn, and walked over to the diagnostics board. Pressure and speed had come up to spec and were standing steady.

"My dad said let it run a quarter-hour and chart the pressures."

Miri nodded, saw that Penn'd already set the timer and turned around.

"What's to do next?" she asked.

Penn shrugged his shoulders. "The 'bike was everything on the schedule," he said, sounding apologetic. "Me, I'm supposed to get the place swept up."

Miri sighed to herself. "Nothing on tomorrow, either?"

"I don't think so," Penn muttered, feeling bad though it was no doing of his—or his dad's. Some extra pay would've been welcome, though.

Extra pay was *always* welcome.

"I'll move on down to Trey's, then," she said, going over to the wall where the heavy wool shirt that served as her coat hung on a nail next to Penn's jacket. "See if there's anything needs done there."

She had to stretch high on her toes to reach her shirt—damn nails were set too high. Or she was set too low, more like it.

Sighing again, she pulled on the shirt and did up the buttons. If Trey didn't have anything—and it was likely he wouldn't—she'd walk over to Dorik's Bake Shop. Dorik always needed small work done—trouble was, she only ever paid in goods, and it was money Miri was particularly interested in.

She turned 'round. Penn was already unlimbering the broom, moving stiff. Took a hiding, she guessed. Penn got some grief on the street—for his glasses and for being so good with his figures and his reading and such, which he had to be with his dad owning a mechanical repair shop and Penn expected to help out with the work—when there was work. Hell, even her father could read, and figure, too; though he was more likely to be doing the hiding than taking it.

"Seen your dad lately?" Penn asked, like he'd heard her thinking. He looked over his shoulder, glasses glinting. "My dad's got the port wanting somebody for a cargo crane repair, and your dad's the best there is for that."

If he could be found, if he was sober when found, if he could be sobered up before the customer got impatient and went with second best . . .

Miri shook her head.

"Ain't seen him since last month," she replied and deliberately didn't add anything more.

"Well," he said after a second. "If you see him . . . "

"I'll let him know," she said, and raised a hand. "See you."

"Right." Penn turned back to the broom, and Miri moved toward the hatch that gave out onto the alley.

· · · ✧ · · ·

OUTSIDE, the air was pleasantly cool. It had rained recently, so the breeze was grit-free. On the other hand, the alley was slick and treacherous underfoot.

Miri walked briskly, absent-mindedly sure-footed, keeping a close eye on the various duck-ins and hiding spots. This close to Kalhoon's Repair, the street was usually OK; Penn's dad paid the local clean-up crew a percentage to make sure there was no trouble. Still, sometimes the crew didn't come by, and sometimes they missed, and sometimes trouble herded out of one spot and into another.

She sighed as she walked, wishing Penn hadn't mentioned her father. He never came home anymore except when he was smoked or drunk. Or both. And last time—it'd been bad last time, the worst since the time he broke her arm, and her mother—her tiny, sickly, soft-talking mother—had gone at him with a piece of the chair he'd busted to let 'em know he was in.

Beat him right across the apartment and out the door, she had, and after he was in the hall, screamed for all the neighbors to hear, "You're none of mine, Chock Robertson! I deny you!"

That'd been pretty good, that denying business, and for a while it looked like it was even gonna work.

Then Robertson, he'd come back in the middle of the night, drunk, smoked, and ugly, and started looking real loud for the rent money.

Miri'd gotten out of her bed in a hurry and run out in her shirt, legs bare, to find him ripping a cabinet off the wall. He dropped it when he saw her.

"Where's my money?" he roared, and took a swing.

She ducked back out of the way, and in that second, her mother was there—and this time she had a knife.

"Leave us!" she said, and though she hadn't raised her voice, the way she said it sent a chill right through Miri's chest.

Chock Robertson, though, never'd had no sense.

He swung on her; she ducked and slashed, raising blood on his swinging arm. Roaring, he swung again, and this time he connected.

Her mother went across the room, hit the wall and slid, boneless, to the floor, the knife falling out of her hand.

Her father laughed and stepped forward.

Miri yelled, jumped, hit the floor rolling—and came up with the knife.

She crouched, the way she'd seen the street fighters do, and looked up—a fair ways up—into her father's face.

"You touch her," she hissed, "and I'll kill you."

The wonder of the moment being, she thought as she turned out of Mechanic Street and onto Grover, was that she'd meant it.

It must've shown on her face because her father didn't keep on coming and beat her 'til all her bones were broke.

"Where's the money?" he asked, sounding almost sober.

"We paid the rent," she snarled, which was a lie, but he took it, for a second wonder, and—just walked away. Out of the apartment, down the hall and into the deepest pit of hell, as Miri had wished every day after.

Her mother . . .

That smack had broke something, though Braken didn't find any busted ribs. The cough, though, that was worse—and she was spittin' up blood with it.

Her lungs, Braken had said, and nothin' she could do, except maybe ask one of Torbin's girls for a line on some happy juice.

The dope eased the cough, though it didn't stop the blood, and Boss Latimer's security wouldn't have her in the kitchen no more, which meant no wages, nor any leftovers from the fatcat's table.

Miri was walking past Grover's Tavern and it was a testament to how slim pickin's had been that the smell of sour beer and hot grease made her mouth water.

She shook her head, tucked her hands in her pockets and stretched her legs. 'Nother couple blocks to Trey's. Maybe there'd be something gone funny in the ductwork that he was too big to get in, but that Miri could slide through just fine.

Even if there wasn't work, there'd be coffeetoot, thick and bitter from havin' been on the stove all day, and Trey was sure to give her a mug of the stuff, it bein' his idea of what was—

A shadow stepped out from behind the tavern's garbage bin. Miri dodged, but her father had already grabbed her arm and twisted it behind her back. Agony screamed through her shoulder and she bit her tongue, hard. Damn if she'd let him hear her yell. Damn if she would.

"Here she is," Robertson shouted over her head. "Gimme the cash!"

Out of the tavern's doorway came another man, tall and fat, his coat embroidered with posies and his beard trimmed and combed. He smiled when he saw her, and gold teeth gleamed.

"Mornin', Miri."

"Torbin," she gasped—and bit her tongue again as her father twisted her arm.

"That's Mr. Torbin, bitch," snarled her father.

Torbin shook his head. "I pay less for damaged goods," he said.

Robertson grunted. "You want my advice, keep her tied up and hungry. She's bad as her ol' lady for sneaking after a man and doin' him harm."

Torbin frowned. "I know how to train my girls, thanks. Let 'er go."

Miri heard her father snort a laugh.

"Gimme my money first. After she's yours, you can chase her through every rat hole on Latimer's turf."

"But she ain't gonna run away, are you, Miri?" Torbin pulled his hand out of a pocket and showed her a gun. Not a homemade one-shot, but a real gun, like the boss' security had.

"Because," Torbin was saying, "if you try an' run away, I'll shoot you in the leg. You don't gotta walk good to work for me."

"Don't wanna work for you," she said, which was stupid, and Robertson yanked her arm up to let her know it.

"That's too bad," said Torbin. "'cause your dad here's gone to a lot a trouble an' thought for you, an' found you a steady job. But, hey, soon's you make enough to pay off the loan an' the interest, you can quit. I don't hold no girl 'gainst her wants."

He grinned. "An' you—you're some lucky girl. Got me a man who pays a big bonus for a redhead, an' other one likes the youngers. You're, what—'leven? Twelve, maybe?"

"Sixteen," Miri snarled. This time, the pain caught her unawares, and a squeak got out before she ground her teeth together.

"She's thirteen," Robertson said, and Torbin nodded.

"That'll do. Let 'er go, Chock."

"M'money," her father said again, and her arm was gonna pop right outta the shoulder, if—

"Right." Torbin pulled his other hand out of its pocket, a fan of greasy bills between his fingers. "Twenty cash, like we agreed on."

Her father reached out a shaky hand and crumbled the notes in his fist.

"Good," said Torbin. "Miri, you 'member what I told you. Be a good girl and we'll get on. Let 'er go, Chock."

He pushed her hard and let go of her arm. He expected her to fall, probably, and truth to tell, she expected it herself, but managed to stay up and keep moving, head down, straight at Torbin.

She rammed her head hard into his crotch, heard a high squeak. Torbin went down to his knees, but got one arm around her; she twisted and dodged, was past, felt the grip on her shirt, and had time to yell before she was slammed into the side of the garbage bin. Her sight grayed, and out of the mist she saw a fist coming toward her.

She dropped to the mud and rolled, sobbing, heard another shout and a hoarse cough, and above it all a third and unfamiliar voice, yelling—

"Put the gun down and stand where you are or by the gods I'll shoot your balls off, if you got any!"

Miri froze where she was, belly flat to the ground, and turned her face a little to see—

Chock Robertson standing still, hands up at belt level, fingers wide and empty; and Torbin standing kinda half-bent, hands hanging empty, his gun on the ground next to his shoe.

A rangy woman in a neat gray shirt and neat gray trousers tucked tight into shiny black boots was holding a gun as shiny as the boots easy and businesslike in her right hand. Her hair was brown and her eyes were hard and the expression on her face was of a woman who'd just found rats in the larder.

"Kick that over here," she said to Torbin.

He grunted, but gave the gun a kick that put it next to the woman's foot. She put her shiny boot on it and nodded slightly. "Obliged."

"You all right, girl?" she asked then, but not like it mattered much.

Miri swallowed. Her arm hurt, and her head did, and her back where she'd caught the metal side of the container. Near's she could tell, though, everything that ought to moved. And she was breathing.

"'m OK," she said.

"Then let's see you stand up and walk over here," the woman said.

She pushed herself up onto her knees, keeping a wary eye on Robertson and Torbin, got her feet under her and walked up to the woman, making sure she kept out of the stare of her weapon.

The brown eyes flicked to her face, the hard mouth frowning.

"I know you?"

"Don't think so," Miri answered, "ma'am."

One side of the mouth twisted up a little, then the eyes moved and the gun, too.

"Stay right there until I tell you otherwise," she snapped, and her father sank back flat on his feet, hands held away from his sides.

"Get behind me, girl," the woman said, and Miri ducked around and stood facing that straight, gray-clad back.

She oughta run, she thought; get to one of her hiding places before

Torbin and her father figured out that the two of them together could take a single woman, but curiosity and some stupid idea that if it came down to it, she should help the person who'd helped her kept her there and watching.

"Now," the woman said briskly, "you gents can take yourselves peaceably off, or I can shoot the pair of you. It really don't matter to me which it is."

"The girl belongs to me!" Torbin said. "Her daddy pledged her for twenty cash."

"Nice of him," said the woman with the gun.

"Girl," she snapped over her shoulder, "if you're keen on going for whore, you go ahead with him. I won't stop you."

"I ain't," Miri said, and was ashamed to hear her voice shake.

"That's settled then." The woman moved her gun in a easy nod at Torbin. "Seems to me you oughta get your money back from her daddy and buy yourself another girl."

"She's mine to see settled!" roared Robertson, leaning forward—and then leaning back as the gun turned its stare on him.

"Girl says she ain't going for whore," the woman said lazily. "Girl's got a say in what she will and won't do to feed herself. Girl!"

Miri's shoulders jerked. "Ma'am?"

"You find yourself some work to do, you make sure your daddy gets his piece, hear?"

"No'm," Miri said, hotly. "When I find work, I'll make sure my mother gets *her* piece. She threw him out and denied him. He's no look-out of ours."

There was a small pause, and Miri thought she saw a twitch along one level shoulder.

"That a fact?" the woman murmured, but didn't wait for any answer before rapping out, "You gents got places to be. Go there."

Amazingly, they went, Torbin not even askin' for his gun back.

"You still there, girl?"

Miri blinked at the straight back. "Yes'm."

The woman turned and looked down her.

"Now the question is, why?" she asked. "You coulda been next turf over by now."

"Thought I might could help," Miri said, feeling stupid now for thinking it, "if things got uglier."

The hard eyes didn't change and the mouth didn't smile. "Ready to wade right in, were you?" she murmured, and just like before, didn't wait for an answer.

"What's your name, girl?"

"Miri Robertson."

"Huh. What's your momma's name?"

Miri looked up into the woman's face, but there wasn't no reading it, one way or the other.

"Katy Tayzin," she said.

The face did change then, though Miri couldn't've said exactly how, and the level shoulders looked to lose a little of their starch.

"You're the spit of her," the woman said, and put her fingers against her neat gray chest. "Name's Lizardi. You call me Liz."

Miri blinked up at her. "You know my mother?"

"Used to," Liz said, sliding her gun away neat into its belt-holder. "Years ago that'd be. How's she fare?"

"She's sick," Miri said, and hesitated, then blurted. "You know anybody's got work—steady work? I can do some mechanical repair, and ductwork and chimney clearing and—"

Liz held up a broad hand. Miri stopped, swallowing, and met the brown eyes steady as she could.

"Happens I have work," Liz said slowly. "It's hard and it's dangerous, but I'm proof it can be good to you. If you want to hear more, come on inside and take a sup with me. Grover does a decent stew, still."

Miri hesitated. "I don't—"

Liz shook her head. "Tradition. Recruiting officer always buys."

Whatever that meant, Miri thought, and then thought again about Torbin and her father being on the loose.

"Your momma all right where she is?" Liz asked and Miri nodded.

"Staying with Braken and Kale," she said. "Won't nobody get through Kale."

"Good. You come with me."

. . . ◇ . .

"GREW UP HERE," Liz said in her lazy way, while Miri worked through her second bowl of stew. "Boss Peterman's territory it was then. Wasn't much by way of work then, neither. Me, I was little bit older'n you, workin' pick-up and on the side. Your momma, she was baker over—well, it ain't here now, but there used to be a big bake shop over on Light Street. It was that kept us, but we was looking to do better. One day, come Commander Feriola, recruitin', just like I'm doin' now. I signed up for to be a soldier. Your momma . . ." She paused, and took a couple of minutes to look around the room. Miri finished her stew and regretfully pushed the bowl away.

"Your momma," Liz said, "she wouldn't go off-world. Her momma had told her there was bad things waitin' for her if she did, and there wasn't nothin' I could say would move her. So I went myself, and learned my trade, and rose up through the rank, and now here I'm back, looking for a few bold ones to fill in my own command."

Miri bit her lip. "What's the pay?"

Liz shook her head. "That was my first question, too. It don't pay enough, some ways. It pays better'n whorin', pays better'n odd jobs. You stand a good chance of gettin' dead from it, but you'll have a fightin' chance. And if you come out on the livin' side of that chance, and you're smart, you'll have some money to retire on and not have to come back to Surebleak never again."

"And my pay," Miri persisted, thinking about the drug Braken thought might be had, over to Boss Abram's turf, that might stop the blood and heal her mother's lungs. "I can send that home?"

Liz's mouth tightened. "You can, if that's what you want. It's your pay, girl. And believe me, you'll earn it."

Braken and Kale, they'd look after her mother while she was gone, 'specially if she was to promise them a piece. And it couldn't be no worse, off-world, than here, she thought—could it?

"I'll do it," she said, sounding maybe too eager, because the woman laughed. Miri frowned.

"No, don't you spit at me," Liz said, raising a hand. "I seen temper."

"I thought—"

"No, you didn't," Liz snapped. "All you saw was the money. Happens I got some questions of my own. I ain't looking to take you off-world and get you killed for sure. If I want to see you dead, I can shoot you right here and now and save us both the fare.

"And that's my first question, a soldier's work being what it is. You think you can kill somebody?"

Miri blinked, remembering the feel of the gun in her hand—and blinked again, pushing the memory back away.

"I can," she said, slowly, "because I have."

Liz pursed her lips, like she tasted something sour. "Have, huh? Mind sharing the particulars?"

Miri shrugged. "'Bout a year ago. They was kid slavers an' thought they'd take me. I got hold of one of their guns and—" she swallowed, remembering the smell and the woman's voice, not steady: easy kid . . .

". . . and I shot both of 'em," she finished up, meeting Liz's eyes.

"Yeah? You like it?"

Like it? Miri shook her head. "Threw up."

"Huh. Would you do it again?"

"If I had to," Miri said, and meant it.

"Huh," Liz said again. "Your momma know about it?"

"No." She hesitated, then added. "I took their money. Told her I found the purse out behind the bar."

Liz nodded.

"I heard two different ages out there on the street. You want to own one of 'em?"

Miri opened her mouth—Liz held up her hand.

"It'd be good if it was your real age. I can see you're small. Remember I knew your momma. I seen what small can do."

Like whaling a man half-again as tall as her and twice as heavy across a room and out into the hall . . .

"Almost fourteen."

"How close an almost?"

"Just shy a Standard month."

Liz closed her eyes and Miri froze.

"I can read," she said.

Liz laughed, soft and ghosty. "Can you, now?" she murmured, and opened her eyes, all business again.

"There's a signing bonus of fifty cash. You being on the light side of what the mercs consider legal age, we'll need your momma's hand on the papers."

· · · ✧ · · ·

BRAKEN EYED Miri's tall companion, and stepped back from the door.

"She's in her chair," she said.

Miri nodded and led the way.

Braken's room had a window, and Katy Tayzin's chair was set square in front of it, so she'd get whatever sun could find its way through the grime.

She was sewing—mending a tear in one of Kale's shirts, Miri thought, and looked up slowly, gray eyes black with the Juice.

"Ma—" Miri began, but Katy's eyes went past her, and she put her hands and the mending down flat on her lap.

"Angela," she said, and it was nothing like the tone she'd used to deny Robertson, but it gave Miri chills anyway.

"Katy," Liz said, in her lazy way, and stepped forward, 'til she stood lookin' down into the chair. "I'm hoping that denial's wore off by now," she said, softlike.

Katy Tayzin smiled faintly. "I think it has," she murmured. "You look fine, Angela. The soldiering's treated you well."

"Just registered my own command with merc headquarters," Liz answered. "I'm recruiting."

"And my daughter brings you here." She moved her languid gaze. "Are you for a soldier, Miri?"

"Yes'm," she said and stood forward, marshalling her arguments: the money she'd send home, the signing cash, the—

"Good," her mother said, and smiled, slowly. "You'll do well."

Liz cleared her throat. "There's a paper you'll need to sign."

"Of course."

There was a pause then. Liz's shoulders rose—and fell.

"Katy. There's medics and drugs and transplants—off world. For old times—"

"My reasons remain," Katy said, and extended a frail, translucent hand. "Sit with me, Angela. Tell me everything. Miri—Kale needs you to help him in the boiler room."

Miri blinked, then nodded. "Yes'm," she said, and turned to go. She looked back before she got to the door, and saw Liz sitting on the floor next to her mother's chair, both broad, tan hands cupping one of her mother's thin hands, brown head bent above red.

· · ·✧· · ·

MIRI'D SPENT HALF her recruitment bonus on vacked coffee and tea, dry beans and vegetables for her mother, and some quality smokes for Braken and Kale. Half of what was left went with Milt Boraneti into Boss Abram's territory, with a paper spelling out the name of the drug Braken'd thought would help Katy's lungs.

She'd gone 'round to Kalhoon's Repair to say good-bye to Penn and drop him off her hoard of paper and books, but he wasn't there. Using one of the smaller pieces of paper, she wrote him a laborious note, borrowed a piece of twine and left the tied-together package with his dad.

Liz'd told her she'd have a uniform when she got to merc headquarters, the cost to be deducted from her pay. For now, she wore her best clothes, and carried her new-signed papers in a bag over her shoulder. In the bag, too, wrapped up in a clean rag, was a smooth disk—intarsia work, her mother had murmured, barely able to hold the thing in her two hands.

"It was your grandmother's," she whispered, "and it came from off-world. It doesn't belong here, and neither do you."

"I'll send money," Miri said, looking into her mother's drugged eyes. "As much as I can."

Katy smiled. "You'll have expenses," she said. "Don't send all your money to me."

Miri bit her lip. "Will you come? Liz says—"

Katy shook her head. "I won't pass the physical at the port," she said, and coughed. She turned her head aside and used a rag to wipe her mouth.

She turned back with a smile, and reached out her thin hand to rest it on Miri's arm. "You, my daughter. You're about to begin the adventure of your life. Be bold, which I know you are. Be as honest as you can. Trust Angela. If you find love, embrace it."

The cough again, hard this time. Miri caught her shoulders and

162 *Sharon Lee & Steve Miller*

held her until it was done. Katy used the rag, and pushed it down beside her on the chair, but not before Miri saw it was dyed crimson.

Katy turned back with another smile, wider this time, and held out her arms. Miri bent and hugged her, feeling the bones. Her mother's lips brushed her cheek, and her voice whispered, "Go now."

And so she left, out the door and down the hall and into the street where Liz Lizardi was waiting, and the adventure of her life begun.

✧ Prodigal Son ✧

MIRI, Val Con thought wryly as he moved silently down the pre-dawn hallway, *is not going to like this.*

He paused outside the door to the suite he shared with his lifemate, took a breath, and put his palm firmly against the plate.

The door slid aside, and he stepped into their private parlor, pausing just over the threshold.

Across the room, the curtains had been drawn back from the wide window, admitting Surebleak's uncertain dawn. The rocking chair placed at an angle to the window moved quietly, back and forth, back and forth, its occupant silhouetted against the light.

"What ain't I gonna like?" she asked, apparently plucking the thought out of his head. Val Con shivered. The link they shared as lifemates made each aware of the other's emotions and general state of mind, and there had been instances of one of them suddenly acquiring a skill or a language which had previously belonged only to the other. This wholesale snatching of thoughts from his mind, though—that was new, and in one direction only. It seemed that Miri could read his mind perfectly well, while hers was as closed to him in detail as ever it had been. He wondered, not for the first time, if this was in some way linked to her pregnancy . . .

"Things looked kinda dicey there for a while," she went on. "From what I could tell."

"It was not without its moments," he allowed, moving toward the

163

window. "Even the presence of Scout Commander ter'Meulen was insufficient to turn all to farce."

"If Clonak was half as stupid as he acts, something with lotsa teeth would've had him for lunch a long time ago."

"True," he murmured from the side of her chair. He reached down and slipped his fingers through the wealth of her unbound hair. "But you discount the joy of the masquerade."

"No I don't. I just wonder why he bothers."

"I believe we must diagnose an excess of energy."

She snorted. Next to her, he smiled into the dawn, then sighed.

"Wanna tell me about it?"

"In fact," he said, dropping lightly to the rug beside her and leaning his head against her thigh, "I do."

"Ready when you are." He felt her hand stroke his hair and sighed in contentment made more poignant by the knowledge that it was to be all too brief.

"The highly condensed version," he murmured, "is that one of the teams the scouts sent to gather the severed blossoms of the Department of Interior . . . " She choked a laugh, and he paused, his eyes on the meager garden below them.

"That's gotta be Clonak," she said.

"Indeed, Commander ter'Meulen was pleased to style it thus," he said. "Allow it, with the understanding that the actual business was not nearly so poetical."

He felt her hair move as she shook her head. "'Course it wasn't."

"Yes, well." Her robe was fleece, soft and warm under his cheek. "This team of scouts obtained news of a situation which . . . lies close to us, *cha'trez*."

Her hand stilled on his hair. "How close, exactly?"

"Close as kin," he answered. "It would seem that the Department deployed a field unit, and perhaps a tech team, to Vandar after Agent sig'Alda failed them."

He felt her grasp it, and the frisson of her horror. Her hand fell to his shoulder, fingers gripping.

"We gotta go in," she said, and he smiled at her quickness. "Zhena Trelu, Hakan, Kem—gods, what if they've already . . . "

"We have some hope that they have not already," Val Con murmured. "A field unit is by no means an Agent of Change. But we dare not tarry."

"We *are* going, then." There was satisfaction in her voice.

Val Con shook his head. "Alas, *I* am going. You, my lady, will stay here and mind Korval's concerns—and our daughter."

"Got a real hankering for a girl, doncha? What if the baby's a boy?"

"Then he will doubtless also be as intelligent and as beautiful as his mother."

Miri laughed, then sobered. "Who's your back-up, then? If I'm staying home to mind the store."

"I thought to travel quickly," he murmured, "and leave within the hour. Clonak is gathering a contact team. He expects them to lift out no later than three days from—"

"What you're saying is that you're going in without any back-up." The rocker moved more strongly; inside his head, he heard the arpeggio of her irritation.

"Not," she said firmly, "on my watch."

"*Cha'trez*—"

"Quiet. I ain't gotta tell you how stupid it is to go into something like this by yourself, 'cause if you'd take a second think, you'd figure it out for yourself. What I am gonna tell you is you got two options: I go, or Beautiful goes."

He could not risk her—would not risk their child. His rejection was scarcely formed when he heard her sigh over his head.

"My feelings are hurt. But have it your way." Her hand left his shoulder. He rolled to his feet and helped her to rise, pulling her into an embrace.

"I will take Nelirikk with me," he whispered into her ear, and felt her laugh.

"That's a good idea," she murmured. "Glad you thought of it."

"Indeed." He hugged her tight, and stepped back. Slipping Korval's Ring from his finger, he handed it to her.

She shoved it onto her thumb and closed her fingers around it.

"Get your kit," she said. "I'll call down to the pilot and give him the good news."

• • • ◇ • • •

IT WAS A GOOD THING, Hakan thought sourly, *that he'd come to university to study guitar.* The storm winds knew what they might have made him do, if he'd come to study walking. Lie on his stomach and march on his elbows, legs dragging in the dirt behind him, probably.

"Zamir Darnill," Zhena Teone, his music history professor, inquired crisply from the front of the classroom. "Is there a problem with your zamzorn?"

Besides it being the most useless instrument in the scope of creation? Hakan thought. A flute made from a full horn, with a range of only an octave, its point sharp enough to stab unwary fingers? No wonder the thing had been abandoned for the ocarina by the serious musicians of two hundred years ago. He sighed to himself and looked up.

"A little trouble with the fipple, Zhena," he said quietly. No matter his own feelings about flutes cut from ox horn, Zhena Teone doted on the thing; and if he'd learned nothing else at university thus far, he had learned that the wise student didn't provoke his professors.

"Zamir Darnill," his teacher said sadly. "The zamzorn represents an important part of our musical tradition. I fear you are giving it neither the respect nor the attention that it deserves."

"I'm sorry, Zhena," he muttered. "Flute isn't really my—"

"Flute? Flute indeed!"

Her pause was worth a fortune of concern, and when she spoke again it was obvious that she was keeping her voice level.

"Zamir, the king has seen fit to send you here, and you will have the goodness to learn. I suspect you have not been carrying the zamzorn on your person, as you have been told this last ten-day, so that it stays at the proper temperature for playing at a moment's notice. In the past the only thing closer to a musical zamir than his zamzorn, was his zhena. So carry yours at all times, yes?"

She caressed the instrument in her hands, producing a subcurrent of stifled laughter in the room.

"You will have ample time to pursue your interest in *stringed instruments—*" she made it sound like a disease, or at least an unpleasant habit that shouldn't be mentioned in polite company—"after you have absorbed the lessons that history has to teach us. Now, then, has your disagreement with the fipple been resolved?"

There was an outright titter from the front row, and Hakan felt his ears heat.

"Yes, Zhena."

"Good. I direct the class's attention once more to the jig on page forty-five . . ."

• • • ✧ • • •

"A GREEN AND PLEASANT WORLD," Nelirikk said, as they broke their march for the meal local time decreed as dinner. "Is it always so chill?"

"Never think it," Val Con answered. "In fact, I am persuaded there are those native to the world who would pronounce today balmy in the extreme, and perfect for turning the garden."

Nelirikk sipped from his canteen. He was, Val Con thought, a woodsman the like of which Gylles had rarely seen: bold in black-and-red plaid flannel, work pants, and sturdy boots, with a red knit cap pulled down over his ears in deference to the chill of dusk.

The big man finished his drink and resealed the jug. "This . . . error the captain sends us to correct," he began.

Val Con lifted an eyebrow. Nelirikk paused, and was seen to sigh.

"Scout, I do not say it was the captain's error."

"Nor should you," Val Con said, surprised by the edge he heard on his own words. He raised a hand, showing empty palm and relaxed fingers.

"The situation—which might, in truth, be said to be error—is of my crafting," he said, more mildly. "It was I who chose to land on an interdicted world. Saying that I did so in order to preserve the lives of the captain and myself does not change the decision or the act. Once here, we inevitably accrued debt, which must of course be Balanced. All of which is aside my decision to See Hakan Meltz. At the time, I stood as Thodelm of yos'Phelium, so it was not a thing done lightly. And yos'Phelium abandons a brother even less readily than Korval relinquishes a child."

Nelirikk was sitting very still, canteen yet in hand, his eyes noncommittal. Likely he was astonished at such a rush of wordage. Val Con gave him a wry look.

"You see how my own stupidity rankles," he said. "I should at least have taken my boots off before leaping down your throat."

A smile, very slight, disturbed the careful blandness of Nelirikk's face.

"We have both made errors, I think," he said. "If ours are larger, or knottier, than the mistakes of the common troop, it is because our training has given us more scope."

Val Con grinned. "*Anyone may break a glass,*" he quoted. "*But it wants a master to break a dozen.*"

There was a small silence while Nelirikk stowed his canteen.

"What I wondered," he said eventually; "is if we will be able to remove these infiltrators without raising questions in the minds of the natives. There are, so I'm told by the Old Scout, certain protocols for operations on forbidden worlds. If we simply eliminate the enemy . . ."

"If we simply eliminate the enemy, Clonak will have both our heads to hang on his office wall," Val Con said. "No, I fear it must be capture and remove."

Nelirikk frowned, doubtless annoyed by such inefficiency. "If they've established themselves, any removal will cause comment among the natives," he pointed out.

"Indeed it will—and the least of the sins I must bear for choosing survival." Val Con stood and stretched. "If you are rested, friend Nelirikk, let us go on. Our target is only a short stroll beyond those trees."

· · · ✧ · · ·

THE PRESENTATION was already underway by the time Hakan arrived at the Explorers Club. He slid into a chair in the last row, wincing when the point of the zamzorn he'd crammed into the inner pocket of his jacket jabbed him in the chest.

"Wind take the thing," he muttered, shifting. His chair lodged noisy protest, and the zhena beside him hissed, "Shhhhhh."

Hakan sighed and subsided. It wasn't bad enough that he was late for the meeting because of having to attend remedial class on the stupid thing, but now it was outright trying to kill him.

He tried to ignore his irritation and focused his attention on the front of the room. Tonight's lecture was entitled, "The Future of Aerodynamics," a subject which at first glance seemed more alien to the interests of a guitarist than even the wind-blasted zamzorn. Hakan, however, had acquired an obsession.

Every free hour found him in the library, perusing the latest industry magazines and manuals. That a good deal of the information he read was so much noise to his untutored mind deterred him not at all. To the contrary, the realization that he had much to learn inspired him to begin attending an entry-level aeronautics course as an observer. He soon found that the acquisition of even the most basic concepts unlocked the meaning of some of what he continued to read.

Unfortunately, this heady taste of knowledge only made him thirstier.

He began to audit an advanced math class on his lunch hours, neglecting guitar while he stretched to encompass this new way of describing the world.

At mid-semester, frustrated by the slow pace of the basic aeronautics course, he considered dropping music altogether and applying to the technical college. It was only the realization that he would have to explain his reasons to Kem that had, so far, deterred him.

It was at mid-semester, too, that Zhena Cahn, the aeronautics instructor, called him to stay after class to talk with her—unprecedented for an observing student. And she had told him of the Explorers Club, and said that he might find the meetings of interest.

In fact, he *had* found them of interest. Even though he kept himself to the edges of the company during the social period, listening to the conversations of people much more learned than he; and even though almost half of the presentations were beyond him, he continued to go to the meetings, and to audit his extra classes.

Little by little, he began to understand, to grasp concepts, to extrapolate . . .

The zhena at the front of the room—he'd missed her name—was not a gifted speaker, but even her dry recitation could not close his mind to the marvels of jet-assisted flight, or heady imaginings of air speeds in excess of two hundred and fifty miles an hour.

All too soon, the zhena stepped down from the podium. The rest of the audience, held as rapt as Hakan, shifted, stood, and sorted out into separate human beings, each heading for the refreshment table.

As was his custom, Hakan took some cheese and a cup of cider—his dinner, this evening, thanks to the remedial session—and wandered the edges of the group, stopping now and then to listen, when an interesting phrase tantalized his ear.

He had almost completed his circuit, and was thinking, regretfully, that it really was time to be getting on home, when he caught the quick flicker of gold-toned fingers, deep toward the center of the crowded room.

His heart stuttered, then slammed into overtime. He put his cup and plate on the precarious edge of an overfull bookshelf, took a breath and dove into the crowd.

· · · ✧ · · ·

IT WAS NOT QUITE FULL DARK. Overhead, the few stars were dulled by a high mist. Val Con moved carefully, all too mindful of the guards—of the garrison!—nearby. His choice would have been to wait until the sluggish early hours for his infiltration. Alas, he had no choice.

He'd left Nelirikk at the entry point, to stand as guard and watcher, under orders not to interfere with the soldiers' duty, unless their duty moved them to interfere with the captain's mission. His own progress was by necessity slow, as he wished to avoid not only discovery, but tripping over the odd spade, hoe, or burlap bag half full of manure. So far, he had managed well enough, but he could only guess at the perils which awaited him as he drew closer to the target.

The terrain had changed considerably since his last visit, and it was difficult to get his precise bearings. His internal map told him that he should be within a few steps of the scuppin' house, though he neither saw—nor smelled—that structure. He did, however, blunder into the soft, treacherous footing of a newly turned garden patch.

He wobbled, and prudently dropped to one knee. It wouldn't do to call attention to himself, no—

But it appeared he had gained someone's attention after all.

Val Con kept himself very still as a shadow detached itself from the deeper shadows to his right, and moved toward him with deliberation.

• • • ✧ • • •

"BORRILL! Wind take the animal, where's he gone to now? Borrill!"

The old woman stood on the back step, staring out into the night. There were lights, of course, at the barracks and the guard stations, but she'd asked that her yard be kept more or less private, and they'd done as she'd asked. With the result that it was black as pitch and her dog with his nose on a skevit trail, or, if she knew him, asleep in the newly turned garden patch.

"Borrill!" she shouted one more time, and listened to the echoes of her voice die away.

"All right, then, spend the night outside," she muttered and turned toward the door.

From the yard came the sound of old leaves crunching underfoot. She turned back, leaning her hands on the banister until, certain as winter, Borrill ambled into the spill of light from the kitchen door, his tail wagging sheepishly, a slim figure in a hooded green jacket walking at his side.

She straightened to ease the abrupt pain in her chest, and took a deep, steadying breath.

"Cory?" she whispered into the night, too soft for him to hear— but, there, his ears had always been keen.

He reached up and put the hood back, revealing rumpled dark hair and thin, angled face.

"Zhena Trelu," he said, stopping at the bottom of the stairs, Borrill with him. "I'm sorry to come so late. We should talk, if you have time."

"Well, you can see I'm still up, thanks to that fool animal. Come along, the two of you and let an old woman go inside before she catches her death."

He smiled, and put his foot on the bottom stair. She stepped into the kitchen to put the kettle on.

"Where's Miri?" That was her first question after he'd closed the door and hung up his coat.

He turned to face her, green eyes bright. There was something . . . odd about him, that she couldn't put her finger quite on—not just the subtly prosperous clothes, or the relative neatness of his hair; something . . .

"Miri is at home, Zhena Trelu. She sends her love—and I am to tell you that we expect our first child, very soon."

She looked at him sharply. "You left her home by herself when there's a baby due? Cory Robersun, you put that coat right back on and—"

He laughed and held his hands up, like he could catch her words.

"No, no! She is surrounded by kin. My sisters, the zhena of my brother . . . Miri is well-cared for." He grinned. "She would say, too well-cared for."

Zhena Trelu snorted. "She would, too. Well, you tell her that I expect to have a visit from that baby, when she's old enough to travel."

Cory inclined his head. "I will tell her, Zhena Trelu."

The kettle sang and she turned to the stove, busy for the next few moments with the teapot. When she looked up, Cory was at the far side of the kitchen, inspecting the molding around the doorway.

He turned as if he felt her looking at him, and gave that strange heavy nod of his. "The King's carpenters, they have done well."

Zhena Trelu sighed and turned her back on him, pulling cups off the rack. "Put it back good as new," she said gruffly. Except the piano in the parlor wasn't the instrument Jerry had loved, Granic's books and old toys no longer littered the attic, the cup his zhena had made was smashed and gone forever . . .

"Sometimes," Cory said softly, "old is better."

The teapot blurred. She blinked, sniffed defiantly, and poured. He came to her side, picked up both cups, and carried them to the table. She turned, watching the slender back. New clothes were all very well, but the boy was still as thin as a stick.

"Hungry?" she asked. He glanced over his shoulder.

"I have eaten," he murmured, and pulled out a chair. "Please, Zhena Trelu, sit. There is something I must say to you, and some questions I should ask."

"Well, then." She sat. From the blanket by the corner of the stove came a long, heart-rending groan. Cory laughed, and sat across from her. He raised his cup solemnly, and took a sip. Zhena Trelu watched him, giving her own tea a chance to cool—and suddenly gasped.

"The scar's gone," she blurted, forgetting her manners in the excitement of finally putting her finger on that elusive difference.

Cory bowed his head gravely. "The scar is gone," he agreed. "I was . . . brought to a physician."

Hah, thought the old lady, lifting her cup for a cautious sip. She'd heard of skin grafting for burn victims; likely there was something similar for scars. New-fangled and expensive treatment, regardless. Well, maybe the Hero money had paid for it. And none of that, judging from the level, patient look he was giving her, was what he wanted to talk to her about.

"All right," she said grumpily. "Out with it, if you've got something to say."

"You are well-guarded here," Cory began slowly. "That is good."

She opened her mouth, then closed it. *Let the boy talk, Estra.*

"It is good because there are some . . . people. Some people who are here, maybe, only because I—we—were here. It is possible that these people will wish to question those who gave us shelter. Who gave us friendship." He paused to sip some tea, then gave her a serious look.

"These people—they are not very careful. Sometimes, they hurt people, break things, when they ask questions." He tipped his head, apparently waiting for her to say something.

Zhena Trelu drank tea and reminded herself that, while Cory had always been a little odd, that had been due to his foreign ways. He wasn't crazy, or dangerous. Or at least, he hadn't been.

"I ask, Zhena Trelu," Cory murmured, apparently taking her silence for understanding. "Are there strangers in town? Who have perhaps come to Gylles for no apparent purpose, who have been—"

"There's Zhena Sandoval and her brother," she interrupted him. "Haven't talked to 'em myself, but—they'd fit your description. Both of 'em got more questions than a three-year-old, from what I've heard."

"Ah," Cory said softly. "And their questions are?"

She shrugged. "You'll want to see Athna Brigsbee for the complete rundown. She's talked with the boy—Bar, I think the name is. From what she told me, he was all over the map, wanting to know about the Winterfair and the music competition, Hakan Meltz and I forget whatall. Athna said she might've thought he was a reporter maybe out of Laxaco City, but turns out he didn't know anything about the invasion, or the King making half the town into Heroes."

Cory frowned slightly. "It is possible . . . I cannot be certain unless I speak to the zhena or her brother, myself."

Zhena Trelu considered him. "Are you going to do that? I thought you said they were dangerous."

He gave her a slight smile. "Bravo, Zhena Trelu," he murmured.

She glared. "What's that supposed to mean?"

He moved his shoulders, his smile more pronounced. "I said these people were . . . not careful. You make the leap to dangerous. Yes, these people are dangerous. The care you gave to us puts you in danger." He paused to finish his tea, and set the cup gently on the table.

"Another question, Zhena Trelu?"

"Why not?" she asked rhetorically. "There's plenty of tea in the pot."

That got her another smile. "The last one, I promise, then I let you go to bed."

Behind them, Borrill gave up another groan. Cory laughed, and Zhena Trelu felt herself relax. She'd missed that laugh.

"So," she prompted him, grumpy in the face of that realization. "What's your last question?"

"I go by Hakan's house earlier, but it is locked; shutters closed."

"Tomas Meltz is at assembly—he's our alderman, remember?"

He nodded. "And Hakan?"

"Why, Kem and Hakan got married just after Winterfair," she said. "I'm surprised Kem didn't write to Miri about it. Very nice wedding. Hakan's aunt on his father's side stood up for him, since his mother's been gone these twenty years, poor thing. Kem was as proud as you can imagine, and the whole town was invited to the feast, after. Next morning, they got on the train to Laxaco."

"I see," Cory murmured. "Laxaco? This would be their . . . their . . . honey trip? That is good. So I should look for Hakan at Kem's house?" He pushed back from the table slightly.

"No." Zhena Trelu shook her head, and he stopped, eyes intent. "You should look for both of them in Laxaco City. They enrolled in university. Athna Brigsbee set it up for them. Got on the phone to the King's minister of something-or-other and came away with two scholarships. Kem is studying the teaching of dance, I think, and Hakan his music. Only thing Kem has to pay is their living expenses, same as she would here."

Cory frowned slightly, and she shivered, which might've been the breeze, except the new house was tight, and double-insulated, too. The only breezes that got in nowadays were invited.

"Zhena Brigsbee," he said carefully. "She told the brother of Zhena Sandoval this? That she had arranged for Hakan and Kem—"

"Shouldn't be surprised," Zhena Trelu said drily. "You know Athna, Cory."

"Yes," he breathed, staring down into his empty cup. "Yes," he said again, and looked up into her face. "Zhena Trelu, I thank you. Keep your guards close. I think Zhena Sandoval and her brother will soon be gone." He pushed his chair back and stood and she looked up at him. He looked serious, she thought. Serious and concerned.

"Going to Laxaco?" she asked.

"Soon," he answered, and came around the table, quick and light. "Keep safe," he murmured, and surprised her by slipping an arm around her shoulder. He gave her a quick hug, putting his cheek against hers briefly.

Then he was gone, walking light and rapid across the kitchen. He took his coat down from the peg and shrugged into it, bent to tug on Borrill's ears—"Good Borrill. You know me, eh?"

Zhena Trelu cleared her throat.

"Cory."

His hand on Borrill's head, he sighed, then straightened, slowly, and turned to face her.

"Zhena Trelu?"

"What's the sense of telling me to keep those guards close when you got 'round 'em like they were sound asleep? If these folks are as dangerous as you say, then they'll get in just as easy."

He drifted a step closer, bright green gaze focused on her face. "You make leaps and bounds, Zhena Trelu," he murmured. "It sits on my head that you must learn these things."

Whatever that was about, she thought, and sent him as sharp a look as she knew how.

"That doesn't go one step toward answering my question," she pointed out.

Cory's eyebrow slipped up a notch. "No, it does not," he said seriously. "The answer is that I think these people will be gone . . . one day, two days. You will get a letter, when they are no longer a . . . threat."

"Is that so? And who's going to take them away, exactly?" She frowned, an idea striking her. "Cory, there's a whole mess of the King's Guard right out there. Why not point these folks out, and let 'em clean house? They're bored here, poor boys. It'll be good for them to have something more exciting to do than watch over an old woman and her dog."

Cory tipped his head. "I would do this," he said slowly, "were these people already . . . breaking things. They are . . . polite, for now. Better that they are asked, politely, to leave."

The boy wasn't making sense, she thought. Or he was and she was too tired and too old to follow. She shook her head. "Have it your way."

"Thank you, Zhena Trelu." He paused. "It would be better, maybe, not to tell your guards that I have been here."

She snorted; he inclined his head.

"Yes. Zhena Trelu, I ask your forgiveness."

She blinked. "My forgiveness? For what?"

"For bringing change to Gylles—and to Vandar. I should not have come here, and put a whole world into danger. Choices have consequences. I know this—and still I chose life over death, for my zhena and for me."

The smooth golden face was somber; his shoulders not quite level.

Tears started; she blinked them back, and held her hand out. He came forward and took it, his fingers warm.

"You made a good choice, Cory. This world's been changing for a long time. Would you believe I remember a time when the nearest telephone was right downtown at Brillit's?"

He smiled, faintly. "I believe that, Zhena Trelu."

"Well, good, because it's true." She gave his fingers a squeeze and let him go.

He went light and quiet across the room, opened the door—and looked at her.

"Sleep well, Zhena Trelu. We will bring our child to see you—soon."

The door clicked shut behind him.

• • • ✧ • • •

HE'D NEVER GOTTEN NEAR ENOUGH to talk to the zhena with the quick golden hands, though he had learned her name from another in the ring of her admirers: Karsin Pelnara. The zhena, according to Hakan's informant, was newly arrived in Laxaco; her precise field something of mystery, though she appeared well-informed in a broad range of scientific topics. The forward-coming zamir wasn't able to tell Hakan where the zhena had arrived from precisely, though he did know that she had been sponsored in to the Club by Zamir Tang.

Seeing that he had little chance of approaching the zhena herself, Hakan had gone off in search of Zamir Tang, finding him in his usual place beside the punch bowl, engaged in a heated debate with two students who Hakan recognized as seniors in the aeronautics college.

He'd hung on the edge of that conversation for a time, first waiting for Zamir Tang's attention, and then because he found himself caught up in the description of the challenges of building a proposed supersonic wind tunnel, until a random remark recalled him to the hour.

Which was . . . late.

And later, still, by the time he had walked across the dark campus, only to find that the trolley to the married students' housing had stopped running hours before.

By the time he'd walked home, it was no longer late, but very early.

Kem, he thought, using his key on the street door, *is not going to like this.*

. . . ◇ . . .

NELIRIKK WAS NOT AT HIS POST

This was . . . worrisome.

Val Con stood very, very still, listening.

The breeze rattled branches overhead and combed the moist grass with chilly fingers. Somewhere to the left, and not immediately nearby, a night bird muttered. From further away came the sound of measured steps along pavement—the garrison guard, pursuing his duty. Beyond that, there was silence.

"Ain't like him to just run off," Miri said quietly from just behind his right shoulder.

"Nor is it." His murmured agreement had been shredded by the chilly breeze before he remembered that Miri was not covering his offside, but minding the clan's business on Surebleak.

He took a careful breath, and brought his attention back to the night around him.

From the right—a soft moan.

Cautiously, he moved in that direction, slipping noiselessly through a scrubby hedge. He dropped to one knee and peered about. To the left, a drift of last year's leaves, crackling slightly in the breeze.

To his right, a shadow leaned over another, and then straightened to an impressive height.

"Scout?" Nelirikk said, softly. "Is it well with the old woman?"

"Well," Val Con said, exiting the shrubbery and moving toward the second shadow, which remained unmoving on the ground.

"A watcher," Nelirikk said, as Val Con knelt down. "And an uncommonly poor one."

Val Con slipped a dimlight from his inner pocket and thumbed it on. The unconscious watcher was unmistakably Liaden; a red welt marred the smooth, golden brow. His hat had fallen off, freeing static-filled golden hair badly cut in imitation of the local style.

"How hard," Val Con asked Nelirikk, thumbing the dim off and slipping it away, "did you hit him?"

"Scout, I only spoke to him."

"Oh?" He sent a glance in Nelirikk's direction, but the big man's face was shadowed. "What did you say to him, I wonder?"

"Dog of a Liaden, prepare to die," Nelirikk said calmly.

Val Con bit his lip. Inside his head, he heard the music of Miri's laughter.

"I see. And then?"

"And then he most foolishly tried to escape me, tangled his feet in a root and fell, striking his head. The guard was at the far end of his patrol, or he could not have missed hearing it."

"Ah." Val Con sat back on his heels. "And his pockets?"

"Empty now. According to those protocols the Old Scout taught me, this person is a criminal many times over."

"As we are. However, our hearts are pure."

The captain's aide felt no need to reply to this truth, instead stuffing the downed man's contraband into a capacious rucksack.

Val Con reached again into his inner pocket, fingered out an ampule and snapped it under the unconscious man's nose.

A gasp, a frenzied fit of coughing. The blond man jack-knifed into a sitting position, eyes snapping open. He blinked at Val Con, flicked a look beyond—and froze, his face a study in horrified disbelief.

"*Galandaria*," he whispered hoarsely, his eyes still riveted on Nelirikk. ". . . an Yxtrang . . ."

"Yes, I know," Val Con said calmly. "He is sworn to my service, which may be fortunate for you, for he will not undertake to pull your arms off without an order from me."

The Liaden swallowed, painfully.

"What is your name and mission?" Val Con asked.

The man closed his eyes. Val Con waited.

"Technician Ilbar ten'Ornold," the Liaden said at last. "We are attached to the Uplift Team, dispatched to the area in order to ascertain if rogue Agent Val Con yos'Phelium . . . " He opened his eyes with a knowing start.

Gravely, Val Con inclined his head.

"Val Con yos'Phelium, Clan Korval," he murmured. "Pray forgive my omission of the courtesies."

Ilban ten'Ornold sighed.

"Field Agent san'Doval and yourself were sent to ascertain whether or not I had left anything of interest to the Department in Gylles," Val Con said, softly, in deference to the guard still walking his line.

"Yes."

Val Con paused, head to one side, studying the man's face.

"You will perhaps not have received recent news of the home world," he said. "The Department—"

"We had heard that headquarters had been destroyed. That does not mean the Department has been eliminated."

"Of course not," Val Con said politely, and stood, taking care to brush the leaves off the knees of his pants. "Nelirikk."

The Yxtrang stepped forward, flexing his fingers and shrugging the chill out of his shoulders.

Tech ten'Ornold jerked backward, feet scrambling for purchase in the dead leaves.

Val Con turned, as if to leave.

"No! For the—you cannot leave me to this! I—"

Val Con turned back.

"Lead us, quietly, to your base in Gylles," he said. "Or I will indeed leave you alone with this man."

Nelirikk paused, and gave the poor fellow a toothy predator's grin, perfectly discernable in the dark.

Ilbar ten'Ornold stared, as if he would keep him at bay with the force of his terror alone.

"I agree," he said hoarsely. "Now, for the love of the gods put me under your protection!"

Val Con looked to Nelirikk, who dropped back a step, with a wholly convincing show of reluctance.

"I accept your parole," Val Con told the tech. "Now, fulfill your part."

* * * ✧ * * *

"THE EXPLORERS CLUB," Kem repeated, her voice calm and cold. Inwardly, Hakan cringed. He'd thought that telling the truth was the best thing to do, though the truth came perilously close to . . . the thing they didn't talk about. The very thing that Kem didn't want to talk about.

Now he thought that he should have lied; invented an impromptu jam session or something else more or less plausible that she could have pretended to believe.

"What," Kem asked coldly, "is the Explorers Club?"

He cleared his throat, looking around their cluttered parlor, brightly lit at this unhappy hour of the morning, and Kem sitting stiff and straight in the rocking chair they'd bought together at the campus jumble shop. She still wore the exercise clothes she favored when she practiced dance, and he wondered if she had worked at it all the time he was away, again.

"Would you like some tea, Kemmy?" he asked, which was cowardly, unworthy, and wouldn't work anyway.

"I'm not thirsty, thank you."

Well, he'd known better.

"The Explorers Club, Hakan," she prompted, voice cold, eyes sparkling. She was, Hakan realized, on the edge of crying, and it was his fault. His fault, and Cory Robersun's.

He was, he thought, committed to the truth now. It seemed unfair that telling it was more likely to make her cry than the comfortable lie he'd been too stupid to tell.

"The Explorers Club," he said slowly, "is a group of people interested in technology and the . . . future. Of flight, mostly. But other things, too."

"Other things," came her over-composed voice, almost sweetly. "Like brewed tea coming out of a flat wall? Or a doctor machine?"

The things she hadn't believed, when he'd told her. The things Cory'd told him nobody would believe. He'd thought Kem would be different; that she'd believe him because she believed *in* him.

"Like those," he said calmly, his hands opening almost as if he gifted her with the information. "Tonight's presentation was on jet-assisted flight. We don't have it yet, but the zhena thinks we will, in ten years or less, traveling at speeds three or four times faster than the aircraft we have today—do you see what that means, Kemmy? At those speeds, Basil would only be a day away; Porlint, maybe two. The world would get smaller, but in a good way, we could—"

He stopped because her tears had spilled over.

"Kem—" Hakan dropped to his knees next to the rocker, and put his arms around her, half-afraid she would pull away. To his relief, she bent into him, putting her forehead against his shoulder.

"Kem, I'm so sorry," he whispered, stroking her hair. "I—the time got away from me. I was waiting for a chance to speak with the new zhena—"

In his arms, Kem stiffened, and Hakan mentally kicked himself.

Why couldn't you just stick with guitar, Hakan Meltz? he asked himself bitterly.

"Which zhena was that, Hakan?" Kem's voice wasn't cold any longer; it sounded small and tired.

He closed his eyes, and put his cheek against her hair. *Get this right*, he advised himself, *or you'll regret it every day for the rest of your life.*

"A new member of the club . . ." he said carefully. "She's from . . . away. Nobody seems to know where, exactly. I'm told she's very knowledgeable, and has a number of . . . creative ideas." Kem shivered, and he went on hastily. "I saw her tonight, and—Kem, she looks like Cory."

Kem pushed against him, and he let her go, though he stayed on his knees beside the rocker. She looked down into his face, hers white and wet and drawn.

"Is she Cory's sister, then?"

"I don't think so. When I say 'looks like,' I don't mean family resemblance—or I do, but not close family. More like a fifth or sixth cousin, maybe. She's got the same gold-tan skin—and she's just a tiny thing, not much taller than Miri, if at all. And when she talks, she moves her hands the way Cory and Miri did sometimes—you remember . . . " He moved his hands in a clumsy imitation of the crisp gestures their friends had used.

"I remember," Kem said quietly. "And you wanted to talk to this zhena."

"I wanted to ask her if she knew Cory," he said. "And I wanted to talk to her about—" he stumbled against the forbidden subject, took a breath and soldiered on. "I wanted to talk to her about that aircraft of his. If she's a countrywoman, and an engineer, she might know—it might . . . really exist," he finished, lamely.

There was a long silence during which Hakan found it hard to breathe, though he kept his eyes on hers.

When she finally, tentatively, raised her hand and smoothed his hair, he almost cried, himself.

"Hakan," she whispered, "why are you . . . obsessed with these things? You're a musician, not an engineer."

"I think," he said unsteadily, "I think people can be more than one thing, Kemmy. Don't you?"

Another silence, with her hand resting on his shoulder. "I don't know. Maybe they can." She took a breath. "Hakan."

"Kem?"

"I would like to go to the next meeting of the Explorers Club with you."

He stared up at her, chest tight. "I—sure, but I thought you didn't—"

"I'd like to meet to this mystery zhena," Kem interrupted. "If she does know Cory Robersun, I have a few things I want to say to her about him."

· · ·✧· · ·

"THE CAPTAIN will have me shot," Nelirikk said, stubbornly.

He's said that once already today, but Val Con had dismissed it out of hand and continued preparations. Now, it needed to be addressed more forcefully since it was actually delaying lift-off.

"Indeed, she will not have you shot. Because, as we have discussed, you will begin calling for aid along our private channels the moment you clear far orbit, and you will not stop calling until you have raised either the captain herself, the Elder Scout, or Commander ter'Meulen. Once you have done this, you will report that the situation is far more complex than we had believed. That, in addition to no less than six field teams and four technical teams, there is at least one Agent of Change stationed in Laxaco City, whose intention is to speedily bring Vandar's technology to the point required by the new headquarters.

"You will report on your prisoners and their condition, and you will say that I have gone to Laxaco on purpose to ensure that Kem and Hakan Darnill are out of harm's way. I will attempt to locate the

Agent, but I do not intend to confront such a one until I have substantial back-up."

"Yay!" Miri cheered in his ear. He ignored her.

"Scout—"

Val Con sliced the air with his hand, a signal for attention; Nelirikk subsided, though he dared to frown.

"If the captain has you shot, you have my permission to bludgeon me to death."

Nelirikk snorted. "A soldier's gamble, indeed." He sighed. "I will send back-up soon, Scout. Try not to do anything the captain would deplore in the meantime."

"It is my sole desire to behave only as the captain would wish."

"Pffft!" Miri commented, and even Nelirikk looked dubious.

But—"Safe lift, Scout."

"Fair journey, Nelirikk."

• • • ◇ • • •

"THERE SHE IS," Hakan whispered into Kem's ear, mindful of the zhena in the seat behind him. "She's sitting next to Zamir Tang—the man with the rumpled gray hair—in front of the pudgy man with the wispy mustache."

Kem took a good long look, her head tipped to one side. Hakan reached inside his coat and tried to adjust the zamzorn so its sharp end didn't pierce him through pocket, sweater and shirt. Wind, but he was going to be glad when the semester ended and he could put the stupid thing away forever or have it mounted as a trophy for his fortitude.

"I see her," Kem murmured. "She does look like Cory, doesn't she? In fact . . . " Her voice drifted off, and she frowned.

"What?" Hakan asked, forgetful of his voice, which earned him an emphatic *sssshhh*! from the zhena behind.

"What?" he whispered.

"Do you remember after the invasion, when Cory went off his head?"

As if he'd forget it soon. Hakan nodded.

"Zhena Pelnara reminds me of him like that," Kem whispered. "I can't quite—"

"If the pair of you don't have any interest in this presentation," the zhena in back of them interrupted in a hoarse whisper, "there are those of us who are."

Hakan looked at Kem. She was biting her lip, her eyes dancing. He grinned and secretly reached down between their seats and slipped his fingers through hers. She squeezed his hand, and he settled back, happier than he had been in many a month. Not even the zamzorn's prick against his ribs cast a shadow on his mood.

· · · ◇ · · ·

VAL CON RELAXED into the shadows across from the slightly seedy shingled building, the *Explorers Club* legend blazoned in bright yellow letters over the door. He had done a quick check of the building, looking for alternate exits, of which there was only one, and that one locked tightly. Not that a lock would necessarily stop, or even slow an Agent of Change, but Val Con rather thought she would be exiting by the front door, doubtless on the arm of the untidy old gentleman who had escorted her inside.

The agent, Karin pel'Nara, if the records he had copied were accurate, had been busy this last while, sowing her seeds of forbidden tech in the most fertile ground available to her: the inventors, visionaries and crackpots associated with the greatest university in Bentrill. That she appeared for the moment to be concentrating her efforts in Bentrill was a comfort, though a small one. At least Clonak and the hopefully substantial mop-up team would have a relatively small segment of the world's population to deal with.

On the other hand, the agent had been thorough, to the point where Vandar might not be recoverable. Val Con sighed. The Department's philosophy regarding young societies had always been one of aggression and exploitation. The death of a few barbarians; the destruction of unique cultures; the upset of societies; or the death of entire worlds—none could be allowed to weigh against the mission.

Well. It was hoped that Clonak arrived soon. A final determination of Vandar's status could certainly not be made until the pernicious influence was removed.

And, truth told, the agent's influence was hardly any worse than his own in allowing a native of an interdicted world onto a spacecraft, in telling him things no man of his world and culture had need of.

Val Con sighed again, quietly.

He had tracked down both Hakan and Kem and assured himself of their continued good health. Indeed, it was the need to be certain that they had not fallen under the eye of Agent pel'Nara that had prompted him to infiltrate the agent's base and copy those very revealing files.

Seeing that Kem and Hakan had not come into the agent's circle, he had reconsidered his own plan to visit them and drop a word of warning in their ears. Better not to take the chance, in case the agent were after all aware of his presence and interested in his movements.

The breeze freshened, rattling the handbills nailed to the post he leaned against. He wondered, idly, how long the Explorers Club would meet.

He was considering the advisability of moving closer when two figures came 'round the corner, moving quickly, their footsteps noisy on the cobbled walk. Latecomers to the meeting, Val Con thought—and then came up straight in his hiding place.

For the two latecomers were Hakan and Kem. As he watched, they jogged up the sagging wooden stairs and disappeared into the depths of the Explorers Club.

Oh, Val Con thought. *Damn*.

. . . ✧ . . .

THE PATTERN of the last meeting held; after the presentation, Zhena Pelnara was immediately surrounded, and there was no getting near her.

"She certainly is admired," Kem said, as they helped themselves to cider and cheese. "How long has she been a member?"

Hakan shrugged. "According to Zamir Fulmon, the zhena was sponsored into the club during the mid-course tests, and scarcely missed a meeting until she was called away on business. The last meeting was her first in some time. I didn't have time to attend meetings during the tests—which is why I'd never seen her before."

"Has she done a presentation?" Kem wondered. "What's her specialty?"

"I don't know," Hakan said. "We could check the event book."

"Maybe—no, look. She's leaving."

It did seem as if the zhena was taking leave of her friends. Zamir Fulmon, Hakan's informant of the last meeting, brought her coat and held it for her. The man with the odd mustache stood with two drinks in-hand, as if he'd brought her one and been overlooked. Another zamir made an offer of escort, but she declined.

"No, it is kind of you, Zamir, but I will meet my brother only a step down the walk. Stay, and continue this excellent conversation! Next meeting, I will want to hear how you have come to terms with this conundrum!"

She moved firmly toward the door, and the group stood aside to make way for her. Kem grabbed Hakan's arm and pulled him with her, heading for the door the long way, around the edge of the crowd.

"What—?" he managed, as they reached the vestibule, coats flapping open in their haste.

"Let's try to overtake her on the walk," Kem said. "It will be a perfect chance to ask her about Cory!"

· · ·✧· · ·

SOMEONE, Val Con was certain, was watching him—and had been for some time. There was no overt evidence to support this certainty, which only meant that whoever it was, they were very good. He didn't believe it was Agent pel'Nara, though it certainly could be one of her team, assigned as backup.

He considered wandering away, to see whether the watcher would follow, but that would mean leaving Hakan and Kem in the agent's orbit without backup. Though what he might do if the three of them emerged arm-in-arm from the—

The door to the Explorers Club opened and Agent pel'Nara stepped out, alone, pulling on her gloves as she descended the tricky stairs. Apparently, his friends had no need of his protection this evening. It galled him to let Agent pel'Nara go, but he judged that prudence would counsel him to walk away in a moment or two, and lose his watcher in the narrow streets to the west of the campus. He could always find the agent again, tomorrow.

Agent pel'Nara was almost to the walkway when the door to the Explorers Club opened again, spilling Hakan and Kem into the night.

Val Con froze.

Agent pel'Nara, apparently oblivious, strode steadily down the walkway toward his position. Kem clattered down the last few steps and hit the walk very nearly at a run, Hakan lagging behind.

"Zhena Pelnara!" she called.

The agent checked, then turned, head cocked to one side.

"Zhena?" she said politely, as Kem came, breathlessly, to her side. "I am not aware of your name, I think?"

"Kem Darnill. I was at the meeting. I'm sorry to chase you down like this, but it was impossible to get near you at the reception."

"Ah," Agent pel'Nara said indulgently. "You have an idea, perhaps? A theory? But you must return and share it with the others. It is with sadness that I must leave early, but—I have an appointment, Zhena. Goodnight."

She turned, and Val Con dared to hope that the encounter was over. Kem, however, was not to be put off.

"I don't have an idea," she said, "but a question. It will only take a moment, Zhena."

Agent pel'Nara was seen to sigh. She turned back. "Very well," she said, her voice a little impatient now. "But quickly if you please, Zhena Darnill."

Kem smiled as Hakan came up next to her. "This is my zamir, Hakan," she said to the Agent. "We both noticed you in the meeting. You look very much like a friend of ours . . . from . . . away."

The agent's stance changed; she was no longer poised to walk away. She was, Val Con saw, *interested* in this. As well she might be.

"I am intrigued, Zhena," she said. "There are very few of my—of us in Laxaco City. What is your friend's name?"

"Corvill Robersun," Kem said.

Val Con closed his eyes, briefly.

"Corvill Robersun," the agent repeated, caressingly. "Now, Zhena

Darnill, I must tell you that I do not know Zamir Robersun, myself. His work, though—that I know well. Do you say that he is in Laxaco? I will ask you for an introduction."

"Cory and his zhena went back home," Kem said seriously. "We'd hoped that you might have word. Also—"

"Do you happen to know—" that was Hakan, speaking quickly, his words all but stumbling over each other. "You said you knew his work . . . " He stopped, apparently embarrassed at having broken into the zhena's discussion.

Agent pel'Nara turned her attention to him. "I do indeed know his work, Zamir Darnill. What is it you wish to ask?"

"He had an . . . an aircraft, he called it," Hakan said, more slowly now, as if he dreaded the answer his question might earn, now that he was committed to asking it. "It wasn't . . . it didn't have a propeller, and there were other things kind of odd about it. But the oddest thing was that it lifted straight up. I saw the snow, and there were—"

"Who's there?" Kem said sharply.

"I hear nothing," Agent pel'Nara said soothingly, but Val Con, at least, knew she was lying.

The watcher was moving, stealthy and almost silent. Moving toward the threesome on the walkway.

Almost unbidden, Val Con found himself falling back into agent training and called up the decision matrix he knew as The Loop. Yes, there it was, the question of what an agent should do in this situation . . . and the probability that the watcher was going into an attack mode was close to unity.

Val Con's reaction was just as certain. Necessity existed.

Carefully, he bent and slipped the knife out of his boot, pausing to listen to the watcher's progress. Then, moving with considerably less noise, he charted an interception course.

. . . ⋄ . . .

THE ZHENA'S FACE had gone frighteningly, familiarly blank, as if she read some inner dialog.

It seemed to Hakan as if time suddenly sped up. He felt a surge of adrenalin.

There was a crashing, a shout from the small dark park beyond them. Zhena Pelnara reacted by reaching out and grabbing Kem's arm, simultaneously reaching inside her coat.

Kem twisted, broke free, and Hakan leapt, spinning behind the zhena, and his left arm was around her upper arms, pinning them, while his right hand held the sharp point of the slick zamzorn firmly against her throat.

The zhena relaxed slightly, as if recognizing and submitting to peril, and Kem dodged in, snatching something from the zhena's hand, and dodged back, holding the odd-shaped object uncertainly.

"That is not a toy, Zhena," Karsin Pelnara said, her voice perfectly matter-of-fact. "Please have your zamir release me."

Hakan saw Kem adjust what she held, as if determining what it was, how to use it . . . and then she held it, surely, as if it were a tiny gun.

"Kem," a familiar, slightly breathless voice said from the suddenly silent park. "Please be very careful. The zhena is correct; that thing is not a toy. Hakan—"

Cory stepped out onto the walk, hair rumpled and coat torn, the knife he used against the invasion force—or its twin—in his left hand. It looked quite as it had during the invasion, too, with its shine mottled with fresh blood.

"Hakan, I will ask you also to be very careful. You have not finished your training with that . . . "

The woman in his grip twisted suddenly, a move Hakan reacted to with his guardsman training. She redoubled her efforts, snarled, and bit at his hand holding the the instrument to her neck. He tried to pull away and the zamzorn slipped and clattered on the cobbles as it fell. Zhena Pelnara kicked, as the move required, but he'd moved and she missed, and spun her attention on Cory, who had dropped into a crouch, knife ready.

"Stop!" Kem shouted, and simultaneously there was a strange coughing sound, followed by the ring of metal on stone.

Zhena Pelnara stumbled—and collapsed to the cobbles at Cory's feet. He knelt down and turned her over, fingers against her throat a handsbreadth above a small stain on her blouse front.

"Did I kill her?" Kem asked, her voice unnaturally calm.

"No," Cory said shortly. "It is a . . . hypnotic . . . a sleep dose. She will rise eventually." He sighed then and said, "The man in the woods, he was not armed with such a benign device, I think, and is not so lucky."

"Hakan, we will need something—a rope, a scarf, to tie her before—"

Very close, someone cleared his throat. Hakan jumped, and then relaxed as the pudgy man in a well-worn jacket smiled at him.

"Peace," he said, his words barely intelligible. "A friend of Cory, me."

Cory sat back on his heels and looked at the man over his shoulder. "You took your time," he said, crankily, to Hakan's ear. "Binders?"

"Right here," the pudgy man with the wispy mustache said, and knelt down beside him, adding, "Had you come inside, you might have found me an hour ago, you know, before I had to sip any of that treacly punch they expected us to drink . . ."

* * * ◇ * * *

HAKAN WAS WIDE-EYED, and Kem no less so. Val Con leaned back in his chair and let them think it through. At the far end of the table, Clonak fiddled with his note-taker, though Val Con was willing to bet there was nothing in the least wrong with it.

"Let me understand this," Hakan said finally. "You, and Clonak, and Zhena Pelnara, and—you're all from *another world*. And Zhena Pelnara broke some kind of law about leaving . . . worlds . . . like Vandar alone, and now there will be . . . *mentors* here to guide us . . . into the *next phase*. And you want *me* to be the go-between—between the mentors and the King, or the assembly or—whoever."

"That's right." Val Con smiled encouragingly. "I know we've given you a lot of information, very quickly. If you agree, we can teach you—and you can teach us."

Hakan took a breath, eyes bright.

"He wants it," Miri commented.

"I—" Hakan started, glanced at Kem, then back to Val Con. "Why me?"

"Good question. Because already you have seen the impossible, already you . . . stretch and accept new ideas. Also, you act quickly and with decision. Not many people could have surprised that zhena, or held her for so long." He, glanced at Kem, noting the tightness of her shoulders, the forcibly calm expression and the eyes bright with tears.

"Kem, you also made a quick decision—to take that weapon, to use it. It is well. This will not be so strange for you—already you are a teacher."

Her face relaxed slightly, though her eyes still swam.

"We'll have to talk it over," she said, sending a look to Hakan. He nodded.

"Yes," Val Con said. "But not too long. I am sorry, but work must start—soon." He rose, gathering Clonak with a glance. "We leave you for an hour. Then we come back and you tell us what you decide."

"Lunch," Clonak added, "comes to help thought." He left the room, presumably to order lunch, and Val Con turned to follow him.

"Cory."

He stopped, and turned toward her. "Kem?"

"That aircraft Hakan told me about, with the tea that's brewed inside the wall, and the doctor machine you slide people into?"

"Yes."

"Is that really true?"

"Yes," Val Con said gently. "It is really true. And if Hakan wishes it, he may be taught to fly—not that craft, but one like it. You both might, if you wish."

"Wants that, too," Miri observed.

Val Con smiled. "That is for the future. For now, you decide the future."

As Val Con turned, Hakan said something quietly to Kem that sounded like, "We may wish to be two things, I think . . . "

• • • ✧ • • •

HE PAUSED OUTSIDE THE DOOR to the suite he shared with his lifemate, took a breath, and put his palm firmly against the plate.

The door slid aside; he stepped into their private parlor—and stopped.

Across the room, the curtains had been drawn back from the wide window, admitting Surebleak's uncertain dawn. The rocking chair placed at an angle to the window moved quietly, back and forth, back and forth, its occupant silhouetted against the light.

"Took your time," Miri said.

He smiled and moved across the room, dropping to his knees by her chair and putting his head in her lap.

"I am glad to be home, too, cha'trez."

She laughed, her hand falling onto the back of his neck, fingers massaging gently.

"Emerging world, huh? Pretty slick way of doing things, Scout Commander."

"It was the only possible solution," Val Con murmured. "Hakan and Kem will do well, I think, as planetary liaisons."

"I think so, too."

"Also, we are to take our child to make her bow to Zhena Trelu, when she is old enough to travel safely."

"Be glad of the vacation," she said. "You don't mind my saying so, you could use some sleep. No need to rush back so fast."

"I did not wish to miss the birth of our daughter," he said, drowsy under her fingers.

"Not a worry. Priscilla says day after tomorrow."

"So soon?"

She laughed, and pushed him off her lap. He made a show of sprawling on the rug, and she laughed again, pushing against the arms of the chair.

Val Con leapt to his feet and helped her rise.

"I believe I will have a nap," he said. "Will you join me?"

"Wouldn't miss it for anything."

✧ Daughter of Dragons ✧

Liad
The Grand Lake Townhouses
Solcintra

"All of these dragons have fangs,
pretty words and comely bodies notwithstanding."
—*From the* melant'i *play* The Harusha Hillside Massacre,
by Norista ven'Deelin

"I FEEL I KNOW OF A CITATION that may answer this question for us," Lady Kareen said slowly, and with a thought spared to the tickets snugged safe in an inner pocket. "It is perplexing, but if I am able to recall the proper book . . . Of your goodness, Scholar, a moment to think and remember—and pray do not let it be known that I sometimes consult my notes before I make my decisions! Please pour yourself a glass of the jade. I'm astounded that no one seems to have touched it, and now that they are gone it would be a shame to waste it. I know it to be rather the best wine out today."

"Thank you, Lady," the scholar murmured. "May I pour for you as well?"

"Indeed you may," she answered, her attention already inward, deliberately putting the ticket and its deadline from her mind, focusing with studied calmness on the matter brought before her, properly, by one of her oldest and most valued associates.

The graying gentleman moved to the side table while she studied the floor to ceiling bookcases with some care. Many of the books here were first editions, one or two were simply irreplaceable, except from within her memory . . .

Some people quietly told each other that she was the most influential person on Liad—carefully making the distinction that, while Korval's delm or first speaker might be the most actively powerful, Lady Kareen yos'Phelium's word was sufficient to certify or decertify an entire clan for a season's visiting lists; and her opinion that this or that person had failed, by reason of Code, to act properly in a certain situation might tarnish a life or even a Line.

In truth, there was no one with more accuracy or memory when it came to the Code—and if she might occasionally be gently—and properly—corrected by one who would some day be Korval Himself, all others came to her or to the books she had indexed and updated to settle vexing matters of procedure and *melant'i*. To the polite world of the Fifty High Houses, Kareen yos'Phelium was the final authority on matters large and small when it came to proper action.

Indeed, the just-concluded annual meeting of the League for the Purity of the Language provided a potent example of the niceness of her judgment. Despite rumors that Korval had fled the planet— rumors well-founded in fact—Lady Kareen had been properly at home to the League, on the date and time long set. Those of the League who had come to her were, of course, persons of *melant'i*, who did not allow ill-bred curiosity into the changes in Korval's business schedules or her own recent notable absence from society to intrude upon the occasion. The agenda of the meeting had after all been fixed for several relumma, and it was treated with all the respect that it deserved.

If anyone present noticed that they had seen the ensemble Lady Kareen wore to today's meeting at least once before, that was something to be discussed and weighed later, at leisure—and in private. Perhaps Korval's fortunes were indeed on the wane. Or, as was more likely, the clothing itself might have been a reminder that the Code, and not fashion, was the center of the meeting. That Lady Kareen was subtle was not to be doubted.

On hand in the lady's capacious library had been thirteen Scholars of the Code—Lady Kareen herself and the twelve other contributors to the latest revision—six librarians, and some few others: the protocol officer appointed by the Council of Clans, two people-of-business, a nadelm of a clan off-planet, and a representative of the dramliz, who took notes and said nothing.

In ordinary times, Lady Kareen might have arranged a dinner party or a tea to follow the meeting as well, but again, those who questioned her arrangements would speak among themselves, later. Indeed, the lack of servants had been the greatest obstacle she had had to overcome in this matter, saving only Luken bel'Tarda's surprisingly strong resistance to her necessity. She had considered calling in one of the two fill-in service agencies listed in the kitchen's low-tech directory, but even that would be depending too much on luck for her taste, with an unknown server taxiing to the lake in haste. Still, she had contrived—and all had gone well.

And now most of her guests had departed, and with them her sense that things were not really as bad as they might have seemed. The meeting itself had been normal and mannerly; the issues worthy of discussion. The out-world version of the Code, based on a centuries-old and centuries-out-of-date edition, had been neatly rectified, to the mortification of the overdressed nadelm, and the single typographical error in the latest edition had been decreed minor enough not to require an entire new printing. Several questions of taste had been properly put aside, while the major issue—use of three words which had migrated over the centuries from the High Tongue to the Low—had been clarified by perusing several volumes in her library.

Only this single guest remained now of the many, posing his vexatious question, the worth of which must be balanced against the upcoming departure time. Still, she thought, as the clock chimed discreetly from its station in the hall; she had a few moments more to give to an old friend.

Turning from the shelves, she received her glass from his hand, raised it, and—choosing a variation of one of the day's perplexities—smiled and said, "To our health!"

The scholar smiled, too, for the perplexity had dealt with the particular "our" that might be used by a master when talking with a student, certainly not indicating an inclusion of the student . . . The scholar and Kareen had been in complete agreement on the matter, as they had been so often in agreement on similar matters, down the years—and so they shared a smile eloquent of long acquaintanceship—even friendship—and each had a sip of the lady's excellent jade.

"Let me understand your question, Scholar," she said now, glass in-hand and gaze abstracted. "You ask, if a clan abandons a holding without properly informing all of the members, are the remaining members still of that clan—that is, may they inherit the clan title and name one from among themselves delm—or are they outcast?"

"That is correct."

"And very complex."

"This is, you understand, the reason I did not wish to bring the matter before the full committee, but rather to refer it to yourself."

"Of course."

There was silence for a moment. The scholar sipped his wine, appeared to take momentary and intense counsel of himself, which was his character—and inclined his head.

"Lady, I believe that I must tell you all. There are a number of us—members of another organization which also believes in the purity of Liaden ways—who are distressed by the unexpected and precipitous withdrawal of Korval from Liad. It appears to us that during the stewardship of yos'Galan Korval's strength, which is at the heart of Liad's strength—as I need not say!—has been dissipated."

"I see," she said evenly, veteran of many a difficult social evening. "Certainly, I can understand how so forward-looking an individual as yourself might become concerned for the health of the homeworld."

"Even so." The man sipped of his wine before continuing.

"And so, you see, my question is a true one, best not shared until we—you and I—come to agreement, with appropriate citations.

"We—my organization—have been in search of the one of Line yos'Phelium beside yourself to have been properly active in society for this last decade, the one who understands the necessities of *melant'i* and Code very nearly as much as yourself, the one who is welcome at all events of social significance . . . ."

She was, in fact, startled, but the dice were hers now, and she must throw in order to understand the game.

So she murmured, in an accent of perhaps slightly bored interest, "You speak, I think, of my heir Pat Rin yos'Phelium?"

"Exactly so! If you could assist us in locating him, we feel that Korval might find itself as strong—stronger—than ever. You, of course, would continue to be the guiding light, elevated to a position, dare I say, more public . . . "

"Ah, but do you know?" she interrupted, maintaining her tone of vague boredom. "I have not been in touch with my son for some time. I believe he travels on pleasure just now—widely, and at whim."

The scholar inclined his head. "Of course. Indeed. We had ourselves thought we had established his location, but apparently . . . ."

Established his location? Perhaps it was astonishment she felt. Perhaps it was—surely not!—fear.

"My son sometimes prefers to game away from the limelight," she reminded the scholar gently.

"As you say. It is merely . . ." His voice trailed off.

Kareen inclined her head in courteous inquiry. "Merely?"

"My organization—we wish, very much, to speak with him; to . . . illuminate his role in planetary destiny. If yos'Galan has fled the planet, we believe that Code and Council together may act to ensure that Korval lives, and thrives . . ."

Kareen bowed.

"I thank you for your clarification. However, I believe I am hardly worthy of the honor of having my son named as Korval. There exists the small difficulty of the lack of a piloting license . . ."

"Ah, but that is why I have come to you!" he exclaimed, his eyes taking fire as they had so often in the past, delighting in the exercise of his considerable intellect. "Surely, one who inherits upon abandonment would not be required to follow the strictures of those who had all but caused the clan to be dissolved. Indeed, to avoid an unseemly and disruptive public challenge to this adjustment we are in the process of insuring that those who have fled Liad, leaving Korval weakened and vulnerable, will not return."

Kareen sipped the wine, feeling the need of it. Really, it was the best in her cellar, and she would miss it, were it gone. Just as she would miss the library, and indeed, the acclamation of her peers. As she missed, from time to time, the outré and unfortunately brilliant presence of her brother Daav, as little love as had been lost between them. Indeed, she felt his lack keenly, just now.

Well.

She bowed a bow.

"Scholar, our discussion has quickened my memory. The answer, I believe, will be found within the Simestan Chronicles. As I recall that Line—"

"But, of course!" he said, his thought taking fire from hers, as it so often had, over the years. "Yes, I recall it! The mine collapse which took the house and all of the clan save the—"

"Indeed. I have the full and certified records here. If you would be so good to ascend the ladder? The volumes are three shelves down from the ceiling, quite nearly before you, bound in lavender leather. I have no doubt that some in Council might be brought to see the correlations . . . "

The scholar, her friend, smiled, and ran to the ladder, moving it carefully across the floor.

Kareen glanced down, admiring the hand-loomed carpet, made some centuries ago for the founder of this library of Code and conduct. She would regret being parted from it.

The scholar had climbed quickly; he was already reaching for the books she had specified.

Kareen sighed, and set her glass aside, quite steadily. She had always wished to see her son properly acknowledged.

• • • ✧ • • •

Jelaza Kazone

THE ROBOT WAS—very likely—the only robot on Liad which was not only capable of doing household chores but of knowing precisely when they needed to be done. It was also the only robot on planet which knew when attending to the social needs of cats was more important than polishing old silver.

Thus, when the annunciator for the phone went off, the robot was stroking several middling cats in the garden rather than working in the kitchen, as the image it projected to the phone suggested.

Although Miss Anthora had been napping, the house told him that she was now awake and on her way to the kitchen viewer, that being the unit where she took those calls which might require direct access to the house net or to the files the robot held of itself. Miss Anthora's abilities being of a different order than its own, though certainly reliable, the robot likewise began to move toward the kitchen, its wheeled chassis considerably slower than her light-footed run—and made slower by the necessity to move or carry cats.

In the meantime, it accessed the incoming call.

"I have the honor of being Lady Kareen yos'Phelium," an entirely familiar voice stated. "Jeeves, please ascertain as best you may that I am who I say I am."

"Working," intoned the robot, quickly confirming the origin of the call and utilizing stored cues, confirming that the call was in fact being made from Lady Kareen's own library. An anomaly was noted: Lady Kareen had never before addressed him directly—or by his name.

The other cues he could take in full or in part over the apparatus: voice pattern, tone, word pattern, partial retinal and other scans, muscle matching—all tended to confirm her identity, as did the fact that the call had bypassed the general screening devices and had activated Daav yos'Phelium's blinking blue "Kareen warning" light on the kitchen unit—an additional fact that he discovered upon his arrival, scant seconds before Miss Anthora.

"Confirmed, Lady Kareen yos'Phelium."

"Thank you," said the lady, and this, too, was the first time she had directed such polite words to him rather than to a human in the household.

"Jeeves, I require assistance. I understand that you may have special knowledge in an area . . ."

Anthora arrived, activated the kitchen view screen—and blinked, clearly nonplussed. She made a quick recovery, however, and inclined her head courteously.

"Cousin Kareen? How may we assist you, ma'am?"

"Anthora." Relief showed in an infinitesimal relaxation of the muscles in the lady's face. "I am in need of information from Jeeves. It is necessary that my house be destroyed."

Stored data told Jeeves that this was an unusual request, even from one of Korval's Line Direct. Clearly, Miss Anthora found it so. "Cousin?"

"I have just now shot Scholar Her Nin yo'Vestra in the spine and in the head; he is not recoverable. I must now insure that he is not easily found and that my library is unavailable to assist the organization of which he was a member." The lady's voice was steady, even stern. It fell to Anthora to cry out, in frank horror—

"Cousin, Scholar yo'Vestra was one of your oldest acquaintances!"

"I will grieve later," Kareen yos'Phelium said, sternness perhaps increasing. "He attempted to bribe me to overthrow the Line Direct in favor of my heir! I must make my library unavailable and do whatever else may be done to hinder this—organization. He-spoke of insuring that those of us who have fled will not return, and I am not fool enough to believe that he simply sought to buy them off. Indeed, the notion that we *could* be bought . . . No. Cousin, let me make haste—permit Jeeves to tell me how to burn . . ."

Anthora shook her head. "That will not be necessary, Cousin. If need be, I can burn your house from here. But your books . . . ."

"In my absence, the books endanger Liad—most especially my private indexes and searches, and the catalog of incomplete debts—"

"Yes, but Cousin Kareen," Anthora interrupted, "why are you here—on Liad? Surely the children . . . Plan B . . ."

The lady made a sign of impatience. "I have been through this once with Luken bel'Tarda! Necessity. Now, attend me, if you please! My library must not fall into the hands of Korval's enemies. I have here, for an example, partial copies of diary entries outlining the early Plan B arrangements. We must not . . ."

"Yes, I begin to see." Anthora inclined her head. Jeeves, who knew her well, was not deceived by her seeming acquiescence to her cousin's necessities.

"If you will permit my discretion in the disposal of your library and house," she continued, "I will undertake the task. How long do you think it will take you to be gone?"

"Please give me to the beginning of the next hour. I will away as I came."

"It will be done as you have said."

"*Flaran cha'menthi*, Anthora," the lady said, fervently. "We dare."

"*Flaran cha'menthi*, Cousin. For us, it is necessity."

The screen blanked.

"Jeeves?"

"Working, Miss. There are signs of attempts to intercept this communications. Someone is aware that Lady Kareen's unit has been used, and when. I find no indication that it was traced past the second relay, but we must assume that they have been alerted."

"Thank you, Jeeves. I will be working from the garden, beneath the Tree. Please ask Merlin to join me there. When I am through, I will wish to have a meal."

"Yes, Miss Anthora."

She had scarcely taken two steps toward the garden door when the annunciator blared again, simultaneous with the flash of the blue warning light. Anthora jumped, her hand slapping the toggle, and Lady Kareen's image came into view.

This time, her face held elements of that emotion known as panic.

"Cousin, I beg that you will not fire the house so soon," she said, her voice perhaps shaking. "The public and the private exits are watched. I believe . . . " She looked sharply aside. "I believe that I am trapped."

* * ◇ * *

The Grand Lake Townhouses
Solcintra

SHE'D BRIEFLY FELT DESPAIR, surely that was the word for it, but as irony would have it, the call on the alternate pocket-comm from Jeeves had led her away from that unproductive emotion and toward some measure of composure. As surely as there were alternate means of communication, there were alternatives available to one of Korval—for one born of the Line—in reaction to the hasty and ill-considered action of an enemy. Panic was not an option. Panic, so she had been taught by her mother, killed: passengers, ships. Pilots.

"Lady Kareen," came Jeeves' voice from the pocket-comm. "Miss Anthora has requested that we permit her some time for thought and preparation while I pursue additional information on the structures and demographics of Grand Lake. We are of the opinion, given that persons of superior *melant'i* attended your meeting, that all interested parties will act with circumspection for some time."

Interested parties. Who knew that a robot intelligence could be so nice?

"Indeed," she murmured into the comm, "circumspection seems called for. For the moment, be aware that I have located several other weapons, and will retire to the stone study, which is not on the house grid"—*and how foolish she had thought that, as a girl!*—"by which I mean to say that it can be locked by a manual set-key. From there, I will have access to the kitchen wing, through a serving closet."

"Position marked and, may I say, strategically sound and defensible." A slight pause, then, "Miss Anthora asks that you activate the in-house intercom to all rooms."

What a strange request! But there! An open intercom might allow her to discover if someone else gained entry, after all.

"Yes, of course. I should have thought of that. Thank you, Jeeves. If I discover a problem, or a solution, I will call."

"Noted. Call ending."

The tone change was sufficient to indicate the call was over, but again she took thought. In these odd and dangerous times, it was necessary for both parties to a call to be certain that the communication had been ended purposefully, rather than cut off by enemy action.

The door into the stone study was rarely closed. In addition to its lack of an electronic lock, that might, Kareen realized now, be overridden by determined persons seeking entry from outside, it possessed sturdy door-bars evocative of the early frontier days of Solcintra that were not, in fact, merely decorative.

Her mother had pointed this out to her in the days of her brief youth, when hope had still been high that Chi yos'Phelium's bright daughter would one day be delm, and Chi had used the Grand Lakes house for quiet parties and meetings in Solcintra. There it was that those who might be uncomfortable being seen entering or leaving the precincts of Jelaza Kazone might still meet face-to-face, or as Chi's appetites dictated, body-to-body, with Korval.

The urgency born of the immediate thrill of dread and death abating, Kareen moved to the door that concealed the closet-passageway to the kitchen, assuring herself that it, too, was secured with a simple mechanical lock, its scrolled key in place. She then glanced out the single tall thin window, which gave an unparalleled view of the lake and the hills beyond, making it feel as if one were in some rural retreat rather than bordering on the heart of Solcintra. On the lake today were several vessels with sails and several without. She wondered if they belonged to friend or foe.

The view grew hazy and she realized she was weeping, that tears were welling up despite the necessity of her action, and that . . . she leaned on the wall as the tears flowed—and that . . .

Her Nin yo'Vestra was dead. He could perhaps have given her as many years as she could have given her absent brother Daav; that difference had never mattered to them. They had first discovered each other at Festival, she near virginal beneath her plumage, his kind and mature attentions both flattering and treasured. When he recognized her some years later at another Festival, they'd gone on as if never parted, their friendship continuing, perhaps not entirely according to the dictates of the Code, into their everyday lives.

But there. Necessity. His studies and family connections took him far from the lists that the Delm of Korval and her seconds had searched; surely he, like her, never was a pilot and never would be, and so her marriage beds had by clannish necessity seen other men, all pilots, in them.

Eyes closed a moment, Kareen found her breath more regular, her hands stiff from pushing against the unyielding stone wall. She nearly fell into the large leather chair that her mother had favored for lectures, the same chair Chi had sat in when she'd explained to the standing Kareen exactly why the delm had chosen another husband and sought another child.

Kareen yos'Phelium Clan Korval, smart as a whip and eager for duty . . . was inadequate to the clan's needs.

What pilots saw when faced with a random tumbling ball, she knew not; how they managed not to be hit in the face with it she could not comprehend—as frequent sessions with the autodoc for too frequent bruises and bloodied noses attested. While numbers blossomed to meaning for others, whispering arcane and delightful secrets, for her they remained mere numerals.

In other words, Kareen was deficient in ways that tutors could not assist her to overcome; her abilities insufficient in ways irreconcilable with the delm's necessities when one was Delm of Korval.

"I must," her mother, the delm, had said, "I must be prepared to bring to the clan my full replacement. It is not the fact of having a child that is important, but of having a child who might be delm."

This said to the child who found only headaches in the twistiness of numbers and joy in the complexity of Code and deed . . .

"Understand me," Chi had continued, "it is not your attention to your studies that is at fault. It is that, as some are born unable to see as many colors as others, and others are born with no ear for music. The equations do not speak to you. The healers have said so, the tutors have said so, and the tests have said so. As we discussed the issue, your tutor admired the time you've spent at the work—she had the logs to hand— while proclaiming your energy high no matter the outcome. She also pointed out that energy alone does not pull an equation into balance."

Here her mother's eyes had gone soft, her voice wry.

"Also, it comes to the attention of your delm that you have given advice to the tutor."

Already numb with the understanding that she had failed her Clan, Kareen had raised her eyes to the delm's.

"I did not 'offer advice,'" she asserted, standing as tall as she might, while bearing the weight of her shame. "The tutor had said to me that an equation she offered for solving was straightforward and without complication, and that for comparison I might see solving an issue her Clan was facing wherein a hasty giving of *nubiath'a* upon notification . . ."

A quick hand-motion by the Delm stopped her.

"I have seen your work, Daughter. The cites were appropriate; the discussion of potential remedies useful and clear. In fact, speaking as one who had been requested to broker the difficulties between those very clans, your solution was by far the cleanest—and one not discovered by three delms after many days of negotiation and research." A slight pause, accompanied by a one-sided smile; followed by a sigh.

"And so, the clan moves forward," her mother said then. "As of today, your math tutor and your prepiloting classes are removed from your schedules. My own schedule has been amended. It is my belief that you have found your calling. Pursue it."

That had been the last time she'd had complete regard of her delm, or her mother.

The intercom blinked, giving out a musical sound entirely unlike its usual alert tone, followed by Jeeves' electronic voice, as clear as if it stood beside her.

"Lady Kareen, you may hear odd sounds from this speaker; we are calibrating the connection. Can you hear me?"

She took a deep breath. When she answered her voice was, of course, perfectly calm.

"Indeed, Jeeves, I can hear you perfectly. You sound exactly as I expect."

"Noted. Miss Anthora suggests we will have a plan of action for you within moments. We have identified several potential methods to extract you and the sensitive information from the situation. Please stand by."

The clock in the hallway chimed.

"Jeeves!"

"Lady Kareen?"

"I have a flight—very soon! It is imperative that I make—"

"Noted," the robot's voice was chillingly mechanical. Kareen inclined her head to the intercom unit.

"Thank you, Jeeves," she murmured, added for herself more than for it, "*Flaran cha'menthi!*"

. . . ✧ . . .

Jelaza Kazone

A SMALL THUNDERCLAP ECHOED off the kitchen tiles; air displaced by Miss Anthora's precipitant arrival, Merlin in her ams.

"Jeeves! I can locate the body easily. But Cousin Kareen . . . she's like fog. No! Like a fog rooted in stone." She leaned heavily against the counter, scarcely seeming to notice when the cat scrambled free and leapt to the floor. There was a certain fixity to her gaze that was consistent with a working trance. She was sweating, which was also not inconsistent with a working state. But this burst of panic in the midst—

Anthora took a hard breath—another; her heart rate dropped, stress hormones leached away. A third breath and her body was soothed.

"The house is," she said calmly to the waiting robot, "as reported, surrounded."

"Noted."

"Suggestion?" she inquired dryly.

"Tactical computations engaged, Miss Anthora. Although nominally engaged as a unit under Plan B, Lady Kareen is currently operating as an independent ally in the absence of Val Con yos'Phelium and others of the Line Direct, until she can return to preassigned duties. She has identified and requested the disposition of certain items of value or concern to the Plan. Tactical simplification is indicated: the orderly disposition of the contents of her house will permit focus on other pending issues."

"Jeeves, are you fully operational at the moment?"

The robot's delayed response brought her pause, but she resisted the urge to scan . . .

"Computationally, I am more efficient and versatile than when originally constructed."

"Do you have strategic computations also engaged then?"

A longer pause, followed by what could have been a short laugh, if Jeeves laughed.

"I do."

"We shall discuss them later. Do you have weather-monitoring capability?"

"Of course."

"Very good. Please monitor the weather in the area of Cousin Kareen's townhouse."

Jeeves initiated the necessary protocols. "As you say, Miss Anthora."

"Thank you. I will work from here, I think."

She settled herself bonelessly to the floor; closed her eyes, and said—to Jeeves or to herself or to Merlin, busily bathing in a spot of sunlight—"first, the blood and flesh."

Based on similar situations in the past, Jeeves refrained from replying as her trance state deepened. He also stationed himself to partially block the doors, since the cats inevitably gathered about as soon as they could when wizard-work was being done.

· · ·◇· · ·

PATIENCE HAD NOT BEEN SO EASY of late. First, she'd been forced to the conclusion that the calling of Plan B, however much she deplored it, fell within the realm of the First Speaker's duties. It was in the diaries, after all, and consistent with the protocols.

Next, she'd found herself dispatched to multiple errands, most of which any servant might have performed in ordinary times. Then, finding that Luken bel'Tarda's role was set as the one who would guide their mission, she'd had to deal with what he called "the grinding and polishing of small wheels" as the children were gathered, informed of their situations, and in several cases, armed.

She had arranged and conferred with what patience she could muster, discovering in the man the delm had appointed her son's protector in her stead—the amiable, babbling rug merchant—someone of quick insight, resilience, and a way with children.

Then had come the machinations placing her as the one to receive this or that of the late-arriving parcels, and providing her with one last chance to add to the confounding of their enemy. Bel'Tarda's contacts were sufficient in the absence of her own staff; smugglerlike, she had acquired three different sets of tickets to the off-world stations, none under her own name.

Luken bel'Tarda had argued strongly against her delaying departure. He had gone so far as to charge her with risking the children. She had waved him and his arguments aside, certain of what was due her own *melant'i*. And in that, she thought now, as the clock chimed the hour of the second ship's departure, she might have been, perhaps . . . somewhat . . . foolish.

At least, there had been no risk to the children. Finding her adamant, bel'Tarda had altered his own arrangements—who, after all, notes the movements of a rug merchant?—and was now several days off-world, with those very children in his charge. Hopefully, she thought with a sudden shiver in the pleasantly warm room, beyond the reach of those others of Her Nin's organization.

She spared a thought then for her own child, whose location had been established, but who had apparently managed to slip out from under the notice of Her Nin's associates. Well. Never let it be said that Pat Rin was anything but clever; and a gambler, so she thought, would have some small skill at defense and misdirection. Surely, he had gone to—

Hold! What was that noise?

Ears straining, she leaned forward in the chair, hands gripping the armrests. The sound came again, from the library just beyond the closed door. A sound like—wind, perhaps, or—

She stood in the doorway of the stone study, with no memory of having risen from her chair or opening the door, staring into the library—knowing that she had carefully taken her shot, and that her victim had fallen thusly. *There.*

As she stared, her library began to . . . disappear. Spirals of dust rose as shelves long filled with books and precious papers emptied themselves with a hazy burping noise. The shelves shook and flexed as their burdens went . . . elsewhere, leaving the dust of paper and people to dance briefly in the slanting light, and settle.

There had been blood, and enough of it to make her gag. Her purpose strong in her heart, she had checked her work and found it potent, before calling for assistance.

Now, there was no sign of blood. There was a mark on the ceiling which might have been new, there, but then the house had a long history, and Chi herself might once have thrown a bottle to make that mark.

Her Nin—Her Nin's *corpse*—was gone, and so were the books that had filled the shelves on the west wall. As she watched, the books on the east wall disappeared shelf by shelf. She folded her hands together, tightly, and wondered if she, too, would disappear in some dusty spiral.

Well, then. She had requested aid from a *dramliza*. It might be said that she had known better.

The ladder Her Nin had died on shivered. It creaked; the rails that had steadied it *twanged*—and the ladder was gone. Next, the chair he had last sat in *phlumphed* elsewhere. The near-empty bottle of jade, the table, the cloth napkins with the tree-and-dragon embroidered in silk. Gone, gone, gone.

She moved then, deliberately, her steps echoing as she made a hasty inspection. There were no beds in the bedrooms, no linens in the bathroom, no rugs on the floors.

Had she been less sure of the world and of her place in it, Lady Kareen might have felt more than a shiver. Indeed, had she another acquaintance to hand she might have been tempted to admit awe or even a tingling of fear. The *dramliz* were a force to be reckoned with, even when doing your bidding.

The door to the stone study stood open still; the furnishings within untouched.

She fled into that comfort; then, too energized to sit, opened the door to the servant's closet.

She had, as a rule, *not* used the closet as a passageway, even as a child, being somewhat uncomfortable with the closeness of it. Later though, there had been times she had been set to minding Daav and Er Thom when a tutor was not to hand. *They*, of course, had delighted in the cramped space, the flour-dusted aprons, and the endless opportunities afforded to spring out at those who searched for them, laughing uproariously, as if it were all a very good game.

Daav, in particular, had had a gift for being someplace *else*: in the servant's closet here, if not in the kitchen, and if not in the kitchen, in the capacious pantry with its huge bags of rare imported flours and mysterious bins, boxes, tins, freezers, and even a stasis box snugged into the stone wall that formed the other boundary of this room, the wall that was the wine cellar itself. More than once, she had been forced to transit the closet in order to extract both of her unwelcome charges from the divertissement of foodstuffs arriving from below.

Chi, though, was wont to use the closet often at parties, and not merely to check on the timing of the next remove.

Kareen sniffed—why was it that a delm of Korval should have felt it better to avoid a guest than to act entirely properly and deal as necessary? But there, that had never been her own condition, and delms must face both necessity and Code in their proper moments.

The staff jackets and aprons in the closet smelled inevitably of the baking as she inched through; Kareen, and Chi before her, always insisted on fresh breads and a choice of rolls and pastries. Until Daav's exuberance ruined a perfect cake, the old cook had joked that he could qualify as an assistant chef if ever he wished to, just by his observations of the kitchen staff.

That had been just before the day when she had been in search of them both—*again*—only to have Er Thom burst upon her, crying out that Daav was going to be recycled, grabbing her by the sleeve and pulling her along at a chancy run, explaining in gulps that there hadn't been room in the dumbwaiter for both of them, so Daav had gone first, cramming himself amid an untidy clutter of outgoing bins and boxes—and it had been a very near thing, indeed, to convince Cook to call down and stop the loading until the heir could be recovered—sticky, befloured, and grinning—from the recyclables.

Kareen stepped out of the passage, even more confining to one of adult proportions. The kitchen felt less than homelike to her, lacking people and preparation for the next meal. Not even a rumble of a breadmaker broke the silence. She glanced at the clock above the main console and bit her lip, the third and final ticket—the ticket she had never thought to need—heavy in her pocket.

The kitchen equipment stood ready, and there beside the service intercom and food consoles was the small staff room, door festooned with traditional paper contacts affixed at what must be traditional angles: lists of vendors, private numbers of on-call staff and notes of travel times, transit routes, and taxi numbers, scribbled on it . . . but there, Cook came from a traditional clan and was classically trained.

There was a modest view through the kitchen window, and through the privacy screen she saw to the north two of the vehicles she had been concerned with, and clustered about them the several unknowns who stood as if they had every right to interfere with Code, custom—and life.

She leaned hard against the window then, recalling that the windows let no sight out. Just as well that, for her tears had started again. The scholar, after all, had been an honorable man, until this misjudgment. Had he not spoken freely, he might now stand at the side of his co-conspirators.

With that bracing thought she straightened. The intercom over Cook's station burbled, and Jeeves spoke.

"Lady Kareen, Miss Anthora has removed those things other than yourself. Please advise on your circumstances and locations of watchers."

Circumstances?

She licked her lips, glancing again through the window.

Circumstances.

"*Flaran cha'menthi,* Jeeves." She paused, drew a breath, and began.

"I arrived in my own vehicle—the landau, of course—with sufficient time to prepare for today's meeting, which began promptly and ended the same. Until approached by the scholar, I saw nothing at first glance untoward, though I was afterward reminded that there had been several vehicles about when I arrived—yet this is not unexpected, being so close to the lake on such a fine day. Those vehicles were still in place when I made my way to leave; random people where there *are* no random people; workmen doing the same work they had been doing when I arrived, groundspeople I had never seen before. Additionally, there were vehicles unfamiliar to me in several of the parking lanes closest to my own, occupied.

"That was at the front entrance. Feeling visible, I returned to our own halls, and attempted to leave by the back entrance, generally used by our staff, and also where there is access to the unit's own runabout. There, I saw a vehicle parked in such a way as to block my garage and there was someone pruning a bush one never prunes.

"At the moment, I have several weapons upon me; I have replaced the charge in my pocket gun and it is fully loaded. I have—"

"Cousin," came Anthora's breathy voice, sounding calm enough considering circumstances and the fey work she'd been performing.

"Anthora."

"Cousin, I am at the end of the removals I can perform directly. A living person such as yourself is not as easy to translate through walls as is furniture."

Kareen bowed sagely to the air, relieved that she, too, was not to merely disappear into an unmarked ether.

"I understand. One works as necessity dictates."

A pause, then, "Of course. I regret to report, however, that necessity is becoming strained. I am arranging a diversion, but it appears that the emergency exits are also covered by the placement of the vehicles you mention."

"Indeed. Might I inquire about the nature of the . . . "

A most discreet musical tone sounded. Kareen recognized the annunciator at the front door.

"I will ignore this intrusion for the moment. Surely you hear it."

"I do. Jeeves will relay . . . "

Another tone sounded: the annunciator at the service entrance.

Her Nin's associates, Kareen thought her heartbeat suddenly loud in her ears, had become bored with waiting.

"Lady Kareen," Jeeves said politely, "we ask if you have thoughts on the matter to hand?"

"Yes," she said, moving quickly back to the closet. A tuque came to her hand; she yanked it savagely over her hair, and snatched up a white jacket, the tree-and-dragon embroidered on the pocket. "I will need a vehicle at my milliner's, to transport me to my next appointment." She paused at the service console, pressed a series of numerals and passed on. "If you have your diversion to hand, for the love of the gods, release it!"

"Now!" Anthora's voice came, though whether in answer or in direction to Jeeves, Kareen was unsure.

Nor did it matter.

She was across the kitchen, the hideaway she had used to take the life of her oldest and dearest friend in her right hand. With her left, she slapped the button—and reeled back a step as the door slid away and the interior of the dumbwaiter was revealed.

It was *much* smaller than she had recalled, nor was she an adventure-blind boy with a child's understanding of danger.

The front door caroled again, chiding her for leaving guests languishing on her doorstep.

She thought that they would not ring a third time.

Teeth drilling her lower lip, she pushed herself into the tiny space, crouching in a most undignified manner, her knees practically in her ears and every muscle protesting. She extended an arm and clumsily slapped at the wall, hitting the button on the third try, barely snatching her hand inside before the doors snapped closed.

· · ·✧· · ·

SHE WOULD, SHE DECIDED, tell Daav alone of this, if he lived and if he inquired. Else it was good to have secrets, after all.

The motion was abrupt, jerky, and her stomach, already at risk from the day's bloody adventure, nearly gave up its wine and pastry. Darkness engulfed her; the drop seemed both precipitous and overlong, the racket of machinery an assault upon her ears. She hung on desperately against nausea and vertigo, the *twomping* sound and shock of the stop all the more unsettling for the continued darkness. Had the mechanism malfunctioned? Was she trapped here, in this small space, in the dark—and above! A noise! Had they broken down her door already? How long would it take them to—

A breath, now! she counseled herself, panting in the dark. *A breath*!

Think!

She groped, skinning knuckles on wire mesh, tearing a nail as she found the latch, and *pushed*. It resisted. She felt a rumble—certainly the thing wasn't moving again?

But there, no, the gate opened suddenly, spilling her out of the compartment, her gun-hand striking gritty 'crete with flinching force, and a knee close behind. Some switch sensed her, and light flared, nearly blinding in actinic purity. She thrust her gun into her pocket, and kept her hand on it.

The room was painted white. Ahead, a platform, empty save for some pallets and a motorized hand-truck. A door, at the far end of the platform. Again the rumble, vibrating in her chest as she hurried toward the door, hating to trust in the luck, hoping that they had not yet set anyone to watching—

She hit the bar. The door popped open, and immediately swung back toward her face, slammed by the wind.

Kareen caught the door on her shoulder, and pushed out into a bewilderment of winds, a rush of rain so heavy it seemed that the lake itself had been upended.

Pausing inside the slender vestibule, she took another breath, and gathered her wits.

There was a flight she must make, and those who wished her not to make.

"*Flaran cha'menthi,*" she muttered, and stepped forward into the storm.

The wind tore, snatching the tuque, and she flailed for a disoriented moment before snatching it back and holding it to her head. Sodden locks of hair straggled into her eyes, and the sturdy baker's jacket was soaked through.

There!

Light beams fought the abnormal weather; the blue cab sat quietly, near the usual service doors.

Beating against the wind, she pressed onward; the driver or some sensor sliding the door to admit her. If there were others she could not see them.

Within, in livery, a wide-eyed taxi attendant spoke in rapid familiar Low-Liaden.

"Are you all in? I've never in my life seen a storm come up like this in Solcintra. You'll need a good stiff drink to dry you out after this . . . "

It was the tuque that saved her, dripping collected water in her eyes.

Yes. She wore the white tuque and livery of her own. Korval's livery.

"I'll have one," she said, answering also in the Low Tongue, though she had to her knowledge never seen the man before, much less counted him an intimate, "as time permits. There's a rush of work needs done first!"

"Oh aye," agreed the driver, "there's always a rush of work."

Mortification set in as she looked at the cab rate info.

"I've come away without payment," she admitted.

The driver—her rescuer—laughed, allowing the cab to accelerate into the gloom.

"Address?"

"But . . . "

"Not a regular for this house, eh? We'll just invoice at end of the relumma, like always. Korval'll pay, just like they always do. Code and Balance. Korval don't play games with their name, is what I think!"

The car stuttered across some standing water, and if the driver saw her sag into the seat, shaking, likely he thought it was because she needed that drink to fend off the dampness.

She looked into the camera feeding her image to the driver.

"Yes," she managed, her voice shaking slightly—but he would surely put that, too, down to chill—"that's what I think as well."

She closed her eyes then and leaned back, the gun weighing in one pocket, the tickets in another.

Flaran cha'menthi.

✧ Dragon Tide ✧

THE PROMISE OF MORNING was brushing the sea as Stregalaar stirred, the down of his forewing barely tickling his outer eyelids, the light barely touching his consciousness.

A breeze was up but fitful, not yet fully streaming in from the ocean, still burdened with upland scent from the river coursing into the sea nearly below his branch. Later would come the salty freshness as both tide and breeze turned and then he would know if his day was spent best scavenging in the hills or fishing along the curling beachfroth.

His usual foraging choice was along the waves, although some days, especially if he woke early like today, he'd have a wanderlust and find his wings set for hills and heights, allowing the sea breeze to waft him as high as the clouds. Those days he'd sight a distant grove and glide there, or perhaps to the one beyond that or the one beyond that.

Again came the awareness of some tiny movement, some minute shifting of weight or a motion he had not made, as when a sharp wind might tug at wings on high.

He opened his eyes more fully then, his neck and head still, wings yet locked, the down fringing his vision momentarily.

Something—not the light on the horizon and not the breeze—had woken him. He listened; it wasn't the usual wind warning that the groves of greenkin might rattle to each other across the fields and ravines, though it held a faint tinge of that, and it *was* of the greenkin.

219

On the rumpled breeze now came the smell of ground-creature fear. Not enough to excite the muscles that made his jaw twitch, not enough to make him turn to find the source. A distant mutter from the tallest tree on the hillcrest suggested that one of the other wingfolk also sensed something, but in the breeze was no message other than unease. Perhaps *that* tree, already lit with full greening light, was already starting its peculiar morning evictions. Not all trees were so populated that they needed to chase their dragons away to preserve pod and leaf.

His own home tree, the Laar, was still in green slumber, and there was no current need for morning evictions—if ever there had been!— for Stregalaar was the only regular resident now that his ancient cousins had flown their final trip into the oceanic mists. Some days— most often at morning tide and sunset—he yearned for company and wished one of the ground-browsing grove youngsters might stay and use his juvenile bedding now that he'd taken up the top nest, as was his right and duty as Tree Master.

True, he was young for it, and true, he was inexperienced in the finer points of tree-keeping. His cousins had done the bulk of the guarding once he'd moved from the groveflock, protecting him to some extent, until that frost-ridden day when Levanlaar's flight became hesitant. She and Hargalaar had gathered in with him, inviting him to add a stick to the top nest and make it his own, and then flown from their ancestral grove and nest tree toward open ocean and the Island of Constant Summer, never to return.

His time so far as Tree Master had been eventful only in that he was still discovering his world and himself: the Laar had already done much to establish itself, after all, being the only remaining greenkin on this clifftop outcrop. The rest of the extended grove was on higher, richer, and more level land where they stood in close formation, inviting root-grubbing rodents, wandering pod thieves, and all manner of lesser pests. There had been other greenkin here on the outcrop, he'd been told, but they had been uprooted by storms. Perhaps they had not the knack of drinking from the brackish waters and giving back sweetwater fruit to their dragons, and so had fallen to root-grubbers, maybe they were merely that much older and unable to root deep because of rock rubble. Surely Laar was fruit of another tree, after all.

Overhead, the patterned night guides gave way to a finer blue-green and the horizon's glow flared with his morning's first sight of the day guide. From his vantage, he could see wavecrests where tide met estuary, and now the telltale signs of fins!

With no repetition of the strangeness that woke him, and with the invitation of a quick breakfast before him, Stregalaar stretched, and then whistled the Tree Master whistle.

No, no response. He rarely had visitors, and usually knew as soon as another dragon landed, even if he was asleep, for his tree was as vigilant as he was. Still, one whistled and listened.

After a few moments he heard other treefolk responding from the grove; as if his call was the first of the day.

Duty done, he climbed to the rim, and fell toward the sea. On his way down, he saw the telltale ultra-green of new leaf cradling a pod.

Wings opening as he sped toward the foam, he tucked the promise of an extra delight in memory and dropped his hunting eyelids into place.

· · · ⬦ · · ·

HIS APPROACH was that of a simple skim-and-snatch. He'd settled on the shadows of three fish swimming together at the surface as a target. As he closed, one of them would be more exposed and he felt the claws begin their tension—but no!

The light reaching him was obscured quickly once and twice and he found two other dragons diving, come from high above, choosing the same fish, sweeping toward him. These were no random beach interlopers but grove members several seasons his senior, now Tree Masters of the tallest tree in the grove. He thought to outspeed them, but they hunted together: Klenveer hunting the fish, Trunveer intent on shouldering him aside.

He tightened wings, not turning away but diving yet quicker, loath to give up the smooth form gliding below. Still, Trunveer came on, now giving out a keening hunting call meant to declare the target as caught and held.

This was where he was weak; with no huntingmate for his nest and that season yet approaching, the older wings could control the beach run all morning if they desired.

With Trunveer's weight and wings pressing him from sunside, Stregalaar let the target slide by, but felt the excitement rising in him as he turned to follow.

"Away, ours!" Trunveer's declaration was a brittle screech.

"My track!" he insisted into the winds, and pivoted against the prevailing breeze in time to see Klenveer miss what should have been a clean strike. The grove wings were unpracticed, sometimes going days without turning to the sea. Why should they interfere when they had as much rodent meat as they could use at root edge on any day?

Klenveer's shriek was clear insult, blaming Stregalaar for his own fumbled approach.

The fish were gone now; the shadows of multiple dragons was enough to drive them down and out.

Still, this was the time for fish and he would fish.

Stregalaar's turn toward the sea was met by the rising Klenveer and Stregalaar felt the tension build again in the claws. This interference was—

"Childwing, stay away!"

Trunveer closed, but she scolded both of them, "Fish and eat, fight later if you must."

Klenveer rose, fishless, squawking complaints, going so far as to spit and show talon with each wingbeat.

"I'll take you down, Childwing," he repeated, unable to gain height on Stregalaar's position. One erratic lurch with talon bared was enough to make Trunveer squeal again.

Klenveer's bluff was obvious, but with hunting partner beside him, they turned toward the beach where the smaller fish were easier prey.

Unsettled, it took Stregalaar a few moments to locate the area he sought, where the sea and the sweetwater met and frothed, where the sparkle fish hunted their own prey and—distant motion caught his attention.

Dragons were streaming toward the same beach stretch as Trunveer and her mate; as if the whole grove flock rose and fell in constant swoops. The yells and screeches were angry, even frightened, as they scoured the beach.

Stregalaar lifted with the grace of the sea breeze, leaned away from the brightness of the day guide, and saw both fish for targets and even more dragons coming from the land. With economic dip of wing he fell, set for the strike, letting the tension in his claws build, and with a quick jarring of talon, grabbed his prey almost before the cool drag of water registered in his brain. Turning speed to height he rose, scanning for other wings, till a convenient turn let him glide at a simple angle all the way to his nest tree.

· · ·✧· · ·

THE LAAR WAS UNSETTLED; Stregalaar could feel it. Sap ran; tiny leaves sprouted ahead of time. The new pod leaves he'd seen before were gone to yellow, and the seeds themselves were ripening rapidly. On the branch opposite, where Levanlaar had preferred to eat, grew another pod, though the tree had long realized he kept the nest alone and allowed that branch to go fallow.

His incoming whistle had been unanswered but with the unsettled nature of the morning, he was not surprised. This was not a day for casual visits.

Stomach full but putting off the usual postprandial half-nap, Stregalaar evaluated the scene before him. He'd seen rare times when the broad fish arrived in huge schools and leapt from wavetops, a dangerous and rewarding prey because they were large enough to offer damage and willing to engage any who ventured to try them. Dragons gathered then to feast and fight the fish, and after that, sometimes each other, for the prey brought with them some strangeness inspiring mating out of season.

This was not that excitement. His grovemates, most older than he, were also not sleeping in the warm sun. Some kept to the grove, standing side-by-side on branches until they threatened to break. Some wheeled overhead, and if they searched for the root grubbers there was no hunt; to Stregalaar's sight there were none to be found. Others departed in a slow and deliberate stream to the hills, carrying with them seed pods from the grove.

Unable to pull reassurance from his own thoughts and finding his tree's reaction as odd as that of his grovemates, the Tree Master finally brought himself to the place where the broad trunk wall nearest the nest had been willfully shaped by dragon and tree.

Here there were claw marks of a dozen dragons who had slept in the nest before him; here was the place he felt his first understanding that this tree recognized and accepted him in ways the rest of the grove trees did not.

Hargalaar had allowed him to roost in the tree the night that he had been expelled from the inner grove, the night that he had resisted Pauveer, the shoving, pod-greedy son of Trunveer and Klenveer, and bloodied him for eating the barely ripe pod Stregalaar had claimed as his own.

The next morning, he had gathered in with Hargalaar and copied the stance shown him, placing his forehead firmly against the Laar's trunk and leaning into it. He had closed his eyes—difficult, when so much information came from his eyes! Still, he could smell and hear—and then he was dreaming. Awake, the dream came upon him, and he stood, forehead pressed to living wood, barely breathing.

The tree's presence had been clear, its welcome brave and bright, the gift of a special pod a bonus unexpected. Since that morning he had been Stregalaar, branch-with-wings to Laar.

Now, with the strangeness of the morning troubling him, Stregalaar pressed his forehead against the spot. The dream was upon him quickly; a sense of concern, and a sense of urgency. Something growing—the pods! The feeling that Hargalaar was lecturing him distantly:

Greenkin can provide only to the limit of our branchlings, and not always that far. Together, young creature, we can withstand many dangers. We are not stronger than the rock that falls, though we may split rock, nor do we prevail always against the flames of summer fires nor against the waters and winds of the great gyres though they may pass us by while taking others. You remove the beasts who would feed from our roots; you peel away the tiny flyers who foul us with toxic sap to weaken our bark and burrow under to eat us from within. Too, by sharing our branches, you protect our seeds from those others who feed without thought.

In thanks, we give you branches for your nests, in thanks we offer to you, Tree Friend, foods of special nourishment in the times of ice, and as learned by the grove, even foods for your time of mating and your times of final flight.

These things we share, Flyer, and we share this as well. Our grove tells us through root and branch of distant hills and other rivers, of places changing—

Here the visions were odd indeed, of flying things which were not quite dragons, of rivers drying to nothing, of rocks rising and great moving walls of snow pushing all before. His dreams had never been so full of terror for him, nor so solid that he felt them to his very bones.

The distant groves we rose from feel what we feel, Young One. The tree that sowed me has long ago fallen and returned to the soil, for the root diggers and the swarms are but life, as we are. The dangers that come from things which are not life—from the rivers and the winds, and the rocks and the fire—these dangers we cannot measure and against which we can give you no aid, other than the pods and a place within our branches.

Growing now are pods for food and pods for seed; other leaf growth is suspended. Waiting for the next year are the extending roots. Bark is thickened as it can. What comes is not fire, nor is it wind, nor does it bore holes to eat us. Sometimes, like the fire, it threatens and does not arrive. Sometimes it arrives without threat. If it happens—when it happens—you must fly to a height and return only when it stops.

The pods you have been eating from, those are yours. Eat and eat more; grasp one in your wing-branch and hold it with you while you fly. The other pods, those are for the flyers who come after you, to make their trees, if what comes takes the grove to rot.

There was an image then, as if Stregalaar was looking through the thickest fog, an image of smoke, shattered trees and fire like a river boiling out of a cave.

He sat still, more moments, but the tree had no more to say to him, and his blood was full of the urge to eat from the new pods, and to fly.

• • • ✧ • • •

THE AIR WAS FULL OF WARY DRAGONS, all seeking something they'd not seen before, all full of a nervous energy fostered by whatever their trees and Tree Masters told them. Stregalaar's calls brought answers from others of his agemates and those younger, and none from the elders. As of his agemates, he was the only Tree-Master, some followed him with noisy inquiry.

"Stones that fly! Fire without drought!" said one circling youngling. "Have *you* seen such?"

He *had* seen fire; Hargalaar had taken him wing to wing to watch it sweep a distant valley, and the pair of them had eaten their fill of the animals too injured to move on, while watching from a safe distance the spirals of dragons around a grove in danger. Seaside they had no drought, for the fog was good to them; and they had no fire.

He had also visited cave fronts, with Levanlaar explaining that some dragons preferred them to trees. Not only rogues, but whole tribes of dragons lived in places where trees were few and far between, or where they would be overwhelmed by the mites, the sticky borers, or the root diggers.

The cave front he'd seen was not one he'd dared enter; the odor about was that of multiple males, anger, and old dead meat as if there were no fresh. He disliked such meals: his greenkin was perched perfectly so that he might choose fish or fur-flesh by whim and rarely tasted the old dead.

"Fire I have seen, and cliffs falling, and rocks," Stregalaar answered the circling young. "Caves I have seen, but none with fire. Rivers, but none with fire."

These were grove-dragons, living among all the trees, not yet of an age to be granted dreams, not yet mated, most not yet recognized by a tree.

This last was a puzzlement to Stregalaar. His first tree knew him as early as he could recall and it was to that tree he had returned nightly until the night he had been disowned for fighting. That expulsion was something many of the grove dragons never knew: they simply slept where they would and the grove kept them as they kept the grove.

His tree, Laar, by accident or on purpose, grew far enough from the main grove to be seen as an outpost rather than a true grovetree. Hargalaar had taught him that, when the trees slowly moved up-coast in the past, it was because the root grubbers had grown too common in the south, so common that they had overwhelmed the attention of even a well-guarded grove, permitting the other pests to gain hold. The root grubbers and other pests were more fond of the heat than the trees, as the former Tree Master had it.

The other reason his tree was an outpost was because of the pods it bore, many of which the dragons disdained as small, and less succulent than those of the main grove. Stregalaar found them of good size, but then he was small—small enough to be miscounted as younger than he was no matter his wing's full color display. He had long outgrown the mottled green-gray camouflage of youth for the iridescent blue-and-silver banded wingtops of an adult male; his head was nearly as white as his belly and talons.

Normally, the other flyers gave way to Stregalaar when close to his tree, while above the larger grove he was grudgingly admitted to airspace. Below the main grove's hill and over the jutting peninsula on which it stood, he was recognized as a power, with only a few of the more flirty females flying close by without permission.

Today, though, the entire space from the smallest of the fringe saplings to the near-beachless cliff to the north of his tree was open to all. Dragons flew until tired and settled where they were to have a moment's rest, or they soared and used the oceanic cliff-face thermals that he loved to ride.

Uncertainty wore on them all; there was bickering but no fighting. As the day moved on, more and more of the younglings settled back to the grove while the Tree Masters mediated with their trees or else gyred at height, watching.

Not all of the younglings rested: several imitated their elders as best as they could within the confines of the grove airspace. Stregalaar caught sight several times of the suddenly graceful Chenachyen, born to the grove's oldest tree. Not as tall as the tallest tree, it was by far the largest with a canopy easily serving a dozen youngsters and a set of older pairs. The flyers from the Chyen tree were orderly, not at all like the current crop from the veer.

As for Chenachyen, the marks on her wings told the story: she'd be strong and seeking her own space, or not strong enough and submitting to another's, as soon as the last of the pale grays faded and her full wing stripes were clear.

That thought took hold and held some fancy for him, even with the strangeness of the day. A tree of special pods could use a strong helper, as perhaps he could.

His tree called; it was in the way the branches fluttered that it hummed loud enough for his attention. Hargalaar told him that the Laar hummed best of all the trees in the grove, and in recognition, he dipped a wing sharply and dove toward the nest-front.

Several top branches were fluttering as he passed by, the notes like those of a pod-offering, and he hurried to grasp the nest and try the newest pod, whistling his approach to the tree.

Our only branch-with-wings, the tree dreamed at him, even before he could close his eyes, *eat and eat and watch and warn and—*

The top branch fluttering grew stronger, but the dream went on, pushing at him:

Rocks flow like rivers, the tree dreamed to him, *rocks have no roots and no wings, rocks sustain with sharp edges and weight, they have no will to touch them, nor claws to hold them, nor do they know the fail or fall. Eat what is here while rocks flow like rivers and shake like leaves—*

The dream stopped on that ungentle image, as if what the Laar wished to teach him went beyond even the thought of trees. Stregalaar grabbed the newest pod with some vigor, the urgent warning calls of dragons filled his ears.

The pod branch was shaking; there was a stickiness on the bark as if the sap flowed at winter-end strength. Deep inside his ears, Stregalaar heard a rumble, and knew it was not just the pod branch shaking but the entire tree. He felt vibrations of some tremendous force through his very leg bones. Around him were popping sounds and great rumbles, as if a thunderstorm was coming up at the tree from the sea below.

He could do nothing against the sudden side-to-side whipping of the branches, except shake himself free, launching sidewise from his perch, more flailing than flying those first perilous moments as he plummeted, until he gained some lift, turning the tumble into a dive down the face of the cliff toward the river, rocks and boulders and dust falling with him—

He arched his back to rise, straining wingtips away from the madness of mounds of water shaking in the river, of some strange tearing noise behind him.

He leveled, beat wings against the noise, turned in time to see portions of the grove crashing to the ground, whole trees sundered, and then *his tree*, twisting against rock and dirt, turning and shaking, sliding down the crumbling cliff face toward him.

With a tremendous shudder, the entire edge of the peninsula gave way, with the Laar engulfed in dust and sliding toward the water below. Unbalanced by the sight of the collapse, and unnerved by the noise, Stregalaar nearly collided with a branch—his branch!—as it slid past him.

The river took the flood of stone and dirt; the tree's descent slowed, and stopped. The sounds like thunder were gone now, but above the hillside were cries of dragonish despair. A glance showed Stregalaar that much of the grove lay at angles, and a new rift in the land split it in two.

In confusion, Stregalaar looked back to his tree, seeing the nest still largely in place, though at an odd angle, as the trunk leaned back against what was left of the hillside it had once crowned.

What must he do? He spun in the air, heard piteous cries, saw the uncertain motion of guard dragons as they dropped down from the heights to survey the damage. In the sudden near silence, he heard a tree hum. His tree. The Laar called.

• • • ✧ • • •

THE TREE'S HUM was odd, strained.

Stregalaar whistled diffidently in response, as if to an injured elder. He would normally circle the tree several times, announcing his arrival as he descended. Now—he fluttered back, hovering against the light breeze.

How was he supposed to behave, after all? This was outside of Hargalaar's teaching. The nest was surprisingly intact, the dreaming place easily accessible even with the tree's unnatural lean against the cliff-face. The smell of sand and saltwater was strong, as was the smell of bruised leaves, but his own nest still had some lure. He was disoriented though, with dark earth between him and the sky where there should only be a view of the horizon, clouds, and distant waves.

He settled finally, for the first time in his life uncertain of the tree's solidity.

The Laar muttered to itself like some scavenging seaflyer arguing with shells unwilling to open. Stregalaar saw dream fragments he could not understand, felt as if he had flowing sap pulled from broken root tips, as if his green leaves bled on the rocks.

Watch, Winged One, from on high. Return to your nest this night, for we are not yet splintered, came the dream, but from beneath came something else: that sound again, and motion. This time the motion was not side-to-side but as if the tree tried and failed again and again to return to its height, up and down, up and down so he was shaken and flung into the air haphazardly. Gathering wits as he gathered air, he pumped his wings, trying to rise above the rumbling danger.

Below, the shaking continued, as before his horrified gaze the entire peninsula shredded, not falling on his tree but subsiding like a dying fish into damp beach sand. The Laar subsided as well, roots awash in the semisalty water, then the crushed branches lay slowly back into the sea, and it was swept into the river current.

His tree! It was moving! The ground had given way around it entirely and now the water it had tapped with long roots had control of it, and was bearing it off!

Unbidden, his flight curved—he knew the Laar lived. He must follow, he must observe, protect. He must protect.

Dragons. Now he could hear the sound of other dragons, some keening with despair, others in terror; the shaking had begun again and the hill the grove stood upon was rent with strange crevasses. Many of the trees had lost most of their leaves if not most of their limbs in the fury of the disaster, and besides the dragons, other creatures rushed about randomly, trying to find someplace not afflicted by this dread calamity.

Below, his tree was picking up speed as it found the center of the current, spinning slowly as it was swept along. He paced it for some time, barely above a lazy glide, using the sea breeze and wing twitches to guide himself. Sometimes he felt he heard the Laar hum. Sometimes the tree's bobbing showed him quick glimpses of pods still intact. The shore was more distant now, the calls of other dragons barely audible.

A freshening breeze from landside surprised him; he rose, and let the wind spin. The tide had turned suddenly, and unlike its usual pattern, the water was retreating rapidly toward the sea, carrying his tree faster and farther away from the grove. The breeze brushed his cheeks. He flicked his inner lids against it as he saw the receding beach, unnaturally wide, and full of fish and wrack. The Laar's leaves stirred as if they were wings on which it sped away from the land now that it was free . . .

Stregalaar flew above the tree, and looked ahead, his eye drawn to the horizon, where a strange line had sprung up, sweeping across the bay with inevitable majesty.

His first impulse reached his wings and he turned to face the threat, to unsheathe his claws that he might rip and rend this thing, or distract it as Hargalaar had told him to distract herd leaders fronting a stampede of grass eaters.

This was no stampede. It was as if the horizon itself was charging, and there was another rumble and roar from below.

It was too much: as much as he tried to think, his wings knew an ancient answer.

He flew higher. He strained to climb away from the madness, for it appeared the whole world was rushing to swallow him and his tree. His wings knew the world was bigger than he was, that nothing but another dragon dares chase a dragon into the sky.

. . . ◇ . . .

HIS GAZE NEVER WAVERED as that wall came on; he let flight take care of itself and observed. As he rose, he could understand what he could not from sea level: this was no moving cliff nor rapid fog, but a wave like no other. It came at an amazing speed and as it came, it rose. It appeared to extend beyond his vision in both directions up and down the coast, as it sped relentlessly toward his tree.

Building, the wave came on.

Then it was by, distantly roaring but unlike the land roars, there was no new damage. His tree was like flotsam after a stormtide; it lifted and then dropped into the following trough with some speed. The wave went on, growing even taller, until it burst upon the land, crashing over the grove spot, seeming to suck from the sky those dragons who dared it.

The grove and the hill beyond disappeared under foam and spray. The sea ran up the river, and then the thunder of that clash of land and sea rumbled to him.

Beneath, his tree, Laar, floated, crushed side down, no longer making obvious headway toward the greater ocean, no longer swirling in circles. Instead it left a slight wake as from somewhere more landwind touched and shook the leaves, the branches leading, the heavy trunk half-submerged, following.

Stregalaar strained to see the land and watch the Laar at the same time; he thought of the grove, but there was no sign of it as the sea ate at the land. He wavered, took two strokes toward the land, torn. He needed to know what had become of his grovemates, but—the Laar.

His wings ached. He was very tired; his nest was near, and dry.

With that thought he spun in air, closed on the tree, and slowed to a near hover as he came over the tangled sticks and branches of his nest. Wings vibrating in the breeze, he allowed his forward motion to fail, and he stepped onto the restless and sea-slicked trunk, barely a step away from a pair of new-formed pods.

* * * ✧ * * *

IT WAS LATE IN THE DAY and still the tree did not dream. If he listened hard, Stregalaar thought he felt mumbles and mutters; sometimes a particular branch or limb would hum briefly, or leaves would flutter oddly, but how much of that was due to the ocean and waves and how much to the tree's will he had no idea. The Laar had rarely done this when planted firm.

They were moving, though. The motion of the tree in the water was somewhat like the motion of branch in a light wind, but the rhythm in it was wrong. Studying the thing, Stregalaar realized it was because the whole trunk was moving—there was no strong point the tree was bending or swaying from.

He inched upward as far as he could, which was not to the old strong trunktop but to the rather bendy end of his own branch, which swayed doubly from the waves and his weight. He would have to dream with the Laar about that, if the tree would listen. Hargalaar had let him know the tree would listen, pointing out the broad platform that used to be beneath the nest and which now worked as a windbreak.

His view from this vantage point was surprisingly limited. He could see waves and clouds and a distant mist on the horizon. He'd felt a touch of fear when he first sighted that mist . . . but this was not a moving wall of water, merely the ordinary motion of fog, a near daily occurrence in some seasons.

In the other direction, when he deliberately searched it out, was the blurred line of land. The clouds he could see building there boded a wet night, and even as he watched, he saw a flicker of lightning in the growing storm.

In the water all about them were signs of the cataclysm they had survived: broken, brainless trees and limbs, clumps of bushes, leaves and berries, even unappetizingly dead animals. Fish and sea things moved among the dead, eating what they would.

He took note of several of the scavengers, who were big enough to be a problem at close range.

The scent of the ocean mingled with the scent of torn limbs and roots, for the tree's slide down the embankment had taken a toll. Too, there were other scents of note: fresh and broken leaves, salt tang, damp earth. Not all of the scents were familiar, and even of those, he knew the proportions were grossly changed from what he was used to.

Gripping the branch carefully in the face of what appeared to be a larger-than-usual wave, Stregalaar turned his back on the land once more to find the mist growing from the seaward side. With weather closing in, he would need to be extra alert in the night. Leaving his perch for a quick snack of pod, he sought the jumbled tangle of the nest, and stepped into it with a will. Granted the Laar's new arrangements, he would eventually need to reshape the nest. For the moment, what he needed was respite.

Tucking claws around the nest's still-firm backbone, he let the ocean's breeze bring him smells until, with closed eyes, he slept.

· · · ◇ · · ·

THE RAIN DID NOT REACH THEM that night, but the fog did, closing in even before the day was done. The thunderstorm rumbled away for half the night, and it wasn't until near-dawn that the fog relented, permitting sight of the fading night guides overhead. Between the movement of the waves and lack of lifelong landmarks, it took him a moment to recognize their patterns as the clearing continued, but before full dawn, he'd seen that nothing there had changed, which was good.

The full morning brought a chill breeze carrying odors familiar and unfamiliar, this one becoming strong enough to flap the leaves and change the progress of the tree through the water. The wave action felt more pronounced, from time to time giving the tree a high end and a low.

If the tree dreamed, it was not sharing.

Stregalaar stretched, nibbled on a pod, and threw himself skyward, the shore invisible until he caught the wind and soared higher.

It wasn't until he gained more height that he saw his tree was part of a mass of stuff, its top branches now gathering in other flotsam. There were other smaller clumps about, but they all seemed to be moving in a wide curve, as if the river's current reached this far and no further.

Tree Gift or not, he knew he could not live only on pods, so he soared even higher, looking for likely schools of fish, or even perhaps some of the small seaflyers. That idea intrigued him, but then he looked down to the tree. The seaflyers, even at half his weight, were able defenders when alone and aggressive predators in groups. Perhaps this was not the time to test his skills thus. Perhaps the best choice would be small fish after all.

· · · ◇ · · ·

FORAGING TOOK LONGER than he had expected. The fish here were less relaxed than those closer to the shore, more alert to shadows. He was accustomed to keeping an eye on the spray to gauge surface winds, and had depended on the breaking waves to bring fish back to the surface. Lacking comfortable reference points, the simple act of fishing required more energey than he was used to.

More, he found himself staying within easy sight of the Laar, concerned twice when he'd misunderstood its motion in the swirling current.

There was also the inconvenient lack of nearby perch or rock on which to *eat* the prey at long-last captured. He could eat some of the smaller fish in flight, but others took a place to work and rend; and of the flotsam available, his tree was the most stable and the most familiar. He had always kept to Hargalaar's rule about not filling the nest with fish bones, but this was problematic now.

Lacking better options, he returned to the Laar to eat. After, he cleaned as well as he could, pushing the scraps over the edge of the nest and into the sea. The meager catch had taken the edge from his hunger, but he knew that soon he would be wanting a larger meal.

His eyes were drawn to an unusual trunkside motion—something was pulling the scraps he had cleared below the surface of the water. This would bear watching: he surely didn't want to attract pests or competitors!

Returned to thoughts about the future, Stregalaar moved again to the dreamspot, closing his eyes against the distractions of outer sight.

There was no muttering to be heard in the dreamplace, no visions, no voices. Rather, there was the feeling of being watched, a feeling akin to the one he'd had when faced with being accepted. The tree was aware of him, the way Hargalaar had known when he slept and when he woke.

Concerned, he tried dreaming *at* the tree—

"Laar, I would sleep in my nest!"

For a moment, perhaps, a hum. A twitch of leaves.

A small pod, bright green, beckoned, releasing a scent of fresh water and clean sweet juices.

Branch-with-wings . . . Stregalaar straightened eagerly. The Laar spoke—but so faint! Almost, it seemed to be his own thought, a memory or—*your nest is here*. He settled his wings noisily. It was, after all, only a memory of what the tree had promised to provide when first he had arrived. Ever since he'd had a nest, and sweet pods, and a thing to do—to be the wings and the eyes of the Laar.

What more did he need at the moment? The tree was providing a place to sleep and pods. What more could a dragon need—

Reality he knew: in a while, he would need food. In a while again, he would need a place to sleep.

In the meantime, the Laar needed what a tree always needed: a dragon to see to the tree's environment as best he could. Were the fishes feeding on the branches as well as the scraps? Would Stregalaar need to eat in-flight and drop scraps randomly?

Working with this dreamless and wordless message, the dragon snatched at the small ripe pod and took again to the air.

· · · ◇ · · ·

THE AIR WAS CLEARER NOW, and the angle of light made it easier to see into the waves. Stregalaar noted that as he caught the wind and soared, tucking the thought away as he had tucked away the information that the long-eared nibblers expected danger from the ground or that root grubbers in a group would put up a dangerous fight.

In this light, he could also see the debris from the land swirling into a pocket of current and moving on, the sand-rich water easily distinguishable from the green-blue of the greater ocean. Higher he soared, and finally he saw land, a misty edge on the horizon.

Between the land and the Laar, much closer to the traveling tree than the misty land, was a mass of green and brown and beige. Stregalaar knew what islands were, but he couldn't recall seeing this one earlier, though he might have missed it in the fog. He dipped a wing and started a long glide in that direction, sharp eyes unable to make sense of what he saw, until he realized that this was like the Laar's progress through the waves, except much bigger. Where the branches, grasses, and flotsam that traveled with the Laar were barely twice the canopy in size, this mass was big enough for a dragon to land on, could he find a suitable spot amid the jumbled junk. And where the Laar's shape could be picked out from its companions from a height, the large mass seemed random, like sticks on the sand on a stormtide morning. Too, there was a busyness—a *motion* around the thing that drew his hunter's eyes without informing him.

A wing flashed and that quickly, he had the pattern. It was a flock of seaflyers playing in the air near the large mass; their motion that had drawn his eye and confused him all at once. Stregalaar slowed his approach. Seaflyers . . . were risky. They seldom came to the beach, which was well for dragon and for seaflyer. While they *could* soar, most of their time was spent close to the surface of the water, from whence they could alight, float, and take off. Unlike dragons, they were comfortable diving for their food if need be. It was rare to find one solitary; they hunted, nested, and slept in flock. These, now that he could see them clearly, were wheeling and diving over the mass in a fashion far from random.

Stregalaar let his wings work the air for altitude; he had no love for the seaflyers. Still, they were hunters, and what one hunter had found was of interest to another hunter.

From his height, Stregalaar could see swarms of fish loitering in the current from the shore, and as he approached the large mass their numbers and variety increased. Was this concentration of prey what had excited—

No, *there*!

A flash of red stripe, a charge of green-gray, and then the surface of the mass was quiet again, but where the movement had taken place, the seaflyers retreated, circled, dived.

The next motion came: a seaflyer skimming in from the ocean side zoomed toward some cavity within the floating junk, dipped with intent, but was torn from the air by—

Dragons.

Now the mass of flyers rose, and their numbers Stregalaar could not count. They swooped toward the large mass in waves, careful of the tattered body of the one who had come too close and so found them their target. Several flyers landed and faced their antagonists, who lunged from the morass with good effect.

Dragons. Stregalaar saw them clearly now. Klenveer was one; Trunveer another. They stood on downed flyers and met the others with tooth and talon!

From his height Stregalaar could see a group of cornered green-gray pressed amid a floating mass of branch and shattered trunks, some cowering, some standing in line to defend themselves and those younger yet.

The line was fronted by Chenachyen, whose adult colors were coming on fast. A pair of flyers attempted to strike through to the young. Her beak caught one, and the second was ripped from the sky by Trunveer, who was up, wings beating the air, her huntmate . . .

Klenveer—Klenveer was not looking good. He dragged a wing, his steps faltered, the second eyelid obscuring his sight.

Wings folded, Stregalaar chose a swarm of flyers swooping purposely toward Klenveer at low level, slid in behind them as they fell into attack formation, opened his sound tube, and whistled a challenge at full volume as he struck the trailing ones from behind with extended claws and collided heavily with three more before pulling up and away. He'd lost little speed, twisting now and skimming the top of the floating mat, striking at the bobbing heads of flyers attempting to land near the dragon lair.

Now Trunveer screamed, her keening drawing echoes from the massed younglings. Stregalaar feared for her mate, but his charge sounded next, and he rose in full fury from the mass, his wing uninjured, willfully plunging into the mass of attackers, leaving falling, failing flyers in his wake.

Stregalaar's turn brought him into a group of the things. Some scattered but two raked his wings with beak and claw; he twisted hard and used the leverage of his weight and speed to knock one of them from the air. That one tumbled soundlessly while others took the time gained to reform a wedge of attack. He turned into it, intending to meet it head-on with his weight but Chenachyen's scream of warning brought him to his senses and he pulled back so suddenly that he struck a flyer whose pounce was interrupted.

Chenachyen was rising now, and the startled flyer whose interception had been interrupted squawked away from her.

Wings grabbing air, Stregalaar rose, circled, and rose again, watching the seaflyers who now confronted four dragons in the air, three low and one high. The noise was tremendous; Klenveer's whistle an amazement as he swooped upon wounded flyers, and the flyers, wounded or not, screamed challenges and threats, the young dragons adding what they could . . .

A scan of the sky showed none of the flyers above him: with his wingspan and speed, it was hard for them to outfly him. The ones lower were no longer crowding the dragons, content instead to circle and scream, staying well-back from Klenveer, so much so that Trunveer took one out of the air who had overlooked her path.

Stregalaar circled, trying not to overfly the crowd of seaflyers, who seemed to be weary of the altercation. The flyers withdrew to the leading seaside of the matted debris while he continued his orbits, and Trunveer settled alertly near the younger as Chenachyen and Klenveer used the oncoming breeze to hover over the landside edge protectively.

Satisfied with the stand-off for the moment, Stregalaar locked his wings and rose, taking time to glance at the aching spots in his wings. There were wide scratches and a touch of blood, but no tear in the membrane itself as far as he could see or feel. Better, his talons had taken no damage; a broken or missing claw being a hazard he could ill afford in these strange and dangerous skies.

A whistle from below. Chenachyen was slowly rising to his altitude, doing her best as well not to approach the flyers. She was aided by something he'd barely noticed in the excitement of the battle: the wind had changed direction, and now the breeze was tending landward.

Chenachyen whistled again, this time indicating a wing survey . . .

Good; they would both look the other over, then, though her sure flying appeared to mask no injuries.

She rose past him, circling slowly, hovering while he peeled hard landward and soared above, then expertly lifted wingtips to circle above and below her, seeing no sign of tear or blood.

He took a closer look then, swooping till their wingtips nearly met.

"Why?" he clicked. "Trunveer and Klenveer? You, here?"

"The fear. The Laar was gone. You were gone and then the trees shook again. Veer lost leaf and nest branch, Chyen's roots shook until it was cast aside, broken on the broken ground. Some of the saplings stood—and then the water!"

They circled, breeze rippling their alignment; they switched wingtips and went on.

"Pauveer flew at the sea, as if to fight the waves . . . but he'd seen Veer carried off. The younglings followed, the Tree Masters followed. There was another shake and more water. We flew and landed where we could."

"So you follow the trees?"

She peeled away at that, wingtips fluttering unreadably, then slowly returned.

"Veer is wood without dream. Chyen is gone to pieces. If the trees live, it is in the few saplings. We would return to the grove and live there with the saplings, coaxing, hoping roots of one of the elders still live to recover, so the trees do not lose themselves."

It was his turn to let the wind-ripple move him away.

"But that is not done—why?"

"The younglings . . . " she began, and then flexed claws with meaning. "The younglings were too tired to fly back, in that light, so we slept and ate and rested, and waited for the badly injured to die. Then the seaflyers came, accusing and fighting and abusing the dying. I stood as brood watcher while Trunveer and Klenveer kept them away. At morning light we meant to return to the grove. They came, as you found us."

"New light, to the grove," Stregalaar said, wingtips quivering. "I will guard with you then, until new light. The young cannot fly against these."

He swooped then, as if diving toward the seaflyers; and from below came Klenveer's screech as he rose, also heading toward the flock.

Almost as one the seaflyers lofted, filling the air with imprecations and boasts, heading down the coast, late-risers streaming behind the front, some few, braver than the rest, turned toward Stregalaar, whose course was now to follow, Chenachyen comfortably at his side—and the flyers turned and joined their brethren, swooping so low over the ocean that even a dragon might have a hard time choosing a target.

The while, Chenachyen clicked her beak, while Stregalaar's whistle echoed behind them.

· · · ✧ · · ·

PAUVEER WAS AMONG THE YOUNGLINGS, a well-cleaned bloody patch on one wing. He ducked his head when Stregalaar hovered and then dropped to the damp tree trunk near him, speaking to the youngsters: "Stregalaar Tree Master was first to lose his tree to the world, but it was not from lack of watching nor lack of courage. His Laar was the first guardian against the sea, and those of the sea respect him."

Klenveer whuffed and turned his back on this, but he said nothing to dismiss Pauveer's story.

Stregalaar clicked his beak, and let Trunveer know his intentions.

"Chenachyen says you return to the grove on morning light. I will help guard until the young are airborne."

Trunveer walked down the trunk of the dead tree.

"Not to the grove again? You might find a tree to groom for your offspring's nest, you know."

He whistled a negative, and again.

"Pauveer, who has no tree, will not fight you for Chenachyen, who has no tree." Trunveer continued.

Stregalaar flapped his wings, resettled.

"The grove guarded me until I grew. I will guard these so you may return them to the grove."

Trunveer flapped once, turned away.

"It happens."

· · · ✧ · · ·

THE MASS WAS NOISY IN THE NIGHT, with wood squealing against wood, complaining younglings full of complaint at the world, even the foam of the sea hissing as waves passed under and around them. Stregalaar felt for the dream source and found none here. These trees were no more, their presence, necessities, and dreams fled elsewhere.

He did as he said he would: acted as guard. He noticed nothing untoward, excepting the lack of presence. He slept between moments, the slow twirl of the tree raft permitting him to close one eye and hood the other, using the sighting of a new star through the second eyelid as a mark to wake, to move about and be aware, then to return to contemplation.

It was during a period of contemplation that he dreamed after all, a dream of his own tree, Laar, pushed by tide and wind into some unfamiliar cove, a dream of the Laar growing into the side of a hill and of him, Stregalaar, carrying pods to mountains as tall as he could fly.

There came a flash of night fire in the sky, then to wake him, and he settled his wings, wondering how he dared dream for a tree.

In the morning, he guarded as well, this time from overhead, while Chenachyen helped feed the youngest and Trunveer, Klenveer, and Pauveer gathered the rest together.

Eventually, Pauveer was airborne, gaining height by circling the matted vegetation just once, and heading slowly back toward the old land and what the sea might have left of the grove. Behind him, the dozen of others rose, gathered their direction, with Trunveer in their midst and Klenveer high behind them.

Chenachyen's flight was not so straight line as the others, and she eventually rose to his height over the empty flotsam.

"There will be need for guards at the grove," she offered gently as they soared, wingtip to wingtip in a slow turn.

"The Laar yet lives," he replied. "I can hear a hum now, from here."

He felt good, nearly giddy.

"I go. It is where I sleep."

He wheeled then, quite confidently, knowing the dragons were well on their way.

· · ·◇· · ·

HE'D HEARD THE HUM, and followed it, knowing long before he arrived there were no seaflyers there.

There were a pair of new pods and new leaves bursting out of the wood; already the nest branch was changing in some way he couldn't name: was it taller? Did it leave him a firmer perch at the new top?

He jumped to the perch, tested it, and then jumped down.

Chenachyen's approach was silent, and neat. Talon briefly skittered on wood, and she was beside him.

Nearly as soon as she landed, the quiescent tree stirred, bringing the leaves of several branches to full hum. Then, perched as he was steps from the dreaming place, Stregalaar was surprised to feel the full Tree Dream arrive, unbidden.

Grove seed, Laar is become the grove that moves, and the season is in change. Elsewhere may be fine soil and settled rocks, with good water unending. Elsewhere may be rocks and drought, else the world is fishes and salt. The grove has long spread, and now must spread again.

Laar seeks a proper rooting for generations of trees and for generations of branches-with-wings. Stregalaar seeks a strong Laar and a long flight. Wing of Chyen, Chyen dreams no more. Chyen's seed pods are no more. Laar's trunk is not splintered, Laar's branches still receive sap. Seasons move; Laar and Stregalaar move. New seasons will bring new growth. Stregalaar sees you. Laar sees you. This nest sees you. Chenachyen you may rest here, Chenalaar, you may move with this nest. There will be pods for you.

Stregalaar stretched his wings and stepped into the nest, knowing this dream to be powerful indeed.

The sounds were waves beating against trunk, and the hiss of sea bubbles. The movement was first of the trunk, and then a firm step toward the Tree Master, and then a wingtip stretch that reached his.

"This nest," Chenalaar clicked with a careful eye to Stregalaar, pulling at an awkwardly placed branch, "will need fresh weaving."

✦ Shadow Partner ✦

IT HAD BEEN APPARENT to Ceola for some days that Min was growing bored with her newest beau. She was hardly surprised; she had never understood why her sister had encouraged the young man's attentions in the first place. Oh, he was pretty enough, though tall, but Min preferred dash, daring, and drama. Shadow was quiet, mannerly, and respectful; so unlike any of Min's previous lovers as to stand in a class of his own.

Perhaps it had been the novelty of a lover who failed to make unreasonable demands upon her time and person. Or perhaps she had felt sorry for him, sitting one among a half-dozen scouts, all senior to him, and the object of a series of increasingly ribald pleasantries. Min did have moments of soft-heartedness, though they usually passed more quickly than the affair of pleasure with Shadow had done.

Whatever her reasons for attaching him, and then keeping him on her string, the signs soon became clear to Ceola's experienced eye: Min had grown tired of Shadow as he was and wished either for him to become someone else and enact her a drama, or that he would take himself off.

Of course, she might send him off herself, though it was not Min's way to put a thing out of one hand until she had something else clasped firmly in the other.

"Elby and I will be going to the new casino this evening." Min was

245

perched on a stool, her elbows folded atop the counter as she watched Ceola do set-up. "You'll be able to handle it alone."

Well, Ceola thought irritably, she had certainly handled the evening shift alone before. Min's lovers were fond of showing their passion by snatching her away to accompany them to shows, openings, and dinners during the hours when she was scheduled to be on the bar, managing what was left of the family's fortune. Except for quiet, ardent Shadow, who appeared perfectly happy to sit at the bar or at a sidetable, sometimes in company with another scout, sometimes with a handheld or a book—and wait until Min's shift was done before whisking her off for pleasure or bedsport.

Which wistful thought reminded Ceola of a thing she had overheard, just a few nights past. She looked over her shoulder at her sister.

"I thought you and Shadow had fixed to go to Noneen's this evening after your shift was done."

Min sniffed. "He may go without me, if he cares for such thin stuff. I have company for this evening. Indeed, Shadow need no longer trouble himself to ask after me. You may tell him so, if he comes in tonight."

If *he* came! Ceola thought, angrily. As if he were ever other than faithful in keeping his assignations! There had been one instance when duty had dictated otherwise, but he had sent 'round a very pretty note and a flower, which really was—Ceola gasped, Min's latest dart at last piercing her understanding, and spun to stare.

"*I* to tell Shadow?"

Her elder lifted bored brown eyes.

"As you will be here, and I will not—who better?"

"Why not she who led him along, and now finds it mete to throw over a kind, quiet lad for a loud popinjay—and break her word, besides!"

"Popinjay!" Min laughed. "Won't Elby like that!"

She looked at Ceola, suddenly calculating.

"It seems to me," she said, "that you might add Shadow to *your* string, Sister, if you value him so high!"

Her string! Ceola drew a hard breath. As if anyone noticed the plain-faced younger sister in the blare and brilliance of the elder's beauty. She might as well, Ceola thought, be a shadow herself.

Another breath, this one deliberate and calm, reminding herself what Grandmother had often said of Min—that she wasn't intentionally cruel, but heedless and caught up in the pursuit of her own pleasure. Indeed, with a little patience, she could often be brought 'round to proper conduct, which surely proved that she wished, in her heart, to behave well.

"Only think how it must wound Shadow, to have such a message from me, rather than yourself," Ceola said, keeping her voice moderate. "I think that—I think that he must truly care for you, Sister. Would it not—"

"Shadow care for me! What an idea! Why, when I said I could not accompany him to dinner Finyal-last, after he had waited all evening—did he act as if that mattered to him, or behave in the least bit put out?" She tossed her hair. "A cool bow and a chaste good-night, *that* was how much Shadow cared to lose my company! You might term him kind, Sister, but Shadow cares for nothing save his own scheming. He deserves neither courtesy nor gentleness from me!"

Ceola stared. Had Min not seen the slight droop of those level shoulders; the frown that had tightened the corners of the generous mouth? Of *course* he had been disappointed—deeply so, as Ceola had read it, though too gentle to rebuke one for whom he surely harbored the tenderest of feelings. Only someone whose heart was engaged, Ceola thought, with a sad lack of sisterly kindness, would tolerate the abuses Min had heaped upon him.

Min slid off the stool, and shook back her plentiful black hair.

"Do what you like with Shadow. You've been wanting a tutor in bedskills." Ceola's cheeks heated. Min laughed, sweetly malicious.

"I must prepare for Elby," she said, strolling toward the backstair that led to their apartment. "Good evening, Sister."

Custom was brisk at the start; when it slowed, near mid-Night Port, she looked around the room and discovered him sitting quietly at a sidetable. His companion this evening was the handheld, and he was wholly concentrated on it. Ceola paused for a moment at the edge of the bar, considering the clean lines of his face, and the errant lock of dark hair that fell across his forehead. Even as she watched, he raised a long-fingered hand and stroked the silky strands away from his eyes, his attention never leaving the screen.

The streetdoor opened and Ceola turned, only to see the potential customer step back, his voice sharp, then muffled as he spoke to a companion outside.

"Not here. Let's try across—"

The door closed. Ceola sighed and walked over to Shadow's table. He looked up at her approach and tendered a grave smile.

Ceola felt her cheeks heat, and silently damned Min's taunting. What was she to say to the man: *my sister is a beautiful fool, but I, the plain and practical, find you fair*? Chilly comfort there.

She made shift, then, to answer his smile and stepped nearer, her hands tucked tightly into the pockets of her apron.

"The usual this evening, Scout?" she asked, because that was commonplace and comforting and gave her a moment to tidy her disorderly thoughts.

The usual was the red wine, which their mother had kept on inventory to please her old and very great friend, Scout Lieutenant tel'Juna.

In the way of such things, Lieutenant tel'Juna had brought his scout friends to drink with him, and they, too, enjoyed the red. As they had good custom from the scouts, so they stocked more of the red, until it came to a solid quarter of their sales.

"I think perhaps," Shadow said in his soft voice, "that it may *not* be a usual evening." He tipped his head. "I hope your sister enjoys her usual robust health?"

Ceola's cheeks warmed further. "I—yes," she stammered, looking down at the worn tabletop. "She is quite well, thank you."

"I'm glad," he answered. "I had feared the worst, with you so troubled."

She looked up at him. "Are all scouts mind-readers?"

He grinned. "Muscle-readers, say; and most have a happy ability to guess well."

"Happy," Ceola repeated and forced herself to meet bright green eyes.

"Min left a message, Shadow. I—" She gulped.

She heard him sigh, very softly. "Did she? Then I propose that we will all be served best by a speedy delivery."

Ceola sighed then, more deeply than he, and kept her eyes on his face. "Perhaps that's so," she said, unhappily. "I—that is, Min, wished you to know that she has . . . chosen to terminate the alliance between you."

There, she thought, *it was said, as quickly and as fairly as one might*. For his part, Shadow neither flinched nor wept, though one well-marked brow slid slightly upward.

"I see," he said; "and has she left you to mind the house by yourself?"

Ceola blinked at him. "Well . . . yes. But that doesn't signify! I often run singleton."

"Do you?" He frowned, more, Ceola thought, like an elder brother annoyed with a flutter-headed youngling than a shattered lover. "I hadn't . . . observed that."

"Oh!" She moved a hand. "That was because you waited for her to finish here before—before . . ." She cleared her throat and added, somewhat inadequately, "Others are not so patient."

Both eyebrows were high now, and Ceola began to worry that she had not acquitted herself as well as she might have done on her sister's business.

"I—Min is heedless, sometimes, Shadow. But, truly—"

"If you would have me understand that her heart is good, I will undertake it, for your peace," he interrupted. The streetdoor opened, admitting a group of three, talking loudly, and more coming in behind them.

"It would seem that the next wave is upon us," Shadow said lightly. He thumbed off his handheld and slid away it into some inner pocket of his jacket, rising as he did so.

"Come, I shall stand your second."

She gaped up at him. "You, wait bar?"

One eyebrow rose, whimsical. "I know the difference between wine and ale," he said mildly.

"But—you're a scout!" she protested.

He looked suddenly forlorn, shoulders drooping and fingers limp. Green eyes sought hers from beneath absurdly long lashes. "I had made sure that *you* would not care about that, Ceola!"

In spite of herself, she laughed. "Scouts are welcome here, sir, and well you know it!"

"Barkeep!" Someone called from the counter and Ceola turned, measuring the room with a practiced eye. Half-full already, and still more coming in the door. It was a tall crew—taller even than lanky Shadow. A Terran freighter just in, then. It would hardly be the first time Terrans had drunk at The Friendly Glass. Situated as they were on the tenuous border between Mid-Port and Low, they were grateful for what custom they got, rough as it ofttimes was.

"Ale, over here!" a woman shouted in Trade from one of the tables. From the corner of her eye, Ceola saw Shadow move toward her, shoulders squared and step firm.

The woman looked up at him from her chair, then 'round at her mates. "Ale, 'tender," she said, in more moderate tones. "My team an' me 're parched."

Shadow nodded, and it came to Ceola as she slipped behind the counter that he would know the difference, too, between good coin and bad; and between exuberance and mischief.

The door opened and more tall, rough bodies pushed in, calling greetings to comrades already in place.

She worked her way down the bar, taking orders, then worked her way up, filling each. Shadow came and went, drawing ale, pouring wine, dropping coins and occasionally port scrip into the till.

Their throats slaked, the freight crews took themselves off in clumps and clusters, in search of food or other entertainment. Some lingered, while a few of the regulars came in, drank their dram and left. Ceola sighed and stepped into the little space behind the casks. She wiped her face with a sleeve, and looked up suddenly, warned perhaps by a movement in the air.

"All's well?" Shadow asked. If he was weary, it colored neither his voice nor his face.

"All's well," she confirmed and inclined her head. "Thank you, for staying."

"No need to thank me," he answered lightly. "I like to be busy."

"Well, I hope you can find some rest before duty calls you," she said frankly. She scraped her hair back off her face. "I can finish up here. It can't be long until—"

A long yodel cut her off. Already? She spun out of her alcove to check the clock over the bar.

The yodel came again, signaling the end of Night Port and the beginning of Day.

Closing time.

• • • ✧ • • •

THE ALARM SOUNDED. Ceola came up onto a reluctant elbow and groped in the general direction of the tea maker. Her fingers connected and she brought the cup to her lips, sipping the hot, bitter beverage and recruiting her determination. She pushed the coverlet back and eventually came to her feet. Her back hurt a little, and she eyed the clock grumpily, sipping.

Don Sin would be around within the hour to change out empty kegs for full. She ought to snatch a quick shower and a quicker sandwich before going down to open the back door. It was her regular chore to oversee the exchange and sign the chit.

But really, she thought with a return of the previous evening's temper, why shouldn't Min take that duty today? *She* had not worked an overfull house last night—and thank the gods Shadow had offered his help, while *the owner* was out on the Port, frolicking—or who knew where it might have ended?

Tea cup refilled and temper high, Ceola walked down to the hall to her sister's room. The door was closed, which might mean that Min had company, but Ceola found that she didn't care. Let dramatic Captain Elby be roused from his doubtless well-deserved slumber, and sent scrambling for his trousers! It might teach him something about how bills were paid.

She rapped sharply, waited for the count of twelve, then pressed the button next to the speaker.

"Min?" she said, her voice sounding raspy and sharp, like a weary kitchen knife. "I need you to take the delivery today."

There was no answer, not even a moan of sleepy protest.

Ceola frowned, pressed the button again, and repeated herself at a slightly increased volume.

No answer.

Well, then. She pushed down on the latch, expecting it to be locked. It gave, and she danced two steps into the bright blare of her sister's room, tea sloshing over the rim of her cup and onto her hand.

Muttering, she sucked her fingers—and only then noted that the bed was empty, untumbled; and that the curtains across the window looking out over the service alley were open.

Min had not come home last night.

Ceola stared at the bed, trying to sort her feelings. She identified dismay, certainly; and an additional flare of anger—*stuck with all the work again!*—but of worry, there was very little. Min, Ceola thought, could take care of herself. Indeed, had she been in a slightly more charitable mood, she might have found it in her to spare some concern for Captain Elby's well-being.

Her eye struck the clock then, and she cursed again. The deliveries!

She quit her sister's room at a run.

· · · ✦ · · ·

MIN HAD NOT RETURNED by opening time, and Ceola, hair still damp from a hasty shower, owned to herself that she was . . . beginning . . . to become concerned.

While it was true that this was not the first time that Min had stayed away all night and into the next day, such complete disregard for kin and the business that fed them both was . . . more unusual than not.

She wondered if she ought to register a lost person claim with the port proctors—and immediately decided against. The less the proctors had to do with The Friendly Glass, the better for all. If one of the scouts came in tonight, she told herself, she'd ask them to inquire along those special routes known to scouts. She sighed then, knowing that she had very little hope of that scout being Shadow.

Ceola shook her head. Kindness was owed kin, surely, and the greater portion of one's affections. But sometimes, it was difficult not to think hard of her sister.

The door opened and she looked up, putting her hands flat on the bar to indicate her willingness to serve.

Two men in the rough, grease-stained coveralls of dock workers entered, walking quickly, as if they had a task in hand. Ceola's foot, hidden behind the bar, moved on its own wisdom, touching the switch that would summon aid from the security company.

The men came on, one slightly in the lead. Ceola turned, too slow; he lunged, grabbed her arm and dragged her toward him across the counter.

She snatched at the underside of the bar with her free hand, screaming, while his partner raced past to the back of the counter. It was the till they were after, much good it would do them. She'd made the deposit—

Her captor yanked cruelly on her arm, the edge of the bar cut into her frantic fingers; her grip held—and the other man bent to snatch the box from its shelf beside her.

"Here!" he called.

His voice was—oddly familiar. Ceola had no time to chase the memory though. She twisted and kicked, her foot in its sturdy shoe unfortunately missing the unkempt head, though it did connect with his shoulder.

"Clanless bitch!" He came up, box in hand, and drove an elbow violently into her ribs.

Breath left her lungs in a thin cry. Weakness roared through her, and ribbons of color distorted her vision. Where was the security team? She couldn't breathe! Her grip loosened, her captor's fingers crushed her arm and she flew across the bar into a rough embrace, face pressed against fabric reeking of filth and engine fluids.

"Go!" He shouted, and she heard hasty footsteps making for the door.

The man holding her twisted his fingers in her hair, releasing her as he yanked her head back, his free hand whipping 'round to strike her, hard, across the face.

Pain exploded; she spun, thoughts spangled into chaos, and fell heavily, stools scattering like twelve-pins.

Through the blare of pain, she heard the door slam shut.

• • ◦✧◦ • •

"WHAT DO YOU MEAN, the tariff hasn't been paid?" She heard her voice keying upward, and swallowed. The security rep averted her eyes, making a show of checking her screens. She had taken one horrified look at Ceola's face when they were first connected, and thereafter found reasons to keep her eyes averted.

"Our records are clear," she said, not looking up. "We have received no payment from The Friendly Glass these last three relumma."

"My records," Ceola said, her voice shaking, "are also clear, ma'am. The fee has been transferred on the day set forth in our contract, never once missed, in more than a half-dozen years."

The security rep looked up, slowly, and met her eyes in the monitor.

"Our records then being so misaligned, I suggest that we commission an audit."

An audit! Out of the monitor's field, Ceola clenched her fists, then bit her lip when abused fingers protested. Her head hurt and her ribs, and—gods abound, an audit? She could no more afford an audit, than—

Behind her, the door opened, and she spoke quickly to the rep, even as her heart-rate increased and her blood chilled.

"Hold a moment," she said breathlessly, and left the screen on as she forced herself to turn.

I should have locked the door, she thought, her palms wet now with panic. *At the least, I should have—but surely, it is only a regular, come in for her usual!*

But it was neither her attackers returning, nor a regular who stood in the center of the room, hands tucked cozily in the pockets of his jacket, surveying the tumbled stools and disordered bar.

It was Shadow.

Relief brought tears to her eyes. She blinked them away as she spun back to the screen.

"I have customers. May I speak to you again tomorrow?"

"If you call on my off-shift, any of my colleagues will assist you, ma'am. I will leave complete notes in your file."

Of course you will, Ceola thought wearily, though she inclined her head courteously.

"My thanks. Good evening to you."

She touched the disconnect, and turned into a speculative green gaze. "Shall I fetch the proctors, Ceola?"

"No!" Her hand rose, torn and reddened fingers spread wide. "I want—" She stumbled, words melting off her tongue like ice. Her eyes stung, and that would be too much, to weep and show helpless before him. Min might employ such stratagems, but she . . .

She . . .

"I don't know what I should do," she said, her voice low. "I— Please, Shadow—what should I do?"

He seemed to become even taller, though he stood there exactly as before, hands in pockets and head tipped slightly to one side.

"You should place yourself entirely in my hands," he said, soft voice decisive. "One moment."

He spun, returning, silent and quick, to the door, which he locked with a snap of his wrist. Ceola began to protest, then bit her lip. She had asked him to solve this for her, after all.

"We will discommode your customers as little as possible," he said briskly, striding back down the room and coming 'round the counter. "But if you will not have the proctors, then we still must find who did this."

He took her gently by the shoulders, and turned her face toward the brighter light over the back bar.

"That wants some attention," he murmured. "Is there any other damage done?"

"My—" She lifted her hand, showing him torn fingers already beginning to purple. "He—he struck me in the ribs, and I couldn't— but I can breathe now," she said hastily, as his lips tightened. "So that's naught, really."

"I see. Ceola, attend me: is there *any other* damage?"

"I—" He was being delicate, she realized, and laughed, the sound high and unsettled in her own ears. "They were after the till, Shadow. It was their whole focus." The tears rose again, and she looked away, misery cramping her chest. "They took what they wanted and ran."

"I see," he said again, and exhaled. "Have you a first-aid kit?"

"No," she answered, and did not add that the ancient unit that had served to patch such minor bruises and contusions as might sometimes occur on a busy night had failed two relumma back, and they had not had enough extra to see it repaired. There were so many things that they had not been able to afford—the newsfeed, a part-time worker, a—

"Very well," Shadow said, interrupting these increasingly tangled thoughts. "Now, these—people—who were so focused on the till. Have you seen them before?"

"No, no—wait." She frowned, which made her face hurt worse. "The voice—last night, the door opened, then closed—you recall it! I thought it only that someone had looked in and failed to find a comrade, but the voice—it was the same."

"The room was too full for them last night, so they looked for easier game," Shadow murmured, perhaps to himself. He released her shoulders, and fished the handheld from its inner pocket.

"Ah, good, you are about," he said into the device. "Bring whomever else you can find and come down to The Friendly Glass, there's been some unpleasantness . . . a first-aid kit and the forensic . . . Yes. I've locked the door; ping me when you've arrived." He paused, then grinned. "Oh, by all means, *quickly*."

* * * ⟡ * * *

SCOUTS APPEARED, three of them, one bearing a first-aid kit, and another a different sort of kit which he immediately unfolded onto an empty table, with assistance from the third.

Shadow brought the scout with the first-aid kit behind the bar, standing a halfstep before her. Ceola looked up at him from her seat on the cold-box. He had, over her objections, wrapped his jacket around her shoulders. She held it close, her injured hand tucked against the plush lining. It wasn't cold—she knew that it wasn't cold—yet she couldn't seem to stop shivering.

"Ceola, this is Tonith," he said, "the best medic among what is admittedly a disreputable crew. Will you allow her to tend to your injuries?"

She did very much, Ceola thought, want someone to tend to her injuries. Her face felt as if she'd scrubbed it with gravel and rinsed it with red wine. Even though she could breathe, her ribs hurt where the thief had struck her, and her arm was throbbing. Those were her major complaints, though there was a growing litany of bruises and minor pains.

"Indeed Shadow, I would be grateful to the scout," she murmured.

Tonith stepped forward, her eyes as warm as if she were approaching an old friend, and with no hint of flinching away from the sight of Ceola's abused face.

"Please, let us be Tonith and Ceola, as I see you are already on good terms with the captain." She glanced over her shoulder to Shadow. "Where may we be private?"

"Wherever Ceola wishes," he answered.

"Well, that's generous, own it!" Tonith said merrily, slinging her kit over a shoulder and offering both hands to Ceola. "Down from the heights with you, now!"

Ceola put her hands in the other woman's and slipped off of the coldbox. She gasped as her feet hit the floor, and found a friendly shoulder bracing her.

"A little ragged, is it, Ceola? We'll soon have everything put right. But first you must tell me where you would prefer to be private."

She thought with longing of her own room, but the stairs—she did not wish to walk up the stairs presently.

"There is the office . . . " she managed, using her chin to point the way. "Just there."

"Perfect," Tonith proclaimed, and slid a firm arm around her waist to help her walk the few steps that were needful.

• • • ✧ • • •

"I AM GOING NOW," Ceola told Jas Per. "Do you have everything needful?"

The big man—taller even than Shadow and with a breadth of shoulder that surely meant there had been a Terran at Festival—gave her a dour nod. "Everything in order, Mistress. Didn't you just go over it all yourself?"

She considered him, suspecting humor or insubordination, but he was industriously racking the glasses, his eyes downcast, his broad hands delicate and sure.

Well, and if he were accustomed to the company of scouts, then it could just as easily be insubordination *and* humor, Ceola thought—and what matter, really? Jas Per worked hard, and though he took most of heavy lifting to himself, he was no mere Port tough, dependent only on his fists. No, Ceola had rapidly come to suspect that Jas Per was as deep as he was broad. He exchanged effortlessly between currencies, scarcely glancing at the 'change board over the bar, and he had at least three languages ready to his tongue: Liaden, Trade and Terran. Though he was not so comprehensive a source of news as Shadow, or even Tonith, yet he seemed to know the goings-ons of Port and city—all without stirring outside The Friendly Glass.

Where he went after the bar closed, she did not know, and he did not say. Shadow had brought him to her, on the day after the till was taken, saying that the big man would "help out." She began to protest—there was no extra money to pay wages—and had been silenced by a raised eyebrow and the quiet information that she need not concern herself with Jas Per's wages at the moment.

That had been five days ago. So short a time; yet time for everything to change. The scouts had speedily found the men who had taken her till. They had made quite an enterprise of the neighborhood, those two, having stolen also from the grab-a-bite at the top of the street, and the trinket shop at the bottom. Her money, alas, had not been found, though it could have been worse. They had taken a full day's profits from the grab-a-bite, and left the owner with a broken head, too.

Of Min, however, or of the dapper Captain Elby, there was no news at all.

"Very well," Ceola said, giving Jas Per a crisp nod of the head. "I will be back in the second hour."

She said the same thing every day when she left him. He must be very tired of hearing it, but to leave the bar, their legacy from their mother, their wealth and their lifeline, in the hands of non-kin—it was not easy for her. And what if Min returned to find a stranger behind the counter?

Yet, if she tarried much longer, she would be late for her assignation with Shadow, and their time together—already much too short!—would be made even shorter by her foolishness.

Ceola gave Jas Per one last nod, deliberately turned her back and once again left her life in his care.

* * * ✧ * * *

SHADOW CAME FORWARD, smiling, his hands extended.

"Am I late?"she asked, slipping her hands into his, and smiling up into his face.

"Precisely on time," he assured her. "How does Jas Per go on?"

"I believe he has mastered the entire trade and will soon release me to my own affairs. He greets the regulars by name, and has their usual waiting before they even find a stool."

Shadow frowned slightly. "That may land him in trouble, should someone chose to vary of an evening."

"Perhaps it might, but the chances are very slender that he would be caught by surprise. Just last evening, he did *not* pour Hantem's ale out for her when she walked in the door. He waited until she had seated herself at the bar and called for wine, then poured with a generous hand. I asked him later how he knew she would not want the usual, and he said, 'it was in her walk.'" She looked up at her tall escort as they strolled toward their private room.

"Now tell me truly, sir! Is he a scout?"

"Jasper, a Scout? No, I fear not—though he is a very skillful muscle-reader."

"Seriously, Shadow, he cannot continue to work for—at The Glass, without wages, and I am in no wise to pay him."

"Has there been no word yet from your sister?" he asked

Ceola looked down at the burnished floor. "I—no. Have you— have your searchers found nothing?"

"Alas, we have not, but you mustn't despair. She may, after all, have gone off-world with her friend for a small vacation."

It would, Ceola thought, be much like Min, though she might have left word! Or perhaps not, considering what else she had forgotten to tell her only kin.

"Tonith was by early today," she said slowly. "You recall that she was kind enough to undertake a trace of those transfers for me." She looked up, forcing herself to meet bright green eyes. Shadow inclined his head, silently inviting her to continue.

Ceola swallowed, for this—this was a wound, a blow to honor that could not lightly be shared.

"The security company rep was correct—we have not made our payment for the last three relumma. The money was transferred, right enough, but it went to—another account. A . . . private account." She cleared her throat. "In Min's name."

"Ah," he said softly.

Ah, indeed. Her sister had stolen from her—had placed the one thing that stood between them and the Low Port in jeopardy. Ceola did not know what to make of it, but it hurt, bitterly.

"Will you hold line?" Shadow asked her, and then—"*Can* you hold line?"

"I will hold as long as I can, of course—I must! The Glass is in Min's name, as eldest. Though how I will manage without Jas Per I hardly know."

"There is no reason to manage without him for some time yet," Shadow said, stepping back and allowing her to proceed him into their room. "Nor will you fret over his wages. There is a matter of Balance between he and I."

Inside the room, she turned to look up at him. "But—"

"Hush," he murmured, holding up a hand as the door closed behind him. "No distractions from the outside world enter this room, correct?"

That had been the mode from the beginning, though how he supposed her able to think at all, once they—

She smiled up at him. "Correct," she said.

* * * ✧ * * *

SOME WHILE LATER, she pushed open the door to The Glass and strode inside, luxuriating in a loose, effortless stride. As always after her time with Shadow, she felt sparklingly *aware*, as if she had slept deeply, instead of exercising profusely.

There was a good early crowd—that was the first thing she noted as she moved toward the counter. The second thing she noticed was

Jas Per, tall and unusually subdued at the center of the bar, as if standing sentinel. He caught her eye and moved his head slightly to the right, even as he turned to answer a call from one of the regulars.

Frowning, Ceola followed the direction of his nod. A woman was draped on the end-most stool, sleek black hair curling over one shoulder, her chin resting on one hand, while with the other she toyed petulantly with a half-empty glass of the red.

Ceola's stomach sank, which must be wrong. Surely, she thought, forcing herself to continue walking brisk and businesslike toward the bar, *surely* she should rejoice to again meet absent kin?

Well, and if her stomach was a fool, at least her head knew what was owed to family.

"Min," she said, softly, upon arriving at her sister's side. "Sister, welcome home; I had been worried, with you gone so long, and no word."

Angry brown eyes met hers, and a shapely arm flung out, pointing.

"*What* is that?" she snapped, heedless of customers within hearing distance of clan business.

Ceola blinked. "Jas Per," she said softly. "He has been helping me keep the bar. I depend upon him a great deal," she added, only then realizing that it was so; "and can scarcely think how I'd go on without him."

"Oh, indeed!" Min made no effort to moderate her voice, which was made sharper by the edge of sarcasm. "And here I thought it was Shadow you had in your eye. Well! If you care for misshapen Low Porters . . ."

Ceola gasped, and leaned forward, her hand perhaps a bit too heavy on her sister's arm.

"Min," she said quietly, "will you shout such things into the ears of our customers, some of whom value Jas Per high?"

For a moment, she thought that Min would continue—and what course stood open to her, Ceola thought, if that came to pass? Surely, she could not ask Jas Per to escort her own sister to the door, like a grease ape in his cups?

Fortunately, it did not come to that. Min slid to her feet and moved toward the back alcove, her uncertain stride speaking of more than one glass of the house red.

She spun unsteadily and leaned against the back wall of the tiny office, crossing her arms over her breast, her face set and hard.

"Why is that abomination working behind my counter?" she asked, her voice high and ugly.

Ceola considered her, and took a deliberate breath. Centering herself, Shadow called it.

"He is here because we were robbed," she said.

Min's face lost some of its rich color. "Robbed?" she repeated. "How much was in the till?"

"Only the 'change money," Ceola told her, keeping her voice even. Gods, had it always been this difficult to speak soft? "However, the security company would not come, on account of nonpayment, and I . . . took some minor harm because of it."

Min shook her hair back. "Nonpayment! Those deposits went out! Check the ledgers."

Ceola felt herself settle into the ready-pose—her weight balanced over her knees, shoulders firm, chin up.

"Do not trouble yourself," she said, and her voice was so cold her skin pebbled. "I've traced the pathway that money traveled, Sister. The deposits went out, right enough, and into your private account."

Min tipped her head. "That was clever work," she commented, without a trace of shame. She tossed her hair again. "But, let us not brangle! I have come to bring you to a meeting, and you have very nearly made us late."

Ceola blinked. "A meeting? I can't leave the bar now!"

"Why not? Surely your charming Jas Per can handle the custom."

"Min, I am not leaving the bar for a *meeting*. Do you mean to stay here?"

"I do *not* mean to stay here!" her sister snapped.

"Then give me your direction. I will come to see you tomorrow during Day Port."

"You will do as you are instructed by the eldest of your House," Min spat, and snapped forward, her hand whipping toward Ceola's face.

She was tipsy with the wine she had drunk, and angry besides. It was no trick at all to catch her wrist, and hold it—tightly.

"Release me, you wretched brat!"

"And be struck in the face? I think not."

Min took a hard breath, lashes fluttering, and looked Ceola in the eye. "Sister, I beg your pardon," she said, sweet and low. "My last few days have been an adventure, and my temper is perhaps not what it should be. Truly, it is imperative that you come with me to a very short meeting, quite nearby. I won't keep you from your duty above an hour. You know I would not ask it of you, if it were not important."

It was everything that was gentle, and surely it should have melted a heart of adamantine—had that heart not been mated to eyes which had observed this very behavior many, many times in the past. This was Min, playing every trick to her hand, in order to get her own way.

Ceola saw a movement from the corner of her eye, and looked to see Jas Per, peering worriedly 'round the door frame.

"Is all well, Mistress?" he asked.

Easy words rose to her tongue; assurances that all was well, a mere misunderstanding between kin. On the edge of speaking them, Ceola pressed her lips tight.

When she opened them again, three long heartbeats later, it was to speak words that were . . . infinitely . . . more difficult.

"Please escort my sister out, Jas Per," she said and each word tore painfully at her throat. "I will cover the counter."

"Yes, Mistress," he said expressionlessly, and stepped in to take Min's arm.

. . . . ✧ . . . .

DON SIN HAD COME and taken the empties, leaving new kegs in their place. It was late afternoon, Day Port time. In another hour, she could expect Jas Per, and shortly after that she would leave for her assignation with Shadow.

Alone for the moment, Ceola puttered, racking glasses, straightening stools, wiping down the bar that Jas Per had seen gleaming before he'd gone off-shift. The unexceptional tasks gave her comfort while she struggled to understand Min's visit.

A *meeting*? And her presence urgently needed? It made less sense in the wan light of afternoon than it had last night. She was youngest; all contracts made for their small family would be signed by Min, the eldest. All contracts made on behalf of The Friendly Glass must likewise be signed by Min, as owner. What other reasons might there be for a meeting?

Ceola stopped polishing the bar, and stood frozen in thought, staring down into the glossy black surface.

Their mother had left the bar to her daughters *jointly*. There was one reason that the youngest's presence might been urgently required at a sudden and mysterious meeting.

Min meant to sell The Glass.

"No," Ceola breathed. "She can't."

Surely not even Min would be so flutterbrained as to cast off their livelihood! Did she think the sale would make her wealthy? A rundown Mid-Port bar, in need of numerous upgrades? True, they had a healthy clientèle, but the money was so slender . . .

Or, Ceola thought, remembering the outflooding of cash identified by Tonith, perhaps the money was not nearly so slender as she had always supposed. What if Min had been taking off the top for . . . some time? Yet, if she had, on what did she spend the money?

Something banged in the back, startling her so that she dropped the cleaning rag.

"It's only Don Sin, who's forgotten to tell me something," she muttered, moving down-counter.

There came another bang, and the sound of hurried footsteps. Not Don Sin, then.

Ceola looked about her. She was in a box, which was not good. On the other hand, if whoever was coming up the hall tried to close with her, they, too, would be in a box. She took a deep breath, as Shadow had taught her, and settled flat-footed to the floor, knees flexed, her weight evenly balanced.

The footsteps acquired a shadow as they approached the end of the hall—and the shadow speedily acquired a face, slightly flushed and not nearly as affable as it had been the last time she'd seen him.

"Elby," she said, marveling at the cool tone of her voice. "Did you break the door?"

"Your opinion of me, Ceola!" he chided her, the jovial tone at odds with his face. "Why must it always be so bad?"

"What have you done to make me think well of you?" Ceola asked, even as she heard Shadow's soft voice in memory: *The best outcome is no engagement. Do not bait your accoster.*

"You do not need to think well of me," Elby said, and his voice was not jovial at all, now. He took up a position at the top of the bar, completing the box that contained her. Reaching into his sleeve, he withdrew a sheaf of papers, which he placed on the bar. "The only thing that is required of you is a signature, Ceola. Surely, that is little enough."

Not bait him, Shadow? she asked silently, and lifted her chin, meeting Elby's angry eyes.

"I will not sign a contract of sale for The Glass," she stated calmly. "Nor will I agree to waive my right of refusal."

Elby sighed. "I do not have time to argue with you, Ceola. You may sign this contract now, or you will sign it not very much later."

Ceola felt her heartbeat increase, and took a breath, seeking her center.

"No," she said.

"Very well. Your sister said that I might find you unreasonable." He came forward, walking heavy, his hand coming up almost casually, swinging toward her—

If your opponent engages, end it as quickly as possible, Shadow coached her.

She moved her head to one side, grabbed his wrist, and twisted, letting his own momentum hurl him into the bar.

"Oof!" Certainly the move surprised him, but it neither incapacitated him nor opened the way for her to flee. Indeed, he seemed to bounce forward from his encounter with the hard edge and his strike this time was meant to do harm.

Ceola ducked, shifted her center to her left foot and brought her right leg up between his legs.

Elby howled and crumbled to the floor. Ceola leapt over him and ran, whipping 'round the end of the bar and heading for the front door, meaning to scream the proctors to her rescue.

The door opened when she was two steps short, and Jas Per stepped in, pocketing his key. Unable to stop, Ceola crashed into him, her nose against his chest.

Strong arms gripped her, holding her upright until she regained her balance, releasing her the instant she had done so.

Jas Per looked over her head toward the bar from which groans still emanated.

"We must—call the proctors," Ceola gasped.

Jas Per spared her a quizzical glance, as if she had spoken in some language he did not comprehend, and strode to the bar. He stepped behind it, bent—and the groans were abruptly silenced.

Ceola started forward—and relaxed as Jas Per hove into sight, Elby held over one shoulder like a particularly irritating sack of sand.

"What should I do with him, Mistress?" he asked.

"Take him to the proctors," she said. "He attacked me. I will go myself—"

"No need," Jas Per interrupted. He put his hand on the counter and took it away, a gleam remained against the wood when he did. "This was in his shirt pocket. Looks like the key to our backdoor to me."

"So it is," she said unsteadily. "Jas Per—"

"I'll handle it," he said, interrupting again, which for Jas Per was an event of epic proportions. He moved 'round the bar, seeming to mind Elby's weight not at all. "You'll be all right?"

She considered, surprised at how very well she did feel. Endorphins, she thought, but so what? She smiled up at Jas Per.

"I will be all right," she assured him. "Hurry back."

He grinned. "Yes, Mistress," he said, and moved past her, out the door, and into the street.

The signal for Night Port sounded as the door swung shut behind him.

• • • ◇ • • •

IT WAS, AS SHE HAD EXPECTED, a bill of sale for The Friendly Glass, building, furnishings and clientèle, made out to one Clarence O'Berin. The buy-out was . . . a significant sum, to her eye, but no such riches as might keep Min in idle luxury for much more than a few Standards.

That being so, still it must be assumed that her sister knew what she was about, for there was her signature on the last page, and a blank line, awaiting Ceola's.

There being as yet a lack of custom, despite the changing of the Port, Ceola unracked a glass and poured two fingers of the red into it. She flipped back to the first page and read the terms again, sipping. The wine was so dry it puckered the mouth, sharpening the sense of taste. Alas, it did not perform a similar service for her mind, which refused to focus on the question of what she was to do now. She did not think that Min would wish to be paid over time.

And, she thought—and it was surely the wine's genius this time— was she even certain that it was Min's wish to sell? It had, after all, been Elby who had brought the paper. Could he not have coerced Min as easily as he had—

The streetdoor opened. Ceola glanced up as Hantem entered and moved slowly down to her usual place. Quietly, she slipped the contract into her sleeve, put her glass below the counter and took a deep breath.

* * * ✧ * * *

IT WAS WELL INTO NIGHT PORT and Jas Per long since returned, freeing her to the alcove office, with the contract and the computer, accounts open on the screen before her. A quiet step brought her out of her chair—

Shadow lifted an eyebrow, leaning his shoulder against the door. "Good evening, Ceola, are you well?"

"Well? Of course—" Her hand flew to her mouth. She had forgotten!

"Shadow—I do beg your pardon! So much has occurred . . ."

"Yes, so Jas Per tells me. It does a teacher good to hear that his lessons are heeded so well. What has happened, though, if you may tell it?"

She plucked the contract from the desk and silently held it out to him. He leaned forward and slipped it out of her hand, glanced down the first page, flipped to the last, read the second, and handed the whole back to her.

"I take it that you have withheld your agreement, and that this was the cause of Captain Elby's . . . annoyance?"

"Yes," Ceola said. "I have been sitting here trying to think what to do . . . "

"Surely, it is obvious? Buy your sister's share from her."

Ceola waved at the screen. "Yes, but it was *how* that I was just now trying to solve. We—cash is not flowing. I think," she said slowly, "that this is a temporary situation that will soon resolve itself . . . " *as soon,* she added silently, *as Min is locked out of the financials.*

"I see," Shadow said. "Perhaps—" He stopped, head turning slightly, and now Ceola heard it, too—soft footsteps coming from the back.

"One moment, by your leave," he murmured and faded out of the doorway.

Ceola rose, hands fisted. From the hallway came a gasp, a murmur, and the sound of footsteps, approaching . . . somewhat less stealthily.

She was not really surprised to see Min enter the room, propelled by Shadow's hand on her shoulder. The scout positioned himself in the doorway, face so neutral it might have been carved from gold.

Min threw a no-doubt beseeching glance at him over her shoulder but his expression did not alter. Ceola cleared her throat.

"If you are come after Elby, I am afraid that Jas Per has taken him to the proctors."

"I know," Min said quietly. "I am come to beg you, Ceola. Sign the contract."

She stared. "Min—does he compel you? You need not accept it, you can—"

Min laughed. "Compel me? No, he does not compel me! I compel myself! This—business, as you call it, as our mother did, as if it were some shining gift for which we ought always to be grateful while it demands our efforts and destroys our strength! It is a stone 'round my neck. I strangle because of it! Sign the contract, Sister, and let us both be free!"

"I do not find it so . . . burdensome as you," Ceola said, wondering. How could she not have known how much her sister hated their livelihood? "I—I wish to buy your share."

Min sniffed. "Mr. O'Berin offers cash. Time payments do me not one whit of good."

Ceola felt her stomach clench. She had guessed as much, and yet—

"Therefore, payment shall be made in cash," Shadow spoke up from his post in the doorway. "What is required is the name and direction of your agent in this matter."

Min turned to stare at him. "I will receive the money myself and sign whatever Ceola would have me sign."

It seemed to Ceola that Shadow . . . hesitated, perhaps to take himself in hand. When he spoke again, it was in that same quiet, measured tone. "The thing will be done properly, or it will not be done at all. Will you go to the Council of Clans with this?"

Ceola nearly choked. Bring it to the Council? The expense would ruin them all!

Min paled, as well, but she accorded Shadow a bow.

"As you will. I shall . . . locate an appropriate agent and send the information to Ceola tomorrow. Is that acceptable?"

Shadow looked toward Ceola, who swallowed and inclined her head, feeling foolishly formal.

"That is acceptable, Sister. I thank you."

* * * ✧ * * *

THE NEXT DAY CAME, and the information regarding Min's agent with it. Ceola sat behind the bar and sipped tea, waiting for Shadow.

He was to bring the money and the contract naming him as her "silent partner" in the business of running The Friendly Glass. The contract was at her insistence; he had suggested an honor loan, but she would have none of it.

"It will be done properly," she had told him, "or not at all!" And managed a wobbly grin when he laughed.

But when the hour of their appointment came, it was not Shadow who strolled into The Glass, but Tonith, bearing a small bag. "Goodday, Ceola!" the scout called cheerily. "I beg that you will accept me as a substitute for the captain, whom duty has called."

Ceola frowned. "Called where?" she asked.

"Off-world," Tonith answered, as if it were perfectly reasonable. "And who can know when he might return—you know what first-ins are!"

As it happened, she didn't. Indeed, she had no idea that Shadow was a "first-in"—whatever that might mean among scouts. Tonith dropped the bag on the bar and hitched a hip onto a stool. Leaning forward, she placed a coin before Ceola.

"Might I beg a glass of the house's finest?"

"Our license is for Night Port," Ceola said sternly, and pushed the coin back across the bar. Then she looked up and smiled. "However, I am perfectly within my rights to share a glass with a friend."

Tonith laughed. "Let us, then, by all means share that friendly glass!" She waved at the packet. "The captain sends this; his tale was that you would know how best to dispose of it."

Ceola poured two glasses of the red, shared the first sip, then excused herself to the alcove office to open the packet.

He had sent cash; more cantra pieces than Ceola had ever seen. There was a note, too, begging her pardon for leaving her to handle the last details by herself, and citing duty as the reason for his absence.

There was no contract.

· · ·◇· · ·

CEOLA STARED UP AT THE NEWSFEED which had been restored to The Glass, along with the security contract and a dozen other small niceties. The story she followed detailed the results of a skimmer race, paying particular attention to the losing team. The news service provided formal clan photos, identifying the white-haired pilot as Shan yos'Galan, and the dark-haired co-pilot as Val Con yos'Phelium, Thodelm and Nadelm, respectively, of Clan Korval. It was the co-pilot who engaged Ceola's attention, particularly. It was difficult to be certain, with the Nadelm dressed in High House splendor and holding his face close, yet—

"It's him," Jas Per said from behind her. "Captain Shadow himself."

Ceola turned to look at him. "Did you know?" she demanded.

He shook his head. "I thought my luck beyond wonderful, that I'd caught the attention of a scout. Korval?" He laughed and gave her a bow. "See how we are both honored!"

"All very well for you to laugh," Ceola said irritably. "Laugh again when you recall that there is an honor debt between us and—and Nadelm Korval."

To his credit, Jas Per did not laugh, though his grin did not fade.

Ceola sighed and looked back to the newsfeed, which had left the race behind.

"I am going," she told Jas Per, "to the Little Festival."

• • • ✧ • • •

ARACELI **HAD WON THE DAY,** and its crew stood in the Winner's Circle, surrounded by well-wishers.

Contract in her pocket, Ceola had started down to the Winner's Circle—and stopped short, abruptly and burningly aware of the enormity of her proposed action. To march up to Korval-in-future and publicly demand that he sign her contract? The mere notion was madness.

She had, from where she stood, feet rooted to the path, a most excellent view of the winners. The dark-haired pilot in his bold orange cloak—she could see his face now, and his motions—there was no doubt that this was Shadow, whom Min had slighted; who had taught Ceola to protect herself, and helped her win free to her heart's desire.

Who am I? Ceola asked herself. *He had his reasons for not wishing to sign the contract, who am I to force him to my will? Why, he has probably forgotten all about us—Min, The Glass . . .*

She took a deliberate breath, centering herself.

I am Ceola tel'Denvit, she thought calmly, *owner of The Friendly Glass. I do business properly or not at all.*

And, really—who but a madwoman would allow one of Korval to buy in to her business without a contract to contain him?

She took another breath, and moved one step down the path.

The dark-haired man in his bright orange cloak looked up from his conversation with a lady, and saw her. Ceola imagined his eyebrows rising. He leaned over to speak to the tall white-haired man, and then stepped out of the Circle.

Ceola hesitated as he came briskly up the walk.

I should bow, she thought, but she never had the chance.

A warm arm swept 'round her waist, turning her with him, orange silk billowing, as they moved up the path, toward the confectioneries and the pleasure tents.

"Hullo, Ceola," he said, and it was Shadow's voice, right enough. "Are you *very* angry with me?"

✧ Persistence ✧

BEBA WALKED FASTER NOW, nearly running; she'd actually stopped and looked around to see if anyone was within range and now she'd be late. For her, proximity was important. Long range was ten or twenty paces of clear sight distance, or just a few paces if a wall intervened. No one there. And she was late.

Ignorance is winning.

Somewhere between five deck and six deck the idea surfaced, and at first she wasn't sure if it was hers or not, it was so subtle, so tentative. She rarely picked up something as direct as a thought, though once or twice she had; mostly when she was young and hormonal. No one was in range though.

The idea was persistent, so she turned it over in her aware mind, saw the signs that it was her thought, and that made it more necessary to think about it:

Ignorance *was* winning.

On consideration, that's what this morning's time with the news round-up had showed: incontrovertible evidence that ignorance was winning. Market flux caused by the industrial committee's decision to favor blue over green this year, the newest student-style of self-lighting ring hats that fluttered in the presence of multiple low-power comm calls to the student accounts that invited conference calls, so that they might all flap together in a spotlight-mocking illumination, the resurrection of the so-called Mind Safety Administration. This run of strangeness, all these things together, illustrated the fact that ignorance was winning.

Beba sighed heavily, a flip of the hand telling the unseeing wall that even the freshly minted shift schedules handed down by the new Bazaar administrators were created more by wishful thinking than thoughtful planning. Orders came down by fiat, by . . . ignorance.

"Persistence."

She said that word out loud, knowing that, after all, she'd done this to herself: created in her own head the idea that there were only two volitional forces at work in the inhabited universe. Those forces were not *necessarily* antagonistic, except that somehow persistence ultimately was superior since ignorance was entropic and the evolutionary dialectic favored life's anti-entropic organizing principles.

Alas, she'd written that in a paper for philosophy class back when she'd still been permitted public schooling and the result had been a severe setback to her grades as well as her social range. Original thinking, it turned out, was antagonistic to her novice philosophy instructor's preordained lesson plans; she could see it in the stiff shoulder and neck muscles when he walked into class, in the way he avoided looking at her shape, in the swirling purple fog that wisped around his eyes and ears, and in the scent.

By then her emotive-control tutor, long since banished off-planet as a threat to world order, had deduced that the scent information she got was as real as the visual, and that she ought not tell anyone about it, just as her sister—off-planet now as well!—should not mention that she *could so* pull names out of people's heads, nothing else, just names they were thinking of.

The so-called philosopher was marked in her memory for his associations of scent and people: her younger self had worried that he'd turn cannibal. It was only later that she'd discovered him on video-share, eating. Eating and eating, very publicly, a meal costing close to a year's tuition. As a ranking member of The Goudry Gourmand Society, he might well have looked at a woman and considered how she'd do as a chaser to roast rump, after a pond of beer.

In a lab session during that course, her ex-lab partner had

managed a search-and-discuss that brought up her family name. From the joyous green cloaking the pronouncement, she doubted it was an accident, and from the response of the locals, she quickly found that friends grew more distant if they thought you knew exactly what they were thinking, though of course there was none of that precision in her family, at least, and perhaps none anywhere save among the legendary Healers of Liad. Damn the healers, that they expressed no kinship, and offered no assistance to those probable kindred living among the Terran worlds.

She pushed the resentment away rapidly: it was Grandmother Varky who claimed to have written message after message and been rebuffed, and to have stood in the foyer of the Liaden embassy and been laughed at. But she'd been well over a hundred Standards and her memories colored by time and the cyclical nature of her peculiar talents.

Diploma school had not admitted the family when Grandmother had been young and she'd deplored it as wasted effort when Beba had aspired to it, just as she'd deplored paying for an outside tutor when there were family members like her with wide experience. That she oft remembered things that hadn't happened yet . . . Mother had gone for the outsider, and Beba's life was the better for it.

The family had tried hard to make things better for Beba and her sister. They'd tried. And then they'd slipped away, most of them, with no word to those not at home. Gone with no forwarding address but a note that tested true: *Grandmother has seen a place for us. Be well.*

And so she'd fallen in with a man with more plan than money, more connections than cash, and a business that needed tending by someone with just a touch of talent. That Caratunk Carpeting wanted to buy that business on the cheap was an on-going problem for Derry Caratunk, who had more than once cast lusty glances at Joshu, was married into one of the triads in new management, and spoke to Beba only because she was part of Joshu's life. She'd made it quite plain, had Derry, that the Sinner's Rug was a detriment to them doing regular business, and a minus to any buy-out.

"You," he said without heat, "are late. That means I may well miss the second seating at Charleschow!"

She laughed, pleased that he wasn't angry, or beset with swarming customers. Charleschow, of course, was so far above their budgets as to be a joke.

"I see then that you have found a major buyer?"

He shrugged at the room, turned and shrugged at her, then pointed with a nod of the head.

"That one, see, who appears to be browsing as so many others, that one is a buyer, my dear. I think, given his coat and manner, that he is not one to buy from the floor bins. I note that he has support staff, which of course a simple tourist will not."

Joshu, who had opened the booth this morning, was an optimist, which was good, for she could not have lived on the shop floor with a pessimist, nor one who dwelt overmuch on failure, delay, or insult. Such thinking was not only unfortunate habit for some, but a burden to one who suffered her family curse of knowing far more and far other than was said.

She'd marked the man Joshu indicated, which was easy enough to do, though he was halfway to the end of the hall. Clearly, he was not looking to find one item of this or one item of that in order to take home a gift; but for something more. And surely, walking the full bazaar from which Bazaar itself took name, one might find anything in profusion.

The gentleman appeared not to *need* random profusion as he stood in the aisle of fabrics and textiles; rather he was examining the cards as well as the goods and if he left far more cards than he carried with him, that was the sign of a careful and deliberate buyer. The kind of buyer who might carry more than a holiday tenbit in his pocket, of which they'd seen far too many in this buying season.

"Joshu, yesterday the large female wearing strings of steel chain was the hope of the day, that we'd unload the last of the Flovint rags. The day before was the cruise ship madness which would make us our season. The day before . . ."

"This is hardly fit topic for conversation: you and I both see this buyer and we can see he ignores the left side of our booth, which is for the tourists and pays for the rice in our bowls . . ." he paused and shrugged his shoulders ". . . at least some days it pays for the rice. But this man, my dear, this man is impeccable. He is discriminating, he . . ."

Unexpectedly, Joshu had run out of energy. He reached into some inner reservoir and continued at a slower pace.

"He is the only one who has come back for a second look at the warebook, who has done more than stare at the pretty images of the Sinners Rug. Truly, I believe it was wrong of us not to have a catalog made up of that rug alone, to sell to the tourists."

"Should I flaunt myself to see if he notices?" Beba swayed her shoulders suggestively, ringed right hand turning palm out in invitation. "The rug provides ample tutoring!"

The quelling look was lost on her, but his words carried some sense.

"Hah, or should I flaunt? Someone as careful of his person as that one may have wide-ranging tastes, my dear."

She laughed, for Joshu believed himself as very private of his personal appetites as he was forward with his wares. The image of him publicly flaunting himself was one she'd not previously entertained, though she suspected Derry Caratunk might.

But there, their wares had not been so much of interest and though they were not destitute they were far from their goal of relocation out-system.

"I'm for my break, and then the commerce office to see if there's any update on those shipments that got lost—so I'm away for awhile. But if that buyer comes around, you pay attention."

She nodded, but he took her hand and looked deep into her eyes.

"Really, listen to your head, Beba," he said, nodding at the man and those two satellites who might also be his people, "and tell me of his mood. I see he stays distant; if you must, yes, gain his eyes."

He took a deep breath. "I have to be elsewhere!"

For one with no measurable talent of the mind, Joshu had instincts which served him well, and she knew that his game of naming this or that top prospect was as much a challenge to himself as a prediction. Often enough, he turned those sales, even without her help.

For a heartbeat, she opened her senses to Joshu. She did this rarely, for it seemed he kept his thoughts secret from himself as well as from others. This time was unsettling, for his mood seemed somber in a way that belied his earlier banter. Colors fogged his face briefly, and the sense was that of a long walk in near darkness, with grays and night-faded greens moving in a deep, distant ravine.

She used the training bought so dearly from the tutor and smiled honestly at her partner as he left, as if in joy of the hunt.

. . . ✧ . . .

THE THREE OF THEM were obviously a team, with the man Joshu had pointed her toward the probable hub. All of them were pilots, if one read their movements, and all of them were alert far beyond the edge of normal, if one saw the very tiny signs and ignored the public ones.

The public signs were thus: the smaller man, with the look of a Liaden, was doing the larger scan of the hall with some efficiency, his eye trained to see the carpet and not the display. The others moved on their own after they spoke with him, always staying within quick distance of the hub but still looking for this or that, likely at his direction.

The larger man. She sighed, for she had been known to be fond of larger men herself; she admired him not only for his stature, but for the way he masked his elegance of walk and motion. He appeared to the public face to be perhaps one as might carry burdens or stand as bodyguard, and truth was he carried a public gun. He was, however, far from the shambling person he projected and his eyes were clear and alert.

He looked at her with a nod, and Beba fought to avoid reacting with other than a polite nod and smile of her own. His form aside, the momentary scent she'd experienced was that of urgent effort, as if the casual tour was far from that. Beyond that was a deeper scent, and she feared that the scent was blood.

And there, a movement of hand, a flash of alert orange across the face, gone; the scent of blood, gone; the orange fading to light blue as if his burden were removed.

She turned, to find the third of the trio rotated between her and the hub; this neat and tidy woman. The woman was no mere servant either, nor dumb. With very fast eyes and hands that carried their own dark color, she was alert as a matter of breathing, as a pilot might be, and it was across her face and gone, the recognition, and the scents were of wood-fire perhaps, and those of fireworks or ammonia, and under it all, the touch of blood persisted, as if the pair had recently seen some tragedy that underscored their lives. This one nodded and approached—no—she *intercepted*!

The hub was being guarded, Beba realized, and glanced to where he stood yet at his own efforts. He dismissed an ordinary carpet with a quick touch and moved on to another of better quality, the eyes taking in a detail—she caught a scent of carpet that was not the carpet around her, but the carpet around *him*.

Then it was gone, the scent. She'd yet to see color there.

"Are you one of the principals of this operation?" The woman's hands moved wondrously smooth, accurately describing their boundaries, the colors of her face almost absent as they sometimes were with those concentrating on a goal beyond the moment.

"Yes, Gentle, I am Beba, co-operator of Joshu's Superb Surfaces." Given the Liaden in the group, Beba's nod was deep, just shy of a bow. The nod-that-was-not-a-bow was mirrored so precisely that Beba was concerned she'd offended, but the colors that flashed across the woman's face now were crisp, businesslike, scentless.

"Our group is relocating our own operations and are seeking quality goods across a range of prices. Inexpensive is very good, for the market we are entering will take some building and the low end is more extensive than the high. Not cheap, mind you, but inexpensive. We will also be looking at a few high-end goods, even uniquities."

Beba listened and watched hard, hearing what one might expect of a customer, remembering the scent of blood earlier. Perhaps she'd been right and there had been a tragedy, now requiring a rebuild.

"We can supply all of that, Gentle," she said. "Quality goods at low cost, and a unique piece rarely available for transport, ready to go. If you would like to enter your order, I'll be pleased to loan you a wireless-entry catalog so that you may purchase at your leisure from our marked prices."

"Yes, I can see that you might," said the woman, and there was perhaps a touch of humor in the eyes, even with the small flash of alert orange, "but our chief associate is of an older school of business than that, and having determined his interest would like to discuss some matter of process in quieter surroundings, it being the way he is used to proceeding."

"Matters of process? Indeed, we might work with appropriate amounts of cash, and pre-approved letters of credit, and reasonable . . ." In the back of her mind, Beba had concerns, for surely Juntava worked this way, and quieter places might not be safe places, after all.

The woman nodded as if hearing these very thoughts, offering open hands as she said, "Surely, there must be a fine place of dining you prefer, you and your absent partner. Name the place, and if you are free this evening or tomorrow at lunch or dinner, we shall be there, pleased to have you as our guests. I have heard very good things of Raleighs, and Panada Paradise, and Charleschow—please name your choice and time."

At this juncture, the large man arrived, nodding to both with the nearly absent air he wore like a cloak over his competence, his colors showing bright points and flashes, as of irritation.

". . . 'essa," Beba heard him say, "we've been offered an extra rate to stay where we are, as I apparently misunderstood the community rules here. They seem to feel I owe some gift or . . ."

Blood scent, clear and clean, from the woman. And why not, for the Bazaar was endangering itself with these games, these so-called second contracts and rise costs.

"We will talk in a moment," she said quietly, "and then I will have the name of the person expecting gifts. But we await word from the lady if dinner appointments might be made, so that we can begin arrangements quickly."

The colors were gone quickly, but Beba was sure she would not want this person facing *her* in that mood. And now, there were decisions to be made. Joshu's instincts must count, but prudence also had a place.

"Might I know the name of your—"

There was color behind her then, and a scent of something more, of carpets recalled and of chocolate and tea distantly, and of blood.

"You may, Lady, if I may be sure of yours?"

He stood before her, shorter by a hand than she, and bowed an exquisite bow. His colors went cool, as if the ritual were calming, and his eyes were on hers when he finished the bow. There was in them frankness, while over all of his face flickered a strength and determination all limned in steel.

She'd never seen color take form like that, down to the shine of metal honed to edge, down to the shape of knife and gun, behind it all the scent of blood and the scent of carpet intermingled. She stepped back, startled, from tripping. She'd found herself steadied, drawn in to his center, his arm on shoulder. Not since training, had she allowed herself to be so overwhelmed by a reading.

"Is there something amiss?" The smaller man looked concerned, the colors were cooled to a mild green tinged with orange, with alert.

She centered herself with great effort and the big man withdrew his hand from her shoulder with a nod.

"Surprise, I think," she managed. "Usually I am not unaware of someone so close!"

There was a flash of hands, speaking that language she'd never learned, and the trio moved a half-pace back, giving her room to stand and be comfortable.

She felt the flush go from her face then, smiled. There were only colors of normal concern, and the blood scent had receded.

"I am Beba," she said carefully. "I am sure that my senior partner, Joshu, and I will both be interested in speaking with you—dining with you. Our section closes at fourteen—let us say at fifteen, at ummm— the places you mentioned are all more than adequate—let us say at Charleschow. If, of course, I may tell him with whom we dine!"

Another bow, complete with sweep of flawless, bare hands. She had the fleeting impression that the hands were rarely thus, and ought to be showing a multiplicity of rings. Not a casual tourist, this one, not an ordinary person.

"Then it is done. We shall meet you and Joshu at fifteen, at Charleschow. If it pleases you, Beba, you may call me Conrad." When he said *Conrad* there was the scent of a distant spice, and hot sand, and a wash of color she associated with someone manipulating their own beliefs.

* * * ✧ * * *

"HONEST. DIRECT. FRIGHTENING." She'd distilled the experience to three words, and brought them to her partner on his return, trying to look beyond his own dark mood as she delivered the news. "We're engaged to meet them for dinner."

Joshu rocked back and forth on his feet as if he were a tree blowing in the wind. He'd once told her how a teacher's attempt to make his inner rhythms match the world's gave him a migraine, which she could well believe if the teacher had been anything like her own grandmother, so she let him twist in the breeze as he thought. There was something he hadn't said, that was certain.

He caught her eye and gave a weak grin.

"So, you think this is a good thing, being asked to dinner by strange people who frighten you?"

Beba closed her eyes, all of them.

"I lack foretelling, Joshu, as you well know. What I have is what you asked for: I have looked into his eyes. Indeed, that is the best way to deal with him, I think, this Conrad. The others are guards and assistants, but they act on his words and his needs before their own, I feel it. I would treat this person properly, Joshu."

She opened her eyes as he sat, hard, on the display of multishade wood-moss-infused carpeting for children's rooms.

"Forgive me, Beba, but I take proper profit where I can. If I did not, we would not still be burdened with your dowry piece nor would management be asking for a search fee to discover the whereabouts of our last two incoming shipments."

"So I am a burden again?"

The last was cruel, and Beba regretted it the moment it left her mouth; the brief yellow blaze of a true strike masking his eyes as he blinked.

"We are faced with ruin within the Standard," he said bleakly, looking more at her shoes than at her face. "Management will be charging a fee to help defray the cost of extra surveillance devices to support the new administration's rulings. The Commerce Center will be requiring search fees for any shipments more than a ten-day overdue, and the lease charge will now include a rising percentage of revenue as our profits rise."

"What devices will they use?"

He stood, rocked, looked her in the face.

"They say they have a source for equipment that tells if someone is being manipulated by—"

Beba *fuffed* hair out of her face, but he only nodded.

"Yes, they're at it again. We have the rug still on display, and anyone with half a word of history knows that it is old and that your family name is all over it. They said, in Commerce, there's talk that your rug controls people's minds by itself."

"That would be the Caratunk effect," she ventured, and seeing him start, asked, "Has Derry made another offer for the company, or for you?"

She read the annoyance and the flutter of indecision across his face; the scent—of Derry's favorite perfume was rather clear.

"Oddly enough, she was waiting for me at opening. Offered for the business as she always does." The flicker then, of confused issues, untouched emotion. "She explained, too, that her triad has been considering expansion."

Ah, well, that might explain the extra levity of their conversation then, for the woman was comely enough.

"She explained this in close proximity?"

He nodded and shrugged shoulders.

"Derry lives on close proximity, you know. Of course she did. She seemed not to hear me point out the Standards you and I have shared."

There was a glimmer of sensual recollection there, and annoyance as well.

Beba shook her head briefly, put on an imitation of Derry's husky voice and then mocked Derry's favorite tactic of holding Joshu's arm with friendly grasp just above the elbow when they were close. She leaned to whisper in his ear. "I knew it. Ignorance is winning."

Joshu harrumphed, and tried changing the topic.

"Frightening, you say?"

It was her turn to look bleak. He rarely questioned her about the process and her own methods were no easier to explain to him than his intuitional leaps were to her.

"Undercurrents. I would not stand in the Con Rad's way. There is a sense of, let me say, a sense of purpose that will not be detoured, of intent that will be followed, and of great need. Too, I hear they have come to the attention of management, which may be bad."

Unexpectedly, Joshu laughed.

"Then surely it is settled! We meet for a quiet dinner and things will be solved. I feel it in my bones!"

She looked at him, saw some glare of concern and another coolness, perhaps of acceptance. No scents. No scents now. The man at least did not smell like blood, which was good.

"Will Charleschow do for you, Joshu? Charleschow at fifteen? Con Rad asks us to be his guests."

He looked at her sharply.

"Will he leave us with the bill after all?"

"No. I'm sure he won't."

Joshu sighed.

"The lady with the chains would have been easier," he said.

"The lady with the chains stank of sweet things she cannot afford. This Liaden, this Con Rad, why as you say, he may solve it all. Else management will see us, deport you penniless, and jail me for my genes, which solves another set of problems."

She'd meant it flippantly, but he just bowed his head, all the colors of gloom running across his face. He stood then, and nodded.

"Charleschow it is. I wonder if Con Rad knows his wine."

• • • ◇ • • •

"NO, THANK YOU, it is *Conrad*, flowing together completely," the man said gently, "though I thank you for your efforts."

They'd arrived at the stroke of five before, to find the big man towering above staff in the lobby, waiting for them. Staff was remarkably unaware of them as they moved toward the quiet rooms one hall inside—and they did not stop there, but found yet another hall with deeper carpeting and lower lighting, and an additional interior space that Beba had not known existed.

She heard the briefest of Joshu's near tuneless whistles, barely louder than a breath. He, too, had no idea that the sanctums got this inner, and now the large man made no attempt to hide his grace. While perhaps no match for the Essa or for Con Rad, he was silent in ways that were surprising, and her attempted read brought only the vague purple of concentration and the distant green of well-being.

"Conrad, like the carpets?" she asked experimentally, and he bowed lightly, in unoffended agreement.

"Indeed. You may make what you will of the coincidence!"

It was a joke of many layers, for she could see it on his face as the colors quickly washed by. The conversation quickly fell to Joshu, who requested Conrad's opinions on the wines.

Those opinions were informed and extensive, permitting the ordering of the meal, and a sampling of wines, to go forth before any hint of business. As host, Conrad had the menu with the prices and Beba was pleased to order freely, though perhaps not quite as freely as Joshu. The big man, who she discovered to be *Pilot Cheever*, was quite comfortable ordering large portions, and if Conrad was less large and thus ordered less, his choices were obviously dictated by desire and not by price.

"You have an interesting mix of products," Conrad said eventually, nodding toward both Joshu and her, his colors going bland, "and, as it would be easier for all concerned if we might single source our purchase, I am much inclined to work with you. In fact, it would be good if we might conclude our business this very shift, if you are able to return to the hall after dinner."

Beba saw the alert colors rise in Conrad's associates, but the man himself was still showing cool.

He looked to her, and she looked pointedly to Joshu, who was showing a true flash of surprise in his colors, and a scent, a rare scent, of—wine.

Her partner raised his hands from the meal, palms up.

"The draymen and longshore, the packers, they are not available so late in the evening, and there will be a charge to open, and perhaps some . . . issues with management."

The woman, Essa, nodded, her alert colors fading somewhat. Her glance was accepted by Conrad, with whatever message it held for him, and he brought his attention back to Beba first, including Joshu with a side glance.

"I will speak with management, should they appear," said Conrad, "and we will proceed. There are two essential things, however, that we must be clear upon."

Joshu's expression said it all: here was where he thought things would fail.

The elegant man leaned forward, watching the pair of them, hand enumerating his points as if he threw dice.

"First, this will be a cash purchase. I will give a single hardcopy list of the items and types we will have, and one or another of my associates will see them and count them with one of you. This will occur once, when we are through I will retain my list and the invoice will indicate that Cash Buyer acquired Lot 1 and Lot 2, assuming that is the case. Is this clear?"

"If you discover discrepancies after, how will you ask for adjustment?"

Joshu was concerned; it did not take a talent to hear it in his voice.

"My people and I are our own witness, gentle sir. We agree on the count with you as we work, and that is the agreed count. There will be no discrepancy."

Beba shrugged. The buyer wished no name on the invoice and no record of exact purchases. Perhaps when the time came, Cash Buyer might agree to lower the recorded purchase price as well, that management would not extract a tithe.

Joshu paused, glancing at the associates, then to her.

She repeated her shrug and added a nod, Joshu forwarded the nod to Conrad.

"Price being agreed on site, I have no problem with this approach."

"Yes. We are agreed on this."

"The second requirement is Lot 2. I must be able to put hands on one of the objects I would purchase, for the sake of determining authenticity. The catalog is quite convincing, of course, but you could hardly allow a Sinners Rug to be in the open, where believers might yet cause it harm. You *are certain*, are you not? You have the provenance . . ."

He looked at Beba. The colors in his face got steely rather than angry, and his question was not to be ignored, whoever he was. She felt a flutter of dread and deliberately calmed herself. The customer had done his research. Of course he had.

"*I am* the provenance," she said quite evenly. "The rug we have on hand, and on sale for the right price, that rug has been in my family for most of four generations, sir. I have the affirmations, the court actions, and the family images from start to finish, if they be required."

"You keep it for more than the curiosity sake then? It is not merely an artifact to show off to top buyers?"

His colors wavered and, for a moment, Beba wondered if he could read her so well as she could read him, if her colors showed through to him, or her scents, or if her muscles had betrayed her.

She sighed, and sipped daintily at her wine. Her very good wine, sitting with the unfinished portion of her very good meal.

"Sir, that is a question I ask myself. Yes, the rug is for sale. It is my inheritance, and since my mother, and her mother too, have left this place, it is mine to deal with. Having not sold it, I cannot say we have used it for more than show."

He looked at her with interest, the steel gone now, and he bowed.

"I do not mean to question your heritage, Lady, yet, as carpets are what I learned from my father, I must see before I may buy, in his honor."

She shuddered even as she nodded. Under that, under all of that so gently said, was blood.

· · · ✦ · · ·

THE ROOM WAS QUIETER than at full-shift, with the lighting at quarter except in their own brightly lit area. The carpet hangers were locked as they'd left them and it took both Joshu and Beba to unlatch the sealing bar for the high-end items. As they were doing that Conrad was giving instructions and copies of his list to his associates, and inspecting the floor carts that Joshu commandeered from the hall fleet. Conrad clearly planned to buy and load tonight enough goods to furnish a small planetary store's opening; if that was the case and he was paying in cash, there ought be no impediment.

As they finished unlimbering the specialty show rack, Joshu murmured, "Life's work, Beba, for a family. Know your worth! No less than three cantra for the rug if his cash is Liaden!"

Three cantra clear had long been their plan; how often had they had an entire extra cantra in place when necessity would appear and eat it away? Yet such a sum!

She thought of her family, and of Joshu, still firmly with her as they were not, and nodded.

The high-end items unlatched, Beba looked to Conrad, who caught the glance, and Joshu, then, went to deal with the associates, while Beba received a bow of respect from Conrad.

"These other items," she said carefully, "are all worthy of purchase as well, sir, if you will pay them mind."

"Surely," he said, the color rising in him was not the calmness she'd expected, but the yellow orange of alert.

The Sinner's Rug was the last on the rack, and each ahead of it must be pulled out and admired. His hands and eyes told the tale: he was no mere salesman seeking stock, but a man who knew fine carpet like he knew fine wine and fine food. His hands touched the right spots on the binding and against the nap; his eye looked for the trim spots if any were to be found, and studied the backing where such was utilized. He named two of the first five on sight, both maker and era, and three of the next four. He was curious of one, and his colors went very strange then.

She caught a scent, but it was not the scent of this rug but some other deep in his memory, for he said without preamble, "This rug is of an old pattern from Brulandia, yet it varies. They have always had excellent teachers there, and the best museum. Have you any information on the source?"

She did not, meekly pointing to the potential dating marks, and—"I have been in close proximity to such a rug, which was deemed genuine," Conrad said. "This feels genuine, yet, yet my references are not to hand. This may be a prototype or a fork. Very nice. Your partner has my bid on Lot 1, which is one cantra solid. Consider this a possible addition to Lot 2. Let us move on, if you please."

Now the fogs flitting across his face were anticipation, alert, and the underlying steeliness.

Joshu's whim was to let several of the early rugs sell later ones, as if the rack were in order of value. At the twelfth and thirteenth hanging rugs, Conrad touched edges and made a noise very much like *snarf* while muttering, "These are sturdy commercial offerings, aren't they?"

The next two interested him not the least, and the following one somewhat, since he felt the binding and sniffed it, and startled her by stretching his hands at shoulder height as he stood with nose to the rug center.

"This is off-size, I think; either a test piece or an excellent forgery from the same period, for the materials are correct. I applaud Joshu's Superb Surfaces for an interesting show."

She nodded, murmured, "Thank you," saw the alert level go up as she tugged that interesting carpet aside, revealing the last rug on a well-illuminated unswinging display rung.

The Sinner's Rug.

Of course it was *a* Sinner's Rug and not the *only*, it was the subject which made it notorious. It did not display the mere sins of food, or of theft or any such inglorious thing. This rug—her rug—was unique: an illustrated guide to sexual possibility as revealed in the dreams, thoughts, and actions of those her great-grandmother had known when her talent was discovered and controlled by the very court that had stripped her of her lands, leaving her and her family a duty to warn people what their thoughts might reveal to mind-reading wantons.

Conrad stood transfixed, and the alert color faded to—

"It is exquisite. May I touch?"

Beba started; she'd been watching his colors at the same time she was celebrating the great work of her family. Look! The joy, the rapture of love and lust and life. The possibilities of touch and desire, the urge to join in so many ways, to—

"Yes," she said, wanting it, for the rug ought to be touched by one who understood it. "Yes, please."

"This will serve me," he said as soon as his hands touched the nap, and then he moved closer, allowing his left hand to touch the front while his right hand pushed and kneaded from the back. The binding, the warp and weft, the colors . . .

Beba looked at him and the steel color was there again, and the sense and scent of blood, and behind all of it, she saw a man who looked not at all like the man before her, and the man was saying, "Dear boy, no house is a proper home without a good rug!" And beneath it was the sense of weapons prepared, of blood already flowing.

Which of course was impossible; she could *not* be seeing so far into this man's mind, into his intent . . .

"This is beautiful. This is perfection! This will serve me!" he said again, and now there was the scent of blood and steel, and the knowledge that some mighty work required the great work of her family.

Conrad turned and looked at her with a killer's eye and said softly, "I grieve, and it colors my thoughts. Forgive me, that I must take it from you. All I can offer you in exchange are cantra. For this rug—I have five cantra. It will be an honor to pay you, and you will honor my father, who loved rugs as much as life."

· · · ✧ · · ·

BEBA STARTED FORWARD when Joshu did, her hand firmly clasping his right, her day bag slung jauntily over shoulder, striding as if she always did this kind of thing, as if *they* always did this kind of thing.

Joshu now, he had traveled and come home, learned whatever he needed to be sure of by coming home, and was set on his plan.

Beba had never been away before, and her first glance of the stars sprinkled randomly among dozen of anonymous gridwork structures with the incongruously slow movement of elegant star vessels as counterpoint stunned her. She'd stood for moments, no doubt impeding experienced travelers, yet around her were others just as star struck at the view.

"Are you sorry?" she asked as they moved toward the lounge their tickets entitled them to, visible down a small hallway, with well-appointed doorkeepers on either side.

Joshu sighed, squeezed her hand.

"Excited is better. But I'm a salesman; I can sell things wherever I go, I can do things. You, I was so concerned for you, Beba, that they'd lock you in finally. You are sensitive and so connected to the world! You've been persistent though, and I admire you the more for it!"

Beba walked straight ahead, keeping her sight off his colors, trying not to pick up the excitement of others, the fear of others, the joy of others—and there were so many! Lights fluttered in front of her, but not the colors of someone's psyche. The lounge indicated that boarding would start on schedule for First Premium passengers on *Vashtara.*

That was them. *Their ship, their release!*

Derry had been positively amazed to hear that they were off so soon, but then she'd been willing to deal expediently. Joshu had signed the papers, wailing the while about the deal, while knowing the price was reasonable, if not good. At the last, Derry made one more effort to recruit Joshu to her bed. He'd parried it, red-eared, able to say in good conscience that yes, he certainly would be in touch with her, when he returned.

Derry, of course, had not seen them at the emigration center, where management, police, and debt services had one last shot at their record and their money, before clearing them as Class D returnables—the least desirable rating.

"Yes," she told the man without a trace of rancor, "I was the last planetary holder of the Sinner's Rug of this court order dated two hundred Standards ago. That rug has been transferred to new ownership and taken off-planet, I so attest."

She'd done that, knowing full well that Conrad Cash Sale had been away mere moments after she'd touched the container that held the rug.

He helped her pack and roll it, watching the care, concerned.

"This is not a theft," he said to her. "You do not do this under duress."

She'd managed to smile at him.

"Not duress. It is apparent that you need this rug more than I. Perhaps you and your friends will sport on it: certainly it deserves the attention and appreciation of people not afraid of joy. Perhaps," here she paused, on dangerous territory momentarily, "perhaps this can bring some measure of relief to your grief, which must be a terrible thing to be so compelling. And for me, this is relief. This is a good thing."

And then they were at the door, she and Joshu, and the door woman nodded to them from behind her glasses, saying, "We're so glad you've joined us for your trip to Brulandia. Your baggage is on-board and will be delivered to your stateroom before you board. We hope you will enjoy some cheese and wine while you wait. Brulandia is only five jumps away."

The door closed behind Beba as she vowed to never again live where ignorance was winning.

✧ Misfits ✧

Day 55, Standard Year 1393
Solcintra, Liad

It was a pellucid, temperate morning. The humidity levels were just a point lower than the theoretical "perfect comfort" zone; the sky was an arcing blue-green bowl marred by neither cloud nor threat of rain. It was, in fact, a fine day for gardening.

As were so many days on Liad.

The gardener was early at his work, having risen betimes from restless, unsettling dreams, and knowing from long experience that laboring in the clan's inner gardens was a potent cure for restlessness. Granted, the work no longer exhausted him to the point of dreamlessness, for which he had only himself to thank. Nine Standards gone, the inner gardens had been a jungle of neglect and ill-considered plantings. Now . . . he flattered himself that it was an oasis, a place of peace and beauty to soothe the spirit and calm the emotions.

To create such a place, that was certainly valuable, he thought as he turned from the portable weather station he had mounted on the garden wall—certainly such a place was of value to the clan.

As he was not, nor ever had been.

An embarrassment to the clan—oh, yes. Many times over; the transgression which had made him gardener under what Terrans so quaintly styled "house arrest," merely the last in the series of embarrassments that had begun with his birth and naming.

293

That he was also the instrument of the Clan's continued financial comfort—well, that was an embarrassment, too.

He took up his hoe and walked to the bottom of the garden, where the pesselberries wanted his attention. A small flock of foraging redbirds flew as far as the garden wall, complaints loud and urgent. One, braver than the rest, held position until the gardener was nearly upon him, and then joined his crew. Within moments their song was back to the constant low twitter he'd become accustomed to.

It was hardly his fault that Clan Lysta had once been on the verge of financial ruin, or that a mad Terran had wanted a ship. Not any ship, but a good ship, a Liaden-built ship, with up-to-date cans and mount points and drives, and—Korval's ships then as now being prebought a dozen or more years in advance—his only choice was to buy from Cochel lo'Vanna, whose clan refused to sell to any but a member of a registered clan.

The madman—one Thrugood Brunner—was not without resources. He set himself to become a member of a registered clan. He had—perhaps by chance, perhaps by reasoned searching—located Lysta, teetering on the edge of dissolution. He met with the desperate delm, an agreement was reached to publish a new Line; a contract was written, money changed hands—hey, presto! as some Terrans would have it—Lysta was saved. And Thrugood Brunner got his ship, which he soon boarded, never to return to planet or clanhouse.

But the contract. The contract had established a trust, a certain percentage of which was to be paid into the clan's operating fund every Standard for precisely as long as Line Brunner flourished in the care of Clan Lysta. This to be proven by the existence, in each generation, of a child bearing the surname Brunner and a personal name from the original Brunner's family history, a list of those names being appended to the contract.

The clan, no longer in debt, found the contract, but not the portion, to be—awkward. By the delm's word, the generational Brunners lived quietly retired, calling no attention to themselves, or to the clan which nurtured them.

Until recently, that was.

"Ichliad!" A glad, childish voice interrupted these ruminations.

He looked up and smiled as Verena rushed down the path, trailed, as ever, by orange Charzi, tail high and whiskers aquiver.

"Why are you all the way down here?" the child asked, depositing herself with abandon on the brick walk. The cat came and stood on her knee, then wandered off, as it was wont to do, to explore what new smells might have developed overnight. The birds quieted somewhat, but still muttered among the branches.

"The pesselberries must have their soil aerated, or they will not bear," he answered.

"That would be a good thing, surely?" she asked. Verena was not fond of pesselberries.

"Not all of us share your distaste for fresh fruits," he commented, wielding his hoe with a will.

"Not all fresh fruits," she objected. "Ichliad, let us make a pact! You may have all of my pesselberries, and I will have all of your kelchin fruit."

He shook his head, a Terran habit he had not been able to break. "You know quite well that kelchin fruit are nuts," he said. He gave her a glance. "And so do I."

She sighed, and squinted up at the sky. "What will the weather be today?"

"Clear and calm and placid," he answered, hoeing. "The weather on Liad is always placid."

"Always?"

"Excepting the occasional tempest along the coasts, yes. We are fortunate in the weather on our homeworld. Others are not nearly so tame."

Charzi appeared out of the bushes then and Verena was obliged to express her admiration of his beauty and prowess for the next few minutes. Ichliad plied his hoe, the rhythm of the work lulling him into a state almost of sleep—and was roused by the child.

"Ichliad," she asked, "will you go back to being a weatherman, when the delm is through punishing you?"

Go back to being a weatherman? he thought, and shook his head once more.

"Child, I have never stopped being a weatherman."

"And you're a good one, too!" she said stoutly. "You're never wrong about—"

Suddenly, unprecedented in this protected place—a downburst of hot, parched wind. The birds went silent. Beneath his feet, the ground shivered.

"Go!" He threw down his hoe, grabbed the child under her arms and yanked her to her feet. "Run! Into the house!"

"Charzi!" she objected and he pushed her, not gently, another blast of wind buffeting them, and a rumble building.

"I'll bring the cat! Go—now!"

She looked up into his face—and ran.

. . . ◇ . . .

THE NEWS WAS EVERYWHERE, driving even his delm's treasured *melant'i* plays off the house screens. Clan Korval had struck against the homeworld, opening a hole in the center of Solcintra itself. Ichliad stayed a short time among his horrified kin, then escaped upstairs to his rooms, where his private screen told the same tale over.

He listened with half an ear to the explanations, the recorded warnings, the speculations as he paced the length and breadth of his quarters, his fingers twisted together as he debated with himself.

He was an authority—an expert. Unlike most of the meteorologists who studied and graphed the subtle, agreeable weather of the homeworld, he had seen, he had studied—he understood— what would happen next. The winds would carry debris and potentially deadly particles, raining them down on others, so distant from the catastrophe that they would not think of their danger.

"They must," he whispered, "be warned."

And by whom? The scouts? Well, yes. But the scouts were stretched thin, as he heard the tale told between the sentences of the news reports. There were evacuations, teams sent in to succor the wounded. It would be—days, perhaps, before the scouts had leisure to think. He—this was his field, and it fell to him to give the warning.

He paused by the window and gazed down into the inner garden that had been his care and duty for the past nine Standards. The terms of his arrest were plain: he was to remain housebound, communicating with no one, calling no attention to himself, bringing no embarrassment to his house. Manage this for ten Standards, his delm had told him, with an ironic bow that indicated such restraint was doubtful, and his confinement would be ended, his debt to the clan's consequence paid.

Six Standard months remained until his parole. Freedom was within his reach.

And yet—

"They must," he said to the empty room, his voice striking the walls firmly, "be told."

His knowledge, his expertise—

His duty.

He had contacts, names. People who would remember him, or at least remember his work. He had only to access the communications module—unlocked, for where was the honor in obedience, if the forbidden were not available as a constant choice?

Ichliad turned from the window, walked over to the desk, sat down. His fingers moved on the keypad, and there was the screen, the program prompting him for an address.

Two relumma to freedom.

But, really, he was a weatherman. There was no choice.

· · · ✧ · · ·

Research Station Number Measton 4
Day 198, Standard Year 1382

"ICHLIAD BRUNNER to Storage Bay Three. Brunner to Storage Bay Three."

It took some moments for the noise to become sound, for the sound to become words, for the words to have meaning, for the meaning to have urgency.

Brunner looked at the remains of his solitary meal—"lunch" this would be by the cryptic schedule on the canteen wall—and realized he was done anyway. Not that the food was bad, but that his mind was far from it, his discovery of yet another bombed-out weather unit filling his thoughts. Someone on the surface was targeting the ground units—that much was certain. Why they would do so, when accurate reporting of the weather was crucial to both—or perhaps he should say, all—sides of the war being waged on the planet below—that was the puzzle.

Well, that and how he would convince the company this time to send him more units.

"Brunner to Storage Bay Three. Ichliad Brunner to Storage Bay Three!"

Sighing, he folded his assigned portable regretfully and slipped it back into its pocket. Somewhere in the latest information might be a key, a pointer, an explanation of the newest weather pattern, the one he'd hoped to pinpoint using the destroyed monitor.

At least today he'd been able to think and study at lunch. Jack was someplace else.

Never good with small talk, even among Liadens, Brunner found station-livers to be largely respectful of someone who was working. Still, there was Jacumbra Edgil—"Jack, just call me Jack and everybody'll know who you're talking about!"—who seemed to wander the station talkative and unfettered at all shifts, doing whatever it was that "Jack" did.

One was warned of Jack's approach by a chorus of subtle clicks, chirps, beeps, and clanks, some of them electronic, some born of the accidental interplay of the objects hung along his several tool belts.

There were other warnings, as well, if one were so engrossed in one's work that mere sound was disregarded. For instance, Jack was very much not of Liaden size, standing a full head taller than Brunner, carrying at least twice the weight; sometimes he blocked the overhead lights.

To hear Jack talk, which was difficult to avoid, he was personally responsible for the upkeep of the station and all its systems. How he could manage this while also being present at people's elbows during breakfast, lunch, dinner, snack, and "canteen cocktails" was hard to imagine. Still, the phrase, "Guess we'd better ask Jack," was said often enough to lend credence to his claims of technical omnipotence.

"Ichliad Brunner to Storage Bay Three! Code Eleven."

Well, he thought, picking up his tray, someone was impatient. And Code Eleven, forsooth! He was expecting no visitors, save the

Phaetera company rep, whose existence he was coming to doubt. And when had the scout designated himself as a mere "visitor"?

He deposited the tray, his thoughts again on the problem of the weather patterns below them. So much unexplained, so much seeming impossible. But there—explanations must exist, revealing what seemed impossible to be merely improbable. That was the hope. It was the reason he was here, and why the station was here. Klamath, in its eccentricities, might well demonstrate a key that could unlock the weather patterns of a thousand worlds.

* * * ✧ * * *

STORAGE BAY THREE was the area reserved for the scout when he made his frequent and largely unscheduled appearances. What the scout did when he wasn't on-station Brunner neither knew nor cared. When the scout was on-station, he dipped his fingers into everything, always asking questions, always being very busy, almost always being annoying, and most often doing all of that in the company of Jack and his clanking tool belts.

Brunner entered the access hall to Storage Bay Three at his usual brisk pace, ignoring the urge to hurry prompted by yet another iteration of the demand for his appearance. This summons was a disruption of his work, his thought, and his schedule. He was obeying it—gods forefend that he bring the scout down upon his work area!— but he would not be goaded into rushing. At least he was not like those who let their names echo through the station for a half-shift.

Ahead, the bay doors were wide open, revealing people, voices, uniforms—and Jack. For a wonder, Jack was standing quiet as the scout and a tall Terran woman dressed in a military uniform peered at something hidden by his bulk.

"Won't be a cause for trouble, then, for you? I mean political trouble. I don't think these—" That was the tall woman.

Jack saw Brunner, and Brunner saw the small hand-sign he made to the scout, one of those signs that pilots and scouts used to communicate in noisy or distracting environments. Brunner thought of the sign as, "Attend, one approaches," but he had never been formally trained in hand-talk, something he greatly regretted. He might have been taught—would have been taught!—had his delm allowed the scouts to buy his contract when he had been at the Scout Academy's meteorology school. Alas, by the time the offer was made, he had been under contract to the technical services company, Phaetera, who had paid for his advanced training.

The scout turned, bowed a polite if minimal bow of equal recognition, close enough to a Terran nod as to be indistinguishable except by one raised in an exacting house. "Tech Brunner."

Brunner returned the bow as precisely as possible. Really, it was saying too much for the scout's clan to concede equality, but perhaps the scout himself was acknowledging Brunner's scout training. If that were so, then he was actually summoned here for some purpose having to do with his work, rather than to engage in yet another rambling conversation regarding the "news" from the planet surface. Brunner knew scouts—and, alas, this particular scout—well enough to understand that those conversations were not as pointless as they seemed, though he was neither sufficiently subtle nor demented to comprehend their purpose.

"Meteorologist Ichliad Brunner Clan Lysta," the scout said now, speaking Trade tongue in deference to mixed company. "Allow me to make you known to Commander Liz Lizardi, of Lizardi's Lunatics."

"Commander," said Brunner, giving what was perhaps too curt a bow to someone of rank, but as she was both Terran and a mercenary, he doubted that she would—

Or perhaps, he thought, he had made too hasty a judgment regarding a mere mercenary's understanding of nuance. The commander returned a bow the mirror image of his own, her face studiously blank.

"Meteorologist," she said, and then, after a very quick scan for signs of rank, including a glance at his hands to see if he wore rings, she added, "Contractor, are you, Brunner?"

"Indeed," he agreed, giving her the fuller bow she had earned. "Like yourself, I assume."

She smiled slightly. "Yes, but not for your boss, I assure you."

"I thought it best to bring you together," the scout suggested firmly before either raised the conversational stakes again, "so that we might all gain advantage from an awkward situation. The commander is bringing her forces into the fray on the side of the Chilongan government. She is in need of accurate weather prediction—and is willing to supply someone to carry special equipment and give reports."

"Special equipment? I have no equipment to loan—" began Brunner—but stopped at Jack's low-key hand-motion.

Six paces to the big man's right, a backpack stood on its rack. A red-headed Liaden youth—as much of an oddity on the station as Brunner himself—in combat dress was examining the pack minutely.

"Tech Brunner," the scout said. "From your training, you will of course be familiar with the commercial version of this Stubbs MicroRanger." He used his chin to point at the backpack. "The scouts will supply this unit on loan to the station, if, in your professional opinion, it will be useful to your work. The station may then lend-lease the unit to Klamath—or to someone representing the legitimate government of Klamath. There is . . . *melant'i* at work . . . in that direction."

Brunner eyed the offered weather machine. The red-headed soldier was bent close, hands prudently behind her back, winged brows pulled together into a frown. "This is no commercial unit, Scout."

"Indeed. In comparison to the commercial Stubbs . . . This one is quite a bit more powerful, and has some additional useful features— we will of course supply the manual. Among the upgrades is the ability to transmit very long distances. It may also be set to do precision positioning and multiremote queries on its own and to act as relay. Is this capability worth the risk to equipment which costs on the order of a dozen cantra to put in place?"

"Worth how much? Maybelle's beard! And I'm supposed to just lug this around in an active zone?"

Startled, Brunner looked back to the apparent halfling who'd been studying the Stubbs.

As Liaden as she appeared, the language she spoke was Terran and the accent was—backworld, at best.

"That's not your problem—" began the commander but the halfling rushed on.

"Liz, this thing could buy Surebleak with change left over, couldn't it? Didn't you say you can buy a ship for—"

The scout laughed out loud, and cocked an eyebrow at the tall Terran at his side.

"I see you have found us willing transport, Commander."

She snorted, made a vague waving motion toward the young soldier.

"Put it on, then we'll see if you've got a worry, right, Corporal?"

The soldier's face was very unLiaden in its mobility and willingness to display emotion. The expression of the moment, if Brunner read it right, was a cross between disdain and awe.

"That an order?" she asked warily. "I can't much afford to pay this back if I drop it wrong—"

"Order," confirmed the commander, though not as sharply as she might have done. "Now, Redhead."

"Yes'm." The soldier bent to the pack.

"The question remains, Tech." The scout's voice drew Brunner's attention. "Is it worth the risk to the equipment to have the corporal carry it in what she properly names an active zone?"

Brunner sighed, shoulders rising in one of the all-encompassing shrugs that formed a great part of station lingua.

"You wish to argue philosophy, Scout? Equipment is to be used in the pursuit of information. This station exists to gather what information we can regarding the unique events upon the planet's surface."

Jack snorted. "See, I told you! Sure he wants the Stubbs on-world. You want the Stubbs on-world. The commander here, she wants the Stubbs on-world—"

"Hey, it ain't that heavy, really, is it?"

The discussion stopped as all eyes focused on the corporal and her burden. She stood as tall as she could, which was not very, and extremely straight, which was . . . admirable, given what she was wearing on her back. The unit's stand was still deployed, and she casually flipped a trip-switch on her left side, retracting it. Reaching to another switch, she said, "This one, right? The antenna?"

The scout nodded. "But not here. The unit will begin transmitting on antenna deployment and I suspect it would give a jolt to the local receivers at this range, even if all it does is protest the lack of its key."

The corporal grinned and gave a half-salute, with a cheery, "Yes, sir!" She moved her shoulders against the rig and strode away at a good clip, as if testing new boots. Out the door she went, down the corridor a dozen steps, then a quick circle back.

Brunner watched the girl-soldier with some discomfort. Certainly, she was young; at a guess, several years younger than he, and—solely in his opinion—far too young to be at war. But there, the planetary news source most usually available to the station insisted that the "free breeders" routinely armed children younger than ten Standards. What the news source did not make plain was if those children were armed defensively, or offensively.

"Security," said the scout, talking either to the room at large or to the commander, "simply means acknowledging that we have a mobile unit on the surface. We can have no secrets about this: all we are doing is making sure that the planet below gets the kind of meteorological coverage it deserves. Given the interconnectedness of all things, weather belongs to the whole world. And the weather where you are bound, my friend, can teach us something, I'm sure."

The scout looked to him; a request for agreement, perhaps, or a reminder of his question?

"Yes," Brunner murmured, directing his reply to both scout and commander. "Yes, if this item is in my inventory, it needs to be used if possible."

There. It was said. And there was another thing that needed, yet, to be said.

He turned to directly face Commander Liz Lizardi, and bowed slightly, promising an accurate account of a problematic situation. "Understand that our channels are sometimes monitored . . . Someone on the surface is searching for weather units, and destroying them. I have no doubt that by carrying such a device you will make your force . . . it could attract the attention of those you may not be sided with."

She smiled, did the commander and gave a casual salute, as if acknowledging the intent of his bow.

"Comes with the territory, sir. We're going down there to

straighten out a mess; happens the folks on the other side might not appreciate us much, with or without your piece of equipment. Weather's a big issue down there—almost another army, by what I've seen of the records. If that machine lets me know what I've got headed my way—well, sir, it's worth the risk, from where I stand."

Brunner inclined his head, accepting her summation.

"In that case, I am in favor of going forward. I require the person who is to carry the unit have some formal training beyond, 'If you push this, the machine will work.' But I myself will need to read the manuals, as this is not the machine I was trained on."

"You would, huh? Well, me too." She looked at the scout, but it was Jack who answered.

"We can hold the docking hub for you for two orbits, Liz. More'n that, it'd look like we're taking sides—"

"Understood." She made what might have been a gesture of dismissal—or a call to action, and raised her voice.

"Redhead! Front and center!"

· · · ◇ · · ·

TECH BRUNNER, the guy who was going to teach her how to use the weather rig, was short—not dumpy, just small and skinny, kinda like her—maybe shy, or maybe just nervous. Hard to tell how old he was—didn't she know how easy it was to suppose years off somebody just 'cause they were short and small? His face was smooth, except for some strainlines around his eyes and mouth, like he spent too much time in front of his screens, looking at things that didn't make him happy. His hair was what they called "ditchwater-blond" back home, not showing any gray; and his eyes were real dark brown, like high-grade chocolate. He had a good voice, firm and cool, and an accent that made it sound almost like he was singing.

He didn't have any service marks on his sleeves; his uniform was basically just ship clothes: a shirt with his name above the pocket, slacks with a name on the left rear pocket, no hatch marks. The shirt did have a cloud with a lightning bolt on the pocket, just under his name. She guessed that was maybe a company or team logo, and didn't help at all with guessing how old he might be.

He amused Liz for some reason, and she held him back to walk with her and her friend the scout, waving Redhead and the weather rig on ahead. That didn't mean she was lonely, though, 'cause the big guy—Jack, his name was—tugged right along beside her, hauling what must have been the rig's shipping crate, and pointing her the way.

Behind, the talk was half in what Redhead supposed was Liaden, half in Trade and probably half in hand-talk, too, but that didn't bounce off the walls, so she couldn't be sure. The whole situation was odd-shaped, off-center and full of politics, in Redhead's opinion. She'd gotten pretty used to odd since leaving Surebleak, even if the politics sometimes escaped her. Being close 'round Liz maybe more than most new soldiers meant she got to watch some of the inner stuff going down, though she didn't savvy all of it.

"There go, kid," her escort directed in Terran with an accent damn close to Surebleak's. "Take the corner there. I gotta bring this 'cause there's a bunch of tech stuff stowed inside, and Mr. Brunner'll be wanting that after the scout finishes sharing out today's mess o' secret. No use us working stiffs hearin' all that; just makes us anxious."

"Call me Redhead, why not?" she suggested, letting the pack settle into the slightly rounded corner of the lift. Damn if she was going back to "kid," now she had chops on her sleeve. "Or corporal."

Jack leaned against the door panel, twitching at a couple of the push plates while he craned his neck to peer down the corridor, then turned back to her.

"Corporal, is it? They must have rushed grades from what I see."

Redhead sighed inwardly, but she knew from experience that the best answer was a joke.

"Nah, not really," she said to Jack, deadpan. "I'm big for my age, is all."

He shook his head.

"You can't be young enough to be big for your age and still carry a gun for Commander Liz," he said in Trade.

She followed that without any trouble, grinning wryly.

"I've known Liz a long time. Guess she knew me longer, really, 'cause she was my mother's friend, even before I was born."

Jack nodded sagely. "Right then, she mighta known you longer—" and cut off as something on his capacious belt beeped and something else clanked. His hands moved as quick as the sounds. The beeping stopped but the clanking didn't, 'cause he was checking the location of some other stuff on the belt. He'd been doing that every so often all the time he'd been in her sight—like he couldn't stand not knowing exactly where his equipment was. She knew a couple of hands in the Lunatics like that: might call it a nervous habit, but they weren't the ones to run low on ammo or suddenly need batteries in the field. Might be Jack'd done soldiertime somewhen, though he seemed even more disinclined to salute than Tech Brunner.

Jack mumbled something and she'd said, "Huh?" before realizing he was talking to his collar. Something twerped on his belt and the lighting in the lift went up a couple notches.

"Sorry 'bout that, Corporal. Lift's got some extra solar shielding so I had to go to back-up to get the lights on. Company don't like to waste power lighting the lifts!" He glanced at her casually, left hand still doing its tour of the belt.

"Must be handy to have the overrides right on your belt!" she said, honestly admiring such efficiency.

He sighed, surprisingly deeply. "You might think so, Corporal Redhead, but answer me this: what happens when you control the overrides?"

She shook her head and shrugged, hands up, the unfamiliar mass on her back making her shift her feet, too, for balance. "Dunno. What happens?"

"When you control the overrides, sometimes you gotta make the decisions. Comes with the territory. Same with pilots, you know?" He gave her a hard look. "Same like maybe you'll hafta do, carrying all that info on your back."

"Yah," she said to Jack, nodding in agreement. "I guess that's so . . ."

Liz hit the lift, then, ahead of her escort, leaned against the wall opposite Jack, and gave him a grin. "Penthouse, if you please!"

Jack said something with his hands that Redhead couldn't see, then the door shut behind the tech and the scout, with Jack and Liz sharing a smile over their heads.

There was a beep, and the car jerked into motion, going sort of northwest according to Redhead's stomach. Jack's belt beeped and the lighting went down a notch.

"Penthouse, next stop!" he said, maybe louder than he needed to—at least, it seemed Tech Brunner thought so, if he wasn't frowning about something else entirely. The scout, tucked into the corner next to Liz, only smiled.

· · · ◇ · · ·

JACK WAS DISMANTLING the shipping crate, piling each piece just so on the conference room floor, making sure that all the pockets and cavities were empty of whatever odds and ends might have been stuffed there. He hummed as he worked, which was annoying, but Brunner kept himself busy by acting the host, quite happy to see the backs of the scout and the commander as they fled for the canteen's small bar after approving the conference area as a classroom, and after the Scout passed him a small blue envelope.

The choice of food available from the conference room fresh-case was somewhat more limited than the canteen's, but since the room was used from time to time for working meetings, it was stocked with some proper teas in addition to coffee, and it held an unreasonably wide supply of *chernubia* especially baked for Tech Brunner by the canteen's cook, who applauded his insistence that each meal should be made more memorable by one or two small sweets to choose from.

The water steaming and a selection of fruited chernubia set out upon a tray, with cups and plates, Brunner turned toward his young student, only to discover her sitting back in the soft, oversized—for her as for him—Terran conference chair, her eyes closed and breath regular. He paused, making use of the unguarded moment to study her more closely.

Her face was tanned and thin, with a spangle of freckles bridging her nose. Unlike Commander Lizardi, who wore her hair cut close and utilitarian, the halfling had made a single thick dark red braid and wrapped it around her head, like the copper crown of a barbarian princess.

Her uniform was tight to her slender throat; any jewels or necklace she might wear sealed away from his sight, but her hands, resting half-curled on her knees, were a garden of small silver and gem-chipped rings, matching those in her thin, blue veined ears. None was a Ring as one might find on a delm or even a pilot, rather they were barely more than fine wire. A child's wealth of play jewels, gaudy and gay. There might be need, he thought, of bright color and friendly glitter in the places this soldier frequented.

In other dress, and with her hair styled more fashionably, Brunner would not have been surprised to find her at Joint School, or at college, or as a passing guest in his own clanhouse.

The annoying hum ceased, reminding Brunner that he was not alone with his sleeping student. He turned to see Jack slowly unwinding from his knees to a crouched stand, where he paused for a long moment, as if feeling his age, or perhaps twinges from an old wound.

"Other stuff's all here, Brunner. I'm guessing you got the key already, 'cause that's not. Me, I gotta check some compressors. Catch you next shift!"

With remarkably few clinks and clanks, Jack stretched to his full height and touched the ceiling with one hand while the other did a quick inventory of his belts. He nodded once to himself, as if satisfied with his count, and departed.

Brunner fetched the tray, and carried it quietly to the table, unwilling to disturb the child, though his duty as well as hers demanded it. As it came about, he was spared the necessity; her eyes opened before he set the tray down, but he could not help but feel a small flicker of guilt for having disturbed her repose.

He bowed slightly, the words coming without thought. "Forgive me for disturbing your rest. I bring *chernubia* and tea, that we might study in comfort, for study we must."

The soldier blinked, and pushed herself up straight in the too-large chair.

"Sorry, sir," she said huskily, in a rush of backworld Terran. "I—uh, I mean, I guess that's Liaden. It's real pretty, but—I don't know Liaden! Terran's best, if you speak it—or Trade." She looked around the room, her eye lighting on the clock and it seemed she reached some further level of wakefulness. "The lesson," she said, cheeks coloring, "we don't have much time!"

Momentarily, Brunner's mind went blank, empty of words in any language. He hadn't realized how much he had been certain that she—how much he had needed someone who would be delighted with *chernubia*, and tea, and who would hear the language of home with pleasure . . .

"Yes," he managed at last, and found a smile for her youth and her obvious embarrassment. "Of course, I speak Terran. How else?"

• • • ✧ • • •

THEY'D SETTLED ON TECH, or Brunner or Tech Brunner; and Robertson or Redhead. So Liaden a name as "Miri" attached to one with such an accent and so misplaced a sense of food as to prefer coffee to his carefully brewed tea—that was awkward, even unacceptable. Corporal Robertson had the Terran habit of trying to shorten names, but he could not hear himself called "Liad," nor would she allow "Ich" as acceptable.

"These are great! Never had anything so good!"

It was the fifth time she had told him so, and it made him feel she was even younger than he had first supposed.

"They help make my stay here livable," he answered now. "It pleases me that they please others as well."

"That's important on something so closed up as this." She stood, snatching one last *chernubia* before donning the Stubbs as he indicated.

"It is important to stay occupied and pleased with your diet," he agreed. "So let us study basic operations. It is unlikely that you will need to deploy the DRAPIN—that is the Direct Report And Pinbeam option—which rapidly drains the energy source and requires a modicum of effort; more on this later. You will be acting as our mobile unit, and while the Stubbs can report continuously on deployment of the antenna, the antenna itself may make your travel . . . less convenient. We shall therefore assume that you will not be simultaneously traveling and transmitting. Instead, let us assume that you have arrived at a destination. Or not even a destination—let us call it not a bivouac but a simple rest stop. You then release the stand . . ."

Here Robertson did as indicated.

"The unit may be set to begin automatic operation when the stand is released. However, I understand from your commander that she prefers the reports to be under your control. To access the basic operator program, one merely inserts the key. To adjust the program from your side—if, for example, you wish to access the location transponder screen, you must insert both keys."

She looked up, gray eyes slightly squinted. "Both?"

He removed from the envelope the scout had given him all three keys; it was conceivable that she might need them all, and the idea of a "manager's key" kept safe on-station to be issued only at need, was ludicrous.

"This one," he said, handing it to her, "is basic. With this key, anyone can turn the unit on or off. You may carry it in your pocket if you like."

The basic key was flat, silver-colored, and recognizable as what it was. Unlike an everyday key, though, it was clad on several levels with a patina of a metallic insulation and had shaped insets at both ends.

Robertson accepted it without comment; her fingers were surprisingly cool as she made light contact with his hand.

"Right then," she said, nodding so deeply in agreement that at first he took it as a bow. "This is a work-day key."

"Yes. Good. A work-day key. This, too, is such a 'work-day key.'" He waved it for emphasis. "Normally, they both must be inserted in order to set local reports or alerts, or to use the unit as a communicator. If you lose one key, you may still access basic functions with the other. I will give you the override instructions before you leave for the surface. This system is to insure that little mistakes do not happen, that alerts are neither set, nor lost, easily. It is perhaps best that these two keys not be carried in the same pocket. If you have an assistant, that person might carry one."

He handed the second key over reluctantly, startled again by the cool touch of her fingers, and more so by her laugh as he held the pair up and compared them by eye.

"That'd be good, wouldn't it? Miri Robertson's assistant! Might be a long time before I'm in charge of anyone 'cept that—what is it?— Stubbs Ranger, what already knows what its doing."

He bowed, acknowledging that he had heard her.

"It often happens," translating a line from one of his nadelm's favorite *melant'i* plays, "that expectation and event are not the same. When necessity exists, conduct follows."

She looked at him firmly, gray eyes serious, and nodded once more.

"That's the way it works everywhere, ain't it? Push comes to shove, that's when you find out what somebody'll really do."

She shook herself then, as if casting off unwanted implications, and showed him the keys.

"So, all I need to do is put these in once a day and you'll get the data and whatever else you need?"

It was his turn to smile.

"If this 'stop once a day' is all that is possible, then that is what we will hope for. But we have hopes for far more than that!"

He produced one of the hardcopy instruction manuals and a series of charts he'd printed out of the station's own records. "You will know about the basics of weather from your schooling. But this world you invade—for many reasons this is not a world of standard weather."

Robertson shook her head energetically.

"Nah, you can't depend on what I know about from school. My folks never sent me to school."

After a moment, Brunner realized he might be said to be staring, and dropped his gaze.

"Surely, some education . . ." he offered, daring to look up again when he heard her short laugh.

"Not so you'd call it school. The money came in, and it went out, and school was on the list for when there was enough. Never was enough, I guess. But I do a lot of reading, you know? My mother taught me how to read. Liz—Commander Lizardi—she gets me classes to study when we got time. And, sorry . . . weather ain't been covered yet."

He raised his hand, concerned she'd feel ashamed.

"School came not easy to me, either," he offered, "for my clan also often felt the money spent better elsewhere." He sighed, and brought his focus back to the necessities of training.

"If I am able, I will send to you information explaining why you are seeing what you are seeing. The equipment can be used that way. The important point, for here and now, is that most weather texts, most weather information we have for habitable worlds, assumes some tectonic activity, some long-term patterns even on worlds mostly ocean, for the ocean has predictable currents."

He pulled a chart and placed it on the table so Robertson's gaze fell upon it easily.

"This is key. For Klamath is perhaps not really a habitable world as we would like to see one. It has not enough core definition; it has not formed . . . say that it has not formed dependable solid plates to top the mantle. Instead, all the land is on rafts! Some, like plates, are stuck to each other; in time, for all we know now, they may become plates. Others merely glance off each other like a transient crowd in a space station at boarding time, moving generally in the same direction but with independent velocity and goals.

"You are experienced at swimming?" he asked suddenly, concerned that this, too, might have been denied her by "folks" who had better use for their money than educating their youth.

"Yep. Gotta be able to swim to be a Lunatic. Why?"

"Because on Klamath, it is as if the plates are swimming. On most mature worlds the plates remain in close proximity to each other, they are bordered and ordered. They may be said to 'stick' on a volcanic vent, or quake when subsurface forces collide. Most short-term motion—that is, motion over a dozen—or a dozen dozen—Standards—that motion is limited to modest amounts caused by the grinding of plates against themselves, or plates slowly being submerged or becoming emergent. But on Klamath, the motion can be—and often is—more considerable. This motion may include 'waves' beneath the lands, making the surface bob up and down, far less stable than one would like, and altering atmospheric and ocean currents in the process."

"Sounds complicated!" The soldier stared intently at the charts, but he despaired of her comprehension.

He sighed, perhaps too loudly, and found her gaze, faintly ironic, on him.

"So what's this mean for what I gotta do, beside not get motion sick?"

He smiled, as her comment was clearly a joke. "Yes, this is good. You cannot fix the world or make the people not colonize it: they are there. So for you to stabilize the populace, for the commander to succeed in her mission, you need weather warnings and weather information. For me—for the station—what you can do is help us by reporting in as often as possible. Understand that on Klamath, everything is changeable. You may camp at night at one altitude and awake in the morning, still comfortable, at another. Each report assists us all!"

She nodded. "Guess you'll want to put that in writing to the commander. I'll do what I can, but she's gonna have to decide a lot of it."

"Yes. That is well-thought. I will make some notes for the commander. But for you, there is also this: another key. This one is a manager's key. It will permit you to leave the Stubbs on auto-function if need be, and return for it later. You might, with sufficient information, also be able to reprogram the unit for specific local necessities. This is unlikely, but you should be aware of the ranges of possibility open to you. Also, this key permits the setting of the DRAPIN, which I mentioned earlier."

Robertson shook her head lightly, as if denying the need.

"Are you sure this thing can send a pinbeam? That'd take a lot of power!"

"Indeed," he agreed. "It does require much power. So much so that it is an option we mention rather than demonstrate. This key, however, permits that." He showed it to her, a small thing, made of slightly phosphorescent blue metal.

"This must not be lost. It must be kept safe and returned to me at the end of your mission. The other keys may be replaced or circumvented, if need be. This one cannot."

He handed it to her. She held it up for frowning study.

"So it's important?" she murmured, perhaps speaking to herself. "Like treasure?"

"Like treasure," he agreed, astounded anew that this valuable and rare equipment was going to war with so volatile and naive a halfling.

"Gotcha!" She slid a finger under the top seal of her uniform and the second, as if, Brunner thought, panicked, she were disrobing!

She saw him start and laughed.

"You're safe, Tech!"

Quick, beringed fingers reached behind her neck, pulling from beneath her collar a flesh-colored cord. Following the sinuous flow of cord came a small pouch, sliding up between the open shirt-top.

"Treasures!" she said as she pulled pouch and cord over her head. She gave him a friendly grin.

"See, all mercs gotta have someplace to keep their important stuff. Some use belts, some use secret pockets, you know, for their cash and gems and cards and stuff. Me, I'm kinda skinny, and I don't own much cash but that's all right, 'cause I don't have that many treasures, either."

She casually dropped the pouch on the table and flipped it open. Within were several small metallic containers and a cloth-wrapped something—

"How 'bout I tuck it inside here?" she said, flipping the cloth open and casually exposing—Brunner stared. A clan badge? But she had denied any knowledge of Liaden! She asked for coffee, and—but the child was speaking.

"This is my best treasure, see?" she said, while Brunner strained to recognize the half-shrouded device. "Got it from my mother. I'll keep your key just as safe, if you understand me."

He looked into her face, aware that she was already folding the cloth over badge and key, returning the pouch to its hiding place while he gathered words.

"*Galandaria,*" he said in low tones, and inclined his head.

"What's that?" She showed no faintest hint of comprehension as she resealed her shirt, her rough Terran at odds with the artwork she'd called her treasure, at odds with her quick bright eyes, at odds with the moment.

Brunner looked away, let his mind run for a moment, cataloging possibility. This was not, as he had supposed, only an ignorant Terran halfling, but a woman acknowledging both her legacy and her isolation. Trusting him with her secret. With her treasure.

He had a moment to wonder why—but, there, the answer was plain. She was about to descend into danger, with her commander and her troop. Whatever necessity required her to act—to be—merely a Terran halfling, yet she could not allow him, a Liaden like herself, to be deceived.

"Yes," he said in soft Terran, accepting the burden of her secret. "I see that you will keep the key as safe as your best treasure, as I would myself."

"Right," she said. "Got that. Tell you what, if all this works out good for you, you owe me a cup of coffee, how's that? Tea's all right with these cakes, but coffee would be perfect."

He smiled at her apparent reversion to simplicity.

"I agree to owe you a cup of coffee, Robertson, and to pay promptly when we meet again."

She nodded happily. "So, you need me to memorize any frequencies or stuff? I got a real good memory."

"Let us first review the basics again," he said. "This unit can function as a communicator if need be. I am, as you know, Ichliad Brunner. You will ask for me if there is need."

* * * ◇ * * *

BRUNNER WAS WORKING ALONE in the meteorology lab when the first transmission from the Stubbs came through. This was not necessarily by happenstance. As soon as Commander Lizardi and Corporal Robertson had departed the station for their posting, he had volunteered to take what Jack called "night-shift" and what the crew in general just called Slot C. There were fewer people about then and there was often work to be caught up on from the preferred "day-shifts," of Slots A and B.

Coincidentally, Slot C was most concurrent with Miri Robertson's expected working hours of daylight.

It took several station-days for the request to go up and down the short command chain. In the interim Brunner managed to stay at work beyond his assigned shift and to arrive before, in case there should be a problem, though what he might do, if there were . . .

But, as it turned out, both his care and his worry were unnecessary.

The Stubbs came online flawlessly, registering locality and altitude, barometric pressure, wind speed, humidity. Allergens were noted, as were pollutants. Cloud cover was ranged and categorized. The somewhat variable mix of atmospheric gases was logged every ten ticks, the air temperature every ten ticks, alternating with the gases. Piggybacked on the databursts was a quick recording in her soft drawl: "The manuals say I should do a base test. Here it is. If there's a problem, the manuals say you can reset remotely or have me recalibrate."

The readings continued for a short time, and ceased in an orderly shut-down, and Brunner breathed a sigh of relief, tinged with anticipation. Now, perhaps they could get accurate—and uninterrupted!—data to work with!

Less than a quarter-day later, a new report came in, and that, too was an orderly report, sans voice, which Brunner regretted. He found Robertson's willing approach to the manuals both thoughtful and interesting. Perhaps her appointment to the weather machine was not mere whim on the commander's part after all.

Days passed, overfull of work; data came in, perhaps half the time accompanied by a recorded message from the operator. Brunner continued on Slot C, and no one complained, save the company's accountant, who felt that he should not receive a bonus for working a shift he clearly preferred. He signed a paper, waiving his right to the Slot C differential, and was left alone to do his work.

To hear the news source tell it, the introduction of "professional warriors" had taken the heart out of the enemy or enemies. All fronts were quiet; even the reports of atrocities decreased. The enemy or enemies had, the news source reported, withdrawn, to pray and to take counsel of such wise ones and elders as they had. The government in Chilonga Center, in the province where Lizardi's Lunatics had been stationed, audibly held its breath.

Brunner watched the weather, made predictions, noted his errors; he collaborated with Dr. Boylan, the planetologist, on a study of the likelihood that there was a long-term subsurface flow echoing the jet stream. The Stubbs continued to report, so whoever had been targeting the stationary weather machines seemed not to have the interest—or the means—to destroy a roving unit.

Betting pools were formed: days until the end of the war, where the next cyclone would form, which government would fall to a coup.

As always, Brunner declined to bet, but found himself importuned anyway, as those who had formed a pool on the probable length of survival of the various mercenary units inquired after the supposed "inside information" he was gaining from his contact on the surface.

In retrospect, it was a time of peaceful repose such as Brunner had rarely experienced during his tour of duty.

* * * ✧ * * *

THE FIRST HINT THAT THINGS might be returning to normal came, not from Brunner's intense study of Klamath's erratic weather systems, nor from his rather less intense study of the news reports, but from his contact on the planet's surface.

"Okay." Robertson's recorded voice sounded breathless. "Just wanted to let you know that we got through it fine, and the machine's good. Some of us got messed up and we had to send a few off to the hospital in Chilonga Center. We had real good luck, though, 'cause I read the manuals, and when I can, I have the local prediction mode up. Caught a march on the Bluebies that way. Anyhow, we're gonna be moving fast so don't expect too many updates for awhile."

What "it" had been he did not know, though he was heartened to hear that she had survived it in good health and with the Stubbs intact.

Automated reports flowed up from the surface, though there was no communication from the operator for nearly a Standard week. Brunner chose to view the arrival of the data as proof of her continued good health—after all, she had said she would be out of contact.

He went back to his work. The pressure systems had undergone a subtle and not entirely comprehensible change. Brunner pulled archives, did overlays, ran projections, sorted and resorted the data, stretching his work shift well into Slot A.

Ten days after assuring him of her survival of "it," Robertson sent another message, short and barely intelligible over a sound like ship's engine cycling.

"Wow! Lotta wind!"

And indeed there had been a lot of wind as a high and a low had fought their own battle over a quarter of the planet, starting at the pole and spiraling down across the equator where they'd formed battle lines over the tortured isthmus connecting Chilonga's embattled territories with those of their bitter invaders.

He had taken heart from that message as well; whatever fighting that may have taken place since her last contact was far from her mind at that moment.

The winds continued to grow; the shift in the pressure systems suddenly painting an all-too-cogent picture. Brunner worked longer hours still, pushing himself and the station's resources, combing the literature.

Something . . . Terran would have it that something "bad" was hovering on the horizon. One hesitated to ascribe such values to the outcome of systemic interactions. And yet something . . . at least, different, was bearing down upon them. Hints whispered to him from the altered pressure systems, from the increasing erratic winds, if only he had wit enough to understand . . .

· · ·✧· · ·

THE SCOUT STOOD BY while Brunner teased a possible pattern from the various historical models. If the scout recognized what he was doing, or knew how it might be done more efficiently, he said nothing, but that was the way of scouts; they interfered as little as possible unless you failed of doing what they wanted of you. So, for the moment at least, the scout wished him to work.

Eventually, Brunner smoothed the touch panel with a reluctant thumb, watching as the images reformed, slowing as the storm moved in reverse, dividing into two smaller storms and a smudge of low pressure. He tapped the screen again, looked up to his silent watcher.

"Service? It will be a number of minutes before the information I seek appears on screen."

The scout sighed lightly, his hands saying something Brunner couldn't read, and then said, quite abruptly, "While the data, which should belong to all of us, is encrypted, the words, which should belong only to the speaker and their intended recipient, are not."

Brunner felt his face heat. He bowed, acknowledging receipt of information. "And this is monitored where beside my own instruments, if I may know?"

"It is recorded, as a side channel, along with all the broadcasts from Klamath."

"This is not simply a science station, then?" Brunner asked sharply, though he had for some time suspected—

"Of course not, except as you allow the study of human systems in disintegration to be a science."

Brunner acknowledged the point with another bow, and looked back to his screen.

"Science can be so many things," said the scout, speaking to the wall perhaps, or to the floor, or to himself. "It can be imprecise and immediately useful and reek of technology and action, or it can be an escape of beautiful equations and elegant systems, backed by theory and distanced by case numbers and modeled meta-statistical analysis."

The scout paused as the screen Brunner was watching reformed. The storm systems moved forward once more, dutifully came together, marched across the planet picking up energy, joined two into one, and again, two into one, the cyclonic motion barely apparent early on and then—

Thumb-tap.

The systems stopped moving.

Thumb-tap.

The screen now displayed four views, all tagged with the same date and time.

The top left showed a widespread storm, faltering, moving northward above the equator with its center diffuse.

The top right showed a tight-knot of mini storms first hugging the northeastern coast above the equator, then following a wide bay north.

The bottom two veered from the northern route and crossed

the isthmus, where both blossomed into monstrous cyclonic storms. While the one on the right rushed eastward and then slowly dissipated, the one on the left veered deep into the Chilonga Mountains after striking the river delta.

Brunner knew the "why" of the blossom into major storm: on the west side of the isthmus, the ocean level was considerably higher and considerably colder than on the east side. Assuming the storm survived the not inconsiderable plunge down the cliffs of the isthmus.

"These are the major models which are now at work." Brunner said conversationally. "One and Two are most standard. Four is the 'preferred' model of my predecessor. She was very climate-oriented in her approach, I think. In going back over her work and comparing it to the standard models, I find that hers were often less wrong than those models, which is interesting given the variability we think we see."

"Less wrong is a useful trait, is it not?" murmured the scout.

They both watched as the images ran again in hypermotion, Brunner mumbling a distant, "Indeed. In theory, it is better."

Thumb-tap. Models One and Two disappeared from the screen. Three and Four immediately resized themselves, greedily filling the space.

Number Four played its image out, giving way to another image, which formed itself with a view of a cloud formation far to the west. That formation, shown as small storms, dispersed into a weak trough, then . . . the trough joined a small storm, which merged with a larger which . . . stopped about where Number Three began.

"My current model," Brunner said, "is Number Three. On screen to the left is the model that predicted the current positions within this . . ." a touch on keypads, a screen tap, an overlay.

The images were not identical by any means, but on a gross scale, storm overlaid storm, calm highs overlaid calm highs.

"Ah," said the scout, executing a small bow.

"My model works from the assumptions my predecessor made initially, modified to reflect my conclusions that we have here in Klamath a planet acting more like a gas planet than a core planet, a planet whose weather is not only driven by surface and near-surface conditions but by core convection and other inconvenient energy sources such as groundswell tides and the like."

"So there might be a paper in this for you? A publication is always good for the career!"

Brunner shook his head, his attention still mostly on the screen and the predicted, coming storm.

"I am not so sure," he said to the scout. "The information may be owned by my employer, after all. If they care to admit that it exists. At the moment, the chief is broadcasting my real-time information, but uses the old model for the official predictions he broadcasts."

The scout raised his hands, palms up.

"Chief Thurton values the neutrality of the station high, does he not?"

Brunner sighed. "Staff is under orders to write a letter of dissent to your involving the mercenary unit in our work. I am to report any actions I perform under your orders or in your name."

"Yes," said the scout, who was pacing the long axis of the room almost as if he were at exercise. "You must, of course, follow protocols. My orders to this point amount to you doing your work, making your predictions, and sharing that information with interested parties. My actions are the same; report them as you must. In the meanwhile, you must be aware that your communications with those on the surface may be public."

Now the scout favored him with a bow of direct instruction.

"As I understand matters, you are from time to time in direct contact with the party carrying your monitor. Continue that association, and share with that group your exact forecasts. You are to make the fullest use possible of the Stubbs unit. Read the manual thoroughly, and forward information as may be required to maintain the unit's performance. Report and forecast the weather accurately. I do not require you to seek out other interested parties with whom to share your predictions; simply make them, forward them to your party on the ground and to the control room where Chief Thurton must see the information shared."

He spun, standing ready on the balls of his feet, as if he expected to need to run, or leap—

"Understand me, Brunner. In so far as you are able, insure the continued performance of the Stubbs unit. That serves the purpose of the organization which hired your company and it serves my needs as scout-in-place. As to the needs of the group carrying the unit . . . inform them that I have forbidden landings by unaccredited spacecraft, and that ongoing scheduled unmanned replenishment may go forward. I have broadcast a request planetwide that civilian populations not be targeted and that I will permit landings on my approval only and by agreement of locally recognized authorities."

Brunner bowed in receipt, and considered his latest predictions.

"Then I am to suggest to—Corporal Robertson— that the Stubbs should be on a protected elevation away from rivers within three Standard days and that wind speeds of up to one-fourth the speed of sound are probable?"

The scout bowed his assent.

"You are so instructed."

. . . ⟡ . . .

"BRUNNER, you guys are life savers!"

"Please, if you are in a secure location do not leave it! You are only in the eye!"

A very slight delay and then: "Oh boy, aren't we. This has gotta be the best weather we've seen on this place. Feels great. Even smells clean, kinda like ocean!"

Yes, of course it smelled like ocean . . .

"Redhead, you are not in the center of the eye—this lull is very glancing. Mere moments. Eat something! And I must say it is very dangerous for you to move during the storm. Please do not do it again unless threatened—You are already—"

But there, he hadn't thought to start a threaded conversation, and the delay was small, so a thread was not really required.

"Are you crazy? I was hunkered right down here the whole time. Haven't moved a bit except to empty water out of my boots!"

Not moved? But, the instruments were quite clear, and quite accurate!

"Say again?"

A sound: footsteps behind him. He waved for quiet.

"I said I haven't moved!" Redhead repeated. "I felt like I was floating a couple times but there's no water here that didn't drain off! We're tucked in a grain storage ranch with everything made out o 'crete! But the rest of your info is right, hey? Been working out for you?"

Indeed, the rest of the information was useful—treasure beyond price. And her report of floating; the fact that the unit reported it had moved by nearly a meter! That required study.

"It is excellent," he told her. "You have done well, and I am very pleased!"

"Good. I'm gonna grab something to eat! Liz says a spotter claims to see a wall o' clouds. Out."

"Out," said Brunner, but she had already gone. He sighed and turned away from the monitor.

The scout stood nearby, smiling.

"The young Terrans, they are amazing. One can hear the excitement in their voices . . ."

Brunner frowned. Was it possible that the scout did not know?

"Terrans?" he murmured.

"Brunner, for this, yes, Terrans. Jack asked me—but no matter. Liz vouches for the child as from Surebleak. Liz is from Surebleak. Surebleak is Terran."

Brunner bowed in acknowledgment, allowing irony to be seen, and turned back to his equipment.

"Your point, Tech Brunner," the scout murmured, perhaps amused. "In the meanwhile, it may be well for you to produce both local and regional forecasts, as usual."

"I have been remiss," Brunner said, without looking around. "In yestermorning's recorded note from our *galandaria* was this message, which you have perhaps not heard." He touched a key.

Flat silence except for the susurration of the room's air-moving equipment, then Miri Robertson's steady voice, "Liz ain't too happy about these new landing regs. Says it sounds iffy as all get out. Wants to know if I can pinbeam a voice message outta here to merc headquarters if things get tight. Dunno what that might do to the power supply and your info." A slight hesitation, as if she was listening, then: "Liz says relay to the scout that any merc transport should be passed, no questions."

Brunner looked at the scout.

"I have not answered."

"I hear this." The scout sighed.

"Ah. Well, hear also that the girl holds the master key. When she is bored she reads the manuals."

The scout glared—and then laughed, fingers dancing out an unread phrase.

"Yes, of course! All honor to you. Were I on a strange world which is doing its best to rid itself of humankind, encircled by enemies who are trying to kill me, I would also need light reading. Liz Lizardi hires quality help. I hear this, too, Weatherman."

* * * ✧ * * *

NO MATTER HOW ENGROSSING the work, a man must sometimes tend to other necessities. Brunner acknowledged that he was becoming a danger to the data when he caught himself reviewing the same data loop for the fifth time.

Dragging himself to his quarters, he fell fully dressed into his bunk, plummeting instantly into sleep.

"Ichliad Brunner! Report to the meteorology lab!"

The words reached him in the dreamless depths, senseless as stones.

"Ichliad Brunner to the weather deck, pronto. Ichliad Brunner—"

That voice roused him, and he pushed upright, still more asleep than awake. The weather deck—Yes, surely! He had told her to call for him by name—

"Ichliad Brunner to the weather deck, pronto!" Again came the demand in Jack's big voice, the speaker at his bedside taking up the cry echoing those in the hall outside his quarters. The door buzzer gave tongue, followed by pounding.

Brunner threw himself across the room, slapped the door open and stepped back as Jack all but fell into the room.

"You're needed. Sorry to wake you."

Brunner stared. "What can possibly be worth all this—"

"Under seal," Jack interrupted. "We'll talk when we're private."

• • • ◆ • • •

HIS LAB ROOM was hardly private. The planetologist's intern huddled near the real-time monitors, openly weeping. Brunner stopped, horrified. Why had she not been given the privacy such emotion required? He looked 'round to Jack, but that noisy person had stepped over to the aux monitors, tool belts silent, for a wonder, as if he wished not to be noticed.

The scout stood with Station Chief Thurton some distance from the weeping girl, his face half-averted, as if he, too, wished to grant her seclusion. Dr. Boylan, the planetologist, stood at the intern's side, apparently taking the part of kin.

She looked up as Brunner approached, face grim.

"Ah, here you are, Weatherman. Estrava," she said, carefully touching the intern's shoulder, "was following up on my request for drift correction. We've been using the dome of the Governor's Hall as a target, it being gold-plated and reflective in a number of useful frequencies." She took a hard breath and nodded at the screen. "We need you to confirm a disaster."

The monitor she indicated displayed a looping series of images, first in false-color infrared mode, then in visible wavelengths. It repeated: an area of relatively lush valley giving way to random buildings, then to an actual urban conglomeration dominated by a bright-lit structure all out of proportion to the rest. Suddenly smoke—or possibly fog—intruded, deepening from a vague white mist to a frothy greenish mass, drifting down from the hillsides, filling the valley and the town until only the top of the building remained visible. The image cut back to infrared—

"An unusual flow," Brunner said slowly. "It seems very dense. Were this some backworld, I would say smog. But this is Klamath, after all; fluke winds might conceivably have trapped a sulfur exhalation and created such a fog."

"Not fog," the intern moaned, half-bent over the counter, like a bird favoring a broken wing. "Not fog. Not fog."

Brunner turned to her, keeping his face politely neutral, which was the least he could do for her distress. He'd had little enough to do with Estrava, the planetologist having laid claim to the bulk of her hours, and she nervous of Liadens in any case.

"It's not fog," she said shrilly, straightening to stare directly into his eyes. "Look at it! The spectrum is wrong, the flow is wrong—people are dying!"

Brunner looked as directed, frowning at the lack of definition.

"What have we, then?" he asked the room at large, stepping forward, his fingers already on the fine controls.

It was the scout who answered.

"Death," he said, his voice neutral to the point of aggression. He bowed, firmly, a bow of duty required.

"As we need to know for certain, Ichliad Brunner. First, please confirm that what we see here is a poison gas. If this is the case we will wish to know of its dispersal range, potential mixing, and to track it if we might—"

"Scout, this station is to remain neutral!" The station chief gestured with his hands, not with sense as the pilots might, but conveying urgency nonetheless. "The treaty requires that we not interfere."

"I require information!" the scout interrupted. "Your station is here at my whim, Chief Thurton."

"I think Phaetera might have something to say to that, sir!" the chief snapped.

Brunner turned from the monitor and raised his hands, one to each combatant, seeking instruction.

Chief Thurton drew a hard breath, turned his back on the scout, and walked away.

"Do as he says, Brunner. You'll give me a full report of all actions you perform for this man, and we will both sign a statement that you act under duress, as I do."

Brunner bowed at the retreating back.

"And these coordinates," he said to the helpful room, "do I have them?"

"In the south," the intern whispered. "Chilonga Center."

* * * ◇ * * *

ON CIVILIZED WORLDS, among civilized people, disasters are accidents or acts of nature; they are not premeditated.

In such times, a meteorologist's declaration of disaster insures the issue of worldwide warnings and unleashes a gathering of willing assistance. Emergency plans bring together medical teams, rescue teams, housing teams—

Klamath hung below the station, uncaring, uncivilized.

Still, it was his necessity as meteorologist to confirm and declare the windborne poisons, the act of intentional war, a disaster.

Perhaps someone would be listening, and thus be warned and saved.

So his thoughts went, and he recorded the thing, and set thumb to it.

The scout bowed.

"A disaster declared, I hereby interdict and quarantine Klamath as a hazard to space travelers."

Brunner stared at the scout.

"You cannot," he said, hearing the protest as if it was spoken by someone else.

"I can and I do," the scout responded, weariness and sorrow apparent on a worn face. "Believe I do it lightly if you must."

Brunner brushed the words aside. They were alone in his lab and had been for several hours. Brunner had backtracked the flow; the scout, on an auxiliary machine, had taken to himself the tedious task of identifying the chemicals by their spectrographic signatures and dispersal fugacity.

"The mercenaries," Brunner said now, arguing, gods, with a scout! "The off-world techs serving the Chilongan government. The natives who have filed for immigration—"

The scout slid off the stool and made the bow of accepting necessary burdens.

"I must," he said, and waved unsteadily at the microphone.

"Tell the girl—you see? I take that burden, as well. Tell her, then get some sleep, Comrade. You will be needed at your board soon enough."

· · · ✧ · · ·

"QUARANTINED," Brunner said into microphone, taking especial care with his pronunciation of the Terran.

"I repeat, the scout has interdicted Klamath, and placed it under quarantine." He took a breath, knowing his words were potentially recorded in records besides that of the Stubbs unit.

"Poison gas has been deployed against civilian targets in contravention of general usage of warfare."

The planetologist's equipment was powerful enough to allow him to see bodies lying on the streets, to see fires burning in the city, to watch Klamath's fickle winds sweeping the vapors out of the city in a strong flow to the south.

Not one, but three aerosol dispersants had been loosed upon Chilonga Center. The first sank rapidly, displacing oxygen, and suffocating some quickly. The second gas, more mistlike, hovered and flowed in every breeze, torturing the lungs and eyes of any who survived, eating at their skins. The third hung higher, and featured a potential late-stage crystallization so that it might precipitate and leave a residue of skin-dangerous toxics.

Cursing the winds under his breath, he had checked the Stubbs' last reported location, all but weeping when he found it east to northeast of Chilonga Center. Miri Robertson, Corporal Redhead— the winds blew past her. In a planetary day, perhaps two, the chemicals would have dispersed entirely, and what was left of the city could be entered.

All of this he told the Stubbs, remote and unreachable, and when he was finished, he whispered, "Please acknowledge."

There was no reply. He told himself that it was the middle of her night; that her pattern was to report in the evenings, and sometimes very early in the morning. He told himself that she was safe, well away from the destruction in the city; that she would call, if she had need of him.

He kept the line open anyway, the microphone clipped to his shirt, the Stubbs' uplink window open in the corner of his workscreen.

In the meanwhile, he started literature searches: toxic flows, aerosol dispersal, plume pollutants, plume tracking, microclimactic poison control, history of planetary quarantines and interdictions, general usage of warfare, strategic poison, tactical toxics, history of Terran Mercenary Units.

The histories held an uncomfortable number of references to merc units being lost without record. He put them aside for later reading and turned his attention to those things he might do that would increase the chances of one particular mercenary unit surviving its odds.

* * * ⟡ * * *

HIS WORK WAS TWICE INTERRUPTED by crew looking for updated information for the on-going betting. He dealt with them—not as they deserved—locked the door, disabled the bell and returned to the literature. Eventually, he found a treatise specifically on defensive meteorology and the tracking of dangerous atmospherics. In the information about aerosols there were unpleasant images, but also some useful approximations he could add to the station's regular monitoring.

He might even be able to—but motion distracted him, and then sounds.

Information was flowing from the Stubbs to his monitor; from the speaker came sharp cracking sounds, then—

"You there, Brunner?"

He touched the microphone. "Here, *Galandaria*."

"Good! Hey, nothing like a little gunfire to get you focused, right?" Despite the cheery phrasing, she sounded . . . breathless. Worn. Brunner frowned, closing his eyes so that he might hear her better.

"Yeah, that was bad, what happened in the city. We lost a couple of ours in the hospital over there. I—not the way I'd wanna go, y'know? Anyhow, business—Liz wants to know what that means if we get a recall, that quarantine. She sent it upline to our employer but no answer yet. Got anything you can tell me? Before I forget—this Stubbs? It's great! Got some dings in it but it took a couple for me and bounced 'em right out. Pretty open here, don't think Liz is gonna keep us—Right. Gotta go. I'm glad you was there. Out."

She was gone, pushed by her necessities, and he had not even said—What? he asked himself. Go carefully? Be alert? Don't breathe tainted air?

Perhaps he should have demanded a fuller accounting of the damage to the Stubbs, but to what end? A glance at the screen told him that the self-test had registered no warnings, so the station's unit must be intact. Unlike Redhead's unit, which had "lost a couple of ours . . ."

As to Commander Lizardi's query—certainly, there was nothing he, caught between the station chief and the scout, could tell her. Chief Thurton was adamant in neutrality, while the scout . . . while the scout played whatever game the scout was embroiled in.

What he could do was have available the best possible wind charts, produce the most accurate weather forecast, and not forget that down there were people relying on him. On him!

. . . ⟡ . . .

LIZ DIDN'T SAY A WORD: just nodded as she went by.

And what was Liz gonna say anyway, Redhead thought, not much more than half worried. Skel was a Lunatic, she was a Lunatic . . . and . . . and. . . damn. She sighed and finished sealing up her uniform.

She'd drawn first clean-up, and now here was Skel already, washed up himself and holding a cup of coffee out to her like it was a prize. That was nice, she thought. Warming. So she took the cup like it *was* a prize, grinned at him, and worried a little more.

There was plenty to worry about, and not just maybe Liz not liking it that she'd partnered up with Skel. Folks had been skittish before word about Klamath being under blanket quarantine had gotten into the general need-to-know pool. Now—hell, Liz was skittish, Skel was skittish, Auifme was downright dangerous, and the liaison the Chilongan government'd given them was scared out of his prayer beads. 'Course, he'd been that way since day one, on account of being stuck all by his lonesome with a buncha Unpious, Outsiders, Orbiteers, Freelovers, and—damn if there wasn't a dozen more not-exactly-appreciative names the man had laid on the Lunatics. Scandal'd said it was a good thing they were on his side, else he'd really be calling in the long guns, which had made the knot of 'em crouched together over quick rations laugh, and the liaison rattle his beads.

Now Skel, Redhead thought, turning her mind to more cheerfuller things, he'd kinda surprised her last night; caught up to her right after she'd tucked the rig in with proper camouflage and getting ready to tuck in herself. Sat his pretty tall self down right there beside where she'd been going over her vitamins to make sure she was up to date and said it right out.

"Hardly like it's a fancy invite, Redhead, but you know, we get along right well and there ain't no time presently for Liz to approve us a proper Hundred Hours to get all perfumed and slinky and everything."

She'd blinked at him, not believing, on account of there was an unofficial moratorium on asking Miri since the Grawn brothers had cut each other awhile back about who was going to ask her—and she'd have told them both no, anyhow. Sorry about them, sort of; died in that damn hospital the liaison got them sent off to.

But Skel'd said his piece, pointed out that weren't neither of them on guard schedule, and that he did have coffee, smokes, and stringent cloth, too, among other supplies what could clean the sweat off and give them some distance from this land that moved like water and the 'way too many crazy people who were trying to kill them.

She'd smiled, felt her heart beating faster—and faster again—when he lost a bit of his seriousness and smiled, too.

"Hundred Hours is right expensive," she said. "Don't know I could buy in to it . . ."

He'd laughed, and relaxed some more, like she'd said something right.

"Oh, hell, I'd pick up the Hundred Hours. I mean, I know what a newer 'cruit's got to worry with, 'spense wise. But like I say, as is, even if we get to town down here, ain't none of these folks'll rent us a side-by-side lunch seat much less a big soft room with a big soft bed . . ."

He'd paused, looking some tentative, and she was sure feeling the same. It was funny, kinda, to see him that way when he could pick up four launch tubes and a long-arm and go wading into battle. She liked Skel fine—always had, and she wouldn't mind—but the man had a right to know.

"Not sure," she said, glancing down at her boots, her uniform slacks, her shirt-front. "Umm . . . Not sure I can give you the best time, see? It'd be learning on the job mostly for me, kinda, not like—I mean."

He didn't say anything but he'd rearranged himself, getting

cross-legged, and close enough that she could see the scrapes on his boot soles and the slot where he'd been knocked off his feet the other day, the bullet just creasing the shoe. Hell, if the shot had struck true, he could have been back there in Chilonga Center with the Grawns.

"Your call, Miri. We can bunk up here if you want, or I got me a spot with three ways out and some quiet, down in a little hollow. You want, you can just sleep."

She smiled and realized that she was smiling so low and slow she was laughing, too.

She looked into his eyes then. Still smiling.

"Got coffee and stringent, huh?"

He nodded, just his eyes smiling, and it came to her, forcibly, that she didn't want to sleep all alone, with just the weather machine to wake up to.

She stood up and stretched, as much like a cat as she could, before reaching a hand down to him.

"Let's see who snores first."

* * * ◇ * * *

"'MORNING." Robertson's voice was softer than usual. Brunner touched the volume control, increasing the gain slightly. "Smokey down here," she murmured. "Been that way the last three days; getting worse, seems like—"

On the station, Brunner nodded, and carefully did not sigh.

"There are large fires burning in the grain belts on both the major continents," he told her, keeping his voice merely informative. She had no need, after all, to carry the burden of his anger. Idiots, fools, and— but, no. That was for later. Now, there were other necessities to be served.

"Some of the forests also seem to have been set on fire. I see plumes all over the planet from installations and communities that have been . . . set afire."

"Yeah, they asked us to start burning things awhile back. Ain't in our job description. Seems they got some kind of fetish 'bout fire cleaning things up—you know, purifying."

Robertson coughed; Brunner pushed a button to download a satellite image to the Stubbs' screen.

"Your location is the blinking green dot," he said. "The other green dots are your most recent report points. The valley directly ahead is very smoky—you can see that there are four distinct plumes which then merge . . . I believe that all of the major communities in your area have burned or are burning; certainly the crop fields have burnt."

A pause, broken by her sigh.

"Guess we won't capture much there. We was supposed to be moving on one of them towns to meet . . . well . . ."

He thumbed the plate, waited.

"Huh. What's this about winter? It got pretty cool last night, even for a girl from Surebleak. I'd have had damn frosty toes without help— Hey! That looks ugly as all get out!"

She was multithreading, though there was scarcely need—or maybe, he thought, there was. Who knew how long she had until the order came to move? Threading was an efficient way to share information.

So. "Winter does come," he said, picking up each thread in turn. "A very strong winter on much of the planet, according to the records. The snowcaps triple in size at the poles. But there are still eighty to one hundred planet days until that is a concern for you. Yes, it is ugly. Easily one hundred and fifty major fires in both hemispheres; on the plains up north there is effectively a single fire half the width of the continent."

A sound came out of the speaker, as if of a boot against rock, followed by a murmured question, Redhead's soft, "I dunno—"

A new voice emerged from the speaker, crisp and tight.

"Commander Lizardi here. My weather reporter says it looks like the locals are burning themselves out of house and home. If the scout is available, relay this to his attention. News of the quarantine has been a catalyst for major upheaval within power structures. Violent upheaval, even by local standards. My groundstation for our tactical satellite has been destroyed by ground forces, and the Chilongan government that hired me has been in transition this last five-day, leaving me with no current contact up-line despite reports that the north is bringing a major invasion force down on the continent. If the government that hired me is gone, I need to withdraw. Repeat: we have no assurance of contracted withdrawal at this point. We also have attracted a few dozen off-world noncombatants who travel in our train. The scout has my contact radio frequencies and I expect them used appropriately.

"We're moving now. Lizardi out."

· · · ◇ · · ·

"BRUNNER, FROM THIS POINT ON you will have an assistant on duty with you at all times while you are in the meteorology lab."

Chief Thurton stood beside his own desk in his own office, hand clenching and unclenching nervously.

"An assistant?" Brunner stared, wondering if he looked upon madness, or only exhaustion.

"We have no such an assistant available," he pointed out. "Shall you assign the intern's hours to mine, it might be possible."

"The intern . . . is on sick-call. She is . . . unreliable. I note that I don't have your letter on file. I need it as soon as possible. You— through the orders of the scout, or by your own choice—are on the verge of violating our neutrality."

"Indeed," he murmured, keeping his voice calm, his posture non-argumentative. "By your direction, I follow the scout's necessity. And the station's—am I not to preserve the function of the monitor?"

"Liz Lizardi is a combatant, as is the operator of the equipment. You should not be carrying messages of a tactical nature for the scout from Lizardi!"

The chief spun, paced; he stared at the monitors with their images of smoke-streaked atmosphere.

"Am I," Brunner asked carefully, "relieved of the command to follow the scout's orders? The equipment on-world was supplied for our use by the scout."

Abruptly, the chief sat behind his desk, still if not at ease. He closed his eyes, and spoke softly, enunciating each word with great care.

"Until such time as we are able to assign an assistant for you, you will record any and all activity within the laboratory, you will forward the text of any and all communications with the ground, with the Lunatics, as soon as it is completed. I have found a dozen or more conversations you've had with that soldier in the files, contacts you've never mentioned . . ."

Brunner bowed, keeping the wave of frustrated confusion in check with an effort. This conversation was far too similar to the senseless interrogations regarding *melant'i*, proper conduct, and "civilized behavior" that his halfling self had endured from delm and nadelm to be borne with true calmness.

"It is as you say, Chief. The conversations were brief and part of the record. It seems . . . profitable . . . to be in touch with the one operating the unit, and in fact to ascertain that the operator is intact enough to operate it properly. The unit is in a war zone, and I am told I am responsible for it!"

The chief opened his eyes.

"I see. In fact, your motives are pure and your thought wise." He took a hard breath. "Allow me to be specific. Do forward messages as they occur. Do not initiate any conversation with the ground which are not in response to their queries or actual operational necessity. Do not contact any other ground units or respond to any outside requests for information; all such must go through my office. Do not argue with the scout, but if he gives you further instructions, report them to me for clarity before carrying them out."

Brunner bowed again and turned to—

"Brunner—" The chief called him back. "Maybe you don't understand your situation—the precarious situation of this station with regard to the—situation on the planet. As a result of the scout's declaration of quarantine, the so-called legitimate planetary government has vanished, giving rise to two entities who now claim to be in control. A third has announced its willingness—and ability— to destroy 'all interlopers in the system.' At one point, this was a civilized world and they had means to back that threat up. A space station, as I am sure I don't need to tell you, is a very, very vulnerable habitat."

Brunner bowed once more, speechless. The chief collapsed against the back of his chair, boneless with emotion and waved an incoherent hand.

"Go!"

• • •✧• • •

REDHEAD shut the Stubbs down and pushed up off her knees. Skel looked 'round from where he'd been watching for her, his face black with ash.

"Get 'im?"

"Just static. I think that roll down the hill might've shook something loose," she said, pulling the now-familiar burden up over her shoulders, and settling it with a wince. Truth told, that tumble hadn't done her a lot of good, either. Skel'd wrapped the ribs for her, but there wasn't much else to do about the bruises and contact burns than ignore 'em.

"Best let's catch up," she said. "I'll try again tonight."

• • •✧• • •

THERE WAS ACTIVITY in the Chilongan isthmus. Heavy equipment working between the mismatched sea walls. Brunner upped the magnification, trying to see what they were about, conscientiously recording to the planetologist's queue.

Could they be digging? he wondered. But what—

Alarms went off, not just in his lab, but all over the station, raucous noise bouncing against walls and ear drums.

Brunner spun away from his screen, trying to catalog the racket— alarms only, no instruction to abandon ship, or report of sections sealed, only—

Jack, clanking in at a run, a device of some sort in his hand.

"What is it?" Brunner yelled, over the unabated clamor.

"Neutrons! Look to your station screen!"

Brunner spun back, slapping the keypad as the alarms reached a crescendo, faltered, died.

"High Energy Particle Alert" flashed across the station information screen. "Check badges now."

"Jack here, we're fine in Science A." A glance showed him listening intently before he said, "Then recalibrate. It's not an error."

Brunner snatched the badge from his pocket, confirmed that it was a perfect, unblemished white, spun back—

Jack waved him 'round again. "Take a look realtime—someone's shooting off big stuff!"

The alarm gave tongue again; ceasing almost at once.

"Are we attacked?" Brunner demanded, his fingers calling up satellites and long-range scans.

"Dunno," Jack admitted, flipping through his beltside inventory. "We're looking secure right now. Bridge didn't mention incoming."

Jack walked around the lab, casually, fingers still busy along his belts. "Yeah, this'll flush out what tech's left, I'm guessing—"

The alarms blared again; Jack flashed his scanner, touched his collar, listened, then wandered over to stand next to Brunner.

"Not aimed at us," he said, as the alarm screamed into silence. "Air bursts, off on the limb. Mostly neutron and gamma stuff but our shielding's up to it . . . you'll have some tracking to do."

"But, the radiation! They'll kill everyone!"

Jack made a noise like a laugh without energy, and patted the top of Brunner's monitor as if it were a pet in need of reassurance.

"Nah. Only if they do it right. Likely they don't have enough N-bombs to do everybody in that way. Gotta hand it to 'em, though; between the gas, and the nukes and burning everything that'll take a flame, they might've figured out how to manage it, anyhow."

Speechless, Brunner brought the tracking screen to full magnification, moving the satellite to cover the area of the Stubbs' last report, while he fingered up the Stubbs' screen. Even as the window came live, data began to flow. Brunner closed his eyes against the wave of relief, took a breath and touched the send button.

"Miri Robertson, please alert. Miri Robertson—"

The response was as instantaneous as the minor lag allowed. "Brunner! Am I glad to hear your voice! Tried to get you earlier, but the machine wasn't getting anything but static! Anyhow, we're ready for a forced march outta here. Locals are gone crazy; had a bunch attack us with sticks—carrying candles like they was going to light us out of the way. Another bunch just sat down in front of us and shot their own brains out—"

"*Galandaria*, they are using nuclear weapons on each other."

A pause; a long, long pause—

"Say again, Brunner." Absolutely serious, her voice, all trace of childish exuberance extinguished.

"We are recording . . ." he said, keeping his voice calm, so calm, for her sake. Jack shifted at his side, making room for the scout.

". . . we are recording nuclear weapons blasts," Brunner said into the microphone. "High-energy particle counts. I have not had opportunity to analyze, but—"

"Right. Hold that there. I'll see if I can get Liz here to—damn!" There were sounds, popping, hisses, explosions. "Bastards coming over the hill! I'll call!" The speaker went dead.

"Redhead!" He slapped at the switch, knowing it futile. On the screen, the instrument reports flowing in from the Stubbs cycled from active, to collate, to archive.

. . . ⋄ . . .

JACK WAS STILL, as it turned out, in the weather room when Brunner returned from his nightmare-riddled off-shift. He lounged in Brunner's chair, feet propped up on the instrument stool. He was awake, as were the monitors, and seemed none the less for the wear. Brunner's mood, already black, darkened.

"Jack, I see now what makes you so valuable to this station. You never sleep and you are always concerned of things you have no need to know!"

Jack grinned and bowed a meaningless, half-reclined bow.

"We're alike that way, aren't we? And yeah—my sleep center took a hit when I was on a mission, back when I was the age of your redhead down there. Well, pretty much all of me took a hit, tell the truth. Got put in an autodoc for about a week . . . and came out mostly better, 'cept I can't sleep more'n about three hours at a time."

Brunner shook his head, looking around at the busy screens.

"What happened?" he demanded.

"Well, I survived and found a job using my unique talents—"

Brunner bristled, strode over to his main screen.

"I know," Jack said, rising with a minimum of clank and clatter. He bowed; a surprisingly apt bow of a colleague relinquishing activity to an equal. "It ain't funny, but it's my only defense right now."

Sighing, Brunner returned the bow. "Now tell me: down there—what has happened?"

Jack rubbed his face wearily. "They're killing each other. Not a peep from our weather station. Every time the terminator hits a new planetary time zone, bombs go off. Looks like somebody's answering somebody else back. There's been a couple of pretty big bombs go off up north, random times, like maybe they had to be delivered in person. I think there's been more gas, too, but it's hard to tell with all the other—Anyhow, I saved it all for you."

Brunner stared at the screens full with smoke, fire, doom and destruction. He leaned against the counter, pushing hard to counteract the shaking.

"To what can they aspire?" he whispered in Liaden. "What can they achieve?"

"I guess," Jack answered, in quiet Terran, "that they can be right."

Still shaking, Brunner took his seat, riffled screens, counted seventeen marked explosions on the charts. He had no way of knowing dispersal rates at this point but many were already thinning rapidly. One in the north was very heavy, and he zoomed the map in to take a closer look.

"Was the south attempting to destroy the rest of the farmlands?"

Jack looked over his shoulder, shook his head.

"That's centered on a small range of hills. Might've been the Chilongans were after a base, a treasure house—something buried for protection."

The door opened, admitting the scout. He waved toward the wall and Brunner reluctantly put the image of the whole hemisphere on the big screen, with the terminator moving relentlessly west.

"That could be bad downwind," said the scout, shockingly matter-of-fact. "We'd need twelve dozen automated Stubbs to begin tracking. Perhaps we could get by with six dozen if we rule out a need to—"

"Rate they're going at it," Jack broke in, "won't be any reason to track it but science."

"We shall see. I have spoken to the chief, who informs me that the station cannot accept more than ten dozen refugees, and that only with the assurance that there be no local interference and that ships will be on the way to offload them soonest."

"No local interference? Surely—" Brunner was watching the clock and the terminator on screen, bringing the satellite online to the old coordinates—

"Nothing there," Jack told him. "Trees, some. Burn marks. Couldn't catch anything moving but the IR isn't that good—"

"There!" the scout shouted, not quite as loud as the alarm.

Jack muttered something, his belt clanked briefly and the alarm shut abruptly off.

"What are they doing?" Even from here there were noticeable points of light, all concentrated.

"Carpet bombing. Nuclear bombing on the isthmus."

The alarms sounded again as two very bright spots blossomed, beeped as several more—

. . . and stopped.

". . . here. Dawn shows us clear; we blew the bridge and—"

"Miri!"

Brunner slapped at the switch.

"Miri!"

"Got static, Tech, are you—There, gotcha. Yeah, it's me. Most of us got through, but we picked up some damage. The Stubbs, it bounced a couple with my name on 'em."

The station alarm sounded, stopped.

". . . so none of 'em are dependable. Hey, sounds like you got some hoorah going up there."

"Miri, Miri, do you know they are still using nuclear weapons? Several dozens or more. All over the world. Many, thirty degrees northeast of you. The—"

"Right, we thought something was going on. Locals suiciding, station control ain't answering—doesn't acknowledge."

The scout made a small sound, and Jack said, "Why you think I'm down here? Tried to answer the phone, stupid old man that I've come to be."

"No," the scout said sharply, "look at the isthmus!"

The low sun angle and remains of expanding clouds made the seeing difficult; but the intent appeared clear. The excavation he had noticed so many days ago had been completed—perhaps by the bombing—and stretching from one ocean to the other.

Brunner took a hard breath. "Miri, it is good that you are far from a coast," he murmured, his fingers keying his cameras to record, while Jack moved away. "We shall need to speak with Commander Lizardi."

The alarm beeped, but barely. Around it, he heard Jack paging the planetologist.

"... with the wounded. I'll grab her when I can. Be there, right?"

"We will be here," Brunner promised. "Next orbit."

• • • ✧ • • •

DR. BOYLAN WAS ... delighted.

"Do you see what they've done? They have removed the isthmus, and that—and that has done something unprecedented on an inhabited world. There are shockwaves registering on the seismographs, and not simply the explosives. They've significantly altered the actual surface structures—and they've created a triple tsunami as well! Something else is going on—but that will take days to confirm, and perhaps millennia to conclude!"

Brunner closed his eyes against this ghoulish enthusiasm while trying to visualize the changes, the—

"I believe the flow of water has upset the balance of the underlying plates," she went on, "and may have even broken the link! They'd be free to float—"

"Brunner! We will need as much as you can get in the way of gas analysis, for they may well have released the oceanic methane clathrates. Oh, that's a delicate balance indeed, and given the odd sediment formations here, and the subsurface temperature variations, we could be looking at a cascade of undersea landslides and quakes, reinforcing a continental redistribution—"

"The jet streams," Brunner managed to get in, "should not be greatly affected, but the currents—much of my database will need to be rebuilt, and we have no reliable reporting scheme—"

Boylan fizzed on, lost in the beauty of the cataclysm. "Imagine! A complete change in the ocean currents occurring nearly instantly! Storm systems and climate disrupted on the spot! Given the elasticity of the plates, who knows but that we might get volcanism out of this?"

"The people," Brunner said, forcefully. "The survivors—"

Boylan's lips straightened. She looked at him, and pointed at the missing isthmus.

"What we need to do now is study and record the processes and phenomena that have been unleashed," she said firmly. "The people will have to be left to historians, don't you think?"

Brunner's glance sought the scout, who took a breath and bowed low—excessive respect for one far exceeding the bower's humble estate.

"Dr. Boylan," he murmured, honey-voiced. "Your enthusiasm for science is well known and manifest. I wonder if you might have the means among your programs, or"—he bowed to Brunner as might one to a comrade—"if you, Ichliad Brunner, might have among yours, a means to predict where these triple tsunami might strike, and when? Perhaps we are best placed to offer warning, if not solace, to those who still live."

· · ·✧· · ·

THERE WAS NO RESPONSE to Brunner's call on the following orbit, and nothing on the automatics indicating that the Stubbs was online. Chief Thurton, apparently again against objections, permitted the station to broadcast a multiband warning to the world below once the scout pointed out that he might do the same from the comfort of his own ship, if the station preferred not to.

As to specific warnings, that was barely possible. A tsunami travels transparently in open ocean, its wave a rapid but nearly invisible swell in an already tumultuous world. They had no resources to determine speed, nor even to insure that the first burst of monster wave against nearby shores had continued beyond the initial coastline.

Eventually, Jack was pressed into service with the satellite, sampling coasts and islands visually, with his observations of specific sites added to the warning the scout gave. What lives were affected by this they could not tell: the surface spoke not at all to them, along any of the regular bands. Periodically he returned to view the isthmus area where a few sandy shoals amidst the deep gash of a river of darker water triumphantly flowing from the west were all that was left of the former barrier.

"An army of liberation?" Jack asked heavily of the room. "Is that what was here?"

"Does it matter?" Boylan answered impatiently. "They are beyond concern at this point, are they not?"

Brunner held to his tasks and said nothing, working as if he could prevent further disaster by the strength and purity of his research.

Eventually, the scout returned, bearing with him a station-issue portable.

Making a bow of respectful request to equals, he waved the portable as if it were a child's rattle or toy.

"The main computer was able to share with me demographic information reported by planetary authorities, and later by those splinter groups claiming authority. Some of it conflicts, some of it is probably purposefully wrong. I would like to use overlays of the various records you have of the last Standard, with particular emphasis on the past three days."

This was said to the room at large.

Jack looked at Boylan, who was tending her screens, working as if the words had not been said.

Brunner sighed and bowed, finding it within himself to add the flourish which brought his acceptance close to that of accepting a comrade's necessity.

"Yes," agreed the scout, "there is some of that, isn't there?"

"Some of what?" asked Boylan, raising her face from her work.

"Must be a Liaden thing," Jack said, rolling his eyes, and nodded at the scout. "How can I help?"

* * * ◇ * * *

LIZ WAS TALKING TO THE SCOUT via the Stubbs, and she was not happy. Redhead hovered nearby, one eye on the machine and the other on the horizon. The air was bad, pollution and radiation levels high—she saw it all on the screen as the Stubbs did its upload.

"The shuttles that brought us down might still exist," Liz was saying, sounding like she'd be mad if she wasn't so damn tired. "So what? They're hellengone back down where the city used to—"

"In that case," the scout interrupted, "they do not exist, my friend. Nothing exists there anymore."

Liz rubbed her face.

"I've broadcast a plea for assistance," the scout continued, "but Klamath has not been a good neighbor these last dozen years and it is painfully clear that there is no immediate commercial advantage to be had."

Liz shook her head. "Merc unit here. I don't have much in the way of bargaining chips, but I do have some off-planet resources. Beam merc headquarters, tell 'em Lizardi's good for the fare—."

Redhead saw it first, the tell-tale wobble in the land.

"Quake, clear and down!" She was parched, and her voice didn't travel; Skel bellowed a repeat before going down flat.

Exhausted Lunatics ran from under tree and makeshift shelters. You didn't want to be under anything when the wave came through and you didn't want to be standing, either—in fact, you couldn't; it was like trying to stand on a tarp stretched out over the sea with the tide coming in.

Whomp!

Redhead was flat when the roll hit, and Liz, already sitting cross-legged, bobbed around as the dirt groaned and a few more trees fell, and that part was over.

Now came the hard part for her: the ground felt unsteady and swollen under her, like it was thinking about splitting open or folding over, or—

The second stage passed, too, and she sighed into the scorched ground before pushing upright. Liz was still at the Stubbs; she swept her hand out toward the scattered Lunatics—

"Injury check!"

Redhead rose unsteadily and hinted at a salute with her right hand while grabbing up the staff she'd picked up from downwood. Her speed and size conspired, giving her a chance to get through tree-fall and such in a hurry. The circuit here was familiar, and this time there were no new casualties among the troops.

The civilians—there were still a few out there, and as long as they didn't actively shoot or throw rocks, it didn't matter if they came along. They'd already been on short rations and shorter morale when they'd stumbled on the Lunatics and their grasp of Trade and common

Terran was less than good. Some of them still grabbed for their amulets and lucky pieces instead of hightailing to open land—and there were a couple more among them injured.

She got back to the Stubbs in time to hear an exasperated Liz snap, "Tidal? We're a good three days' march from anything approaching shoreside, assuming I can still read a map. Unless things have changed—"

"The tsunami made some new dents, but nothing that extreme," the scout offered. "The underplates themselves are doing something we can't quantify yet. The planetologist and the weatherman are working to define—to predict. Moment . . . Ah. Tech Brunner shows me that your location gained altitude in the last upheaval. Higher by about the height of your redhead, I think."

"That's interesting," Liz grated. "But it doesn't get us out of here."

The line buzzed empty, then the scout was back. "It does not," he admitted quietly. "Give me the headcount at your next check-in—your people and the civilians. I do not wish to commit insufficient transport—and I would prefer a better landing zone."

That, thought Redhead, sounded like he was going to get them transport—and apparently it sounded like that to Liz, too.

"Will do," she said, sounding easier. "Here's your connection!"

Liz waved her over. Redhead muttered a quick report: "Lost three of the locals overnight but everybody else came through fine. Might've been a sprained ankle there . . . but that's livable."

Liz nodded and moved away, hand up to grab somebody else's attention.

Redhead sat down and punched the "talk" button.

"Redhead here."

"Here's Tech," she heard, followed by his calm, unflappable voice. It was like easing in for a swim after a hot, horrible day, his voice; the water so cool it felt like silk.

"Redhead, you are untroubled by the earthquakes?"

She laughed, hand to face.

"That's not true, Brunner. I hate 'em. I feel like the whole damn world's trying to shake me off it! And that's when the locals aren't praying for me one minute and shooting at me the next."

"You have a good commander, Redhead," he murmured. "I think you will not have those problems much longer. If you have a portable, or paper to hand to record this—we think you can expect waves of about the same strength as you recently experienced at approximately every nine Standard hours. I stress that this is approximate. Recent events are—unprecedented, which makes prediction—difficult. So, there will be a resonance, if we are right, a larger kick-in-the-pants, as Jack calls it, perhaps every fourth or fifth. Also, there will likely be random sharp waves."

"Got it," she said, memorizing what he told her; she'd lost her portable, with her books and games and all—gods, it seemed like years ago, at that firefight at—

"And so," Brunner was continuing, "the rest of the information is that in the short term, we see no major precipitation. This is good; it keeps some of the fall-out radiation above you. You are not under the jet currents carrying the worse loads yet. The long term is much harder."

"Snow?" she offered.

Brunner laughed.

"Not snow, no. What is happening is that we have new water flows in the ocean, new and unstable. This will affect the . . . the . . mesoscale events, the regional weather and possibilities for local and regional. Weather we cannot predict so well. We are um . . . perhaps aided in that we know where you are and will be able, to some extent at least, to concentrate our efforts in predicting for you. It would be best for us and for you, if we can receive frequent updates. They needn't be nonstop, but perhaps a reading each orbit or two that we travel overhead—"

"That's what—about fifteen times a day?" She chewed her lip. "I'll see what we can do. Might need to add somebody to the talk list—but if mostly you need the unit switched on, we ought to be good for that."

A pause, and then Brunner's voice came as if he was partly turned away from the mike.

"Yes, we will monitor at all times, but will expect voice communication as you need, else three times per day. Perhaps you should take our tide warnings and we will set a schedule from there?"

"I can do that. Send away!"

• • • ✧ • • •

BRUNNER WOKE, his body already calling for tea and *chernubia*. He kept time now by the next time he was needed at the microphone, or what sort of weather was imminent. It happened that this time, his waking and first meal coincided with the day's first scheduled report from the surface, where Lizardi's Lunatics slowly moved through the smoldering remains of what had once been a vast forest toward an abandoned hilltop farmstead, hoping to find shuttles waiting to bear them to the station.

That there would actually be shuttles—that sat between the scout and the station master.

He heard raised voices as he approached the weather room, one of them Boylan's, one the scout's. Then Jack chimed in and the level rose.

"We have to go in!"

"There's nothing we can do."

"The chief insists that we cannot land." That was the scout, and it hurried Brunner's steps. Cannot land? But—

"It's disturbing the science!" Boylan shouted. "We knew from early on there was little chance—"

Brunner ran, boot-heels noisy against the floor.

"What has happened?"

His three associates fell silent. The scout bowed, slowly, as between equals.

"I see we need not wake you for this news."

Jack stepped up, ushering Brunner toward his seat.

"I slept late and had a meeting with the intern," said Boylan defensively, "and when I arrived, we were beyond range already."

Brunner turned to face her, his stomach twisting. "What has happened?"

She turned away from him. It was the scout who leaned forward and touched the pad, started the recording. There was noise, bursts of sounds that once he would have mistaken for thunder.

"Tech! Recon squad found us a nest of leftovers. Liz tried to talk to 'em but you hear what they're saying. Hold them ships till you hear from us 'cause it looks like they got themselves some anti-air stuff. Bastard's tried to sneak in through—damn! Out."

"Last orbit?" Brunner demanded, though he could see the time on the scan. "This happened and no one told me?" He spun, coming up out of the chair so quickly the scout fell back a step.

Boylan turned to face him. "What could you have done?" She shouted. "Nothing! There's nothing you can do for them, Brunner, and the sooner you stop pretending—and him, too!—the better, for you and for the mission! Mercenaries are paid to die!"

Breath caught, Brunner took a step, his hand going out of its own accord, snatching up a coffee cup left on the counter—

Jack moved, clinks subdued, caught Brunner's shoulder and pried the cup from his hand.

"Sorry, Tech." The hand squeezed his shoulder, perhaps meaning comfort, then Jack turned, cup yet in hand as he nodded to the planetologist.

"Let's get some breakfast, hey? We'll be able to work better after we've had something to eat."

Boylan looked at Jack, then at Brunner, her eyes wide and her face hard.

"Later today," she said, and her voice was soft. "I marked it in the event file. Later today, the tides will be bad. Ugly. I'm not sure they're survivable. I'm sorry, Brunner."

He stared at her, vision spangling. He blinked and felt the tears, hot down his cheeks.

"Right." Jack took Boylan's arm and steered her toward the door. "Coffee. Coffee'll help us both, and company, too—"

Weeping, Brunner watched them leave, then turned back to his instruments, tapping the event file up.

"The times are there," the scout said quietly. "I believe that the quakes are due six orbits from now. Before that, there is the enemy. With the right weather, with luck, perhaps they may sneak past to a place of safety. It would be wise of you to prepare a forecast, my friend. I go to see if calls for assistance will be answered."

The scout bowed, gently, and Brunner replied, "Comrade."

· · · ❖ · · ·

THE CIVILIANS WERE DEAD; the gun took the couple the land had let live. Liz pulled what was left of the Lunatics back some, and sent scouts out, looking for a way around trouble. Joey came back, reporting no joy. Auifme didn't come back at all, which Redhead guessed amounted to the same thing.

"We got no good choices," Liz said. "Weatherman upstairs says there's bad weather coming—worst we seen. Weatherman's a cheerful boyo, but he's not being cheerful about this. Wants us to get to a safe place pronto, by which I gather he means off-planet and maybe out-system.

"In the meantime, the scout's guaranteeing transport, but we've got to make the rendezvous point before that weather hits."

Scandal shook her head. "Hell, Liz, that ain't no choice; it's one choice!"

There were a few laughs from around the circle. Miri finished up her half of the last ration bar in her pack, had a drink, and passed her water jug to Skel. They'd stripped down to necessaries some while back, taking just enough to get 'em to the rendezvous. That was before they'd run into the crazies with the Forsbo 75, o' course—not that anything they'd had left would've answered it for good.

"There's a little obstacle between us and the rendezvous, in case you hadn't noticed," Skel said to Scandal, when Liz didn't.

"So, we run for it," she answered, pushing her helmet up off her face with a grimy forefinger.

"It's an option," Liz allowed. "I'd like to up our odds some, though. I'm thinking in terms of a diversion. Something to draw the gunner's fire while we're sneaking past in the direction we need to go." She looked 'round at them, taking her time.

"I'm looking for a volunteer."

Miri took her water jug back from Skel and snapped it onto her belt. Outside the circle, a baby wind twist swirled into being, stirred the dust, threw a couple of stones and dissipated. Inside the circle, nobody said anything.

"I'll do it," she said, and heard Skel draw in a hard breath, exhaling it on a laugh.

"Hey, no, now. Stealing my thunder, Redhead?"

She shook her head at him, but she was looking at Liz. Liz, whose face had gone still, eyes narrowed; who'd gotten her off of Surebleak and given her a fighting chance.

Well, and sometimes you fought, and sometimes you lost. Even she knew that.

And, besides, she didn't intend to lose.

"Makes sense," she said to Liz's hooded eyes. "I'm smallest. I'm fastest. Got the best chance of getting in, doing the job and getting back out."

Liz took a breath. "You got a distraction in mind, I take it?"

"Yes'm." She nodded. "I do."

· · · ✧ · · ·

"TECH BRUNNER, I have news which may—ease your burden somewhat."

Brunner turned from his screen. The scout was disheveled, even unkempt. He was, however, smiling. Brunner felt his own heart lift in response, which was surely not wise, but hearts were not known for wisdom.

"What has happened?" he asked.

"We have shuttle craft fueled and standing by, we have pilots volunteered from among the crew."

"Ah. And the permission of Chief Thurton, you have that, as well?"

"Pending receipt of a message from Phaetera headquarters. If the hour comes upon us and the message is yet unreceived, we go. This by the chief's own word."

Brunner's knees wobbled. He sat abruptly on the stool.

"This is . . . an astonishing reversal," he said slowly, and took a breath.

"Earlier, when I spoke to her—they are still pinned. Commander Lizardi had pulled back, and sent recon to seek a way around." He took another breath, remembering. "She said, this morning's count was twenty-seven. The civilians—they did not survive the night."

The scout inclined his head. "All honor to them," he murmured, then straightened, eyes bright. "We have been in contact with others who are also making for the rendezvous point. We will take any and all who meet us, but . . . I fear we will not be able to wait for those who are not there."

"Understood," Brunner whispered. He cleared his throat. "Understood."

• • • ✧ • • •

"TECH? Ichliad? You there?"

"I am here, *Galandaria*." As if he could—would—be anywhere else until this was over, however it came . . .

He leaned his head against edge of the monitor, the plastic cool against his skin.

"I wanted to tell you," Miri Robertson said, her voice as clear as if she stood next to him in the weather lab. "Couple things. First, you done real good by us; we wouldn't've got this far without you helping us so much—"

Brunner closed his eyes, hand fisted on his lap. "Child—"

"No, hey, listen. And I gotta tell you—having you on the other end of this thing, talking to me, an' all? You didn't have to do that and it—I don't guess I can say out how much it helped, so you're gonna just hafta believe it did. A lot. We sit down and get that coffee, after this is all over, I'll try to 'splain it better, okay?"

Brunner swallowed. "Okay—"

"Good," she said. "That's good. Now, the other thing I got to tell you? We're gonna be moving real soon. Gonna strike for the rendezvous point—run like hell, that's the plan. Good one, huh?"

"Indeed. A most excellent plan."

"It's got a lot going for it, mostly being the only plan we got," she said, sounding amused. "But, see, the Stubbs here. I'm gonna—"

"Leave it!" he said violently. That she should worry over mere equipment when—he took a breath.

"*Galandaria*, listen to me. Set the unit to automatic and leave it. I will gather what data I may, while it functions. Promise me that you will do this."

"No—can't. I—Brunner. Look, I need this thing, okay? What I wanted to tell you is—you're prolly gonna lose the signal. Don't worry 'bout that, right? Promise."

Gods, Gods. He took another deep breath, and when he spoke, his voice was calm, never hinting at the tears running from closed eyes.

"Of course, you will do as you deem wise," he told her. "You have never given me cause to doubt your judgment. Now," he said, more briskly, "you should know that the scout has just recently assured me that there will be ships at the rendezvous point. They will board any who come, but they will not wait, *Galandaria*. Do you understand me?"

"Got it," she said cheerfully. "Right in line with the plan, huh?"

"Yes," he murmured. "Run like hell."

· · · ◇ · · · · · ◇ · · ·

"GET 'IM?" Skel hunkered down next to her and held out a square of chocolate.

"Did. Told me to get my ass to the rendezvous point or else." She nodded at the chocolate. "You better have that."

"Already did," he said, and if he was lying—which he probably was—he was good. "Saved this out for you. Least I can do, huh?"

"Thanks." She took it and gnawed on a corner while she pulled up the Stubbs' manual, ran the search and pulled up the page.

"You tell 'im it ain't likely you'll be with us to meet the pilots?" Skel asked harshly.

She looked up at him, shaking her head. "Not planning on getting done just yet. You?"

"What *are* you planning, then, if you don't mind sharing with a friend?"

She nodded at the screen, gnawing on her chocolate. "This thing here? It's got a power supply capable of powering a pinbeam."

Skel sat back on his heels, face attentive. "Does it, now?"

"That's what it says here." She tapped the screen. "An' if I was to do a series of something stupids, like it warns me here in this manual never to do? Then it might give up all its power at once."

Skel didn't say anything. She gave him a look and a grin. "Want your chocolate back now, don't you?"

"You got everything you need to pull this off?"

She nodded, and reached 'round with her free hand to pull the grubby cord up over her head. The key was right where she'd put it, nestled next to the enamel disk her mother'd given her. She palmed it and let Skel put the string back over her head and tuck the pouch away.

"You tell 'im up there you was gonna blow up his equipment?"

"Told him he was gonna lose the signal, and not to think anything 'bout it."

"That'll be a comfort," Skel said dryly, and Miri sighed.

"I'll make it up to him. Now, gimme a minute to read this part again, right?"

* * * ◇ * * *

THE DOOR OPENED and Jack strode in, tool belts clanking.

"Tech," he said, nodding, and wandered over to the supply cupboard, casually opening a hatch that was coded to Brunner's thumbprint, and placing something within it.

"I see that I am wise to lock important items away," Brunner said.

The big man shot a grin over one shoulder. "Little testy? Well, you got a right, I guess. We all do. Just gotta remember that I hold the overrides. You're safe from everybody but me." He closed the hatch and walked over to the monitor shelf, hitching himself up on the stool.

Brunner sighed and turned back to his screen. "If you are here for a purpose . . . ?"

"Come down to see how the work was going, is all. Heard from that girl of yours lately?"

"Indeed. She informs me that they intend to make rendezvous. I have assured her that the ships will be there."

"Did you, now," Jack murmured, and Brunner threw him a sharp look.

"Will the ships be there?" he demanded.

"Said so, didn't you? Now, you might be interested in knowing that the chief, he got his answer from the company. And—following the letter of his instructions, y'know, just like he ought—he's had the scout arrested and thrown in the brig. I expect to be—yeah, here it is, now."

Footsteps rang in the corridor outside; the door opened and three people in Phaetera security colors entered the room. One stood by the door, stunrod held ready, the other two advanced on Jack, who docilely held out his hands to accept the restraints.

"Phaetera Company orders Jacumbra Edgil removed from his position and the company payroll. His access to the station is restricted and he will be removed from the station at the earliest opportunity." The security guard looked up from the portable from which she had been reading, and looked hard into Jack's face. "Phaetera Company also wishes you to know that there will be no involvement in the situation on the planet below. Promises of rescue or succor made by Scout Commander Kon Rad yo'Lazne and/or Jacumbra Edgil are not binding on Phaetera Company."

"What? But—"

Jack's shoulder lifted minutely and Brunner stopped himself, biting his lip. Jack rose at the prompting of his guard, bound hands held awkwardly in front of him. The other guard looked to Brunner.

"We apologize for disturbing your work, Technician Brunner."

"Jack—"

"See you, Brunner! Hey, it's about time I got a vacation. Don't expect the scout to be such good company, though—"

He passed through the door on the heels of his guard, the others following.

The door closed, leaving Brunner alone with the equipment.

• • • ✧ • • •

GETTING IN CLOSE ENOUGH to kill the gun, Redhead thought, as she rested behind the scant cover of a charred bush, that was gonna be tricky.

But not half as tricky as getting back out before the Stubbs blew.

Liz, she'd laid down the law, and it was the scariest thing Miri had heard so far in her life.

"Soon's Redhead's diversion goes off, we're running, and it's every hand for themselves, you hear me? If your partner falls and don't get up, run. If I fall—run. If you get hit and fall and it ain't fatal—get up, damn you, and run!"

Miri figured she'd be a little behind the general race, what with having to set the Stubbs and all. She had the route to the rendezvous set in her mind, so that was okay. Skel, he'd wanted to stick with her, but she'd told him to look out for himself, like Liz'd said, and she'd see him at the shuttles, or for sure on the station, after.

Time to move. She took a breath in deep, got her feet under her, and moved.

. . . ◇ . .

BRUNNER LOCKED THE LAB DOOR, went to the cupboard, set his thumb in the lock and pulled the door open.

Calmly, and not at all surprised, he removed the non-station communication device and a data stick.

Returning to the monitors, he cleared one, inserted the stick, and touched the "talk" button on the communicator.

"Jack?" Cautious. Low.

"Brunner," he answered serenely. "I am the meteorologist of record. You and your compatriots are in place and willing?"

"We're willing, sir, but the dock's locked up."

"Security?"

"Not now."

A schematic blossomed on the screen as the feed from the datastick kicked in. Brunner looked at it, understood what he was to do, and spoke into the communicator.

"You can move at once."

"Yessir, but—"

"I will take care of the airlock and the bay door. If anyone should ask, you do this on my orders, which you believe I am able to issue. You understand this?"

"Yessir."

"Good. The airlock will cycle in three minutes from my mark. Mark. What is your name?"

"Jamin Fowler, sir."

"Jamin Fowler, fly well. The weather will be unsettling on-planet, bear in mind that it will soon be worse. Be quick, and bring everyone you can."

"We aim to do just that, sir."

"Good," Brunner said. "Good."

He glanced over at the weather screen, saw the window for the

Stubbs open, and data begin to flow. Surely not! he thought, suddenly not calm at all. There was no time now to stop and—

The data continued to flow, he reached out, touched the speaker plate—

Static from the speaker was abruptly cut off. On the screen, the data flow ceased, and the window reformed, displaying the legend: NO SIGNAL. CACHING HISTORY. ARCHIVING. DONE.

. . . ✧ . . .

Day 57, Standard Year 1393
Solcintra, Liad

"WE HAD MANAGED," Delm Lysta said, "to quiet the problems you have caused. We brought you home to the clanhouse, fed you, clothed you, kept you from prying eyes and wagging tongues. You have, in return, tended our inner gardens, and for the most part you have been respectful."

His delm turned on him suddenly. Brunner recognized the play, and the actor whose stance was but poorly emulated.

"Tell me why you thought, what gave you the least reason to assume, that you would be permitted to broadcast your name to the world now? You fall yet short of the ten Standards we had agreed to retain you in-house for your own protection. Have you no sense of propriety? Is it that you specialize in disasters?"

The delm pounded a key, sweeping the on-hold play from the wall-screen taller than he and replacing it with:

Scouts Confirm Meteorologic Concerns Over Blast Aftermath read the teaseline, above a wonderfully colorful and overwrought full motion graphic representation of the beam blast and the resultant dust plume. Below that was his paper, exactly as he had written to yo'Lazne, detailing his concerns regarding trace timonium and other radioactive by-products, the assumptions of dispersal difficulties, the recommendation that nearby residents be tested for pollutants at least and perhaps treated to a prophylactic stay in an autodoc.

There was more. He was quoted from his letters of testimony regarding the investigation into the actions of Phaetera Company in the matter of Klamath, his certifications were listed. As he had given his opinions in his *melant'i* as a professional and an expert, he was signed as I. Brunner, Master Meteorologist, with neither clan nor even city of residence appended.

His analysis, including jet-stream particulate distribution, fall-out rates, half-lives, everything he'd sent to the scout, were included by link.

Brunner sighed and turned to his delm.

"By warning the people of Liad of the peculiar nature and dangers of the blast plume, and showing potential areas of concern, I have shamed the House?"

His delm stamped feet, twice. Brunner wasn't certain of the play from which the gesture was borrowed, though the mood he knew far too well. The delm being a forever-hopeful playwright, all actions were seen through another author's eyes.

"Ten Standards. Ten Standards you were to remain silent to the world, and then to remove yourself to a quiet occupation. This morning, already, I have had three comm-calls and a piece of mail inquiring if this is the clan home of I. Brunner.

"We have an orderly house." The delm sniffed. "And we will have an orderly house. This—" waving energetically at the wall "—is not a quiet occupation, do you understand? I am willing to acknowledge you ten years a gardener, and to divert a portion of the trust to set you in that service."

Brunner bowed, acknowledging that he'd heard.

The comm-line blinked; the delm ignored it in favor of staring toward the door toward the outer halls, where a rarely heard chime echoed discreetly.

"This, if this is more of your doing we shall—"

The what of the doing was interrupted by yet another comm-call; this one, at least was known to the house for the comm emitted a quiet *chirchirchir*, stolen from the sounds of chiretas closing out the last act of *A Clan Dissolute*, the extended critical version.

The delm said, "Answer," and the comm dutifully did so.

"Cousin," started the voice, and Brunner winced. "Imagine my surprise—"

"Hold Cousin, there's a knock."

Brunner winced again: Act II, Scene 6 of *The Interminable* as echoed in Act I, Scene 4, of the current rage *False Melant'i*.

Verena stood at the door when the delm opened it. A polite if rapid bow followed, and a sweep of words.

"There are visitors to see Ichliad. They ask by name and they have—"

A stamp of feet.

"Ichliad does not receive visitors. Not from friends and not from the curious! This House does not permit."

Brunner still stood, wondering if the child would break and run. He was pleased to see that she did not, nor did she look at him.

"My delm, please. I have cards." She showed them, two, fanned between small fingers. "Also, the lady sends this—" She raised her other hand, showing a slightly phosphorescent blue key.

Brunner's stomach went into freefall.

Lysta snatched the cards, reached for the key, but Verena stepped sideways, extending her hand to Brunner.

"The lady said that I should place it in Ichliad's hand, for she had promised to bring it back to him, when her mission was done."

He moved, received the key, and stood for a moment staring at the imprinted Stubbs logo in archaic Terran script.

"She died," he said, perhaps to Verena, perhaps to his delm. "On Klamath. I—she was not listed among the survivors and—"

"Korval!" His delm's voice carried shock without artifice. "We cannot receive Korval. They are—"

"—thrown off-planet for being bad boys and girls," an ironic voice concluded in backworld Terran. A red-headed woman in working leathers stepped into the room neatly between Verena and Lysta, followed by a slender, dark-haired man wearing a battered pilot's jacket.

"Hi, Brunner," the woman said to him, gray eyes measuring him, head to toe.

"Redhead," he whispered. "Is it you?"

She grinned, and he saw the halfling soldier. "'Fraid so. Amazing what some people'll do to get a cup o'coffee, ain't it?"

She reached behind her, took the man's arm and brought him forward. "Ichliad Brunner, I make you known to my lifemate, Val Con yos'Phelium Clan Korval." Now she spoke Liaden. Her accent was Solcintran, pure and perfectly clear.

Korval Himself bowed, a bow most exquisite in its exactness and in its brevity: The bow of one owing a debt beyond paying.

"Ichliad Brunner, I am most glad to meet you," he said softly.

"And now that you have met him," Lysta said sharply, "I will ask you to remove yourselves from this clanhouse." The cards were thrust out imperiously, exactly the famous gesture performed by Nadelm Casaro in *A Clan Redeemed*. Brunner closed his eyes.

Korval turned and bowed again, delm to delm. He seemed unaware of the attempt to return the cards.

"Lysta, forgive us for coming to you in such a state of disarray," he said smoothly. "There is a long history between my lady and Meteorologist Brunner; many events to be told over, several Balances to be crafted and weighed. You will have heard the news; we do not have much time here."

Val Con glanced at them, his free hand executing a sign Brunner took to be "Continue."

"Too long and too short," Redhead murmured from her place next to Brunner. She sent him a quick look from beneath her lashes.

"You and me got a lot to talk over, like the man says," she continued, as Korval walked Lysta over to the other side of the room, still talking, his posture one of concerned respect. "So, quick question—you looking for work?"

Brunner blinked. "Work?"

"Yeah, work. 'Cause, see, where we're going, we're gonna need a weatherman, and I want to hire the best there is. I'll tell you right out, the weather ain't as interesting as Klamath's, but we're figuring to set satellites, warm the place up. Going to need some studies done, and—"

Did he want work? he asked himself, and almost laughed. His fingers itched for a portable, so that he could begin making notes. And yet—He lifted his head, watching his delm speaking with Korval.

"Your choice, Weatherman," she murmured, and he did laugh,

then, loudly enough that Lysta turned to stare. "And look, I mean we can get you going today, if you want. But really, just say no if you don't think it'd be a fit. You'll have to work with some pretty strange folks, like us, and some mercs, and some scouts, too."

He raised a hand a moment, and held the key she'd brought back to him to eye level.

"I think, I need to know something first. How is it that your name was never on the station rescue list?"

"Well," she said in Terran, "I got rid of that gun that was holding us down and then . . . I took some damage. When they brought me up, they didn't bring me in-station. While the crews were getting Jack and the scout out of the brig, they just took me right to the scout's doc. I really did mean to bring that thing right back to you!"

He sighed and it turned into a slow smile and a gentle laugh. "Scouts, mercs, strange people, Redhead and her partner. And odd weather . . . "

Redhead bit her lip as he paused, vaguely hearing something his delm was saying to Korval about how Solcintra's theater could be improved if new plays were sometimes brought to stage . . .

"Yes," he said, and bowed to her. "Indeed, I would very much like to have work. And very much, I expect it will be a fit."

✧ Hidden Resources ✧

Runig's Rock

The ship was still there, hanging just inside the sensors' range. Not a ship of the clan, certainly; nor yet the ship of an ally, the captain of which would have been given the passcodes, hailing protocols, and some understanding of the capabilities of this, Korval's most secret and secure hidey-hole.

This ship . . . This ship only sat there, making no attempt at contact, seeming to think itself both hidden and secure—watching.

Waiting.

The urgent question being—waiting for what?

Alone in the control parlor, Luken bel'Tarda leaned back in his chair and rubbed his eyes, wearily.

His wager, slim as it was, rested on the square marked "orders," while Lady Kareen, his collaborator in maintaining the integrity of Korval's treasurehouse, had her coin on "back-up."

That the fruition of either choice would do more than inconvenience themselves and that which they guarded was assured. With Plan B in effect, he and Lady Kareen were their own safety and rescue. Even if they had been inclined to endanger others of the clan in these uncertain times, the news that reached them was not encouraging. Liad in turmoil, trade in disarray, murmurings even of the Juntavas, which in saner times certainly took care to keep itself and its business far from the news feeds . . .

No, even if they had been so minded, there was no certainty that any of the secure message drops remained so, and they could not risk what they guarded on anything less than certainty.

They were not without resources—weapons, that would be. And so it was that he and Kareen had decided, uneasily, to wait, though at an increased level of alertness.

Luken rubbed his eyes again and looked once more to the screens. The ship was gone.

* * * ⋄ * * *

SYL VOR WAS SNORING.

To be perfectly truthful, it wasn't so much a snore as a sort of *puff puff puff* sound that Quin customarily found . . . comforting. If his small cousin were sleeping thus deeply, it must after all mean that they were perfectly safe, no matter that they were in hiding, and deliberately cut off from clan and kin.

Tonight, though—say that tonight, thoughts of kin weighed heavy on Quin's mind, magnifying the small sound of Syl Vor's sleep into an intolerable annoyance.

He had tried turning onto his side, and putting his head under the pillow. But then it was hot, and he couldn't find a comfortable place for his hands, and his feet kept twitching, and—

Syl Vor sneezed, tiny and sharp, like a kitten; he muttered, bed clothes rustling as he resettled himself without really waking up.

Quin took a careful breath, loud in the sudden silence.

There was no sound from the bunk beneath, where his cousin Padi slept as if all were well, as if they hadn't just today—

Wel, it wasn't *her* father who hadn't reported in, after all. Cousin Shan had missed several call-ins, but then began reporting again, just as usual.

Pat Rin yos'Phelium, however . . .

Pat Rin yos'Phelium had never once reported in. Which meant . . .

Quin swallowed, hard.

It does not mean, he told himself, that Father is . . . is—anything could have happened! He might be safe with, with an ally, or . . . traveling! Or . . .

But his inventiveness failed here, and after all he wasn't a youngling like Syl Vor. He knew what Plan B meant. More, he knew that people could die. That people *did* die.

Even people one cared about.

But not, he thought, *Father. He's far too clever. He will have—he will have done* SOME*thing* . . .

He swallowed again, and it was abruptly intolerable, lying here with his thoughts whirling, and the children asleep around him.

Syl Vor sneezed again.

Quin gritted his teeth and sat up in his bunk. He put the blanket aside, and swung silently over the edge.

. . . ✧ . . .

LUKEN HAD WALKED THE ROCK for the third and last time during his shift, manually verifying every reading. It was, in its way, a soothing routine, and by the time he let himself into the family quarters, he was fairly calmed. He might, he thought, be calmer, if he could *know* what had moved that ship, *now*, and whether it had gone for good, or for ill.

It might be, he told himself, that the ship master had never harbored any intentions regarding themselves. There were reasons enough for a ship to drop out of Jump and tarry a time. Urgent repairs would be one reason. An importuned or wounded pilot, another. Also, a ship and a pilot might from time to time find it necessary to lie low for such reasons as tended to beset pilotkind. It was an odd eddy of space they sat in, and far out from usual traffic. Still, they were not *hidden*, only inconveniently located. Despite which, a pilot of Korval had found it— the place and the Rock—and so another pilot might also.

A clatter drew his attention as he turned into the main hall. A clatter and a light, glowing green over the door to the galley. The lady's constitution was excellent, as was her discipline, but he had once or twice met Kareen yos'Phelium awake during the latter part of his shift. An early riser, she styled herself on the first such meeting, with a wry modesty much unlike her usual mode. She had offered him tea at that first, and perhaps, not-quite-chance, meeting. He had accepted and they had talked the pot empty. And so it was on the second meeting, and the third. On the subject of their shared duty, he came to know her as a stern and subtle thinker, and was glad of her insights.

Indeed, he thought, putting his hand on the latch, he would be glad of her insight just now.

Nor would a cup of tea be out of the way.

The door slid aside. A slim figure in a rumpled robe turned from the counter, teapot in hand, opal blue eyes wide in a thin, golden face.

"Quin," said Luken, smiling.

"Grandfather!" the boy gasped, looking conscious. He smiled, then, and nodded down at the pot.

"Would you like a cup of tea? It's fresh made."

* * * ✧ * * *

GRANDFATHER LOOKED TIRED, Quin thought. No, more than that, he looked *worried*. That was an honor. Grandfather was treating him like an adult, not like a child or a halfling to whom an untroubled face must be shown.

It was also deeply disturbing, which Quin had noticed was the case with many of adulthood's honors. He sipped his tea, watching Luken do the same, and wished that there was some way in which he could ease that all-too-obvious worry. His father, he thought, would know exactly what to do.

But his father wasn't here.

Heart cramped, Quin put his cup down.

"Would you like some cookies, Grandfather?" he asked.

Luken lowered his cup, and smiled gently. "Thank you, Boy Dear, but I think not. The tea is very welcome, though." He sipped again, appreciatively, and placed his cup on the table. "Now, tell me, what brings you awake so early in the morn?"

When they had first come here, Grandmother Kareen had insisted that they keep the homeworld's hours and maintain a strict division of day and night. She said it was their duty, which Quin supposed it must be, since Grandmother knew everything about duty and how it was most properly fulfilled. For himself, Quin could have done with a little less duty and a little more Luken, though it worked out well enough once the two elders began to rotate shifts, "so that we do not become stale and accustomed," as Grandfather had it.

"Quin?"

He started, and sighed. "I was . . . thinking," he admitted, and suddenly leaned forward, his hands gripping each other painfully. "Grandfather, do you think—do you think it goes *well*? It's been so long . . . "

"Has it been *so long*?" Luken murmured. He patted Quin's arm softly. "I suppose it has been some time, at that, and your year is longer than mine by reason of you having so few of them. Well." He picked up his cup.

Quin forced himself to sit back and picked up his own cup. The tea *was* good, he thought, but he didn't sip.

Neither did Luken.

"I think," he said slowly, as if he were considering the matter deeply, "that it goes as well as it may. Understand that some matters require more time than others. The First Speaker will surely wish to be certain of Korval's position and of our allies before she calls us to her side."

The First Speaker—Cousin Nova, that was, who was almost as much of a stickler as Grandmother Kareen. Quin had once remarked to his father that Cousin Nova was no gambler, and received a sharp set-down for his impertinence.

I should hope that the one who holds the clan's future in trust for the delm is everything that is prudent. Gambling with lives is for Korval to do.

Quin bit his lip. "If it—If the First Speaker needed pilots, she'd remember to send for me—wouldn't she, Grandfather?"

"Things would be desperate indeed, Boy Dear, before the First Speaker deprived us of *our* pilot."

Our pilot. That was, Quin thought, with some bitterness, him. Not that he'd been allowed to pilot anything more than a sim since they came here, and done enough board drills to last him a long lifetime. He held a second-class card, but, he thought, he *should* have been a first class by now. *Would have been*, if Plan B hadn't caught them all in its net of duty and boredom.

"I'm scarcely a pilot if I'm not allowed to fly," he pointed out, his voice sounding churlish in his own ears. "Your pardon, Grandfather," he muttered, and sipped tepid tea.

"That's only the truth spoken," Luken said, pushing his cup across the table. "Pour for me, Child."

He did, first filling Grandfather's cup, then his own, and put the pot aside.

"You recall the protocol," Luken said gently. "If I fall, the keys are yours, whereupon—"

"No!" Quin interrupted, so forcefully that his tea sloshed over the edge of the cup and onto his hand. "Grandfather, *you* are not going to fall!"

Luken raised his eyebrows. "Well, if it comes to that, it is my duty to fall, if it will buy the pilot and the passengers time to be away," he said mildly, and inclined his head. "Do you know, Quin, I think that I will have some cookies after all."

"Of course, Grandfather." He rose at once and went to the cabinet, had the tin down and took a moment to arrange the cookies on a plate. *Just because we are in exile, Grandmother said, often, is no reason to descend into barbarism.*

He took the plate to the table, offering it first to Luken, who took a single cookie, daintily, and bit into it with obvious enjoyment.

Quin put the plate in the center of the table, and reclaimed his chair. The cookies were his favorite—vanilla and spice seed—but he wasn't hungry. He sipped his tea.

"Now," Luken murmured gently, done with his treat, "what news?"

Quin blinked.

"I—news, Grandfather?" he managed.

Luken sighed. "You must forgive a man grown old in the ways of Liad. It had seemed to me, Boy Dear, that you placed a subtle emphasis on *you* in the declaration that I would not fall, which suggested to me that you have had news, perhaps, of . . . someone who may indeed have fallen."

Quin sighed. It was useless to try to hide things from Luken; he knew that. Really, Grandfather probably knew all and everything, even about Padi helping him crack the datalocks.

He sighed again and looked up into his Grandfather's eyes.

"Father hasn't signed in," he said slowly. "Not once since—since Plan B . . ."

"Ah, I had forgotten that you held the access codes to the Roster," Luken said gently.

Quin pressed his lips together and said nothing. If by some chance Grandfather *didn't* know about Padi's assistance, he wouldn't hear of it from Quin.

"Very good," Luken said after a moment. "I must say that you surprise me, Boy Dear. I would have thought you knew by now that one who listens at doors hears nothing good."

That was a lesson long ago learned, true enough, but—

"I had to know," he muttered.

"Of course you did," Luken replied courteously. He reached for another cookie and raised his eyes to Quin's. "Now, tell me: what it is that you know?"

"I—" He gasped, feeling tears rise, swallowed, and forced himself to meet Grandfather's calm, gray eyes.

"I know that Father hasn't signed in," he said steadily. He took a breath. "The rest is speculation."

"I see. Well." Luken bit into his cookie and sighed. "I agree that it is extremely vexatious of Pat Rin to have ignored protocol. His mother, your grandmother, is certain to ring a peal over him, when they are once again in the same room. For myself, I have determined to do nothing of the kind, for he will have had his reasons, you know. Your father does not much resemble an idiot."

Quin considered him, the heavy misery that had settled in his chest lightening somewhat.

"You know that he is . . . safe, then, Grandfather?"

Luken sighed and picked up his teacup.

"Child, I know nothing of the sort. I merely hope."

"Hope." He hadn't meant to speak so scornfully, not to Grandfather, and yet—

"It's no shameful thing," Luken murmured, "to hope. Nor would you be alone, did you take up the habit. We each of us hope for a Balanced outcome, and a speedy return home. Here, we hope for the safety of those who actively expose themselves to danger, while they hope to prevail, so that they and we will be reunited and that soon."

Quin cleared his throat, thinking of the last time he'd seen his father. They'd said their public goodbyes at the foot of the gangway; his father had pressed his hand, and abjured him to study well, wearing what Quin thought of as his card-playing face. All very ordinary, and he was only going back to school, after all, and would be home again at the end of the term.

There had been no reason for it, but Quin had paused just as he was about to enter the shuttle. Paused and turned his head.

At the foot of the gangway stood his father still, his dark hair riffled by the evening breeze, his face . . . attentive. Quin caught his eyes, and Father smiled, wide and sweet, as he so seldom did, and never in public. Quin had smiled back; Father raised his hand, fingers rippling in the sign for *soon*. Then the steward called and Quin had to clear the door, find his seat, strap in, and lean back, all the while glowing with the warmth of Father's smile.

"Quin?"

He looked up into Grandfather's eyes. "It would be good if we were called home soon," he said, gravely. "And in the meanwhile, Grandfather, it doesn't quite seem like Father to have allowed anything ill to befall him."

Luken smiled and put his warm hand over Quin's cold one.

"No, it doesn't, does it?"

• • •✧• • •

"THEY'VE GONE?"

Those were Kareen yos'Phelium's first words when she entered the control parlor to relieve Luken as guardian on-duty. A sharp-tongued stickler she might be, and what she had done to his boy never to be forgot, or forgiven, but no one could say that the lady was dull or that her ability to do sums was in any way impaired.

"Directly before the last manual survey," Luken said, glancing again at the screen, yet innocent of lurkers. "I admit to a certain dismay."

"One would prefer them in eye," Kareen agreed, taking the second's chair. "Perhaps they grew bored?"

"I could find no ease along that road, though you might do better," Luken answered cordially.

Kareen sighed. "I expect I shall find none, either. It's an ill road, beginning to end." She frowned at the screen.

"Shall we take to the ship?"

According to the First Speaker's wisdom, he was the elder-in-charge; thus the question came properly to him. Of course. Nor was it an ill question, only annoying in the way that questions which have no clean answer so often are.

Certainly, one felt increasingly exposed, in this supposedly rarely traveled corner of space. Certainly, a ship afforded flexibility, *mobility*, that their current situation did not. And yet . . .

"A destination?" he murmured, inviting her suggestion.

Again, she sighed. "Without proper access to certain information . . ."

Precisely. A ship might also, of course, gain them the newsfeeds that their stable fortress location lacked. It was no use thinking of sending one out for news, of course; they had but a single ship. If one went, all accompanied.

There were, of course, subplans to guide them, committed to memory long ago, and each assuming a catastrophic impetus. This . . . uneasiness was formed by a circumstance that, despite the instincts of two grown old in society, might yet be only happenstance.

"If we formed a less vulnerable grouping . . ." Kareen murmured, perhaps to herself.

Oh, they were vulnerable, Luken agreed silently; never think otherwise! Two silver-hairs, two halflings, a younger, and a pair of babes-in-arms. Had they been more grown, or less old—

Well. Had they been more grown, Korval's treasures, there would have been no need to hide them away.

Luken looked to the screens . . . blinked and looked again.

"It may be," he said slowly, "that our decision has been made for us."

• • • ◇ • • •

IT WAS NOT THE SAME SHIP, and it was possible that they had overreacted in sending the children to the ready room, the ship keys usually on Luken's belt in Quin's hand, and the back-up keys in Padi's. Lady Kareen waited with him in the control parlor, one hand on the back of his chair, watching the screens over his shoulder, ready to move on the instant through the panel directly behind them.

On the screen, the ship approached, slowly, inexorably.

"Now . . ." Kareen breathed, and as if in response, the first beacon sent its challenge.

The approaching ship made answer, properly. On the master board, Luken saw the beacon begin its countdown from twelve. If the ship were still in range of its sensors when it came back online, it would die, friend or—but there, it was past and on course for the second beacon.

A ship of the clan, Luken thought, but found scant comfort in the thinking of it. Ships, after all, could be captured; and pilots subverted. The codes that held their doors against those who wished to gain Korval's treasures for their own enrichment were not invincible. And as much as he wished the vessel that was now past the second beacon and on its way to the third and last, to be the answer to all their waiting, the closer it came, the more he mistrusted it.

"Does it seem to you, good Master bel'Tarda," Kareen yos'Phelium murmured in his ear, "that the ship we see is somewhat too . . . apt?"

"It occurs to me," he answered, his voice hushed. "One does so *wish* it to be a Korval vessel . . ."

"Precisely," she said, suddenly crisp.

Luken drew a careful breath, and watched the ship in the screens. *I am too old for this*, he thought, *and not nearly clever enough*.

"The docking computer's been fairly answered," is what he said aloud. "Will you step aside while I go to greet our guest?"

"I'll remain here, I think," she said, not entirely surprisingly, "and monitor the situation. If matters . . . clarify, be assured that I know my duty."

None better, he thought, and pushed out of his chair, suddenly feeling all of his years and the accumulated weight of the childrens'.

"I daresay, I won't be but a moment," he said with false cheer, and left the control parlor, heading for the dock.

• • • ✧ • • •

SYL VOR SAT WITH THE TWINS, who were being very good, very quiet, in their separate carriers. That was precisely as it should be, Quin thought approvingly; Shindi and Mik were Syl Vor's job until they had to move. If they had to go before Grandmother was with them, then Syl Vor would pick up Shindi and he would take Mik, and they'd run as fast as they could, with Padi bringing up the rear. That was as it should be, too, because Padi was co-pilot; her charges, the pilot and the passengers.

Quin, watching the screen, thought that Grandfather and Grandmother had—perhaps—been too enthusiastic in their duty. Indeed, it was all he could do to hold to discipline and not open the door. For surely, *surely*, this was recall at last, for here came a ship whose pilot held all the proper codes . . .

"Why don't we have an all-clear?" Padi demanded, echoing his thought. "The systems accept the ship—it's docking! What more does Aunt want? A calling card?"

"They want the pilot to prove the door code, too," Quin said.

"Why?" Padi was fairly dancing from one foot to the other. "He had all the others. What proof can one more door hold?"

Quin touched the screen's keypad, accessing the camera on the hall outside the forward dock. It would, he thought, be Cousin Shan, or perhaps Cousin Anthora. Or . . . if Cousin Nova—if the First Speaker couldn't spare any of the Line Direct for the errand, then it would certainly be Pilot Mendoza, or . . .

Familiar and firm. That was what Grandmother said. That the pilot the First Speaker sent to them, when it was come time to go home, would be familiar to them, and firm in their loyalty to Korval.

For long moments, the bay door remained sealed, ready light glowing green above it. Quin's stomach clenched. What if the pilot failed, after all, to have the proper codes for the door? That would mean—gods, *would* it mean that the ship had been stolen? Or that the pilot—*their* pilot, familiar and firm—had been stolen, and—and coerced into revealing—

"Quin?"

Padi was frowning at him, and that would never do

He took a deep breath and gave her a smile. "Don't *you* want to know who has come for us?"

Her face relaxed into a grin.

"The pilot could," she agreed, "take our feelings into account and make some haste."

As if the pilot had heard her, the ready light snapped to yellow, and the bay door slid open.

"Syl Vor!" Quin hissed. "Count of twelve!"

He had never in his life seen the woman who stepped, soundless as a scout, into the hallway.

· · ·✧· · ·

THE SHIP REJOICED in the name of *Fortune's Reward;* a ship of the line, lately assigned to the wastrel cousin, whom Korval's great enemy and the Juntavas alike had thought to be easy meat.

Not so the Office of Judgment, and in that they had been proven wise. Never an ill thing, to have the sagacity of the judges proven.

It *was* ill, the pilot thought, releasing the webbing, but not yet rising from the chair . . . It was ill, indeed, that she came thus into Korval's most secret treasurehouse, alone, and unknown to those who stood guard. It had been better—but no matter. Done was done, and, truly, she had finessed more volatile situations. She would need to win them, that was all.

Win them.

She rose then, with no need to check her status. Her weapons were old friends; each of their caresses known and unique. They would not disturb her, nor unbalance her; and they would come to her hand when they were needed.

So, then, the codes; last in the series she had been given to memorize. She would in a moment open the door and step into Korval's treasurehouse, where she would doubtless be greeted by one of the vigilant guardians.

Win them.

· · ·✧· · ·

THE DOOR ACCEPTED THE CODES, whisking out of her way. Beyond, the hall was empty, saving the cameras and the vents that she did not doubt were an active part of security.

Happily, whoever monitored the camera, and presumably held the decision as to what sort of gas might fill this hallway, appeared to be of a deliberate nature. She had, after all, demonstrated mastery of the codes. The guard might grant an extra few minutes of life to such a one, awaiting . . . confirmation.

There was another door at the top of the hall. She did not approach it; certainly she did not try it. Her information regarding what might happen, did she attempt either, had been specific.

By necessity, then, she waited.

For the cameras, she adopted an easy stance, proud without being prideful. She was a pilot, and pilots had pride. As did judges, of course, and certain of the better class of Juntavas assassin.

Scarcely had she counted to eight when the door at the end of the hall—the door that led to the interior, and all the treasures collected therein—opened, admitting a man no longer young, his hair silver and his eyes wide and gray. Childlike, one might say, in ignorance.

As she was very much *not* ignorant, she bowed, supple and sweet, as she had been taught from a child.

"Master bel'Tarda," she said, in her soft, accented Liaden, "I am Inas Bhar." She gave him that name—the one her father had bestowed upon her at birth. Her other names were such as might impart little comfort to a man with so much duty weighing upon him. Yet, there was room for comfort on both sides.

"Called Natesa," she added, straightening. She raised a hand, slowly, specifically unthreatening, and showed him the token. The tree-and-dragon flashed in the light, then held steady.

That should have been enough to seal the thing. She should have received from Luken bel'Tarda a bow, and perhaps a courteous word or two, and a pass into the rocky heart of the station.

What she received, instead, was the barest of nods—scant, even meager, courtesy—and a question, harsh in the mode of Stranger to the House.

"Who sent you?"

It was, on its face, a reasonable question, as she was, indeed, a stranger to this House, and to this guardian. Yet the mode—not one of the kindest, no, but yet without an inherent harshness; that was from the man himself. And that—gave one pause.

To cover her moment of calculation, she bowed again, youth deferring to years.

"Master, I am sent jointly by Korval Themselves, and by the Boss of Surebleak. Their personal names are, perhaps, known to you: Val Con yos'Phelium, Miri Robertson, and Pat Rin yos'Phelium."

Luken bel'Tarda's face tightened. It could not be said that he was inept, or in any less control of his face than one would expect of an elderly Liaden who was, in addition, a merchant of renown—still, Natesa felt that what she had seen was hope, sternly suppressed.

"Why did they not come themselves?" Luken demanded, keeping still to a harshness that must, from all she had been taught of his nature, pain him considerably.

She did not bow this time, though she inclined her head slightly, and sent him as soft a glance as she might manage from beneath her lashes.

"You may not have heard that the Council ordered Korval to depart the homeworld, declaring the Captain's Contract void. The clan, therefore, seeks to set down roots on the planet Surebleak, where they have the advantage of kin to aid them."

She paused. He waited, his silence reminding her that she had not answered his question.

"Korval is needed at the forefront, as they are the face and voice of the clan. Yos'Galan is likewise required to show themselves good for business, and also, to supervise the peaceful settling of the House. It was thought that I would accompany Pat Rin to you—in fact, it was quite set, until there was a difficulty among his jurisdictions which could neither be ignored nor left for a lieutenant.

"It was then decided that a young cousin—Gordy Arbuthnot— might sit my second; another emergency claimed him when we came to the Port itself." She did bow this time, feeling that it was proper.

"Thus I came alone, Master, trusting to what I have been given to know, and to the goodwill and uncommon sense of yourself and Lady Kareen. The delm's order must be obeyed."

"That is, of course, true for we who stand within the delm's honor, Inas Bhar, called Natesa," Luken said, his intonation less harsh, his mode unchanged. "You must forgive me for wondering why you feel thus."

Natesa sighed. She would very much have preferred to answer this particular question in far different circumstances. Preferences were not spaceships, alas, and only truth and candor would win this old man's trust. Pat Rin had told her as much.

She met his eyes firmly. "I have the honor to stand as Pat Rin yos'Phelium's lifemate," she said.

Luken's eyebrows rose, but whatever he was about to say in answer to such a bold claim was cut off by the opening of the door.

She had seen a picture of this young pilot, but even if she had not, there was no doubting who he was. Far too much of his father showed in his face—his father in a temper, if every truth were told.

Natesa bowed, pilot-to-pilot, that being the least challenging of the modes readily available to her, and one that observation had shown to be acceptable—even soothing—to all of Korval, of whatever rank, saving Pat Rin himself.

"Quin yos'Phelium, I greet you."

He did not return the courtesy, though he allowed himself to be stopped by Luken's outflung arm.

"Why hasn't my father reported in?" he demanded.

· · ·◇· · ·

IN THE END IT WAS THE RECORDING, hastily made and poor in quality, that won them. They heard it, all together, in the control parlor, Luken standing shoulder-to-shoulder with Lady Kareen, a spare woman with iron-gray hair and hard dark eyes. Quin and the others of Korval's treasure were ranged behind them. Even the babes were silent as the brief message played; and Quin was seen to blink rapidly several times, as if to vanquish tears.

"Father, Mother—I greet you and I ask forgiveness, that I do not come to you myself. Necessity demands that I be elsewhere—a fuller accounting will be made when we are all again enclanned. In the meanwhile, I desire you to accept the protection and escort of my lifemate, Inas, also called Natesa. It may seem madness that the children are desired in the midst of such disarray as she will acquaint you with. Be assured that it is the delm's madness, and very much the lesser of several risky paths.

"We are, every one of us, safe, a happier outcome than I would have predicted only a few relumma gone. Come home, now. The delm desires it no more than I do.

"Until soon."

Despite the tape, Natesa could tell that neither of the elders was entirely at ease with her—for which she blamed them not at all. She asked them to trust much, and recordings, after all, could be forged— or forced.

And, yet . . . There was something—an undercurrent between them; something, Natesa thought, that they knew and which the children did not. Something that was inclining them toward her, even more than Pat Rin's voice, or her possession of the codes.

"I think that we must," Lady Kareen said at last. "If the delm is mad, it is no more than Korval has ever been, and yet the clan endures."

"I agree," Luken said, and looked to Natesa.

"These other risks of which the boy speaks. What of those?"

What of those, indeed.

Natesa spread her hands.

"There was a story told in nursery when I was a child, of a peculiar beast which had seven heads, all savage. It would seem that the best— indeed, the only—way to defeat such a creature was to strike off its heads—"

"I know this story!" cried the smaller boy—Syl Vor, his name was. "Every time one of the heads was cut off, the creature grew two!"

She smiled at him, where he knelt beside the babes in their baskets.

"Precisely so." She looked to the lady and gentleman, waiting with edged politeness. "To stretch the simile full-length, Korval struck off the head of its enemy—perhaps even the greater one, that ruled coordination, schedules, and necessities. But in doing that, it has freed dozens of lesser heads to act independently."

The elders exchanged a speaking glance.

"We go," the lady said decisively.

The gentleman inclined his head. "I agree."

He nodded to Natesa. "We have a ship, which of course the delm will not wish to lose. Quin here is rated an able pilot. Let us—"

"Grandfather?" the young girl, Padi, interrupted. She was, Natesa saw, staring at the screens.

"What ship is that?"

• • • ◇ • • •

GUNS—in Grandfather's hand; in Grandmother's hands.

Father's lifemate—her hands were held before her, slender fingers spread, declaring herself no threat.

Quin threw a glance at the screen, at the ship approaching Beacon One along the proper vector.

"You have shown them the path," Grandmother said, her voice so cold that Quin shivered.

Pilot Natesa tipped her head. "Please explain," she said.

It wasn't Grandmother, but Grandfather who did that, in a clipped, hard voice nothing like his own.

"This same ship has been lurking at the edge of scan range the last four-day. It vanished, you appeared."

What? Quin pushed forward.

"Why didn't you—" he began, and gasped when Padi stamped on his foot.

"It is possible that I did show them the path," Pilot Natesa said, calmly, "or some part of it." There was a sharp *snap*, which was the safety coming off of one of the weapons.

It might have been someone cracking a nut, for all the attention Pilot Natesa paid it.

"If they have the proper codes," she continued, in her calm, musical voice, "then you may dispense with me. If they do not have the codes, I beg that you will allow me to assist."

Quin bit his lip. *Father has lifemated a gambler,* he thought. Of course he had; like called to like.

"Assist!" Grandmother snapped. "If they do not have the proper codes, there will be nothing to assist with, as the beacons will have—"

Syl Vor gasped.

Quin turned, his eyes leaping to the screen that showed the ship, which had not moderated itself in the least, nor, according to the legend at the bottom, broadcast any code.

A thin red line came from what must be the stranger ship's forward laser cannon.

Beacon One exploded.

Grandfather slid his gun away and bowed to Pilot Natesa.

"We accept your assistance," he said.

• • • ✦ • • •

QUIN SAT AT THE PILOT'S STATION; Padi at second; Grandfather in the jump-seat between, where he could see both boards, though he had none of his own. Grandfather might only be a third class, but he had been a pilot for longer than Quin and Padi together had been alive, and experience, so his instructors had impressed upon him, counted.

It was not their own ship they piloted, but Father's *Fortune's Reward*, that Pilot Natesa had brought to them. He and Padi had done a rapid board check, and he had found those pre-sets that Pilot Natesa had told him of, coded precisely as she had said. A quick check with the navcomp verified that their course was for Surebleak nearspace—again, precisely as the pilot had said.

He fingered the keys, bringing the presets into the active queue. One tap and they would load. One tap . . . but not quite yet.

Padi had the audio wide on all the bands. He himself was connected by private line to the control parlor, where they had left Grandmother and Pilot Natesa. The screens showed the docking bay, live, feeds of nearspace . . . and the terrible approach of the wolf-ship. All three beacons were gone, now, and the ship was on-course for the opposite-side dock.

Quin chewed his lip, and wiped damp palms surreptitiously down his thighs. What was to prevent the wolf-ship from loosing their weapons on Runig's Rock, breaching it, killing . . .

He ground his teeth, tried to bring his ragged breathing under control—and felt a hand, firm and warm on his shoulder.

"Pilot Natesa seems to be fully capable," Grandfather said, as calm and unhurried as if they were discussing whether or not to go for a walk. "And her reasoning is, by my reckoning, sound."

Quin swallowed, inclined his head, recalled the pilot's explanation.

"They have been brutal with the beacons, yes—but the beacons are merely mechanicals—barriers to their progress. This place—is a treasurehouse of many kinds. They will not wish to undermine it, nor to destroy that for which they search. Their first goal must be yourselves, for hostages have a high value. However, they must also be on the hunt for any small thing that may give them an advantage, or a grasp upon Korval."

"Dragon by the tail," Padi had said, irrepressible even in this hour of danger.

Pilot Natesa laughed.

"Foolish, are they not?" she asked, seeming almost merry. "Yet, they must be answered sternly, for their foolishness cannot be allowed to endanger us. Thus—"

She had turned to Quin then, keys in hand and her eyes serious. Quickly, concisely, she had given him the boardcodes and the key under which the presets had been filed.

He had his doubts. Especially he had his doubts about leaving Grandmother behind.

She, however, had brooked no argument.

"The pilot is wise, and I make no doubt, experienced," she said coolly. "I will remain, as I know the systems, and may provide back-up."

"Grandmother—" he began, and stopped when she held up her hand, imperious.

"I know my duty, as you know yours, Pilot."

There was no answering her in this mode, Quin knew, yet to leave two—one of them his Grandmother—to face who knew what kind and number of savage crew? How would he answer his father for that?

It was then that Pilot Natesa placed her neat hand upon his arm.

"So soon as this small task is completed, Pilot Quin, we will be away, in the very ship of the clan, so that the delm will have no cause to scold either of us for losing it," she said softly, her dusky face calm, and a smile in her dark eyes.

Obviously, the pilot anticipated nothing more than a few moments' inconvenience. She was his superior, in rank and in age. And, as Grandmother had said, he knew his duty.

"They're docked," Padi said, jolting him back to the here-and-now of his board. A moment later came Grandmother's confirmation, for his ear alone.

"Our visitors are committed. On my count of six, Pilot yos'Phelium. One."

Padi hit the in-ship.

"Syl Vor, are you strapped in?"

"I am!" he called back from the cabin he shared with the twins, who had already been made secure.

"Stay that way until we sound 'all clear.'"

"All right," Syl Vor answered, amiable as always. "Do you think Mother will be at the port? And Uncle Shan?"

"Remember, the pilot told us there was a great deal of busyness, Boy Dear," Luken said, leaning forward and directing his voice toward the mic. "We shall see them, soon enough, though. No fears."

"No fears, Grandfather," Syl Vor agreed.

"Six," Grandmother said, calm and purposeful.

Quin reached to the board, and *Fortune's Reward* dropped away from Runig's Rock.

• • • ✧ • • •

"THEY'RE AWAY," Pat Rin's lady mother said.

"That is well," Natesa replied, leaning over the back of the chair. The dock light glowed a steady green in the screen; the hallway she had entered so short a time ago empty and bright.

"Am I correct in assuming that the hallway may be filled with something other than plain air?"

"You are," said Lady Kareen.

"It would be simplest," Natesa said, "if they would fall at once. Do you watch here and when they are fairly into the hall, release your most potent, nonlethal mixture."

The lady tipped her head, as if she might question this, as well she might; prisoners were always a risk, and yet—

"The delm will wish to speak with them," Kareen yos'Phelium said, and inclined her head. "I shall do as you say, Pilot. And yourself?"

"I?" Natesa shook her head. "I will assume that they are clever enough for suits, and shall be devising a secondary plan."

The lady was seen, faintly, to smile.

"Very good, Pilot," she said, and looked to her board.

• • • ✧ • • •

THE JUMP-POINT was coming up. *Fortune's Reward* was steady as she went. Screens in all directions clear, saving those to the rear, which showed Runig's Rock, sitting quiet in its little eddy of space, to all appearances inert.

"Approaching Jump," Quin said, unnecessarily. He glanced to the rear screens again, hoping to see the second ship—*their* ship—tumbling away from dock.

What he saw instead, in the instant before normal space blurred Jump-gray, was a jerk, as if the station had been hit by space junk, or—

The warning chime sounded, and he brought his attention to the board.

* * * ✧ * * *

THEY HAD BEEN CLEVER ENOUGH for suits, and not nearly as careful as she had hoped they would be.

Natesa fell back as they entered the main hallway through the shattered door, weapons ready, spread out in a pattern that told her they knew their business well.

She regretted, for a moment, Pat Rin's mother, then gave over regrets altogether.

* * * ✧ * * *

THE WARNING CHIME SOUNDED, and *Fortune's Reward* was out into normal space.

Crowded and unfamiliar normal space.

Quin snatched at the controls, bringing weapons up, demanding answers from the navcomp.

"Padi, grab the beacons, please," he said calmly, because he was too frightened to be anything but calm. "Then get the local feeds. We're off-course."

A moment's wrestling with the navcomp showed that they *were* off-course, though not as much as he had feared. More, the reason was perfectly obvious—in fact, it surrounded them.

Surebleak nearspace wasn't merely crowded, it was *crammed* with ships. Scout ships, small traders, large yachts, and a great number of mid-sized craft, not meant for long-Jump, but well-enough for short trips.

Padi fed him the beacon locations; he pulled the chart, located port and fed the numbers to the navcomp. That done, he began to calculate a course of his own, and winced when Padi brought audio up a little too strong.

"Tree-and-dragon," someone close said, and that was—maybe that wasn't good.

"Kill our ID," he told Padi, and saw the appropriate light at the top of the board go dark.

He felt Grandfather shift behind him, as if in protest—and then still. The pilot made those decisions for the ship, and Quin was the pilot.

As it happened, he hadn't been quick enough.

"Message from Tower, welcoming *Fortune's Reward* home," Padi said. "They request access, and promise a quick descent to the . . . the boss' own pad."

"The . . . boss?" Quin said, memory stirring, but failing to fully wake.

"That will be your father, Boy Dear," Grandfather said from the jump-seat. "The Boss of Surebleak, Pilot Natesa styled him. You recall it."

Now he did, at any rate.

Cheeks warm, he addressed his co-pilot.

"Please thank the tower, and allow access."

· · ·✧· · ·

TOWER PULLED THEIR FILES, and routed them the promised fast drop to port, whereupon they busied themselves with shutdown, not to full sleep, but to twilight. That had been Grandfather's suggestion, and while it was undoubtedly a good one, Quin felt his stomach cramp with renewed worry.

If Grandfather had second thoughts about Pilot Natesa's tale *now* . . .

Shutdown complete, they gathered the twins and Syl Vor. By then, the hull was cool, but it seemed that none of them wanted to open the hatch.

While they were standing in the piloting chamber, looking uneasily at each other, the comm pinged.

Padi leapt for it, got the bud in her ear, listened, and stammered, "Yes, sir, at once," she licked her lips. "Pending pilot's approval."

She turned to Quin. "Tower relays a message: The boss requests that we open the hatch."

Quin stepped forward—and stopped, his arm caught by Luken, who handed him Shindi.

"I'll go first, Boy Dear."

Quin looked to Padi and gave her a nod. She fingered the sequence and the hatch came up.

· · · ✧ · · ·

THREE MEN IN PILOT LEATHER stood in the hatchway. The biggest man was Terran, Quin thought, and he stayed well to the rear, calling as little attention to himself as a big man might.

The man nearest—

It was Father, after all! Father wearing a pilot's jacket, with his hair in need of a trim, and his face chapped, as if he spent a lot of time out in the cold wind that blared through the open hatch.

He embraced Grandfather, and Quin looked to the man who stood a little to the side. That man was . . . strangely difficult to see, as if he were somehow thinking himself invisible. Once one had him in-eye, however, he was found to look like Grandmother; dark hair going to gray, and ironic black eyes.

"Quin!"

Padi snatched Shindi out of his arms and he was caught in a strong hug, cheek to cheek.

"Quin. Child, I am all joy to see you!"

Father stepped back. Quin sniffled and blinked, embarrassed to be found crying, but then he saw that he had no need, because Father was weeping, too.

"Welcome," he said, "to your new home."

He turned, then, holding his hands out to Padi and Syl Vor.

"Welcome. Your parents send their love, and their regret that duty keeps them so long away. Directly, we will go to Jelaza Kazone, as soon as—"

He raised his head, looking beyond Syl Vor, as if expecting someone to emerge yet from the interior of the ship.

Quin gulped, and stepped forward, his hand on his father's arm.

"She's not here," he said, his voice wavering.

Father looked back to him, his face suddenly still. Frighteningly still.

"Is she not?" he murmured.

"There were intruders," Grandfather said, turning from a low-voiced discussion with the pilot who so looked like Grandmother. "Truly, the pilot came to us in the very nick of time, Boy Dear—and stayed behind with your mother to deal with the problem. Neither would see wolves among the clan's holdings, nor would they have us pursued."

"Of course not," Father said, his voice cool and smooth. His gambling voice, Quin thought. He shook himself, then, and looked back, to where the big man tarried on the gantry.

"Mr. McFarland," he said in Terran, "I shall be returning immediately to Runig's Rock. Pray you take my father, and our children under your care, and see them safe to the delm at Jelaza Kazone."

"All right, sir. Daav sitting second?"

"I wouldn't miss it for worlds," the pilot who looked like Grandmother said, his voice deep and rough.

"I'm coming, too," someone said, as Grandfather and the rest sorted themselves without question, preparing to accompany Mr. McFarland.

Quin blinked, recognizing his own voice—and the rightness of his assertion.

"Oh?" Father considered him, one eyebrow raised. "By what right?"

Quin cleared his throat, and glanced at the elder pilot, who gave him an encouraging nod.

"I left them there," he said. "Pilot Natesa and Grandmother."

"You can scarcely argue the pilot's *melant'i*," the elder pilot said.

"Can I not?" Father gave him a cold stare. The usual effect of such a stare was a glance aside and a bow of submission.

The elder pilot laughed, then looked to Quin, black eyes glinting.

"I have the honor to be your grandmother's brother. My name is

Daav. You will address me, please, as Uncle Daav, as I don't feel able to support Grand-Uncle." He returned his attention to Father. "Pat Rin, do you go?"

"At once."

"Excellent. I engage to talk the tower into giving us a quick lift while you, Pilot Pat Rin, look to your course. Pilot Quin, the jump-seat for you, sir; you've flown enough, and there are two here able to relieve you."

Uncle Daav had an oddly decisive way about him, for someone who proposed to sit second, Quin thought, but he folded into the jump-seat with a certain amount of relief.

He considered the screens as the pilots began their work, and so it was that he was the first to have eyes on the neat, and very familiar ship coming down near to hand.

"They're here!" he cried, snapping upright. He pointed—and then froze, looking to Father's face.

"It may not be—"

Uncle Daav touched the toggle and the general port babble filled the cabin.

"*Shadow Drake*," came Pilot Natesa's soft, calm voice, riding a wave of argument over an extended wait time. "We are down and locked. Shutdown proceeds immediately."

From the pilot's chair, a sound between a laugh and a cry.

"Bother," said Uncle Daav, sweeping his hand down the board. "I had so been looking forward to a flight." He sighed, theatrically, reminding Quin of Cousin Shan. "Well, I suppose one must make the most of it. Shall we go over and display our manners, Pilot Pat Rin?"

Father gave a long sigh, and reached out to trigger the final shutdown.

"Indeed," he said, his voice not quite steady, "we should."

* * * ✧ * * *

"IT WILL REQUIRE HOUSEKEEPING," Natesa told Pat Rin, after they had embraced and he had assured himself that she was well. "And—I regret—there was damage to the clan's holding."

"Damn the clan's holding," Pat Rin said into her hair, and sighed. "Such terrible risks, Inas."

"Nonsense," she answered. "And, you know, I would not have your mother think me faint-hearted, or unworthy of you."

He laughed at that, which was well, and allowed her to step out of his embrace, though he retained a grip on her hand.

Elsewhere in *Shadow Drake's* piloting chamber, Quin sat, palpably patient, and studying the board as if he had never seen one before. Daav yos'Phelium lounged against the back of the co-pilot's chair, to first glance completely at ease.

Second glance, however, marked a certain tension in his shoulders and the cock of his hip, and the way his glance returned, time and again, to the door that led to the passenger's section.

"Lady Kareen," Natesa began, and paused as the door flicked open, admitting the lady herself, none the worse for the wear, saving some singed hair and a neatly bandaged scrape along her arm.

One step into the chamber, she paused, dark eyes on the tall shape in his lounge against the chair.

"Kareen," he said, his voice quiet, his tone absolutely neutral.

The lady took a breath deep into her lungs.

Sighed it out.

"Daav," she temperately, in the mode between kin. "Well met, Brother."

✧ Moon on the Hills ✧

Surebleak

Yulie had the frights pretty bad this time, bad enough that he'd waited, tucked down and froze-quiet in the rugged hatcher-nut grove in the hills well above the road, shaking, until long after the noisy threesome from somewhere downroad rushed to the clearest of the paths to the south in the face of impending darkness.

What exactly his visitors had been doing he didn't know—they'd called out *hullo* and *whoha whoha* a few times, like they didn't know if the place was empty—and one of them called out "Captain Shaper" twice, and that made no sense since Grampa had been dead for so long, Yulie could hardly remember his face sometimes without looking at the image files. Likely someone had the house-spot listed somewhere as a leasehold to the dead company, but heck, that was so far back it shouldn't matter to no one. They'd called *his* name once or twice, too, he thought, but by then he'd been moving away and it might just as well have been a trick of the wind.

"We need to talk with you!"

Maybe those were the words he'd heard, but even as he'd thought to come down, he hadn't—there was dread in his way. He hadn't had any company since Melina Sherton had walked up some butter awhile back, being a good neighbor like she was, for all that she was a boss. But he'd known her since he was a kid. Strangers—no, he wasn't much used to strangers around and it did make him worry.

They'd probably been in the house if they wanted, since the door didn't lock beyond mild, and he could only hope that they hadn't searched too hard—if he was lucky, they'd left him the gun on the wall. Real luck was that they'd probably believed the ancient outhouse shoved against the outcrop was what it looked like.

The whining of the overloaded buggy died down along with the temperature, and still he waited, hearing the regular sounds return as the mindlessness of fear receded. He wilted against a tree then, aware of the tiny movements in the leaves and drying field grass, of the wind's sigh, super aware of his vulnerability. The visitors all had guns, and he—he'd left his hand gun back in the safe and the long-gun locked into the rack. He hadn't carried them with him for quite some time.

He knew better, he did, especially since some of the city folk thought they could come up and hunt anywhere that wasn't in the city. He didn't mind them shooting at rats or wild dogs or whatever *someplace else*, but here—here they had no dogs, and the field creatures were few and far between mostly. The other potential targets—well, Rollie'd explained it to the neighbors the year of the problem, and they'd posted signs, and it ought to be clear he preferred being left alone, him and the cats.

And they hadn't looked to be intending assault . . .

Not that he had reason to be assaulted, but they came from down the road, and Rollie'd gone down the road one day and never come back, dead from not knowing one boss from another, or from not having the sense not to antagonize a Port City block-boy at a tollgate.

The odd thing was that the road—the road Rollie'd gone down, the road that grew to carry edibles for city folks, the road that ran all the way to port—that road, it started here. Here, on the property he called his, running right by the door of the cabin, right by the vegetable patch, right to the very cliffs that marked the first dig—and Rollie, like always, was the one wanted to wander the other way. He'd looked over World's End enough that he wanted to get away from it, down the road with the 'lectracart in front of him, cart full of produce and him full of ideas.

"I'll have news of the doings, when I get back. Big changes, you know. Big changes!"

His brother's last words to him, "Big changes!"

Yulie shivered, more from the memory than the weather. *Mud, mud, mud!* His old grandfather'd been a spaceman and that was the worst thing to him about being on a planet—the dirt and the mud and the rain—and here he was, the last of his Grampa's line as far as he knew, what with Rollie dead in the city, down the road.

That reminded him that he still owed a fetch of onions and maybe some grassnip to the lady, but he'd been pretty well shook to a standstill recently, and the debt was his accounting and not hers, anyway.

The debt-letter was still in the house, walked up from Boss Melina Sherton's closest tollbooth by a kid with a swagger. It felt like weeks ago, not like a year, like it was. Some things stick with a man, some things don't.

"You relative to Rollie Shapers?"

He'd nodded, standing at the door, annoyed enough to insist— "Shaper, that 'd be. Don't sizzle at the end of it."

The kid had shrugged, unslung his day-sack, pulled out a letter and a bag. He handed over the letter, held onto the bag, eyeballing the cats around the field edge before bringing his attention back to Yulie.

"Down to the big whorehouse they had these to send on up— 'spose to be for you, I guess. If you can write, I ought have your name here on this line to give back to Miss Audrey so she know I done it."

So Yulie had gingerly taken the big fancy pen and signed the proffered clean white sheet of real paper *Yulian Rastov Shaper*. He *did* know how to read and write, because Grandpa had made that rule for all of the family. If he'd had kids he'd teach them. Rollie—he'd been Roland Yermanov Shaper. He'd not much been interested besides half-day gardening with side trips to The Easiery or girlfriends—he'd also known how to write, and sometimes Yulie came across odds and ends of notes on recipe cards and such, notes that weren't from Grampa or Emily or Susten or—any of his ladies, so it must have been Rollie.

He handed the signed sheet to the kid, who'd sealed it in one quick finger rub into a certiseal, his thumb hard on both sides before negligently dropping it into his sack, and handed over the bag.

Inside the bag, Yulie'd been given a big, fancy, sealed, brown envelope, with a return emblem at the top of "Miss Audrey's Deluxe, Port City, Surebleak." It wasn't an address he recognized but he'd never really been deep to the city, so names weren't much connected.

Inside the envelope was a letter, hand-writ, with a date and the same return address as the outside, that started "Dear Kin or Friend of Rollie Shaper."

He'd got that dread feeling then because hardly anyone wrote to him, ever—mostly just folks requesting extra greens or hoping for something out-of-season—and Grampa had spoke about how he'd had to write kin-letters more than once, and how hard they were to write even if there really wasn't much to say.

Sometimes he could push that dread back so he could see, and that's what he did, pushed it away hard.

Dear Kin or Friend of Mr. Rollie Shaper, the letter went, *Rollie was a patron at Portside Deluxe some days ago and on expiration of his room rental his effects were collected and placed in storage, where we have them now. Unfortunately, it later became clear on evidence that Mr. Shaper was the previously unidentified victim of an altercation, and had died of his injuries before medical assistance could be sought. The block clean-up committee's report should be attached; they had a working med-tech known to me with them who certified the negative results of revival tests and the clean-up committee's standing disposal instructions were followed, with ashes included in the weekly south garden run.*

The letter went on of course, and he'd read it through, requesting him to come on down to the city to pick up the effects. What would they be? Could his Grampa's Musonium still be there? The good blade that Rollie'd always carried though it was supposed to stay at home? Cash in bits or dex or maybe gold weights? Her name was at the end, and businesslike as it was, the lady's signature was bold and delicate at the same time.

He'd had to think a moment about the ashes, because it was a strange thought, that sweaty, noisy, busy Rollie could be something other than he'd ever been, but they said so, and had bothered to write to him, which was probably proof enough. The *south* garden, that was one on the far side of the port itself, down toward the flat of the land.

He'd never been there, but the maps and Grampa both said that's where the small gardens were supposed to be back before the spaceport was plopped dead center on the best growing land the continent had, on account of it being convenient.

Then he'd started to look at the report, but it wasn't something kin wanted to see, really, about how many cuts and—so he folded it in, and held himself a second or two, knowing that he wanted to know and that he didn't want to know, knowing that he'd seen something like that once, entrance wounds and exit wounds and—

The feeling was building as the boy stood there, the feeling that something was going to happen, that more bad was going to happen, that the clouds held weight beyond rain, and that something really *really* bad—

When it hit, the panic, it was solid, like a crashing wall of rock falling on reason, to the point that he saw that gray nothingness where vision should be, where if he concentrated and stared hard, he found his shoes and his hands fearfully far away, like looking the wrong way through Grampa's optical telescope.

He'd held on, still, so he wouldn't run. He'd stood there long enough for the kid to ask, "You got anything to send back? Got any smoke or . . ."

But as much as Yulie'd gotten to feel his breath run out, as much as he'd felt his hands go numb, and his eyes begin to search for the way out, that much so, with all that, he'd managed to scrape together the proper and secure, "We don't got smoke here, boy, nor want it. Got something for your trouble, though, and something for Miss Audrey."

For Miss Audrey, the spice herbs, prime grassnip, just picked. They'd been going to go to the city on Rollie's next walk down the road, so they might as well go now, anyhow, and then he'd picked up two of the prettiest spudfruit he'd seen in awhile—easily a meal or two for the kid and his family—and he'd handed them over.

"For your trouble," he'd said, "but you better go now."

The kid heard a warning, grabbed the offerings and packed out, and Yulie'd managed to get the letter and report inside, grabbing at the door, grabbing at the table, scattering cats, scattering thought, the panic rising so bad . . .

And then he'd given it direction, and lumbered out the door, knocking shoulder on door frame and on the door, gathering speed, running across what Grampa had named "the meadow", and heedlessly over the small bed of field beans and through the bluefruits, entirely without thought for the value, or for anything but getting away, of running, of—

He'd run so far and so fast he almost ran off the edge they called World's End, which wasn't the end of the world, after all, but the carved cliff a hundred times his height and more, the first place the mining company had stripped bare with the mining machines to tug out the tiny veins of timonium in their matrix of junk rock and near uranics.

Below, the suddenly tempting vista of scrag rock, rubble, sand, and several twisty, barren streams of water. The colors of the lip of land he trembled on were the scrawny green and yellow of the local ground-grass, a touch of thatch, the dark flutter of a blowing leaf. Below was shadowed rock and water the color of the cliff walls and … nothing else, a scar a century and more unhealed.

He'd stopped, sweating, barely able to catch his breath, barely thinking, but starting to think that maybe this time, this would be the time—but no, not now, he couldn't. The nuts would need harvest, and the—and—but what would he *do*? Rollie'd always taken the stuff down road once Mom had gone away. Rollie'd always—

Dead. Rollie was dead. He'd took all their money and used it— used it at the whorehouse without telling him!—and now he was dead and dust!

Rage then. A black leaf spun past into the gorge, and he'd kicked a rock unsteadily at the abyss, and almost slipped in his breathless weakness, and the fear rose in him again, and now he was afraid of World's End, and of himself.

He'd run, as best he could then, in the back of his mind recalling that kid game where they'd counted, "four thousand big steps from the stoop to the end of the world!" His run was sometimes no more than a heedless willful stumble in the right direction, gathering scratches and bruises, feeling afraid of the sky, feeling afraid of the road, feeling like he couldn't find breath, *knowing* that he couldn't find breath. He'd skinned his shins crossing the stoop, falling into the house, and barely shouldered the door shut, locking it three times behind him.

It was three days before he'd managed to get outdoors again, two of them spent huddled in the threadbare bed, staring, thinking, letting impossible things and small noises frighten him into stiff, senseless panic, closed eyes worse than open. That first night, only Nugget, the frail very skinny cat, had come to sleep with him, and then not really sleep, but sit at the bottom of the bed with big eyes, worried and unpurring. On the third day, Yulie managed to eat, and then to remember that the crops would need in, real soon.

Some days, he kept track of time, some days he didn't. The crops and the cats and the auto-calendar helped him keep up, mostly. Almost a year to the day since Rollie was gone, and things still needed doing.

Today . . . today, he'd actually contemplated walking all the way down to the first tollgate, but then the searchers had showed up while he was in the field, and he'd fled.

Stretching, finally, letting the leaf-fall and rough, browning grass comfort him, Yulie curled his head on his arms against a wind-breaking rock.

· · ·✧· · ·

MR. PEL'TOLIAN'S NOTE, franked as it was with a pristine Korval seal, looked out of place amid the piles of local paper, envelopes, and mismatched inks. He'd moved it aside several times, knowing that it could wait, knowing that the business of Boss Conrad of Surebleak was far more pressing than the business of a Pat Rin yos'Phelium, man-about-town on the distant and increasingly inhospitable world of Liad. The note had arrived on the overnight, likely brought in by a scout ship or a Juntavas courier; possibly it had arrived via Korval's own packet vessels. Surely it was not more than a day or two out of Solcintra Port, unlike many of the items in these piles which had taken days to travel up from the port or down Blair Road, hand to tollbooth to hand to end up here, with him, in a pile. A pile which had waited patiently while he was away to Liad, but which demanded attention now that he was returned and despite that he'd rather be walking arm-in-arm with his lady to his casino, or even just having lunch with his planning committee.

Piles—piles were his bane. Back home—on Liad—his mail came in neat bundles, a few paper newsletters and such, invitations more frequently, business items—rarely more than a piece or two—and already sorted by likely priority by the early and steadfast action of Mr. pel'Tolian himself. The mail and news came self-sorted into the proper channels and databases of his day-screen, where it could be added to his carrybook or not.

Here, there were piles. And in the piles . . .

Some were letters on paper to begin with, others were letter-size now because anything of on-world interest that needed to be shared beyond his own staff likely would need to be in paper format to facilitate that sharing. And paper format needed to be logged, signed, notated, carried, stored, lifted—and piled.

Once that happened, of course, and items were acted on, there was a multiplication rather than reduction of piles—

Pat Rin sighed. Across the room, Silk, the resident cat, stirred, and opened one eye enough to check on the boss and his work. Ensconced in a pile of paper land records from the old days of the mining company, *his* work was going fine, thank you.

For himself, Pat Rin stretched, pleased that there was neither pain nor ache when he did. He was aware, too, that his family included healers . . . and that a recent three-breath, closed-eye hug from Cousin Anthora, followed by a smile and a simply-said, "You've been taking chances, Cousin. I knew you could," meant that she'd gathered to him healing that a month of Surebleak clinic could not.

Well, then.

Now in-hand, Mr. pel'Tolian's note had more weight to it than he'd expected. Unsealing it, he saw that it contained not only a letter but several visiting cards. He laughed—ah yes, Shan would have no doubt much enjoyed dispensing these—after all, they still carried the soon-to-be eliminated Trealla Fantrol address.

Lord Pat Rin, the letter began without flowery preamble, *this day I received in your name a visitation by the yos'Galan lifemates and Miss Anthora in the pursuit of the final removal, as we previously discussed.*

I have secured passage for myself as well as the entire contents of your Nasingtale Alley establishment. In keeping with our ongoing arrangements, I include Mistress Miranda in these travel plans and am assured that she will find the trip comfortable; rest assured, she will travel in my suite and will not be paraded about the ship.

Your clan rug was rightfully of special interest to your guests and my bindings on it were checked by all. Miss Anthora and Lady Mendoza also did a "security walkthrough" inasmuch as there have been several efforts by the curious to obtain a glimpse of the interior since your shot to the capital. Miss Anthora located several items long missed by Master Quin; these have been included in his desk, which is sealed for shipping. The final containers for the more precious items have also arrived. After some discussion, I have permitted Lord yos'Galan to take several cases of the finer bottles of your Lordship's sherry and port for safekeeping in Dutiful Passage's *own wine cellar. Several bottles travel with me, and the rest will be in the general safeguarding of the* Passage, *which will carry nothing but Korval's own household goods and necessities this trip.*

Odd, it was though written, the words carried the weight of pel'Tolian's voice with them. Odder, perhaps, was how welcome that voice had been when Pat Rin had stood shoulder-to-shoulder with Val Con and Miri, accepting visitors the second evening after the blast. On the door were scouts as security, in the corner were scouts and pilots of Korval, all armed, all dangerous, and into this midst, unbidden, had come pel'Tolian—through the security, through what surely was a madman's pattern of traffic and confusion leading to Korval's valley.

"Lord Pat Rin, Nasingtale Alley stands firmly with you."

Of a moment, he'd nearly doubted the voice, for the irony of having his houseman declare for him and for his actions was not lost on him. Neither was the man's rapid appraisal of the pilot's jacket Pat Rin wore, and of the flawless faux delm's ring he wore on the wrong finger, a ring now a fixture, against all odds. The fact that his man had come armed to this reception of allies, friends, and spies—but yes, Pat Rin had heard the tales of the dea'Gauss taking on the enemy. Why should he be surprised that the man who'd made sure young Quin ate when his father was not to home should be prepared for such duty?

His own bow had been crisp with acceptance.

"How fares the Alley, my friend?"

"As always, Lord Pat Rin—we have a quiet neighborhood. Should you require, we are ready this evening to drive you home ourselves and—"

The laughter from Miri was unexpected, but—

"All honor to you," had come his cousin's voice. A step and a bow had brought Val Con into the conversation. "Even such a secure place as Nasingtale Alley is at risk in these times, Mr. pel'Tolian. In addition, his delm has need of Lord Pat Rin's expertise at immediate hand until matters settle somewhat. Be assured that we do the best we may at feeding and housing him!"

Pel'Tolian's bow had been as precise as any could want: acknowledging a delm's right to order things yet prepared to press for his own necessities and those of his employer. If . . .

"Surely the situation is not so dire?"

That was Miri, of course, in her best Solcintran accent. He'd discovered the delmae something of a wonder, speaking Terran like a mercenary, commanding the respect of an Yxtrang, and catching the fine points of Liaden—and able to do all with a sense of underlying good nature.

"Your employer is also our kin, and his presence is both welcome and an honor. May one inquire if you've ever used that?"

Miri's point, not to the handgun sealed beneath a weather guard on pel'Tolian's belt, but toward his offhand pocket—

His man hesitated visibly, proving he was more a houseman than a gambler, and bowed a simple yes.

"My grandfather's," he said. "Now mine."

"Too large for a pocket, sir. It is a good plan, but it needs refinement. I firmly suggest you speak to the very large man over there," here she'd pointed out the Yxtrang, "and tell him the captain sent you—see if he's got something more portable for local carry. Else ask Pilot Cheever."

And then there'd been more people to meet and deal with—a matter of confirming landing access on Surebleak for a retired scout and—but Pat Rin managed to convey his appreciation, and his concern, and to confirm that pel'Tolian was not interested in staying on Liad, or in leaving his service. Later, Nelirikk was pleased to give as his judgment that pel'Tolian was alert and dutiful; fully worthy of carrying a weapon in Korval's troop.

Thus did pel'Tolian increase his worth even as his station altered—from a fribble's houseman to majordomo of a backworld dictator's prime establishment.

Well, yes, that was true, the boss told himself. It was only true. And, then the letter finished:

I look forward to arranging the new house to best advantage.
Vesker pel'Tolian.

Pat Rin folded the letter and slipped it into his pocket.

"Changes, Silk, and soon. I'm afraid we will no longer get by with the modest guidance of Natesa and Mr. McFarland. I assure you that Mistress Miranda and pel'Tolian will not consider our current unruly arrangements sufficient, and will insist you work for your living."

Silk opened his eyes, flicked an ear and settled in. Silk knew how to deal with changes. And he already worked for his living.

Closing his eyes again, he left the boss to his duties.

The boss, for his part, saw that the day's green Action File was not yet delivered, although it was late in the day, and frowned. True, he'd barely returned from Solcintra, but surely procedures hadn't slipped so far so quickly. He rang the small bell he kept on a shelf above his desk, which would summon someone, likely a recruit from Miss Audrey's, to find Cheever McFarland or the green day-file, or perhaps both.

* * * ⋄ * * *

THE SURLY GAZE of the double star Chuck-Honey barely a lightyear away was flickerless in the breeze when he woke, more proof that the wind had turned and came now from the northwest rather than the southwest—none of the road's smoke and smudge in the sky now, none of whatever latent heat the city and its spaceport might contribute to shimmer the sky.

This sleeping outdoors would have to stop, should have stopped now that Rollie was gone—no one to remind him of the dangers of sleeping himself to death in the cold. And it was cold . . . or at least cool, despite his shirt and jacket. He pulled himself to his feet, using the rock he'd sheltered against as leverage. He'd managed last winter though, him and the cats. He'd get through. Boss Sherton told him when she'd walked up with some butter just a a few days back that he was a good neighbor, and besides, he traded her fresh coffee, and she told him the news.

This last time, she'd tried to get him to walk to town and trade direct, but Rollie'd got caught up in all that and never come back. And him, Yulie, he'd never been down to pick up the stuff Miss Audrey had. If he'd have really needed it, he would have known Rollie'd taken it. But trading direct was supposed to be better and safer now, said Melina. There was a new boss—a Boss of Bosses! Not only was he a boss, but he *had* brought ships to port, which had to be good for business. This Boss Conrad was a man who was making changes.

Changes—Yulie didn't like changes all that much. Didn't *trust* changes all that much.

Frost well before dawn then, that was his prediction, and the skittering he could hear in the leaves provided more evidence of the season and the weather. The wind on his face would quiet sometime before—ah!

The flash of a meteor: a momentary scintillation fading into a green line fading into the gathered darkness, the light a comfort rather than a threat.

Rollie'd thought he spent too much time with Grandpa watching the sky, and Yulie wondered if he spent too much time now, on account of he knew the sky. Most of the changes in it were cyclical— the sky would look much the same this time next year, aside from the barely perceptible flight of the double stars. His full panic came on him easily in the open day, but not as often in the night. Under the stars, it was as if he sat more firmly in the universe, as wild as the universe was.

A flash—meteor?

No, what had caught his eye was—what? It clearly moved at an orbital speed, low to the horizon, but if he read it right, it was easily as large as the largest ship he'd ever seen orbit Surebleak, maybe larger. There was more going on in the sky; it was as if a swarm of ships had arrived nearly at once—a host of ships, orbiting almost in a stream or a ring, there were so many. He felt a flutter of energy, pushed the panic back. Boss Sherton had explained that the Boss of Bosses was busy, and that she trusted what Conrad was doing, and that there were ships. The big one that caught his eye was in a polar orbit crossing that stream; a small halo of other ships about it—it might even be one of the legendary Korval trade ships Grampa'd always talked about.

Changes!

Yulie shivered, unsure if it was the weather or the times. Grampa had taught him to be wary of change. Change had taken away his ship, and then the settlement agreement he'd made with the company had turned into a debacle as the whole organization evaporated shortly after he'd set down to take over his property, prepared to lease out . . . well, a regional depression did nothing to make *that* work.

Yeah, change was difficult. Certainly Rollie'd never helped, always managing to take an advantage when something new did happen, from taking the newer bed when Mom left to pulling a muscle right at the time Grampa was setting work schedules so it ended up Rollie on perpetual light-duty, it seemed.

Started down that thought road, Yulie rolled on, right up to Rollie helping him choose a nettle-vined hideaway for one of his few forays into hunting oversized feral Cachura pigs—apparently one of Rollie's least successful jokes on account of Grampa finding out about it—and for that matter, for taking such an interest in his attempts to talk to the twins hanging around the small farm market near the inner tollbooth to Ira Gabriel's blocks that Rollie'd made it a threesome, leaving Yulie out of the mix entire, claiming of course that he'd been misunderstood. And once he'd made *that* connection . . .

Yah, that's how it was, often enough, Rollie doing what he wanted and when, and now this, right out of Grampa's dreams, traders coming here, big traders. Ships coming, lots of ships. That was the change he'd been told, that the new big boss, Boss Conrad, was building the port up in part so he could bring in the trade. And Rollie, he'd missed this good thing, pushing too hard too soon. The road was open, now. Not so much of tariff at each tollbooth, not so much hassle.

Yulie shivered again and heard a distant complaint. It was likely the gray one. Some cats told time better than he did. Yes, he was late, and some people around here kept schedules, even if he didn't.

But he should. The strangers might be back tomorrow, and besides, he needed to walk down to Melina Sherton's and see if somebody would talk to him, assuming he could get that far. He had tubers and late greens and cabbages that needed to go to market, some way, and the folks down at Boss Sherton's stands understood that sometimes it took him awhile to get a conversation going.

* * * ✦ * * *

THE NEWS WASN'T GOOD, and it didn't come until he was at Prime. Pat Rin was unfond of the Terran habits which broke meals, though often as not here on Surebleak, necessity was necessity.

Cheever's nod prespoke a problem, and though he needed no permission to sit at the evening's communal table he seemed unsure . . . and then decisive, making his way directly to the boss.

Low voice, a touch of hand-talk—a glance to make sure his large person was between the room and his words.

"The plot's tended, and the door's locked. We called, but it was getting late, and Sherton's people were a little unsure, on account of the guy's some strange, they say. Like you figured, Sherton wants the thing cured proper beforehand, and so does Boss Ira.

"No use spooking him or annoying a good neighbor. The road itself—the thing is, I don't know how stuff is going to fit together there, but it looks like a straight shot from the tollbooth to the ditch. Road goes right there."

Pat Rin looked away, not angered, but frustrated. On his left Natesa asked, "The door locked? How locked—could they have been inside?"

The big man shrugged, palms up.

"Wouldn't think so, catwise. Couple or three right there, wanting us to let 'em in, kinda sleek. Some out cats was around while we searched—pretty much ignored us, but the ones at the door, I'd say they were wanting someone to let 'em to supper." He shrugged again, looked to the boss.

"Should I have forced the door? Didn't seem neighborly."

Pat Rin waved the hand-talk, *Negative Negative Negative* with a touch of impatience.

"Surely not, Mr. McFarland. I may already have an aggrieved party on my hands; it clearly wouldn't do to give him any other advantages in negotiation."

"My take, too." Cheever glanced meaningfully toward his place at the table.

"Tomorrow, it should be done, even if it means I go out myself. *The Passage* is in orbit and soon enough the logistics of the landings will be organized. If need be, you can fly surveillance for us."

Cheever cleared his throat, hard.

"There's more?"

"Boss, if you go, take somebody with you. He's supposed to be a real fine rifle shot. Real fine. Boss Ira says that, anyhow. Boss Melina says he's doing better now. Hasn't fired on people for a couple, four years, far as anyone knows."

Pat Rin nodded.

"Would I could say the same, Pilot. Thank you for your information."

. . . ⟡ . . .

FARMING WAS LIKE THAT, day comes after the night, sometimes it rains and sometimes it don't. This time of the year favored rain, so Yulie was just as glad to be up early, almost on schedule, the gray cat having forgotten to wake. Just as well, a few extra minutes was good, and he'd been a little tense anyway, when he came in, and the single glass he allowed himself did help . . . but he'd been a few minutes late getting to bed. The little *Blair Road Booster* newssheet yesterday's visitors had left him was a curiosity—he mostly didn't take any of the radio feeds, and now this: talk about a clinic going to full-time, all day, all night, all the time, and something that made him laugh—an image of road sign they called a stop sign that drivers were supposed to pay attention to even if there weren't a tollbooth and a gunman behind it.

But there was more interesting news: a new bakery, and a new school, and a meeting of the bosses about a general safety patrol to take care of the road. And an events listing, which looked like so many times and days and things going on that it couldn't be his Surebleak.

He'd gone to sleep with a twitch of irony. That safety patrol was good from the port all the way out to the third Blair road intersection. But the road, the big road, it came all the way out to him. Was he gonna end up with more cat hunters?

That germ of an idea had brought nightmares to wake him up— flashbacks, Rollie'd call them—ten of the cats from the greens field, laid out neat in a row, mostly shot, like they was food, laying on a bag. The sight of them made him throw up. Then he'd heard another shot and gone back to the house.

He'd always liked to shoot—it relaxed him immensely. This time though, he'd brought out the rounds Grampa called military tops and loaded up, and walked calm as could be back past the dead cats, and found another one, along with some of the skulk rats it had taken, and so then he went to hunt mode.

Wasn't much to hunt, really: six of them, a couple with pistols, stupid about moving. He was going to try to stop them, that was his idea, but he come on them when two were sighting on a hunter cat at work, and there, clear as could be, was *his* shot.

Five of them were dead where they fell; the sixth tried to pull a hideaway on him, way too late.

He'd gone back to the house with the dead cats, planning to bury them, and roused Rollie—who'd been late getting back from a jaunt to The Easiery—and told him he'd got himself some bad varmints, and Rollie'd better look, which Rollie did.

Eventually a couple of city-types claiming kin and friend came looking, and Rollie'd pointed out the signs about no hunting and told them there'd been a hunting accident that got out of hand, told them the farm didn't have any food animals no how.

Rollie'd already sold the intruder's guns to Boss Ira, anyhow, and wasn't much to show them, and that had been that, except of course Yulie'd spent every day for a year walking that route, back and forth, counting the cats, and some nights took the rifle out, waiting for people. Nobody else came, and eventually he'd learned to sleep again.

And so he'd got up, last night, and walked out to the disguised growhouse. He talked to a couple of the cats who guarded the coffee plants there in the cavern, told them he was sorry for not doing better by them. If they didn't say nothing back, at least they listened to his apology; then he slept well and woke up sharp, and ready to work.

The morning wake-up being what it was, he was standing at the window watching the gray horizon verging on pink, his coffee just warming his hands, gray cat leaning companionably against the back of his legs, when this *thing* appeared in the sky, dusty bright in the coming sunlight, unscheduled.

No meteor. No spaceship he knew of. Not even a Korval spaceship, big as Grampa had made them sound—this thing looked like it had craters on it . . . and then it was out of sight.

He stood there for some time, feeling the gray cat against the back of his legs. He sighed, wondering if that hadn't been in the events columns there in the *Blair Road Booster.*

This time he was waiting for it, and since the world had turned under the orbit, caught it in just above mid-horizon, and he stopped tossing the cabbages to stare.

It wasn't a ship, and it *was* cratered, but it wasn't a big thing by any means, "big" being a relative term when it came to objects in space, even in nearspace. Yulie'd heard of constructs that might be that size, but not constructs of rock; whatever it was, it was not the size of a tidal satellite, by any means.

Still, he was hardly an expert, having only the hand-me-down lessons from Grampa, and the optics scope. The sky was brilliant though, and blue, and it was still visible, with Triga and Toppa not yet risen to confuse with odd shadows. Not that Surebleak's two tidal moons were all that bright, but they both were capable of casting some light and when they were in-sync were quite a spectacular sight, especially when they were in conjunction with Chuck-Honey.

Yulie checked the chronometer, almost doubting. Right. It *was* orbiting, and it wasn't high at all. Something that size could make a heck of a hole if it was on the way down. A heck of a hole.

He felt the panic gnawing experimentally at his vision, but no! There, an aircraft, flying low over Melina Sherton's land, or maybe over Ira's back farms. Almost noiseless, it banked, headed his way. He thought to run, but the thing banked away, obviously interested in the growing little blocktown Melina and Ira'd been working on, just in case the fools in the city actually did themselves in. Interested? Hah—it might be it was landing somewhere over that way.

Yulie threw the striped orange cabbage from his hand to the crate, willing to call the thing full. That ought to do it. Five full crates—time to get things moving. No time to be worried about aircraft, and—

He twisted, catching a glimpse of some low clouds coming from the northwest, which could portend a rainy morning on the morrow, perhaps even a snowy tomorrow night.

The moon-thing was out of sight now, but he was going to watch for it. Meanwhile, it was time to go if he was going to hit Boss Sherton's farmer's market before the last of the day-buyers left.

· · · ✧ · · ·

THE WALK WAS DOING YULIE GOOD, even if the plane had come by for one more pass before disappearing for good. He knew it was too soon for the return of the new moon, but scanning the sky was helping him keep the world in perspective as he trod down the slope toward the farmers market. His backpack held six cabbages—one each for the two local bosses, and one each for the tollbooth crews to share. The other two were promise-proofs for the farmers who might come to help, knowing good food when they saw it.

The slope got steeper, and then the road went through a short valley, still tending downhill, with rocky hills acting as a kind of weather break and demarcation for the land below.

Originally, of course, that natural wall the valley pierced made for good siting for the test dig that had become World's End, and for the company's first management zone. Once the dig got going, management was inclined to prefer the portside bar and restaurants and then—and then the company had gone slowly into decline as the commercial timonium need drove the independents, and later the big boys, to follow the joint trail of creation and destruction that was the legacy of Chuck-Honey's rapid path through the regional space.

Somewhere Chuck, or Honey, or the pair together, had swarmed upon a stony-cored brown-dwarf remnant of the same monster cloud that had formed Surebleak and its system, and that dwarf's bounty lay in the metals and transuranics—and the encounter, sundering the dwarf, created a rogue field of rocks and high-grade ore, loosely trailing behind. Asteroids and comets and potential moons, the rocks now transited interstellar space. Lucky ships could come up with lumps of near pure timonium, or gold, or lead. Hardworking ships and companies could mine instead the broken chunks, needing no excavation equipment to speak of, no investment in people and governments and law—

The company stuck with appurtenances—excavators and law clerks and straw bosses and crewship pilots and—it had contracts and plans and goals enough to get it through a couple of financial ripples, but in the end it was easiest to sell the company to a shell corporation and merge that with another and drag what funds there were in transit out—and then abandon to the tender mercies of the jackals of interstellar finance the remains. The people stuck onworld belonged there after all—who needed dirt miners in a good clean space-rock roundup?

Grampa—Grampa had been owed big-time when the company was going to dust, and he'd fought for what was owed him for the ship he'd bought, fought for his plans to retire to a nice planet somewhere with lots of water and lots of willing ladies . . . and filed liens and lawsuits.

The company capitulated and in a final act of law, after seven years, offered a settlement. They gave all the company's current right, title, and interest to all its holdings on Surebleak to Grampa. That included the original administrative area, and the marshaling yards . . .

Like so many others, he'd been swindled: the ditch was worked clean and worth nothing, and the marshaling yard had long been converted into farms for the portside executives.

In the end, Grampa moved to his holding, found himself a wife and a girlfriend and some monographs on farming, and dug in, sure that eventually, things would turn out. It wasn't long before he was doing well enough, in the strange way that things worked on Surebleak. His daughter, of course, was brought up to farm, and then her sons, after she left...and now Yulie walked to the people next door, hoping for a boon. He had good food, what he needed was transportation and trade for it . . . especially now, a way to replace the lighting that Rollie'd always traded for.

It was a trick of geography that could let him arrive first at the market and then at the small streets and buildings, and then go through the tollbooth, if he were so inclined—but really, since he wasn't much interested in anything but the market and the farmers, he headed that way, the day warming on him in a way that warned of incoming moisture. He walked more slowly now, not liking to overheat if he was going to be seeing people, the road now a sandy gravel as he approached the market.

Yulie could just about identify the stalls and stall owners when the edge of his hearing was tickled by an odd sound. It was not one of Surebleak's rare birds, but it bounced around considerably, and it wasn't an aircraft. It was a more like a moan, speeding up and then down, rising and decreasing in volume . . .

Whatever it was, it traveled the road, a tail of dust behind it, rapidly approaching the dimly seen tollbooth, and just as rapidly charging through, all the guards standing aside.

The distant market folk were as transfixed as he, and the sound grew both closer and louder, and downslope he could see the glint of the vehicle. It came on, shiny as dew on the grass, scattering walkers and small carts out of the way. It rushed at him, silver glinting from all the polished surfaces, and he stepped into the gully, trying to push back the panic that rose in him.

The vehicle charged on, not pausing.

Unless the driver was mad, there was only one place it could be going.

To his house.

Yulie turned and began running, uphill, toward home, the cabbages banging at his back.

* * * ✧ * * *

THE MORNING HAD BEEN considerably hectic and much more uncomfortable than expected. Pat Rin had never expected to *miss* the wallow of his mother's landau but the rattle-filled car was simply not up to the paving, or lack thereof, on this section of the road he supposedly controlled. He'd gone to the road's end once before, at a stately pace, some twelve days before his expedition to Liad, but that ride had been marked by ceremonial stops at each of the tollbooths, exchanges of gifts, small sips of whatever the local boss thought potable, and the inevitable meeting of the first three or four ranks of each tollbooth crew.

This expedition was frantic from the outset. The portacom call had shattered rest, and the breakfast thrown onto the table soon after had been functional and little else. In need of speed, they'd all drunk some of Cheever McFarland's blend of coffee, which no doubt multiplied the current feel of dangerous speed. McFarland's unfinished mission of the day before haunted them now.

Awake on need, he heard the unmistakable timbre, not of Shan's voice or of Val Con, as he might expect, but of the rapidly socializing brother of his cousin.

"Boss Pat Rin yos'Phelium Clan Korval, Master Gambler, I give you greetings. I have sighted the landing zone indicated and, following my brother's wishes that this portion of his art be conducted as smoothly as possible, I have entered into a course arriving there this day. I look forward to seeing you again as we walk together with my brother."

And that was that: the tree was landing.

He'd tried of course—

"There are preliminaries, Edger, yet undone. I do not seek to school you in haste or—"

Uncharacteristically, Edger had spoken over him.

"My brother is in the throes of what may be his most elegant and urgent artwork yet. I will not fail him in this, as my delay in earlier matters of art interfered in the work in progress. We will walk together soon, you and I, and discuss this art."

"Wait at least until—"

"Before the local sun sets on the site, you will assure me that the way is clear."

And that had been the end of the conversation.

"How many more?"

"We're not there yet, Boss. Two more."

"Excellent!" is what he said, but the ceaseless cry of the siren drowned him out as he fiddled with two piles, one printouts of old company records and the second hastily written legal papers based on the admittedly thin standing his title of Boss gave him. The other standing he held—he looked down at his ring—*that* standing was certainly an odd one as well. For the first time in memory there were *two* Korval clan rings. Val Con wore his, the proper original, worn and fractured as it was, while the one recognized here on Surebleak was the wonderfully crafted counterfeit given him by the Department of the Interior. Not that the materials were counterfeit, but that the whole of it was part of a scheme to turn Korval into a puppet of the Department. And now . . .

And now Korval was depending on him as much or more than ever.

"Can we go faster?"

Gwince managed to shake her head and avoid a lumbering truck full of squash at the same time, eyes briefly on Pat Rin through the rear-view.

"If you say so, Boss. The car's already gonna need fixing when we get home."

"Do it."

They could and they did. Cheever McFarland's overflight had spotted the apparent landowner to home and not carrying a long gun, and now they rushed past Boss Ira's second tollbooth without acknowledging the various attempted salutes as well as the gestures that were not, quite, salutes from those clearing way for him. Ahead, when he looked, the Boss could see farmers hurrying to the side, and the occasional lurch showed that not all of the travelers used enough alacrity, even with the siren. They'd have to push on the emergency vehicle protocols.

"Little more coffee up here, Boss," Gwince told him. "You want it?"

"I do not. If it keeps you sharp, I suggest you use it."

They came that quickly to Melina Sherton's hold, and screamed through it, still scattering people before them. Gwince said, "Last one, Boss," rousing Pat Rin from an inner debate on how many items of Code he'd broken today. When his mother arrived from her missions, no doubt he'd receive particular tuition in his faults.

One last straggler before them, knapsack bouncing, gained the gully ahead, and then open road past the farmer's market, and perhaps some chance of a successful negotiation.

• • •◇• • •

YULIE WASN'T LIKE ROLLIE—he spent no time swearing—but he was running now on adrenaline, a situation that always put him prepanic. Not good to have strangers in the yard, not good to try to do this all himself, not good to—

He stopped his rapid march, stomping his feet at himself. The "not good" was more dangerous than anything, right now, because it took thought from him

Closing his eyes, he took a deep breath, felt his feet on the ground, the knapsack on his back, the growing breeze on his face. He opened his eyes, slowly, and stretched.

Overhead was the new moonlet, bright and motionless in the light, larger maybe than it had been, but, motionless.

That, of course, was unlikely. Anything that size in low orbit should visibly move. He craned his neck and saw no evidence that it moved.

He closed his eyes again, staggering when he opened them, and the moonlet remained there.

The other option was that the moon was larger than he believed, and in the synchronous orbit, always to remain overhead.

He faced forward, looked up.

No change.

He held no confidence in the idea that the moonlet was hovering, but—

He shook his head, saw his shadow, looked to the sky where a small cloud's shadowed underbelly came between him and the moon. And then revealed the moon, giving the momentary sense that the thing was moving . . . but then as the cloud distanced itself, it was clear that again, the moon was not moving perceptibly.

He felt like bolting, like hiding and covering his head until everything went away. That hadn't worked though, and he'd gotten behind—

"Doing something is better than doing nothing," Grampa had told him more than once.

He'd been doing something. He better just do it.

Keeping his head level, eyes forward, he snugged the knapsack and took a step. Then another, a little faster, and then another, faster, not quite coming to a trot. The cats needed him.

. . .◇. . .

THE KITCHEN WAS TIDY, if one ignored the cat on the countertop. Pat Rin had been trying to ignore it, but it was large enough to do damage if provoked, and who knew what might provoke it, as skittish as it was, and the landowner alike.

His eyes were brown and wary, and he had a right to be wary. His movements were disturbing in some odd way—skittish. Like he suddenly might jump for the door, or for the gun on the wall, or for Pat Rin himself. It was by main force of will, Pat Rin thought, that the man Yulie sat at all.

"Melina told me about you," he said. "She told me I should send to you. She told me I ought to go see you, but I didn't. She said you were an even-handed boss, the best she's seen."

Pat Rin spread his hands slowly, turning the extremely modest bow he'd started into a nod.

"I'm pleased she speaks well of me," he admitted. "It makes one feel worthy of being boss. Boss Sherton told me of you as well," he said. "Of your holdings. Of you, as a farmer. She speaks highly of you and that is why I am here, you see, because I have taken it upon myself to hold the road open, with the help of the other bosses. It is good for farmers, it is good for the bosses, and it good for the port."

"But this thing about the road—"

Pat Rin nodded.

"Yes. I have asked you if you are fond of the old ditch, and you tell me no. I repeat that what I need, as boss and as member of Clan Korval, is a place for my kin to live. It will be a change for you, to have such near neighbors, I know, but understand, these are neighbors who will appreciate your right to privacy. In addition, they will assist in the upgrading of the road, and they will assist in Boss Sherton's plan to take the road, starting at the farmers market, toward the sea."

He'd begun, had Pat Rin, as soon as the man's cat had stopped stropping at his legs, as soon as the man had managed to catch his breath in front of the low house, with the baldest statement of his mission he'd been able to formulate on the bouncing ride.

"I am Boss Conrad, also known as Pat Rin yos'Phelium. I come as both to purchase access through your land to the abandoned pit, for my kin. Your own lands and fields will be untouched."

They'd stood in a tableau for some moments, both aware of the unnatural moon hanging above, neither admitting it was there until finally the cat had stretched to Yulie's hand, seeking a head rub. Gwince remained around the car, talking complaints into a recorder, saying things like "quarter panel scrape passenger side, gonna need filling. Door gonna need . . ."

The man had glanced at Gwince, and pointed toward the house, saying, "And I'm Yulie Shaper. I guess we better talk. Come on in."

There were on the table ten cantra pieces, all of which had been examined minutely, and two tested with a knife, and there were two cups, one of which held coffee of a very potent scent, and the other, which held a fragrant tea.

"Melina Sherton never told me you was crazy."

The laugh came unbidden, a natural and not a social laugh, and Pat Rin nodded the point.

"Nor did she say that you were. It appears that the times make us crazy, Yulie Shaper."

Yulie's skittishness lessened, which put the cat at ease. The cat retracted feet until it rested like a furry log on the counter, eyes on Yulie.

"That's real money," said the farmer, touching the coins again. "Out there, that's World's End, and that's real. How's anybody going to live there? Nothing there but old bedrock and streams that don't go nowhere. Let's look at the reality of the situation. How can ten cantra be Balance for all that empty?"

"*That empty*, as you put it, that is precisely what is needed since Clan Korval has contrived, with the assistance of relatives and friends, to bring the house itself, much as the company brought here prefabbed units, growing chambers, stasis storage bins—"

Yulie sat straight, bringing the cat to sit straight as well.

Pat Rin raised his hands away from the table and looked the farmer directly in the eyes, speaking soft-voiced.

"Yes, we do have those records—we know—but it is of no matter. Please understand that I am far too involved with other matters . . ."

The calm voice seemed to help, and Pat Rin spread his hands, ring bright. He tapped the ring thoughtfully.

"Mr. Shaper, had I personal designs on being a farmer, I'd have thought no better place exists on Surebleak. You have the lands that were prepared with excellent soil by the company to sell stock, the equipment meant to hold food for ten thousand workers, and likely active grow sheds and prep rooms . . . and I come to you and request you sell access because building other access routes would be difficult, and unpopular. Personally, I have no designs on being a farmer, and farming has never been a family business. You might inquire of Boss Sherton, who is assured I have no interest in holding farms given the many I might have owned by now all in the hands of those who know what to do with them."

The man settled, nodding. The cat settled, too.

Pat Rin sipped at the surprisingly good tea, no doubt due to those stasis bins he'd mentioned. Yulie Shaper sipped at his fragrant coffee.

"Your world will change somewhat, when the house is . . . installed. For some measure of traffic, there will be traffic, but it will be passing traffic. The clan is not large, and historically we spend much time in travel. But the location of *that empty* is perfect for us, and I think for you."

"Suppose I want to sleep on it?"

Pat Rin declined to put on his card-player's face, and kept Boss Conrad as tightly controlled as he might.

"That would be unfortunate from my viewpoint, as my kin are in transit, along with the house. The clan's ships are arriving even now . . ."

"Saw that," Yulie nodded. "Big ship orbiting. Did you use that to figure out the spot?"

Pat Rin sighed lightly.

"We used that to bring the clan and possessions. We used it to leave our home world and come here. Mr. Shaper, the only practical place for the clanhouse to go is someplace very close to the road, yet not in someone else's territory. Boss Gabriel tells me he has no plans for the place you call World's End. Boss Sherton says the same. Your claim here is perhaps the strongest claim on a piece of land on all of Surebleak, the port notwithstanding. It is impractical for us to move the port, as you must know. We tried to reach you sooner, but you were not speaking with visitors."

"This is sudden—"

He stood up, did Yulie, jerkily, pushing away from the table with a clatter. Pat Rin wished he'd brought Anthora or Shan, or Priscilla, all of whom were healers. Clearly, there was need here for calm—

Yulie spun around, touched the cat. There was a pause, and Pat Rin wondered if the gun on the wall could actually be loaded, since the man looked at it, touched the cat again, before he sat down heavily in the chair, pulled it to table, eyes staring into the distance, troubled.

The fist that hit the table was firm, and not impudent.

"Didn't answer," Yulie said.

Pat Rin bowed. Boss Conrad sighed.

"Mr. Shaper, my kin *will* be taking over that location. They *will* put the clanhouse and all that comes with it there. And they will do it soon. What we ask is for an access road. The contract is clear: ten cantra now and one per Standard Year in the future to lease access as long as the clan uses it."

He paused, suppressed the pilot's clear-the-board hand motion, continued.

"If you say no, the clan will put the house there and take away a hill or hills and do whatever else is necessary to reach the city over on the farside, through wastelands."

"Why don't you just take it?"

Pat Rin sighed then.

"Mr. Shaper, I have done many things to make Surebleak workable. I *have* taken things. What I wish to do is to make things work well, and to deal honorably with the world. I wish not to take it. I wish to trade for it, just as you wished to trade your cabbages for what you need."

Yulie was holding on to his coffee cup now as if he was afraid it would jump from his hands, a lucky thing that he'd had so much of it already.

Pat Rin stood up, bowing.

"*I will not just take it,*" he said so quietly that it might have been for his ears rather than Yulie's, and reached for the pile of cantra on the table.

Now it was Yulie's turn to show placating hands. Pat Rin saw them, left the coins where they were while Yulie's unschooled face showed decision crossed with doubt before finally giving way to words.

"Promise me—write it in the contract—that your people won't shoot my cats. And I want you here when they put the house in, and you'll tell them so there won't be any—accidents. Write it and sign that, and I'll sign it."

Pat Rin glanced up at the cat on the counter, thought about Silk, thought about Jonni, who some called his son . . . and nodded.

"I can do that, Mr. Shaper. I may need a moment or two in order to compose it, of course."

"Take your time. But when do you think you'll be back?"

Pat Rin lifted an eyebrow.

"Be back?"

"Yes. When will they put the house in?"

Pat Rin lifted a hand to stay the query as he wrote, and then signed with a flourish, which became an offer of the stylus.

"Here, Mr. Shaper, do you agree as well, if you would."

Yulie read the words several times and mumbled "Good cats," or something like, after reading "welfare of cats shall not be imperiled" and nodded, and signed a scrawling hand that nearly filled the bottom of the sheet.

"Good, here." Yulie handed the sheets back as if they were precious, then asked, "When will they be here—I should move some of the rocks on the edge and . . ."

"When? I expect just before dusk."

"But *when*? What day?"

"Oh, I expect before dusk today, Mr. Shaper, today."

· · · ◇ · · ·

THE ROCK, THE MOON, was almost down now; they'd followed it bright in the day, and then seen it shine through from behind light clouds. Now it was half-enveloped as the light faded, and so close that it seemed it might crush them all were one wrong move made by the pilot.

Sounds came randomly: booms of lightnings from planet to moon, echoes of the winds, crackling noises as small portions of the moonlet were shed in puffs of dust. Surebleak had few birds, but they all appeared to have gathered in welcome, the preternatural light of a setting star bounced off a descending moon giving the birds' shadows the length of an avenue.

The word from the city was that all was quiet; which was good— the news that Boss Conrad was in charge was unreasonably accepted as evidence that there would be no problem, no matter the appearance of a moon falling ever so slowly on the upcountry tilt of land that supplied the city with food.

Boss Conrad himself stood in a crowd of cats—several dozen by his estimate. He'd been warned that the proximity of the clutch drive might have unexpected effects, and certainly the sudden appearance of so *many* cats, streaming from the fields, from the sheds, from the rocks—was unexpected.

Also unexpected was the absolute calm Yulie Shaper exhibited, as if whatever demons he usually had to deal with were exorcised by the drive's beneficent fields.

Pat Rin, for his part, was well-traveled; as passenger and pilot, he'd been shipboard many times when approaching foreign worlds, satellites, and stations, and he found the experience just barely containable: there were no walls, no comforting calls of station managers, nothing ordinary whatsoever about this vision. He knew more than most what the size of things were and the size and expanse of this was beyond his knowledge. Something that size should not move, that was what he knew. The moon nearly touched the planet's surface, the wind rushed and carried odors of space and time and strangeness with it.

Whatever downward progress had been made, it all paused at once, though stones and ice, dust and clouds continued to fall. Something very strange was happening now, as the bottom surface of the moon appeared to vibrate and—but there was no human word for the process, which occurred within their sight over the yawning chasm of the place they both now called World's End.

An earthquake's worth of sound beat at them, the ground shook, trembled, bellowed, vibrated—and was calm.

For a moment or two, the only sound was that of cats, huddled now near the people in as much awe as they were, and then a hiss, and more wind, and the surprisingly familiar odor of wood and leaf.

Almost imperceptibly, the moon-thing that filled their vision and covered the land rotated, spinning very, very slowly on an axis and then it was rising . . . rising, rising, the sounds of falling dust and noisy birds and earth trembles giving way to a rush and almost a thunderclap as the moon, disgorging the impossible thing within it, lifted, and spinning more strongly, wafted away.

Amid the haze and winds stood a massive new tower of green, the upper fronds of the tree catching the failing light as the base was in shadow, the whole seeming now to have been too big to have landed within the moon, far too alive to have come through space. The birds, still alight from the rising of the moon, swirled toward it, their calls echoing from the land and sky.

Pat Rin yos'Phelium Clan Korval, bowed to the clan's still-astounded new neighbor.

"The tree's roots grew with the bounds of the house, you see, and so we brought both. Necessity, sir, necessity."

Using his chin, Pat Rin indicated the low structure beneath the branches. "The house is there, where the dust settles even now."

Pat Rin sighed, waved his hand toward the lip of World's End, now full to within paces of Shaper's land.

"I believe that, if we start walking now, we can explain the rules of the contract to my kin very soon. As a clan, we're somewhat familiar with contracts."

✧ Skyblaze ✧

Solcintra, Liad

IT WAS PERHAPS a nonsense phrase, but around fares and administrivia, Vertu dea'San Clan Wylan, who was in fact Wylan Herself, Delm of her small Clan, allowed it to amuse for most of the early shift, finding the ease with which it shifted between Terran and Trade, with at least some meaning attached to it, an instructive counterpoint to the utter inability to phrase it properly in any of the modes Liaden provided.

Somebody ought to do something.

It was the "ought" of course, providing the information that *melant'i* required an action without indicating in which direction it flowed, nor from which necessity, nor from which source, the "somebody" being a particular problem for the Liaden sensibility.

The phrase had become common recently, the port being unusually beset by Terran travelers left behind or inconvenienced by this or that ship, change of schedule or sudden rerouting—and had today intensified with the sudden advent of a large vessel full of boisterous mercs with only the most modest of language resources among them.

Not that they—tourists and travelers and mercs every one—weren't good for business, especially at the hours when they were the only business, but they tended to want *something to be done* about signs in Trade or Terran where clearly they were on a Liaden port and should expect Liaden custom to prevail.

It was, Vertu acknowledged to herself, true that the two places most likely to be accessible to non-Liaden speakers were the elegances of High Port, and the depths within the shadow of the Tower—Low Port, where small businesses, some barely above begging shops, trembled to bring in every last coin, not disdaining Terran bits or other Terran custom.

This insight came to her as she finished a bowl of noodles and cheese with the last sip of wake-up tea from the corner shop that supplied her meals whenever she had the shift—the insight that she, too, did not disdain Terran bits.

For that lack of disdain, she supposed she would forever be among the last and least to receive invitations or acknowledgment from the Council, but there—she was Wylan, and would remain so for some time, and in that she was secure. She did her best to keep the clan, and if it had meant that over the relumma she'd opted to add respectable Terran and Trade lettering to her vehicles, and to choose the larger rather than the most elegant, and if *Most Serene Travel Experience* became *Wylan's Port Taxi* in translation, so be it. That the High Houses disdained her survival was not her concern. That they expected her to bow to them out of other than necessity was absurd.

Well, perhaps she ought to bow, just for practice.

With that thought, she bowed vaguely in direction of Korval's distant Tree, it being the closest point she could see that was not of the port and thus not of the Council, and turned on the comm-retrieval, in case there was commerce.

· · · ◇ · · ·

THE PECKING ORDER at the taxi line was nearly immutable, with latecomers—meaning those firms or clans with three generations or less experience—sitting on the second line for manual wave-ins, while those older—the "holding clans" who had permanent transport licenses with no expiration date—shared the first line in an intricate dance Vertu could call, but whose logic was born of something other than service to the traveling public.

Clan Wylan ought, perhaps, *not* be be among those called latecomers, being not recent to the trade, but to the location, but there—that was an old battle, lost some generations back when a racing park gave way to manufacturing in a slyly executed move by an Olanek—and the Balance for it would come from someone else, for her need upon retrieving the Ring from the insensate hand of her predecessor had been to preserve the clan, which to this point she had done.

The current Wylan license would grow to a holding license in only another twelve Standards; Vertu's personal goal was to take that first drive for the clan and retire, her duty done, with daughter to take up the Ring. But for now, within her clan, port duty went first to the one who'd had least of it within the last twelve-day and she'd been the lucky one for some time, finding on-call work from the scout back office, from the Binjali repair shop, from people traveling anywhere but to or from the port's pick-up line.

For that stretch of good fortune, she today had the on-port line while her daughter, Fereda, did the outer routes and her no-longer-halfling son, Chim Dal, still likely partied his night off with friends who might well make him late tomorrow morning. Ah, to have such energy—and such friends!—as he did.

Dutifully, Vertu pulled her taxi into the secondary line, watching the first line's ballet as they accepted or neglected fares. A quiet shift, she was perhaps seventh in line as she waited, allowing the car's music system to wake up the day. Soon she was sixth, and then fifth, and fourth . . . fourth behind three drivers sitting for the morning meal as they waited.

That, of course, was one of her advantages—she did not eat nor game while on wait, nor drink, smoke, or chat for more than a moment or two with other drivers—and so she was not in the wrong to move forward when the manager of line one waved frantically at line two, despite the shiny row of on-duty line ones, all disdaining the next fare.

And so, there must be a reason.

She blinked as she pulled to the front, for the next fare was not one but two uniformed mercenary Terrans and their luggage. Clearly too large for many of the top-end cabs—even without their hand-carry—with it, they would have needed a moving service, or indeed, a multicab like the very one she drove.

The Terrans nodded to her, and the darker one held out a Unicredit card as she slowed to a stop.

She popped the doors, intending to assist, but they hustled into the cab without aid, depositing their luggage between them, the dark one still holding the card out.

"We need to visit this address," he said in what might be flawless Trade, but who knew, after all, Trade being a language without a home. He pulled out a folded sheet of hard copy which he held for her to see, adding, "We may be some time at the location."

She bowed a slight acknowledgment, pointing out, "Traveler, time and distance are what I charge for, and so we are Balanced."

She accepted the proffered card and waved it at the reader, which happily beeped and accepted the charge, for one Howler Higdon, if she read the transliterations correctly.

"Soonest is better!" the larger of the two said.

"Yes," she agreed, "soonest is always better."

* * * ✧ * * *

UNUSUAL TO SAY, the address was one she'd never delivered to before—in fact, she barely recognized the subquadrant, much less the crossroads, and was pleased to find the vehicle map knew more than she did. The quadrant was hardly one visited frequently by anyone, especially not sudden Terrans, but she accelerated away from the line at a heady pace, wondering what they might want to see in the overgrown semi-wild sections of Solcintra's abandoned old lands.

The in-cab camera showed the Terrans at peace with themselves, watching the trip with interest but unconcern, quiet. She'd anticipated perhaps a visit to a brothel, or a gambling hall, or even a shopping extravaganza—not any of them out of the way destinations for Terrans, in her experience. This was perhaps even beyond the last unusual request she'd had—a Terran starpilot demanding a direct ride to Korval's holdings—but there, she'd learned from that trip to take the money, drive . . . and let the traveler take care of the details.

Routed through minimum traffic once away from the spaceport exit, the cab quickly passed through the usual areas of tourist interest—the largest buildings, the gaudy townhouse estates of the most overreaching High and Mid-Houses, the quaint rows of elegant shops where the rich shopped, the fastidiously landscaped inner and mid-parks, the—

The Terrans spoke low among themselves, and if the language was any she'd ever been schooled in, it was not recognized by her ear at this level, at this cadence.

"Your pardon, Driver."

She glanced to the screen, found his eyes waiting.

"Does the Serene Taxi Agency employ other vehicles? Might you be able to summon more if need be? Of this size or larger?"

She blinked, which he must have seen—he had enough Liaden to see the true-name, and hence to read her own on the driver-slot. Not, perhaps, a common Terran, here . . .

"I have several cars in my service," she admitted, "though availability depends upon prior routings and arrangements. Have you an immediate request—does your friend need another destination?"

That made the dark man smile and the larger man chuckle.

"No, Driver," the larger one said. "It is that, if we find our destination as we envision it, we may wish to invite others to an event." He paused, glancing with some meaning she did not grasp to his companion, who suppressed a smile as he continued, "The word for such an event is *picnic* in Terran, or call it a lunchfest, perhaps, in Trade."

She had Terran, to an extent, and this word *picnic* had come to her along with others of use to her trade and security—*rob, take, orgy, bash* . . . The destination they had chosen seemed an . . . odd . . . place for a picnic.

"Ah," she said, to indicate that she had heard, but not wishing to add more. She watched the city wind down to the true old houses and abandoned shells of things long left to the elements as Greater Solcintra had grown. Some of the area actually belonged to this or that clan, other parts had been early communal areas built shortly after landfall and ostensibly under the benevolent oversight of the Council of Clans. They called much of this area a park, but as so many things the Council did it was a convenient sop to appearances rather than a reality to be enjoyed by the average Solcintran.

Here, when they arrived, was a sharp corner leading into a sudden ridgetop. There was a short cross-street; perhaps buildings had adorned each end at some distant moment in history. After that came a turnabout overlooking hills falling away so sharply that at least one of them might be called a cliff, hills that fell in green profusion to wild streams and scattered rock below. It was in its way even more unregulated than the wilderness around Korval's valley, and a little disquieting, for it showed dissolution rather than desolation. The edge of the turnabout nearest the cliff lacked a buffer or curb, and there were marks there as if someone used the spot to push unwanted items into the ravine.

Vertu stopped on the side of the pavement with a curb, car and timer running, finding the address matched perfectly the one the dark Terran had given her. She looked into the camera then, finding her passengers looking elsewhere.

"Here we find your address. Shall you depart from me here, where there are neither people nor businesses, lost in the the backwoods of Solcintra?"

She trusted that Trade might somewhat hide her amusement, for surely she'd had worse fares. Still, as a destination it . . .

The larger Terran said in a Trade undertone clearly meant for his companion rather than her, "This could do it."

She glanced up, meeting the dark man's gaze in the camera, amusement flickering about his lips and eyes.

"If you might hold for us a short while, Driver. We must take a few readings . . ."

She bowed toward the camera, turned as if to show them the functioning of the doors, which, the cab being still, were able to be opened by either of them.

"You are my fare, and so I will await you, as the cab is empowered to charge you for time as well as travel."

"Yes, that is so." He smiled into the camera, and the pair moved quickly, opening the doors and exiting, pulling their luggage with them.

She watched as they walked to the paved edge, speaking too quietly now for her to overhear, gesturing in directions that indicated the sweep of the streams below, and of hills on the farther side.

A piece of luggage was snatched up, zipped quickly from its

sheathing—and there stood on a tripod, an object from another piece of luggage mounted to it—and another. The dark man stood back from it, staring into a hand-held, free hand moving as if he counted seconds.

The larger man moved to the cliff edge, staring into the distance, hands to face as if he shielded his eyes from glare, or held some small object to peer through.

"There!"

The larger man pointed, and made some kind of hand-signal, and both of them were at the tripod, hefting it just over the rim to the hillside, sliding down the dirt there, urgently doing things she couldn't quite see, until half of the tripod was out of sight, and half held its head above the paved plateau.

The larger man lurched up the side of the hill to the pavement, taking businesslike strides past her and the taxi to the cross-street where he turned, surveying the view like a tourist, and then with purpose. He stooped, staring toward the tripod and his friend with a solemn expression.

"And so?" he called out.

The smaller man replied across the distance, clearly saying:

"We're synched. Port-comm, ship-comm, Higdon Central. Enough to start on, I'd say."

"Got your recall on?"

"Can activate at will."

"You know the drill, then. You'll probably see me before you hear from me."

A wave and the Terran near the tripod moved down the slope, disappearing from view. The large man strode back to the cab, opened the door smoothly and slid in, carefully engaging the lock.

"Thank you for waiting," he said as he adjusted his lanky form to fit the seat. "Please start driving," he said carelessly, hand perhaps pointing toward the greater city.

Vertu bowed, put the car in motion. There were not all that many routes from here, after all . . .

She glanced into the camera, let the car straighten into the main road.

He watched, his face nearly Liaden in neutrality.

"I'd like to return to the spaceport area, but not to the point you picked us up. I'll show you where as we get near, if I may. Also, I'd like to discuss hiring this vehicle for the next Standard Day, and another fifteen vehicles like it, if they may be had. I am able to pay cantra, in advance, at triple day rate, if you prefer."

Returning her attention to the road, she bowed vaguely toward the camera.

"This discussion, we shall have it," she allowed in careful Trade, "when we have a stop on the road."

* * * ✧ * * *

WYLAN LET THE CAR'S TAXI-CHANNEL chatter to itself as she turned off the direct route. The noodle shop made an excellent stop on the road, and the location was agreeable to the Terran. He, nameless, had been quite patient with her short quick inquiries over timing and locations once she'd admitted she'd be dealing with—she used the Trade term *allies*—to fill in the cars her own agency could not provide. That most of those would not be directly under her command she'd not let on, but there, the details need not concern him.

Into the camera, she began—

"Your need must be great, oh traveler, and you have many friends. I must, you understand, be sure of my necessities before committing so many of my resources . . ."

Also into the camera, the Terran: "May I speak in confidence with you, and ask, if you find my offer not to your liking, that you permit me to make the offer to others—"

She bowed lightly in her seat, also raising her left hand with a slight shoo-away sign.

"If my *melant'i* finds your offer unfortunate, I will tell you so, carry you to a destination, and be done with it. I cannot be responsible for the *melant'i* of others, says the Code, nor should I wish to!"

"I appreciate your understanding," he said, "and your honesty." He paused, reaching about his person as if in search of something, finally arriving at a bent card—yes, very much a card such as she herself might convey upon meeting new acquaintances of worth.

"It seems that I am come with a less-than-presentable card, and ask you to forgive my haste. Let me share this, if I may, as is—"

She opened the port and took the flimsy, which was a very high-quality paper indeed.

The card was two-sided—one side printed in Trade, the other in Terran. Simple typography conveyed extremely chilling information.

Commander Octavius Higdon
Higdon's Howlers
Military Missions. Security to mayhem.
Guaranteed Service.

There were contact numbers listed, and the man in her cab's passenger compartment—this *Commander Higdon*—quietly awaiting her reaction.

Vertu met his eyes in the screen.

"And you wish to invade our park?"

He sighed openly, which surprised her, but then Terrans were complicated, it was well-known.

"I wish to expose my acquaintances to a larger experience here on Liad, and the park is an excellent location for it. In fact, my compatriots will carry their lunches and be prepared to enjoy them there, at my direction. Additionally, we are involved in a . . . situation of Balance—and my understanding is that by showing a presence *here* we may arrive at an equitable solution in a timely fashion."

It was likely that she blinked at him, so unexpected was his declaration.

"Balance from off-worlders . . . is not something one often sees, here on Liad," she managed, "since so many things that follow the Code are subtle and enforced by . . ." she paused, seeking the right phrase in translation.

"Social pressure?"

He'd leaned forward, had the commander, offering his suggestion with deference.

"An accurate turn of phrase," she said. "I thank you."

He nodded then and, perhaps, threw in a shrug of indeterminate meaning, and made a hand gesture indicating, perhaps, motion.

"As we noted before, soonest is better. A quick Balance sees you paid ahead and permits my friend at the gully to sleep indoors tonight! Thus, permit Higdon's Howlers to charter your vehicle at the three-times rate now, and we shall add the others as you may arrange or broker, understanding that the request is on short notice."

Vertu paused, considering, staring into the slightly thickening sky above, measuring her need.

Fereda, of course, was her need—it would be well to solve the girl's urge for the soonest marriage. A single heir was all she required, of a good—if not High—clan.

The candidates were there, for Fereda kept track of those most eligible, as she kept track of the most likely contract price. And it was not as if Fereda had either a fear or a distaste for those she preferred as a father to her child—it was that her *cha'laket* was an artist and near-healer, fragile in *her* necessities, and would not willingly abide a frequent parting. That Fereda thought this possible—well, that would be hers to mend.

The price of a husband had twice been within reach, and lost each time to business. This time, *this* time, it would not be so. Three-times day-rate for each of Wylan's three cabs, plus the broker fee from those others she enlisted. She would not—could not—name the sum entirely, but that it would be of use to Clan Wylan—*that* she could say with assurance.

"I will broker this," she said, "and since Balance requires care and concern, for this my own retainer will be five times the day-rate. My other cars, and those of my associates, they will be paid for at your offered rate, per car, in advance, as they arrive to work."

There was a pause and a glance, and a hint of a smile.

"This can be done, if we may adjust the number of total vehicles to a dozen."

She bowed agreement.

"Here is five cantra," he said, showing them to the screen before placing them in the pass-through tray, "to seal the arrangements."

* * * ✧ * * *

IT WAS THE THIRD RETURN TRIP from the park to the port, and by now the fact of their passing was drawing attention, despite the window shields hiding their cargo of potential mayhem. Vertu's cab was in the lead, with Fereda just behind. Vertu was sweating, despite the climate-controlled driver's space.

They'd ferried the soldiers and their weapons, yes, to the hidden park—and they had done so several times, with the other dozen allied cabs assisting as they might.

Something had happened there, fighting and such, but the signs she'd seen of it were all on the rim of the park: soldiers tired and rumpled, some without the weapons and objects they'd carried in, soldiers dirty despite obvious attempts to clean up. Soldiers injured, who were assisted into passenger compartments by their undamaged comrades.

On this, her third return to Port, a wounded man occupied the seat behind Vertu, laughing with his mates, arm and shoulder bloodied. He included her in his conversation—a distraction, for he spoke Terran in a thick dialect that was almost as thick in Trade.

"Don'cha worry, ma'am," he said when his mates had hustled him into the car. "Don' feel a thing. Don'cha worry 'bout Tommee, no'm. I'll wrap this up some so's we don't getcher pretty car dirty. 'Mander made sure we know this ain't like it's a zone transport or nothing."

His comrades folded him gently into the backseat, for he was a big Terran, and they chatted with him, trying to fix his attention, and free her to drive.

"Tommee, tell me about breakfasts, keed," they said—and when he laughed and said something half-finished, they had at him again, "What's the name of that girl waiting for them Hundred Hours?"

"Here," one said, soft-voiced under the rambling reminiscence of that lady's charms. "Just a shot, keed, so's ya walk on yer own, an' don't go falling over on us."

Tommee laughed, hearing that, or some part of it. "Hellno! Don' wan' me fallin' that's sure! Take a platoon to carry me, eh?"

The soft-voiced one agreed, and there was the hiss of an injection, then a device came out of pack or pocket, and went around his arm—

a monitor of some kind, Vertu thought, and dragged her attention back to her contracted duty.

The taxi-call channels were jammed with people trying to escape *something*, of hurried visits to the country. Regulars were calling her in vain, for the call channels were reporting her cabs out of service, except for perhaps Chim Dal, who had never answered his call to assist in today's event.

Traffic was strangely light now, as if the Port and Low Port were emptied of all those who could go, as if the "side door" Commander Higdon had arranged truly opened upon some hidden corridors.

He had appeared, the commander, as Tommee was being loaded into her cab, and thrown what she thought might be a salute in her direction. She lowered the window as he leaned down.

"We've had a recall," he told her. "Balance achieved."

The boy, Tommee, for Vertu realized that for all his length, he was young, no older than her missing son . . . Tommee was singing now, and didn't even stop when a pair of noises erupted from the men on either side of him, each grabbing for a comm of some kind, and then each searching about themselves for—

"Tommee, where's the sidearm, my boy?"

"Right leg storage pocket, Danil, just like regs. Just cause I got hit a little don't mean . . ."

Beneath Tommee's voice, continuing at length, came a chime from Routing Info indicating information incoming. Vertu looked to the screens, at routes blocked out, streets unavailable.

Unavailable?

"Ma'am," said the one called Danil, catching her eye in the screen. "Our guys are seeing something a little bit like a riot, where we're going. You may want to just drop us off a few blocks away and we'll—"

The voice was respectful, and also his words. This did not hide the fact that he and his uninjured companion on Tommee's left both had weapons in-hand.

Vertu moved her foot, touching the floor stud that locked the partition, and brought the handgun out of the console.

"Is this an order, a robbery?"

The handgun . . . she'd fired it twice, the day she'd bought it, wondered if it would still work after all these years.

She drove on, knowing the cab's protection was meant for urban dangers, civilians . . .

"No, ma'am," Danil said. "Just that things may be out of hand towards the end of the trip . . ."

She barely spared him a glance as yet another route blinked out as impassable.

"I drive to Low Port, sir; a riot there is nothing new."

No sooner the words were said than she regretted them, for Tommee, who by now held a firearm in his undamaged hand, began singing something in loud Trade about Low Port Tramps . . .

They were now just two blocks from the exit point, she and her fares, with Fereda behind, and several more cabs still continuing on in train. The city around them was darker than it should have been, the streets becoming crowded with what might well *be* a riot, with people of mixed station standing on the walks, and cars left idling on the side of the street, with—

The road in front of them erupted, scattering rock and road against the windshield.

"Grenades," said one in the back, but by then she'd stopped the cab and unlocked all the doors.

"We're out!"

That was to her, no doubt, and the two able soldiers *were* out, dragging Tommee with them, and the cabs behind were disgorging their passengers as well.

Vertu saw her daughter's car begin to move—she'd not had a casualty disembark, after all. On the sidewalks, the soldiers were forming up.

"Anti-armor, get out of there!"

Vertu looked up, and there before her, perhaps three cab-lengths away, stood a man, an ordinary Liaden, well-dressed and calm. He met her eyes, his face perfectly composed, as he brought a tube to his shoulder, pointing it toward her, no—toward Fereda's cab! There were sounds she knew were guns, sounds she knew was small-arms fire—

Her cab leapt forward under her command, Tommee and his

comrades scattering as she aimed it for this calm, ordinary man. It was satisfaction she felt, in the instant that he changed his stance, and moved the tube, acquiring her cab as his target.

Vertu slammed the controls forward; the cab roared—

All around was brilliance and sound. The cab was lofted, tumbling backwards, restraints flashed into being, holding her tight and safe.

The odors were incredible, immediate. Dust covered her. The cab was wedged at an unfortunate angle, but around her the sounds continued. The windscreen was a spidernest of crazed glass, the whole car shaking with the force of Fereda's pounding against the door. With her were Vertu's last fares, the soldiers, with Tommee, who had not fallen down.

The door was jammed. Trussed tight in safety tape, there was little Vertu could do to aid in her own rescue. One of the soldiers took Fereda's place, another pulling her back with a gloved hand on her shoulder. There was a scream of tearing metal, and the door—was gone.

Vertu had time to blink the dust out of her eyes, before the crash-tape retracted and she fell into her daughter's arms.

"Mother!"

"Daughter, I am well."

"You could have been killed!"

"So I could, and you! A moment!"

Amid the chatter of gunfire and larger sounds, Vertu snatched her gun from its holder and returned to Fereda's side. Around them, the riot was a war zone; the soldiers gathering in positions against whatever enemy there was. The man with the tube, there he was, leveling it again, this time at her—

There was time to shove Fereda behind her; to raise the gun, to see his face, his anger and his intent

"Whoa, now! Civlins!"

Something struck her in the ribs with enough force to knock her from her feet to the ground, and Fereda atop her.

A very tall man stood above them, gun leveled.

The explosion deafened her, disoriented her. Fereda went limp, and she feared—but no, it was only the shock. They shoved against

each other, untangling and grasping at arms and shoulders, climbing
to their feet, staring again at a street in disorder, and—Tommee!

The Liaden with the tube lay like an empty bread wrap, bloody
back and side to them. Tommee was forward of his position, fallen
after all—swearing, swearing, *surely* swearing in his peculiar Terran
and in Trade, his legs—his foot—too far away from the rest of
him . . .

He saw her—saw them—made a grimace that might have been a
smile, saw the direction of her gaze, and followed it.

For a long moment, he looked at the red ruin of his leg, at the
disconnected foot in its overlarge boot. He raised his head and met
her eyes.

"Ma'am, thanks for the ride. 'Preciate. Reallydo."

The soldier's face, already ashen and staring upward, went pale
and then bright as shadows flashed out of the day and color washed
out of everything.

Vertu looked to the light above her, above them all, and there in
the sky over the city was a dancing lance of purplish light, and another
and perhaps more; and a boom like a thousand thunder strikes at
once washed over her. Her eyes involuntarily shut against the assault
of sound and light, and then she opened them, looking up to find the
source, but there was no source now, just a blazing brightness in the
sky. She thought it was done, but another lance of light fell upon the
city, and another until at last the sky was full of sudden cloud and
billowing smoke. The skyblaze was done now, but the world and the
people still shook in aftermath.

• • •◇• • •

"DERE'S A KINDAL DECENT WYMAN comm street edge . . . cah
checked . . ."

The news came from a guard with a comm set in each ear, who
stood nodding and scanning, nodding and scanning—

Vertu looked up from the comfort of the gun and leather, the
sounds coming together oddly, with almost as much meaning as
"somebody ought to do something . . ." and for the same reason—it
meant something to another, and she needed to respond. She was
sitting on the curb, drained of energy, with blood still wet before her,

in the street, strange clouds and a lingering scintillant light behind the smoke still rising from the strike zone.

This guard was not one she'd carried to the battle zone—this one was female, not quite as large as Tommee, with a multigun in open readiness—and she had only the barest distinguishable Terran, no Trade nor Liaden.

The words came again, this time perhaps aimed at Fereda, who leaned against her whole cab behind the shambles that had been the Delm's Own Cab, but Fereda had not heard; was not listening, as Vertu could see with a quick glance. The girl stood with a gun-grip perilously showing from her jacket pocket, staring into the sky where the flash had taken color from the world and where now rose a column of darkness unsullied by the light of the setting sun.

Fereda had been crying, which was unseemly, but the mercs had the dignity not to notice, which gave Vertu a relief far beyond reason. That gave her strength enough to look into the guard's eyes as she stood awaiting an answer, and replay the sounds she had uttered, seeking a sense which was suddenly plain.

"Chim Dal dea'San Clan Wylan," she said, speaking as clearly as possible.

The guard blamed the headset for a miscommunication by tapping at it seriously—but again she nodded, and used her chin to point toward the Mid-Port end of the road, which was now unblocked of the half-dozen cabs still mobile.

"Yes'm, gots it, and 'mander Higdon gives goheath foyah, pair."

Translation this time was easier. Vertu moved her hand to show that she had gotten the message, understanding that they were to go now. The gun and belt were heavy in her hand, but she had tried to give it back several times, and was every time refused. Tommee had been clear as they gathered him up—

"No'm," he said. "I'm f'surgery, an' got my backups. You had this, we'd all be better off. You take it, my gift. That's mine own, an' I give it to you, f—for your care. Pleased to be alive, ma'am, an' you taking on anti-armor! You'd make merc if you wanted! I'll sing your song, I will."

They'd known what to do, his comrades, and she'd felt helpless as they'd used belts and tubes and collected what obvious parts of his legs as they could, and bore him away. The commander had come by a few moments later as she was still clutching her daughter to her, the two of them perhaps weeping into the privacy of the other's shoulder. His face was clean but the uniform had been busy; there was blood—perhaps even Tommee's blood—on his sleeve.

How someone could be businesslike under these mad circumstances she did not know, but he had been, and she returned it as best she could.

"You have my card and you have my thanks. Smitty told me you sent your cab against anti-armor, and saved his life. By the rocks, you could have been killed! Good work, ma'am. I'll make it good—you understand? A new cab; repairs. You have my card. Get to me with a bill, hear?"

He'd attempted a bow, gave it up, saluted, and was gone. His aide also refused to take Tommee's gun from her. "Ma'am, he knows it might be the last thing he gets to give if you have my meaning, and you took damage for him. He's a newbie and his paycheck and his sidegun, it's what he owns. If it was me, I'd keep it and sleep with it under my pillow!"

Vertu sighed, made sure of her grip on the leather belt that held Tommee's gift, and walked unsteadily over to the cab, and her daughter leaning there. It had not escaped damage, this second of Wylan's three vehicles—there were holes stitched down the driver's door, a shattered window, a list to one side that spoke of blown stabilizers.

A bill, she thought wearily. For a new cab, and repairs.

Tomorrow, she would bill Higdon's Howlers for the damage they had caused her. For now . . .

"Fereda," she said, extending a hand to touch her daughter's pale and soot-streaked face.

The girl blinked as if she suddenly came to her senses from a swoon, stepping sharply away from her cab, away from Vertu's hand.

She turned her back, arms crossed tightly over her chest.

Vertu gasped, heart stuttering at the violence of the act—worse than any she had witnessed this day. Worse even than that flash which had dazzled everyone and everything, more violent than the ground-shake, more violent than the noise when that arrived.

Heart-struck, Vertu drew a careful breath and exhaled. Surviving that, she drew another breath . . . and a third.

The leather was real in her hand, and she had to do, *now,* with what was real now.

There was a stain on the belt, and the gun was twice as heavy as her own, the one that Fereda held in such low esteem as to pocket it so clumsily that it might fall out. But it was hers, this gun. A gift, for her care. That was real.

The fighting had been short and sharp; she'd shot once or twice with the gun Fereda had, not because she knew who was shooting but because they were shooting at her, or her car, or her daughter, or bloody Tommee . . .

She did not look at the street. Instead, she paced forward until she faced her daughter, trying to ignore the dark clouds overhead and in her daughter's visage.

"Fereda dea'San," she said to set face and distant eyes, "we shall leave here together. On the morrow, if the planet is still here, we shall sit and speak together, telling over my errors."

Her daughter shied away from the offered hand, but she began walking through the dust toward the end of the road, Vertu dea'San Clan Wylan, the Delm Herself, threw the gunbelt over her shoulder, and cinched the strap, walking as firmly as she could, stride for stride with her daughter.

This world, it made no sense any longer.

Tomorrow—tomorrow, she would do something about it.

• • • ◇ • • •

Port City, Surebleak

THE WIND WHIPPED BY, the now-familiar sound rushing down the narrow sidestreets, becoming a brief moan before turning to a continual rattling susurration of air, grit, and weather. Her well-used coat wrapped as tight as the seals allowed, Vertu dea'San forged ahead into the morning, the dim light of the promised dawn aiding her very slightly as the day's snow began with a gust and a swirl.

The coat was a regretful purple color, with a collar imitating any of five different animal pelts, none convincingly. Despite its age and aesthetic deficiencies, it was warm, hung well on her, and swept the path she walked without impeding her Liaden-length stride. Her tall-peaked hat was hand-knit and accidentally color-coordinated with her coat, with purple symbols of good luck splashed around the red-orange that was so often seen as winter colors here.

The hat was pulled down over her ears and tucked into the collar wrapped with the heavy ugly purple-and-orange scarf, which was also hand-knit locally. The hat peak was stuffed with an extra pair of light gloves in the top pouch, while her so-called wind gloves were still in her pocket, where their bulk warmed her hands and helped disguise her size, and perhaps her capability.

Being no-nonsense, she tried as much as possible to put aside the recognition that this morning might well be the coldest morning she'd experienced in her life, just as she'd put it aside yesterday. The boots did as advertised, being the most expensive of her recent acquisitions, and the only certifiably (as much as anything might be certified on Surebleak) new ones. Her other outer clothes were used and comfortable, for she'd bought early, having whiled her time in the long lines by listening to the chat of those who were native. The wisdom of the natives was also to buy clothes somewhat large, for oversize became the perfect size when layered and layered again. The boots, of course, were harder to layer, but with them she wore thick socks—and had been glad of both on the first morning that the mush in the street tripped her—mush gone stone-hard and jagged on the overnight.

The weather had been unrelenting, windy and cold, for the past seven-day now, and the forecast for the morrow was much the same. The night winds would move over the seacoast, pushing moisture into the swamp regions, where it would gather energy from the barely frozen rivers, then push to and over the bowl of the city as the winds changed with the morning—and it would snow. The local at the bakery—Granita—promised Vertu that it had been a warm year so far, and that when *real* winter arrived, she'd wear her hood, sight loss or no, lessen she got herself some working blizzer goggles to hold on her face.

The street was not empty, but it being the dark of morning rather than the dark of night, it was much safer than it might have been a quarter spin before. The doors of the open bars were far fewer, and the doors of the day businesses shone with the white blue of guide-lights.

The door she wanted was across the street, and she looked both ways for traffic of vehicles, and then for people within intercept distance, and crossed to Brickoff Flourpower, where the door recognized her and whined open as she approached.

Behind the counter, Granita looked up with a grin. "There you are, more on time than I'd guess!"

Vertu bowed in her direction wordlessly, letting the warmth comfort her as she read the words to be a welcome. It was good to expected and greeted, and she found it happened more often on Surebleak than it had in Low Port, and more often in Low Port than many of the Higher places she'd frequented in Solcintra. Who expected the ragged to recall one's usual time of arrival?

"Why so, Mother of Baking?" Vertu ventured, pulling her hat off and checking the room in the same motion. The Hooper sat in his corner, hands cupped around his mug of 'toot . . . she knew it was 'toot because he asked for it by name, and sometimes she was here before he was. He got "'toot and crackers" most mornings, the "crackers" being yesterday's flatbread covered in a pasty flour sauce with soy crumbles.

Granita extended a hand with two fingers straight up, which meant, here, "hold that thought" and rushed to the back to do something in response to a quick triple-beat beeping noise. The ticking wall clock chimed about then—it did count the quarters—and Vertu wondered if the clock-count was part of Granita's secret to good service . . .

Vertu's usual morning dish of Ronian Cheese was warming, it being a port-staple at all hours, and a proper-sized cup sat on the counter side among a triple-dozen of other unmatching and mostly oversized cups, the one waiting on Vertu, as had become a custom at the Flourpower these last seventy-seven mornings.

The Hooper said little to anyone, save Granita. In respect of his station, and also in acknowledgment of a service done her, Vertu accorded him a nod, and a half-raised hand, which was considered a "good morning" here.

Chatter overheard from others of Flourpower's reggers taught Vertu that The Hooper was an "organeer"—a musician, so she gathered, though the precise instrument eluded her understanding. Still, it would seem that any life event of importance—births, deaths, trothings—was made more so by the presence of The Hooper and the blessing of his art. There were such on Liad—*galan'ranubiet* they were called: Treasures of the House.

True enough that The Hooper little looked like a Treasure. His clothes in winter-come were the same as in winter-coming—a brown hat with a brim all around and a small crown festooned with tiny green and white feathers—and a coatlet half as thick as hers, which he took off without fail upon entering, to reveal a vest with two dozen varisize pockets, each pocket showing the tip of something metallic. He rarely took off his hat, which covered a half-bald spot in a head of otherwise bushy colorless hair, and when he did, it was to neaten the thick sideburns of the same no-color that stopped abruptly in a razor-sharp line, giving way some days to a light stubble and others to a face as smooth as hers.

Vertu had thought him an elder when first she had seen him; an impression that persisted. Others of the reggers called him Old Fellow, and others his proper name—and none with anything but respect.

Some mornings, The Hooper bent over his mug as if hoarding it, sipping his 'toot with no crackers, and those mornings his hands moved restlessly over his pockets, as if he counted, as if the contents were pets that required gentling. On other mornings, he sat relaxed with his 'toot and crackers, and a side of morning beans, and even engaged in an odd kind of conversation with others of the reggers, though never with Vertu herself.

Quite outside his obvious status as a Treasure, Vertu acknowledged a debt to The Hooper. Her first morning worldside, cold beyond any previous experience, disoriented and lost, she had someway stumbled after The Hooper, who had walked as a man who knew his street and also his destination, entered Flourpower in his wake, and stood behind him at the counter. He had ordered his meal, and she, tired and ragged-minded, uncomprehending the menu scrawled upon the pale blue wipeboard, had scarcely managed a whisper—"What he is having, I will have."

That was the second from the last time she had willfully ordered 'toot, though of a day she might yet ask for crackers, and now that she was an acknowledged regger, she owed him too for the information that, "Dems reggers that brin thanown cup, dems saves a cup of fife!"

The fifth filled cup was free if you had your own cup, brought to the counter and offered, that stayed on the premises. Both Granita and her late-help, Bets, knew each cup by its owner, and knew, too, what went into each without fail.

Vertu's beverage might be the oddest of all, for into her cup now went a measured haspoon of the local Yellobud tea, which was acceptable if brewed half as long as the locals did, the boiled water tempered by a cube before it was poured.

By now, besides The Hooper, she probably knew most of the reggers by face, and could tell if they'd been in, as they'd know if she had. If her cup wasn't on the counter and she wasn't at one of the two back tables she favored, then she'd "comin-gawn," because usually dishwashing happened once per day at close.

The reggers sometimes talked about the years with numbers of the local calendar, and it had been those discussions—forwarded perhaps for her edification, who knew?—that had convinced her of the good boots. They had told over people she saw sometimes daily, walking with a gait they'd "picked up on '66 and they'd lost the little toe for burnfrost," or "backta '59" when the rains came for a week in mid-winter and toes and feet had mildewed or molded along with the clothes, until the thaw died.

Granita returned from the kitchen, her skinny face coming back to a smile from its work-a-day lines, as she answered Vertu's question.

"Huh, Girl. You come in here wif snow in your curls and boots, and down inside the collar. That's a day with wind, and newfuns sometimes takeaback when the real weather gets in. Still, you're a worker, I can tell, and bet you don't let no boss-down timewise."

The bow fell from her shoulders along with the nod—*here* at least, no one was annoyed if she might have Liaden habits, nor asked. Here were reggers, locals, strangers, or flights, and reggers might share a confidence, or might never. She'd seen some of the reggers in the wider world, where they'd sometimes think to raise left hand to left eyebrow in recognition, but else reggers mostly left reggers be, if not invited to converse.

"Not my best sun, this morning," she said, using one of the common phrases, "but bright enough to get in!"

Granita's smile broadened, and she pointed toward the warming tray.

"Got's some starcheese just in to spice our Ronian Cheese if you want some, or the crackers haven't been hardly dredged yet 'cept for The Hooper, if you want something ribstickers."

Vertu blinked, considering. She'd be early in line if the snow slowed folks down: early-in and, as likely, early-out.

"Ronian Cheese, that be fine."

The bow came to her shoulders again, but the woman was already fetching the cube for her cup, and missed it.

* * * ⋄ * * *

HER EARS BURNED, and not from the wind and snow.

Vertu held herself at her fullest height, glad for a new reason that her collar was high and her coat voluminous. She continued to look ahead as well she could while the man behind her muttered to the man behind *him* in a Terran so odd even that one had requested a sayagain.

There were things on Surebleak of which she was still unsure and finding answers was not always as easy as asking the person in line behind you, nor reading an infoscreen.

"*Hworked treedays, mysel, liddle miz, donya haz to hwork toady yuwon booznrazzle. Payada ferya, feedsya an feelya fine. Gotz heat, gotz smokes, gotz dembigbed, yez, no bliz tashov, no dreamslong.*"

That was as clear as she'd made it out after he'd tapped her diffidently on the shoulder—he'd apparently been repeating something that she hadn't understood was directed at her.

She shouldn't have asked for a sayagain, for it came with a wide gap-toothed grin and the clear odor of alcohol and smoke and rampant decay.

The hurt of it was that his face was comely with mouth closed, and his person elsewise no more unkempt than any of the seven in line behind him.

She'd managed a "Nothangya," accented as well as she might recall from bakery talk, holding back the bow as much as it hurt her nerves to do so, for the bow would have brought her closer to the lips with their near-blue inner smoke stains.

For the first time *this day,* she doubted her decision to leave Liad and then shook herself with a derisive inner laughter in recognition that the choice had barely been hers.

Still, of the outcomes she'd considered, public solicitation for prostitution was proof that she'd erred—

NO!

She stamped her foot, the act stinging for her and unremarked by others here—who knew when one needed to rid the boot of snow or ice or mud, after all?

Well, at least the foot was warm, if still tingling from her anger. She bowed a tiny bow to herself, permission to admit error. That was a trick her only social mentor taught her a bare day before she was off to be contract-wifed: *sometimes the only real person in the room is yourself, but manners must be served even so.*

In fact she was being unfair to herself, for she'd had such offers from travelers and drunks from the time she'd first driven for her clan, in fact since her second fare. Well she recalled that, and moreso since that person was seated yet on Liad, comfortable and honored on the Council of Clans, while she, Ring stripped from her finger, stood in danger of—but, again, no. She would not permit herself to believe that this banishment, this mercy from her daughter the delm, might yet end in the death for which the Council had sued.

The line moved, with the work-pair who'd stood in front of her moving now together toward a table to the left while four other tables with work supplicants in place were revealed to her. A very short line; apparently the weather was expected, indeed, to "turn bad."

The man behind shuffled close and whispered toward her, and

she glanced at him, hard, pushing the lingo through her teeth, near as she could.

"Nothangya, heerit?"

He mumbled and backed away a half-step, lips tight.

Compared to the offer from a clan head to pet her face with tongue and tumescence, this man's offer was downright honorable: *"I've worked three days myself, little miss. You don't have to work today if you want to booze and wrestle. Payday for you, food for you, feels fine for you. Got heat, got smokes, got a damn big bed. Yes, I say no blizzard to shovel, no dreaming alone."*

Her delm had been unimpressed by her outrage—a lesson well-learned, that. A Lower House could hardly bring such a complaint against one of the High without evidence—and such evidence, were there any, would hardly survive the impoundment.

Here, the offer was a passing of the time of day. Practical and even, perhaps honorable. That she had living funds for less than a Standard more in this place weighed on her, but work was in fact available at times . . . and she was in no ways desperate, this day.

The table to the right cleared, a man of middle height and middle years smiling and hurrying off with a bright blue chit in hand—going to do something for the street association, she'd figured out over time. That would be day-pay and not long-term, she'd heard in the bakery, but day-pay was day-pay, after all.

She took the vacant spot with alacrity.

"Heavy manual labor?"

The man behind the table was familiar; his voice was brusque and impartial as ever. She raised her head in consideration, and made a counteroffer, staring at the seven bright blue tubs behind him, each mostly empty, and the brown one, with scraps in the bottom.

"Mechanics, systems, detail work, Trade-writing, Liaden-writing, light stock and inventory, driving."

The man pursed his lips.

"Picked up anything new overnight? This ain't being a busy day."

"Translation? Garden design?"

He shook his head, muttering, "Don't think so."

He turned dutifully and pulled the few sheets of hard-copy out of the brown tub, fanning them, glancing up with a sigh and going through the sheets one by one, the first quite dismissively.

"I got armed security, long-term—bring your own gun, night work. I got 'crete formula mixer, experienced." He paused, shook his head. "That one I bet you can do, sound of you, but they want experienced, which I'm betting you can't."

"This is true," she admitted. "I can learn—"

"No on-the-job training, they're right clear, since wintertime set-up is nothing for beginners."

He pulled another sheet. "Whorehouse needs all positions, mixed hours."

She closed her eyes. *Not yet.*

"Serious work there," he said earnestly. "An' they got need for some folk who ain't doing the customers . . ."

She moved a hand, cutting him off. "And else?"

He dropped the cards back into the tub with a shrug.

"Guess else is tomorrow, if we can keep the doors open."

A half-bow she offered, and then gave a second thought.

"Security, night work? Is it experienced?"

The man sat back, looked at her shrewdly, appraising.

"Bring your own gun," he reminded her, but he reached into the tub for the flimsy.

"If necessary, I can do that." She straightened, and took a deep breath. *Be assured*, she told herself. *Show no doubt.* She had done well, Skyblaze night, had she not? She could—

"Yeah, I mean we all can, right? But they're looking for serious hardware . . . damn, I was impressed when I read it coming in."

He flipped the sheet, then pulled free the clip-attached sheet, with notes on both sides, running his gaze rapidly down first one side, then the other.

"Here it is, let's see . . . dumbty *here* it is . . . 'Must be Nordley, Bangtu, Lademeter, or certified genuine Resh & Rolfe or Zombin.'" He looked up into her face. "Big guns, ma'am; not streetwear."

She held his eyes a moment, then half-bowed, hiding her sigh, and her hand.

"Do they mention caliber or charge-range?"

He glanced down, then again to her.

"It says here, 'service rating'. That's a gun that can be shot every day and—"

"Yes," she said, drawing close as if to peer at the paper, at the same time briefly displaying her cradled hands.

His eyes widened. He nodded, several times, and cleared his throat.

"Oh, yes, umm, a Nordley Thirty Pack would do, but . . ."

He turned the papers over; finger tracing the details.

"You gotta supply your own night-sight gear, too, combat-status. And a cold-weather suit."

She said something very potent under her breath and he held his hands up, palm out, placating.

"These things grow on trees on Surebleak?"

He blinked, eyes flicking to her hands. Vertu smiled, deliberately, and tucked the weapon away.

"Forgive, it was not to threaten you. But work is good."

He nodded, relaxing visibly, still using his hands for emphasis.

"I was hoping we had you a match today, much as I seen you in here. Maybe come winter-gone, if you can get in with 'em. It's port security, they're beefing up big time, but best come here unless you get an in with a boss to put your name through."

She made a puffing sound with her lips as the gun found its inner pocket.

"Security is not my first choice, please."

"Got that," he said, nodding. "Yes, got that."

He opened his hands wide—and went on, "Far as I know, all the others is digging, shoveling, construction, work-crew things. Even the forefolk gotta be able to stand shoulder-up with the rest of the crew . . ."

"Ayes and more," she said, drawing from the bakery, and making his eyes widen again. "I understand."

"Good. And sorry. You best get on to cover by lunch, 'specting a bad one, I hear."

"Heard it, ya." She nodded and turned at the dismissal, striding with unexpected purpose past the man who'd been behind her, who must have seen or heard something of her discussion, because he cleared room for her, hissing, "Seery, seery, ma'am, nothinmen."

Nothing meant.

Perhaps she should break into her precious capital to buy herself a coldsuit and dark goggles? Work was, truly said, work, and the contract had been long-term. Weighing the matter, she nearly walked all unsealed into the storm.

Warned by the clatter of the door and the frigid breeze that kissed her face, she stopped there in the vestibule to seal her coat against the wind and snow. She pulled her hat on, and gloves, being sure that the coat's collar was well up around her face.

Think, Vertu, can you really report to your daughter, the delm, that you've hired on as a gun-hand? That report she must take to the Council and Wylan is not yet safe from the price of your errors. You are a dangerously unbalanced radical, in league with the villains Korval. Gunhire is the last thing you want—even less than the whorehouse.

Mouth tight, she slapped the door with her palm, unnecessarily hard, and stepped out into the storm.

She hesitated then, at the side of the door, considering her best route. Her first day, her first purchase, save The Hooper-imitated meal, was a set of maps: port map, city map, country map, world map. The disorientation she had felt, disembarking from the ship, the understanding that she knew where *nothing* in this city was situated, nor the three best routes to gain them. Then, at that moment, she had almost carried out the Council's first judgment, that her delm had appealed and fought and argued until Vertu had her life back, but not, never again, on Liad.

The moment had passed, and she had resolutely gone forward, trying to feel out a new life—a life without Clan—on this strange and bitter world. There were moments—of course there were moments, of doubt, and of loneliness. Those things she endured, as befit one who had once been Wylan Herself.

Now though, just this instant, staring out into the swirling snow, and the street near empty of traffic—gods, how she wanted her cab, to feel the controls in her hands, and the seat that knew her form, and the whole of the Port in her head, as familiar as the face of a lover.

The snow swirled, wrapping her in impenetrable whiteness, then parted, revealing—a cab.

That it was not her cab was quickly and painfully apparent, yet it proceeded as a cab should, businesslike and foursquare down the snow-filled street, the yellow ready-light set atop it turning the dancing flakes into gold.

Breath caught, Vertu watched its progress, the driver a silhouette inside the cabin. She watched until it had passed her and made the turn at the end of the street, left—toward the port proper.

Only then did she breathe, looking down to find her coat growing a second coat of sparkling flakes, and realized that she was cold.

Flourpower, she thought, thinking of warmth and companionship and food. Before they closed, she would go there, and spoil herself with new food. After all, she thought, setting out with care for the slippery walk, today she had almost found a job, and that was already better than yesterday.

· · · ⋄ · · ·

VERTU'S MUG SAT, steaming, before she'd had her coat off. The coatracks were full since the room, too, was almost full, so she laid the snow-rimmed coat beside her on the bench seat she'd ended up with, back in the colder corner, away from the kitchen, near the sealed and covered sidewindow—so dealing with the coat had taken time. Her order of soup of the day was acknowledged with a wave, and promised as up in a minute.

It was good to see the room so full, and the sound level elevated. Good for this hour, at least. She'd probably not want so lively a place early in the wake-up time of the day. Granita deserved a good day if the morrow was going to be a snow mess, and talk was of little else.

"I ain't putting a screen in, Lesker. No, I am not! You wanna keep up, that's for you. But folks come here to eat, not to stare at sat-pics of show-tops. Just 'cause they got themselves a weatherman don't mean I gotta do one thing about him."

Well, *they* did have a weatherman, and apparently Surebleak hadn't had one before—*they* being the so-called Road Boss, the Delms Korval—and now there was real-time forecasting and interpretation, too, instead of the antiquated six spot condition reports that the port had been using the last fifty Standards to approximate how a day might shape.

Delms or Delm, Korval they still were to Vertu, no matter the mythic transition that had, for Surebleak, made the prime yos'Phelium into his cousin's little brother, and gained him a new title. Korval still lived under Tree, which was well enough, and from spot and spot around the city she was pleased to see the crown or more of that great Tree, and still—as light or cloud formation drew her eye to it—she bowed to it from time to time as she had in Solcintra.

As in Solcintra, too, the gambling cousin lived in the city, gambling still; his stakes being no higher than a planet's survival. That story she had only in pieces, how Boss Conrad had come from nowhere and, one by one, toppled the most abusive of the bosses, turning the patchwork territories into a more congenial whole, using talk and gun and explosives as required, and only as much of any as was needed. Thus he'd become legend before she'd arrived as a 'comer.

Legends. As a gambler in Solcintra he had been quiet, even cordial in her cab the time or two he'd traveled alone in it; and when he traveled with a companion in the late evenings, as he had from time to time, he had been nothing but exacting in his attentions—to the companion.

Her cup hand flat on the table, Vertu sighed, acknowledging the lack of Ring on her finger. The boss—Boss Conrad, who had been Pat Rin yos'Phelium, Clan Korval—he, of course, wore the Ring wrong-fingered, while his "little brother" wore another, properly. She no longer wore a Ring, nor wanted one in this place where having even such a modest Ring as Wylan possessed might leave one throttled and motionless of a night-time sidestreet.

Vertu shook those thoughts away, and deliberately looked about the room. She recognized some of the reggers, was rewarded with nods and finger waves by them, and waited patiently for her soup. The clock chimed a quarter—and as if that was a signal, folk around the room began to rustle themselves about, to rise and start donning coats, or to hurry-sip the dregs of their cups, or some to wrap what was left of their lunch into bags or napkins to take with.

It was, she reckoned, not quite closing time, but—oh. Several of the nearby bars opened for day-business soon, and on a day such as this, some of the reggers would be trading one seat for another about now.

Snow squalled into the room as four patrons left together, the small outer welcome way doing nothing to dim the ferocity. Vertu shivered involuntarily. She had been hoping for moderation, but if anything, the weather had gotten worse in the short time she'd been sipping her tea.

Ah, and the door had not only been open to let some out, but to let The Hooper in. He all but fell into his no-doubt warm, just-vacated regular spot, his hat uncharacteristically flung to the table top as he mopped snow off his brow and face.

Vertu watched him as other patrons filed out, until finally it was just the two of them, the sounds of the wind outside and the clatter of the unseen kitchen work. He was visibly more comfortable now, though she saw a couple of fleeting half-suppressed reaches toward his vest, but not the full-fledged search she'd seen him do at other times, when clearly agitated. Merely a trifle out of sorts then . . .

"'Toot?"

Granita's voice was muffled as she peered at the room from behind the back counter, and she repeated herself, louder.

"'Toot? I got your cup here if—"

The Hooper beat his hat against his knee and pulled it on, only then admitting that he'd heard her.

"Guess so, if's time."

"Extra few minutes ain't a problem, you know. Girl here's got about the last of the food though, less you want some biscuits. Fact, I'll bring you both some, on me, 'cause they won't wait so good for tomorrow."

The soup came, a bowl for her, delivered with a nod and three cheese biscuits, while a hot cup of the same and three more biscuits went to The Hooper, who had leaned his chair back against the wall while he ate, his foot twitching time to a tune only he could hear.

Granita might have seen his nerves, because she paused, waving her hands toward the door.

"A little too long a walk down to the Stadium today, or they run out of lights already?"

The Hooper shook his head, took a sudden interest in one of his biscuits, stuffing it into his mouth all at once while he moved his hand as if he explained something the whole time he was chewing.

"Got lights, but not my best welcome right now," he said, biting into another biscuit like he was afraid it might get away from him, following Granita with his eyes as she straightened chairs and wiped down tables.

"Looked to be Bopst Eckman and High-Man Prezman hanging at the Stadium door, it did, the pair both. Thought I saw your Harley Irsay ahead of 'em, going in. Hasn't seen them twonce since I dunno— no I do, it'd be the Wicky and David wedding day, same day as when I saw them together at Cholo's wake, when they took the casket bottle and thought no one saw 'em. Not my best welcome, any of themselves, you know it."

The soup was hot and nourishing if not up to the standards of a fine Liaden restaurant—certainly there were too many beans and tubers, and too much salt—but with the butter and the biscuits, Vertu felt on the cusp of content, despite the coming frosty trudge to her small apartment in the Hearstings. Vertu concentrated on her food, trying to be inconspicuous—she'd never heard The Hooper open up quite so much, nor speak quite so clearly.

The door shook with the wind, and then opened roughly—not the wind, but a large man in a rustic black coat nearly as long as her own, and wearing a hooded overcape so covered in snow as to deaden the loud stripes to spots.

He looked in and around, pushed the door against the wind and noise and yelled "Get in!"

Two more snow-covered forms trailed behind, and the last of them pulled the door to with a will, slapping at the day-locks like a guard before stamping his feet and shaking the snow away.

It wasn't her imagination: the sound The Hooper made was close to a sob, right then, overwhelmed instantly by the loud and bitter "Get out!" that Granita the baker offered them as she brandished her slops tray like a weapon.

· · · ✧ · · ·

THE BIG MAN looked past Granita, right at Vertu.

"You belong here, do you? Just eating? Or you from the Patrol?"

"Get out," Granita repeated. "Closin' time; we're done."

The big man casually turned to her, laughing.

"You got no right to run me out, Girl. Just shut up!"

For a moment, they stared at each, and then the baker fled toward the rear of the place, leaving a pile of dishes on the table.

The other men were noisily looking about and taking coats off, but there was no doubt that this one, hand to the inside of his coat, was both wary and dangerous.

Her voice caught in her throat for a long moment.

"You talk at all? Speak up!"

The words formed, finally, on her lips.

"I eat here. Often. I—"

"She got herself a mug, Harley, so she's a regger. Pretty little regger, ain't she?"

"Quiet, gots to be sure. Patrol?"

She shook her head, Terranstyle.

"Not patrol. I just eat here."

"Don't know you, so you're new. Good. Bidness is good all over they say, 'cept for the dead bosses who ain't saying nothing. You work for a boss?"

She shook her head again, aghast at his rudeness, unable to marshal a fitting response to it. The cut direct, she suspected, would be lost on this person. And that left only civil answers to his questions as defense.

"Looking for work," she said.

The man turned his back on her, to look at The Hooper, huddled in the corner.

"More than you do, old man," he said, pointing at Vertu. "Least she's looking for work. All you do is make silly sounds and trouble for people. You know what I mean, old man. More than once the news spread I did this or that and the only one might know was you, can see right through them closed eyes of yours when you're drunk, can't you? But we can work this out, 'cause there's a great storm here right now, and we'll all be here for a good long time while this new patrol's out looking for us."

Vertu had caught a movement out of the corner of her eye and saw Granita, face pale and stern, standing behind the counter with a strange looking weapon—"Out, Harley! Get out!"

He turned on her, his hand full of a gun of his own.

"I staked you to this, Girl, and we was just about married, and that means this is my place, too. You got no right to—"

Granita raised her weapon, and it was her turn to say, "Shut up."

"These things," he said, ignoring the gun entire and picking up one of the mugs; "These are mine aren't they? It was my idea, I told you how they did it, off-world." He smashed the mug into the pile of dishes, picked up another and smashed it, turned the tray over and laughed as they fell, kicking at the remains.

He moved his hand, and his confederates rushed into The Hooper's corner, lifting him effortlessly and dragging him to stand before Harley.

"Can't rightly aim that, can you?" He said to Granita. "Your old regger here—him and me got a lot to talk about. Might as well put that down—we got what we need for a snow party now, don't we? We can have some music, and we got us a couple women, we got food and 'toot, and since the old man don't need none, that's enough women to get us by 'til this storm's done in a couple days, all comfortable and snug."

"Let him go, Harley—this ain't his fight."

"He don't get fight, he just gets hurt." One of the followers that was, suddenly launching a flurry of strikes and blows at The Hooper while his mate held the sobbing man.

Vertu stirred, then, not sure how to best interfere, how to help—

"See? You can't do it! You had a knife on me and you couldn't use it!"

They were slapping the The Hooper now, one after another. He made no move to resist, only holding his hands down over his vest, over his precious things—until Harley stepped in, snatching at pockets, fishing out one, two, three tiny objects, slick and silvery as fish as they fell to the floor. Heavy boots rose—fell . . .

The Hooper yelled, wordless, fighting now the one who held him laughing as he twisted the old arms harder.

"Stop!"

Authority rang in that voice, and for a moment Vertu thought that the patrol had arrived.

But no, she realized, standing tall with Tommee's gift ready in her hand—it was only Vertu dea'San, playing the fool once more.

She hit the side switch that would throw the weapon power, the hum adding itself to the racket in the room.

"'Ware! Gun!" The follower pointed, too far away to interfere with her.

Harley turned, his weapon shining in the light, his eyes targeting her as he moved.

There were two explosions, then perhaps a third . . . a rush of smoke and whining, zinging things. There came a groan, the room was full of smoke, and Granita shouted, "Don't shoot!"

· · ◇ · · ·

THE PATROL ARRIVED, stepping in through the door the moment Granita snapped the locks back. Two went immediately forward: one to The Hooper where he knelt on the floor, moaning as he picked up bits of silver and what might be reed, and placing them in a startlingly white 'kerchief.

The second patrolwoman went to Harley and his mates, standing cowed beneath the baleful glare of Vertu's gun, unsnapping wrist restraints from her belt as she walked.

The third—was Liaden, and walked with the soundless step of a scout, to Vertu's very side, taking care to be seen, yet not be in her sights. He paused at the proper distance for speaking to a stranger and bowed gently.

"*Galandaria*, I am grateful for your assistance, and regret that it was necessary. I am Scout Lieutenant ter'Volla, detached to the Surebleak Street Patrol. My crew and I are tardy, but now we are come. You may stand down, if you please."

In truth, the Nordley had grown heavy, and it was all she could do, to hold it on target. Vertu inclined her head to indicate that she had heard, averted the gun's gaze, and touched the power-stud.

The hum died, and she slid the weapon away before turning to face the scout and showing him empty palms.

"It is well," he said. "Again, I regret. I will need your name, for the reports, and also, please a description of what has happened here."

· · · ◇ · · ·

THE WIND HAD LESSENED, and the snow fell silent and bewitching in the meager day-light. Vertu dea'San stood at the crossroads, her hat pulled low and her gloved hands tucked into her coat pockets, checking her direction against the maps she had memorized.

The patrol, having gained names and reports, had dispersed, two taking Harley and his mates on foot to the so-called "stationhouse," while the scout and Granita coaxed The Hooper into the Patrol's own car, for transport to Ms. Audrey's whorehouse, where it appeared he had call upon a room at need, and folk to give him the care due kin.

That was, in Vertu's view, only proper—a Treasure of the House deserved nothing less.

For herself, she had been left staring at the white 'kerchief and its burden of bits and splinters, and one instrument nearly whole so that she might say with authority that she had never before seen its like.

"These," she said to Scout Lieutenant ter'Volla. "The Hooper is *galan'ranubiet*. These are the instruments of his art."

The scout moved his shoulders. "He has others, yet safe in their pockets. The lack of these will not silence his voice."

"Only limit what he might say," Vertu answered, perhaps more sharply than was required.

He looked at her, the scout, and abruptly he bowed as to one who has spoken a pure truth.

"This is so. Have you an interest?"

An interest? She looked at the broken bits, stark against the white 'kerchief, remembered The Hooper checking his pockets of a morning, gentling his pets.

"Somebody," she said, "ought to do something."

"Ah." The scout looked toward the ceiling, as if seeking advice from the lighting, then looked back to Vertu. "If you find that it falls to you to serve one who is, in truth, a Treasure, then you may bear these to the Port Repair and ask for Andy Mack, who may, or may not, be inclined to repair them. Say that ter'Volla sent you, and that these are rescues." There was a pause, and perhaps the glimmer of a smile, before he added, "Say also that, yes, I do know that he is busy, and that he may call upon me for Balance."

So it was that Vertu dea'San found herself at the crossroads, consulting the map in her head and counseling herself that it was too far, at this time, in this weather, to walk.

The pieces of The Hooper's instruments, tied up in their white 'kerchief, were sealed into an inner coat pocket, safe from the snow. For herself, however . . . she was cold, and the port no small distance from where she stood.

Truly, she thought, one needed a cab.

And as before, precisely as if her thought had summoned it, there came a cab, the very same garish yellow cab she had seen earlier, the roof-mounted light telling all who might care that it was available for hire.

Vertu's hand signal flashed out and up as the cab proceeded down the street, and past her to about its own length, before it pulled aside and stopped, the door nearest the walk popping open.

She—did not run; the footing was too uncertain for that. She did, however, hurry, noting as she entered the passenger compartment the name painted in too-thin letters on the side door: Jemie's Taxi.

"Where to?" a cheerful voice asked her as the door sealed behind her.

"The port, if you please. The repair shop of Andy Mack." Vertu said, looking up to find, not a screen, but merely a glass partition with a speaker set at low center.

The figure in the driver's slot was thin and gave the impression of extreme youth. An impression which was not amended when the driver turned to face Vertu through the glass, shaking ragged black bangs out of brilliant blue eyes.

"Port's outta reach right now, sorry to say. Road was open, but what's some amateur gotta do but put his delivery wagon right across all lanes at Vine's toll—at what *ustabe* Vine's tollbooths. Word comes down—" she leaned to her control board and tapped what Vertu took to be the router—"that the road crew's working on it, but the weather ain't makin' things easy. Don't suppose you got a backup plan?"

"In fact," Vertu said to that absurdly young and open face, "I do. If traffic is stopped at Vine's tollbooths, then we may reroute down Fuller Avenue."

A startled blink was her answer, followed by a look of concentration.

"Yanno . . ." The driver paused, possibly checking the map in her head, even as Vertu rechecked her own.

"Yeah, that'd work. Thanks!"

She faced front, and gave the vehicle its office, moving inexorably through the snow.

"Weather update says storm's about done," she said over her shoulder. "So, not as bad as we'd braced for, but plenty bad enough. I'm Jemie, by the way. You?"

There was no need for the driver of a taxi to know the name of a particular fare, except insofar as Unicredit or some other voucher might record it within the payment system. Nonetheless, Vertu answered, choosing to see the question as a pleasantry born, perhaps, of a slow day.

"My name is Vertu," she said, giving only one, as Jemie had done.

"That's pretty. Liaden, huh?"

"Indeed."

"Pretty good idea 'bout goin' around. Fuller's nice and wide—oughta be able to get down there, no problem. You drive?"

It was Vertu's turn to blink. "Your pardon?"

"You drive? Like a cab, or maybe a delivery wagon? Don't meet many who got the streets laid out in their head. Meet more who think it's kinda funny that I do."

"Once, I had owned a small fleet," she said, slowly. "Three cabs, and thinking of a fourth."

"Yeah?" blue eyes met hers in the rearview mirror. "What happened?"

"There was . . . a war action. At—on Liad, they name it Skyblaze. I—my cab and I—picked up the wrong fare."

"Hey, that's tough." There was a moment of silence, as the driver maneuvered them around what appeared to be another car, abandoned in the center of the road.

"Amateurs," Jemie muttered. "Could at least've pulled it to the curb. So!" she said a moment later, the hazard to travel safely behind them, "you lookin' to set up?"

Vertu shook her head. "I have . . . limited funds."

"Don't we all? Worse luck, too. What've I got but the colonel, hisself, willin' to stake me a cab, but I gotta find a 'nother driver. With references. 'Nother driver's bad enough. References—well hell, I'm the first legit cab ever, less you count them little jitneys they're usin' to move folk around Port proper." Another blue glance in the mirror. "You don't happen t'have references, do ya, Vertu?"

For a moment, she sat there, thinking of the references she could have produced, before Skyblaze, and the Council's judgment and her banishment from clan and kin . . .

"As a driver, locally," she said, keeping her voice steady with an effort. "I fear not."

"Well hell," Jemie said again, making the turn from the Port Road onto Fuller Avenue with commendable caution. "You're for Mack's shop, though, right?"

"I am, yes."

"He know you?"

"No. I am sent to him by the patrol."

"Well, maybe we can talk him inta letting you do a—whasit called, when you try somebody out and see if they can do the job? A parole?"

"Probation?" Vertu suggested, wondering after the connection between the colonel who staked cabs and Andy Mack of Port Repairs.

"Right." Jemie sighed, and the cab made a smooth turn out of Fuller Avenue and into the Port Road. Behind them, Vertu could see the blinking red lights of emergency equipment. Ahead of them was the entrance to Surebleak Port.

"You gonna need a ride back, Vertu?"

She looked out the window. The snow had dwindled to a stop, and the star was slightly more robust in the graycast sky.

"I believe that I'll walk."

"I b'lieve that you'll freeze your tail, you try it," Jemie said frankly. "Tell you what, I'm gonna stop at the Emerald and eat m'supper. You finish with Mack, come on over—it's just 'round the corner. I'm still there, we'll work something out for pay-maybe you can drive f'me one night I need to be elsewhere. That suit?"

"That—suits, But—"

"No buts, woman! We'll work it out. Later. Right now, here y'are. Get on out and let a girl get something ta eat."

The door opened at her elbow. Vertu reached into the pocket of her coat, fished out the few coins she found there and put them in the pass-tray.

"Hey—"

"For the cab," she said, overriding Jemie's protest. "The cab costs, and those costs must be covered." She pulled her coat around her and exited.

"Thank you!" she called and closed the door.

* * * ✦ * * *

THE MAN WAS TERRAN and grizzled, and he'd hauled himself out from beneath an obscenely large and smelly piece of something that appeared to be an engine of some sort, the while complaining, "Whoever used this scooter last is gonna have to learn to adjust it proper!"

Vertu heard the same thing three times and was still not sure if "this scooter" was the item with wheels that he rode flat on his back as he came out feet first or if it was the object he'd been under.

"I'm Mack," he said brusquely. "These are rescues, eh? I guess someone thinks that's important, but it ain't like I don't got a hundred dozen other rescues to deal with—"

He looked at the knotted 'kerchief she held, and let her continue to hold it while he stretched several times, as if being under things was not what he was best at.

"This thing's a rescue, too," he muttered, "and damned if I know why they found it now and not a generation ago when we might still've had parts somewhere here or in half the ports nearspace. But no, *now* they find it, and it's up to me to get it running." He shook his head, glared at her and demanded, "Who'd you say sent you?"

"Scout Lieutenant ter'Volla sends me. These—" she held up the 'kerchief, "are rescues. They are all from the pockets of a crime victim. They are important because they belong to a *galan'ranubiet*."

Andy Mack blinked.

"I got lotsa vocabulary, young lady, but that's one I don't know. And who are *you*, by the way?"

"Vertu dea'San," she said, biting the clan name away.

He shook his head again. "Everybody's important, you ever notice that, Ms. Vertu?" He shook his head once more. "'Specially when they want somebody else to do something for them."

Vertu inclined her head, the smile coming. "Scout ter'Volla gave me to say that, yes he did know that you were very busy and that you might call upon him for Balance."

He snickered, waved one hand toward the ceiling.

"Ter'Volla, is it? Well then, I can see who's climbing the gantry next time I need some lights changed!"

Vertu laughed, which was needful; such sounds had not come willingly to her since her son had dropped her and her scant luggage at Solcintra Port in obedience to the Council's order.

"All right, then, since the scout's willing to pay. Bring what you got over here and I'll take a look . . ."

Vertu bowed then, thanks to a master, but if he noticed, or knew, he offered no bow in return because he was already striding toward a roomside table. The place echoed with their steps, and there were other noises in constant background hum—heaters and blowers, perhaps, and maybe a device compressing air, and perhaps the hiss of air leaking from someplace that was not the cold outside but a spherical tank.

"Ms. Vertu," he said over his shoulder, "what is a *galan'ranubiet*, and what's it doing owning a hand 'kerchief full o'junk what needs repair?"

She strode with him, impressed that for one who claimed not to know the word he'd managed to both recall it and pronounce it. True, it was not a Solcintran accent he used, but he'd been taught by a native speaker. The clicks and sounds of the place were not sufficient to hide a facility with language.

"A *galan'ranubiet* is a person, Andy Mack, a person with an extreme *melant'i* . . . an earned recognition, that would be. Someone with, let us say, knowledge or skills of importance to a whole community."

"Well, hand it over," he said, "and if that's the case, I pity the person because no doubt they got more to do and less to do it with than they ever did."

Vertu placed the 'kerchief on the desk, and was surprised to see him reach not for it, but for a small pad of paper and a writing stylus.

In good, round script he wrote, "Received of Vertu dea'San, one bag of community treasures . . ." then he looked up—"Who're these from?"

"The man's call name, what they know him as on the street, it is 'The Hooper.'"

Andy Mack's startlement was clear in the near explosive intake of breath.

"Crime victim? The Hooper? Is he in health? What happened?"

There was no playfulness in him now, but full attention.

"The patrol wrote in the report that he was 'beat up by punks.'"

The colonel's expression got even more serious, but if he was going to speak his words were swept away by the deep voice of a large man who was suddenly, otherwise silently, beside them.

"Beat up by punks? Guess that's a report waiting for me!"

. . . ✧ . . .

THE JACKET WAS BATTERED and totally incongruous for the weather; the face somehow familiar. That she'd reached for her gun as a first reaction wasn't lost on the man who owned the face; his hand twitched but he suppressed it instantly.

Her hand had been slower to stop and closer to acting; perhaps in a public place, it wouldn't have been noted.

She blushed even before Andy Mack started chuckling—

"'Swat you get from sneaking in a back door like a galoot 'stead of coming in like folk!"

Recognition stirred on the galoot's face as he dragged a handy stool from beneath the workbench, the gunhand going to forehead in a salute to all present. Snow fell from creases in his jacket; in other spots, it was already going to patient waterdrops that held on as if frozen by a root. He sat fluidly, his size having nothing to do with his grace.

"Andy, you give me a key and leave to use the door, I'm gonna. Save my ears and brain from freezing, using the back way—"

"Too late on that save?" Andy Mack's mischievous grin got the best of him, and turned into a chuckle.

"It ain't froze yet. If it was we'd both've drawn. And pardon me, Driver, for giving you a start. I'm McFarland."

"Pilot McFarland, yes, it is good to see you again."

"And you, Driver. Got some bunch of lightyears 'tween you and . . . Solcintra, I think it was."

"I am Vertu dea'San, Pilot—"

Andy Mack interrupted, holding a hand toward each of them.

"Damn if you didn't make me forget my manners, Cheever. But looks like you met before—"

"Briefly," Vertu managed. "It would have been a taxi ride from the small private-ship side of Solcintra Port to some place unexpected—I think Korval's valley, to yos'Galan's house. We have not met in a social way, Andy Mack."

The mechanic stood then, shaking the foot he'd had tangled around the chair as if it had been asleep.

"We have here," he announced formally, "Vertu dea'San, deputized by ter'Volla on patrol to bring items of interest to us all to me in order to make something wrong as right as it can be. I'm pleased to be receiving such visitors, I am."

He nodded, then turned with a flourish. "This here—this is Cheever McFarland, Master Pilot, come as Boss Conrad's Right Hand, if I have that proper."

Cheever McFarland nodded, and Vertu answered with a seated bow, each murmuring appropriately.

"Good, so let me see what we got here, if you can be patient, Cheever, and then you can get to whatever brought you out in the snow."

· · · ✧ · · ·

THE PLASTIM OF TEA was better than she'd expected, and it was even recognizably a Vertuna blend, as promised—the tea her namesake, due to a prior Wylan's whim. Empty now, she moved it aside as the pilots told over the contents of the 'kerchief. Drawing her more and more into conversation like comrades rather than strangers, they'd made as sure as they might that The Hooper's physical injuries were minor.

"So they roughed him up because they could, was that it? Thing is that if he said what he did, The Hooper, in front of trusty witnesses, them boys have got themselves a mess of trouble anywhere there's someone for the block. Took the casket bottle? Stupid—"

"But what happened next? Patrol show up?" That was McFarland.

"Not until I had pulled my gun, and Granita fired hers. Harley was struck with—the Patrolwoman said 'bird shot'—instead of a charge from this."

She showed the gun in explanation, and there was a whistle, and an, "Ah."

"I see we should talk," Andy Mack said. "You tell me your campaigns and I'll tell you mine!"

Cheever it was who understood her quick questioning look—

"Not been on campaign? That's a heavy-duty merc weapon for a civilian taxi driver then. Can I see it?"

She checked it for safety, and handed it over to the Hand of the Boss, who held it appreciatively.

"Real one, Colonel—not one of those cheap look-likes they sell down the Low Ports."

McFarland made a gesture, which she interpreted as asking permission to hand the weapon to the other man, and she nodded.

"Not more'n two Standards old, by the serial number. They don't usually sell a Nordley on Liad though—and I know you can't often pluck one up out on the dock here!"

He returned the weapon, respectfully.

"It was a gift," she explained carefully. "On the day of Skyblaze, a solider gave it to me, in thanks for the ride. His mates insisted I should have it—"

Neither of the men said anything, and she felt like there was something more she needed to tell them.

"The soldier, he'd been wounded already when I picked them up. Then, we got back to near port and a man came at us; there was shooting, and he pointed—umm, they called it anti-armor, at us! I could do one thing to protect my fares—I ran the car at them and he shot wild."

They waited, and she wished there was tea in the cup.

"This Tommee, this boy, he was wounded and trying to shoot, too, and then he said, 'Thank you much for the ride ma'am' . . . and gave this to me, since I might need it, and it was all that he had."

The colonel pressed his hands, then slowly spread them with tips touching its opposite twin, staring into the cavity as if some truth existed there, and nodded slowly.

"He made a good call, the boy," he said after a moment. "His mates were with him to sing him home?"

She closed her eyes, hearing the question fully, shaking her head with the Terran not-so.

"They said they could get him to medics, that he had some time off coming, and a vacation—"

Her voice drifted off, remembering Tommee's wounds, the still, bloodied form of the man who had targeted her cab, and, later, standing before the Council, hearing their judgment come down. So much lost, that day, by so many . . .

"It was for my part in the rebellion—carrying enemy soldiers who were in league with those ships that fired upon the homeworld—that is why I am here. On Surebleak." She took a breath and met Cheever McFarland's eyes. "If I was to aid Korval in their madness, then I might go to them in their banishment."

He frowned. "That was your sentence? The Council sent you to Surebleak?"

"My daughter, who is now delm in my place by the Council's order, sent me to Surebleak. The Council wanted my life."

There was a long pause, then Andy Mack said carefully.

"You go to Korval, once you hit planet?"

She laughed. "To what end? I did not fight for Korval. I fought to protect my cabs, my daughter, my life. Before that, I negotiated in good faith to ferry a group-client from the port to a city park, and return them, at need."

"When my daughter—my delm—sued for my life, the Council offered this, as leniency: that I might not show my face in Solcintra for twelve years Liaden, nor to be seen anywhere on planet in control of a vehicle until such time as the Council of Clans credited that I had been cured of my errors and was no longer a rash and conspicuous danger to the populace and institutions of Liad. I would be disallowed from forming alliances, making contracts, or adult decisions without the written consent of my delm, or the nadelm if appropriate. That was to be revisited at the end of the dozen years, if the Council of Clans pleased."

There was silence—for a moment. Then Andy Mack sighed a heavy sigh for her, putting aside the minute metal piece he'd been studying, moving his hands as if he now rubbed his wrists against unseen shackles.

"House arrest for a dozen years? No time off for good behavior? That's hardly a civilized way to be—"

"Happens," said Cheever sharply, "and we've both talked to a man on-world who had his delm do the same." He looked to her.

"What about your cab—could you bring that?"

She shook her head, Terranstyle.

"*My* cab," she said, "my cab that carried you to Dragon's Valley— that was destroyed on the spot where Tommee exited; we took pieces of sharpness—" here she paused, not knowing the exactly correct word . . .

"Shrapnel," Andy Mack said. "That could hurt a civilian vehicle pretty bad."

"Thank you. The Commander Higdon, an excellent man for all that he was banished forever from Liad on pain of death, he offered to replace my cab, but that replacement vehicle was—" here she sighed out loud against her own wishes—"That vehicle was *dedicated*. It is to be used for carrying the Council Speaker only, and to be manned by drivers furnished around the clock by Wylan."

There was a loud snap then as McFarland stretched both hands, interlocked, to the ends of his arm with quite some energy.

"So they stole your cab, took your Ring, and took your name. Then they tossed you randomly off-world?"

She looked down to her Ringless hand.

"That last, no, not that. Even a madwoman must obey her delm.

So it was that Wylan commanded me to go off-world, for she knows my limits perhaps not so finely as I do myself, but near enough. Twelve years a drain upon my House—that, I would not, could not, abide. And so I was granted capital, and a berth arranged—to Surebleak. I think Fereda—my daughter, though perhaps not my delm—had hoped that Korval's wing would unfurl."

"But you didn't ask."

"This is not of the Dragon's *melant'i*, but my own."

They exchanged glances, the two Terrans, and it was Cheever McFarland who asked, "So, what're you doing for work?"

"I have just this afternoon had an offer of work," she said, "but first, I must ask—" She looked to Andy Mack.

He nodded, watching her.

"Are you also called the colonel, and have you offered to stake Jemie a cab, if she hires a second driver?"

A grin spread slowly over his face.

"Now, then, happens I am and happens I do. You applyin'?"

"I am, if—" She looked to the other man, who was watching interestedly—"if Pilot McFarland may give me a reference."

He laughed, and her stomach sank, hearing in his merriment the last and best of her slender hopes dissolving.

"Give you a reference? Hell, I'll buy you a cab!"

"No, hey, now—none o'that! Competition's all well and good, in its place. What we need right now is a Port-N-City taxi squad that's honest, strange as that word might fall on your ear, there, Pilot. If Ms. Vertu's willin' to take Jemie on, then I think we're on the way to solving a couple problems right now."

"I would welcome the work," Vertu said, looking between the two of them. "Wylan has driven cabs for many generations. We have experience that, perhaps, Jemie might find to—to our profit."

"Startin' with gettin' the name of the taxi service big enough to be read 'cross the street," Cheever said.

"That," Vertu admitted, with a smile, "is one of the first things I will speak of with her."

"All right, then," Colonel Andy Mack said. "Soon's I can get the news to Jemie, you got work."

"Jemie had stopped at the Emerald for her supper, and asked me to come by when I had finished here. She proposed to take me home as a free fare, with the debt to be paid that I drive for her some day when there was need."

"Well, now she can drive her partner home and bring 'er back to port tomorrow to pick up 'er cab."

Andy Mack grinned and stuck out his hand, Terranstyle. Vertu blinked, then placed her hand in his.

They shook.

"Done!"

"'Bout time," Cheever McFarland said. "Speaking of the Emerald, I'm heading back that way, Ms. Vertu, and I'd take it kindly if you'd have some supper with me before you go on home. If Jemie can't wait, I'll drive you back."

"Thank you," she said, rising. "That is very kind, but—"

"No buts," he said firmly, and bowed her toward the back door ahead of him.

. . . . ✧ . . .

IT WAS SPRING AT LAST, insofar as Surebleak entertained the season. Vertu dea'San sat in her cab outside of the Emerald Casino on the port, awaiting her contracted fare.

Who was . . . about to be late. She lowered the window, settling back into the seat that by now knew her shape, and considered starting the meter. Spring had brought the addition of a third cab to Jemie's fleet, and a new driver, known to the colonel, for he had grown up on a Surebleak street. One leg was cybernetic, but that was no handicap to the cab, and he held the streets in his head like a driver born. Soon, they would need a fourth driver to stand at call, and she and Jemie had discussed the possibility of branching out into the ground-courier business.

The Emerald's door opened, and a big man exited, crossing to the cab in a half-dozen long strides, and settling familiarly into the seat beside the driver.

"'Evenin'," he said, pulling the door closed and giving her a grin. "Ready?"

She nodded, looking down at herself—a white shirt and a dark sweater under a spring-weight jacket; new trousers and boots. She was as presentable as she might be, for this trip out to the end of the road, and an introduction she thought never to receive.

"Know the way?" Cheever asked her, waking the echo of memories.

Vertu grinned and put the car into gear.

"I know the way," she said. "The question becomes—can we afford the fare?"

He laughed, and she did, and the car slipped into traffic, heading out the road, toward Korval.